MW01287461

Edited by Andie Edwards of Beyond the Proof
Proofread by Shannon Shacka
Illustration by Yibi of @yibiart
Cover design by Milos Jevremovic
Paperback chapter art by Ginotage Sandaru
www.oliviahayle.com

Between the Lines

OLIVIA HAYLE

To all of our past selves.
We were doing the best we could at the time.
Thank you for getting us here.

CHAPTER 1
CHARLOTTE

The water pressure in this hotel shower is fantastic.

The cost of a night here is worth every penny for the hot water alone, as I wash away my earlier hike. I'm already looking forward to ordering the best pasta dish the hotel restaurant has to offer and falling into bed early.

It's the perfect end to a day of exploration on my solo road trip from Chicago to Los Angeles. An entire week all to myself, with new parts of the country to see.

I lean against the tiled wall behind me and turn my face toward the spray of warm water. This is one of my favorite places to be. The in-between state, with one city and ghost-writing job behind me, and another looming. It's freedom of the best kind.

There's good water pressure here. I wonder...

I turn on the handheld shower nozzle and wash my back, my stomach. Move the showerhead down between my legs and shift until I find just the right angle.

That's good. That's really good. Closing my eyes, I think about nothing but pleasure. Shadowy figures from my past flash through my mind. Not the specific men I've been with, but rather the situations. Like the time I had sex standing up against a camper van in the middle of a national park in

Arizona. I'd only seen Simon for a few weeks while working on a book down in Tucson. He'd been a hot commitment-phobe who liked to laugh. Perfect for my tastes.

I don't date. I don't stay long enough in one place for that, and even if I did, I doubt dating is for me. Casual and noncommittal work best. Fun, until it stops being fun, and where I can't get hurt.

I change the angle a bit, and pleasure flows through my limbs. It's slow and syrupy, growing with every passing minute. My mind shifts to another fantasy. One I've had but never fulfilled. The idea of a man tying my hands to the head-board, my legs on either side of his head. He bends me in half and goes to town.

I moan. The sound echoes through the bathroom, and I let it. There's no one but me here, in this large hotel room. For some reason, I was upgraded to a suite when I checked in, and I'm not one to complain.

I reach out to rest my hand against the glass shower wall. My eyes close, and I imagine someone inside me, filling the ache...

"Hello?" a voice rings out.

I only have time to open my eyes. Then he comes into view, stopping in the open doorway of my ensuite bathroom. Tall. Dark hair. Leather jacket. A keycard in hand.

Staring straight at me.

I scream. The shower nozzle falls out of my grasp, spraying water in every direction. I cover my breasts and shove my now-free hand between my legs.

The man closes his eyes. There's a flush of color on his cheeks as he reaches out blindly for the bathroom door I'd left open. He shoves it shut.

"What are you doing in here?!" Embarrassment runs through me, hotter than the water still flowing. It chases away the high of my near-orgasm.

"I could ask you the same thing." The voice, even through

the door, is deep. Almost a bit hoarse. "I checked into this suite earlier today."

I shut the water off and step out of the shower. Wrap a towel around my body. Water drips from my soaking hair and onto the stone floor. "I was just given this suite an hour ago!"

"Must be some mix-up." He curses, loud enough for me to hear every syllable. "I'll... leave you to it."

My cheeks are flaming. I can't remember if anyone has *ever* seen me masturbate. It's not something I've done in bed before.

My hand hovers on the doorknob. Should I ensure he leaves? Tell him off? Right now, I don't know if I can look him in the eye.

I don't know if it's better or worse that the man is handsome, too.

Still doesn't make this his room.

"Bye!" I call.

I hear the heavy front door of my suite open and then shut with a final *snick.*

Breathing a sigh of relief, I look over at the mirror. My entire face is red, and I don't know if it's from the hot water, the pleasure, or the shame.

Probably all three.

I don't finish with the nozzle. Instead, I blow-dry my hair halfway and then throw it into a low bun. Then I get into my jeans and a black sweater. The book I'm reading beckons from where I'd thrown it on my bed. It's by one of my all-time favorite commercial non-fiction authors. One of the writers I most want to be like... if I can manage to impress my editor at Polar Publishing enough to finally get a contract of my own. Not for ghostwriting a memoir, but for writing my own investigative story.

All dressed, I take a long, hard look at the front door of my suite. Someone came in. They shouldn't have been able to, and if anything, that's something I should tell the hotel staff. The front desk needs to know.

But someone also saw me *naked*. A very attractive, very tall, very male someone. Not just naked, either. But my mind can't quite linger on what he saw me doing, or I'll die of embarrassment.

Humiliation is a feeling I'm well aware of. It's something I've been running from for almost a decade. But this time, I hadn't done anything wrong. I had taken a shower in the hotel room *I* was assigned. Upgraded to, even!

I psych myself up and leave the safety of the suite.

The resort is massive and decorated like a Western frontier dream. It has log siding walls and stone floors, and a giant fireplace in the lobby. It's lit, but the leather armchairs in front of it are empty. It would be a great place to read.

I walk straight up to the reception desk. The bespectacled woman behind the long oak counter smiles at me. Her grin disappears as soon as I tell her I'm staying in in room 128.

"Yes, we're so sorry, Ms. Gray." She twists a little, looking behind her at her colleague. He's glancing at me with cheeks that flame red. "This is a very unusual situation, and we've got, well... there's actually been a double-booking," she continues. "Both you and the gentleman in question had been assigned that room."

"I've never experienced this before."

"No, it's very unusual, and we do our best to avoid it." She clears her throat and looks supremely uncomfortable. "The thing is, the resort is fully booked. It's Easter weekend, and we don't have any other rooms left."

It takes a moment for what she's saying to sink in. I've never even heard of this happening before. "What?"

"I'm so sorry." Her voice wavers. "This is unprecedented for us, too, and we will of course refund you the entire sum."

"What does that mean? Who gets the room?"

She glances at someone behind me, a quick look before

returning to me. "That's the problem. The gentleman had, in fact, checked into room 128 before you. We shouldn't have been able to check you into it again, but like I said, this is unprecedented for us. I promise we'll be thoroughly reviewing just how this happened."

Well. That's great. But it doesn't help me now. "There was no one in that room when I arrived," I say. "It was untouched."

"He'd just dropped off his bags in the room and then headed out again." Her cheeks are red now, too. "Truly, we're so, so sorry, Ms. Gray. I've been authorized to offer you extra reward points and a free weekend at a later date. To make up for the inconvenience."

There had been a double booking. He was first. That damn man was *first*? How had I missed a bag in the room?

I'd been tired and dirty from my hike.

I'd gone straight into the bathroom and hit the shower.

"I'm really sorry. The entire team apologizes," she says again.

Don't get irritated. Don't get irritated… "So I need to go back into what I thought was my room, pack up my things, and leave? With nowhere to go?"

She blinks rapidly. "God, I'm so sorry. But… yes." Then her gaze fixes on a point behind me, and her frown deepens.

A man comes to stand beside me at the counter and leans against it. A familiar leather jacket. Black, messy hair. Tanned skin. He puts his keycard on the counter.

"We'll talk this out between us," he tells the receptionist. "Don't worry."

Her shoulders sink. "Okay, absolutely. However you'd like to solve it."

The man smiles at her and then turns to me. Up close, his eyes are green. "Come with me, and let's see what more chaos you'll create."

My eyebrows rise. "*Chaos*?"

"You've caused a lot of it today." But his voice is dryly amused. I follow him over to the fireplace and the two empty chairs there. He gestures for me to sit. As if we're about to open negotiations.

Somewhere right there, between the fireplace and the front desk, my irritation gives way to a fierce embarrassment.

Not even an hour ago, he had seen me naked.

I sit on the very edge of my seat. He smiles a little and sinks to the chair across from me. He occupies all of it. Settles in, long legs stretched out, both arms draped along the armrests.

I focus on the sleeve of his leather jacket. His hand, curved over the edge.

"So," he says. "We're two people, and there's only one room."

"I've never been at a hotel where this has happened to me before."

He nods. "Yeah. Me neither. But it seems like the water pressure at this place is excellent."

Heat races up my cheeks, and my gaze snaps to his.

"How are we going to settle this?" he asks. "Only one room, and the sun has already set outside. It's a long drive to the nearest vacant hotel."

His implication is clear, and I cross my arms over my chest. "I'm not sharing."

"Oh, of course you're not." He leans forward, and something glitters in his eyes. "We'll play a game for it."

CHAPTER 2
CHARLOTTE

"A game," I repeat slowly.

He looks around the lobby. For a moment, I suspect he's going to flag down a waiter, but he just makes eye contact with one instead. Nods his head a little. "Yes. A bit of friendly… betting."

"You can't be serious." Embarrassment and irritation make my words come out sharper than I intended.

"Why not? This makes the evening more interesting." His lips tip up in a half smile, and it makes him even more handsome. "Have you eaten?"

I shake my head mutely.

"We can start with that." The waiter arrives with menus and the man orders a bourbon. He looks at me.

A punch of fear hits me, right below the breastbone, accompanied by adrenaline. It makes everything feel sweeter. "A glass of red wine, please."

I look at him over the edge of my menu. Noticing the thick black hair and the straight eyebrows. His beard looks good, and his face has a light tan, the look of someone who's spent a good week outdoors.

He's large. A few inches taller than me. Broad across the shoulders, something that's emphasized by his leather jacket.

I suddenly feel acutely aware of that. Just like the fact that he saw me naked only a while ago.

Pleasuring myself.

I should win an award just for having a normal conversation with this man, without blushing or racing out of the room.

He's looking at his own menu. "I don't know your name," he says without lifting his eyes.

I hesitate only for a moment. "Charlotte."

"Charlotte," he repeats. "*Chaos* fits you, then."

"That's not my nickname."

A smile plays at the corner of his lips. "Sure it's not."

I want to roll my eyes; it's with a valiant effort that I manage to resist. I'm sure I've sprained something in the effort. "What's your name?"

"Aiden."

The waiter returns with our drinks. I hold my wineglass against my chest like it's a shield. "You want us to play a game for the room?"

"Why not? We're going to have to settle this somehow."

"I'm not giving up my room," I say.

"Neither am I."

I narrow my eyes. "What kind of *game* are you proposing?"

He leans back in his chair and looks around. Other guests are eating in the dining room, and, outside the large windows, the world is pitch-black. The great mountains of Zion are standing silent guard, hidden beneath the blanket of darkness.

"We're limited on options," he says. "But there should be a deck of cards around here. I don't suppose you know how to play blackjack?"

I make sure to keep a smile off my face. Pinch my face a little, as if I'm concerned. "I've played it a few times. It's pretty simple."

He nods and reaches for his drink. "We'll play a few rounds. Winner gets the room."

I reach for my drink and, very deliberately, take a sip. Just like him. Can't drive anywhere now.

"Winner gets the room," I agree.

We order food and Aiden somehow finds a deck of cards. It lies innocent between our plates as we eat.

I do my best to seem slightly confused about the rules and ask him to explain them in detail.

"Okay, I've got it. This will be fun." I look up at him through my lashes. I've been taught well. You never play your opponent—you always play the odds.

A strange sort of excitement takes root. The unexpected. The adventure. It's what I've been chasing for years. Never knew it would come in this form and after one of the most embarrassing moments of my life, but here we are. You play the hand you're dealt.

Aiden has a thick watch on his left hand that seems expensive and hiking boots on his feet. The leather jacket looks fine, but worn.

"You're studying me," he says, cutting into the last part of his steak. "Good tactic."

I reach for my wine. Look at the dark-red liquid rather than at him. "You've seen a whole lot of me today, so I think it's only fair."

His movements pause, and that smile tugs at his lips again. That almost-smile. "Valid point. I didn't look for very long, though."

"But you saw more. So it's justified."

He nods, and that curved smile widens. "Another fair point. Any questions?"

"What are you here for?"

He takes a moment to answer, like the question is a hard one. Then, he lifts a shoulder in a single shrug. "I'm hiking.

Wanted to go somewhere without people. Get away from the... noise."

"This resort can't be to your liking, then."

"No, it's rather crowded. I still prefer the room to sleeping outdoors, though," he says.

I put my cutlery down, finished. If I don't win this game, I'll have to sleep in my car. It's always a possibility. But the wine has taken hold, settled around the edges of my mind, and with it my drive to win.

He had embarrassed me earlier.

Let me try to embarrass him.

The plates are cleared. "Another bourbon," Aiden tells the waiter. He glances at me. "And for the lady... Another glass of wine?"

I nod. "Yes, please."

Aiden cracks open the deck of cards. It looks unused, and he shuffles the cards with more ease than I would have expected from a man with hands that large.

He has no accent that would place him clearly from a certain area of the country. No distinguishing features that lean toward either coast.

He's likely my age. Around twenty-nine, but maybe a bit older. No more than thirty-five, I think. "You're studying me again," he says even as he deals the cards.

"I thought that was an essential part of poker."

"It certainly helps."

"How many rounds do we play?"

"Let's say... best of five. Might take a while." His eyes narrow, and there's a thrill of competition in them that sends energy surging through me. "I hope you don't have somewhere to be."

I reach for my cards. "I do. I just need to win access to it first."

He grins and reaches for his own cards.

The first game takes longer than I'd expected. He's a confident, forceful player, but not stupid. He doesn't make silly mistakes.

I make one, right off the bat. Risking it when I already have sixteen.

There's no need to clue him into my past. Or that I just spent four months working with the world champion of online poker, helping him pen his memoir. I recently left him in Chicago after turning in the second draft of the book.

Sure, blackjack is much simpler. No chips. Closest to twenty-one wins. But you still have to bet with the odds.

Aiden wins the first round. I shake my head. "Damn."

"The night is young," he says.

The people around us clearly feel differently. They have been dropping off—table after table—wrapping up their dinners. Unprompted, the waiter comes by with a bowl of nuts for us and silently pours Aiden another bourbon. I'm still on my second glass of wine.

"Maybe we should up the stakes a little," I say. It's my time to deal this time, and the emotions have made me brave. I feel like someone else, someone who knows how to have these kinds of conversations and say these kinds of things.

Aiden raises an eyebrow. "Oh? What are you thinking."

"I know nothing about you," I say. "I think it's only fair that the winner of a round also gets to… ask a question of their choice. And the other person has to answer."

"Do you want to get to know me, Chaos?"

"That's the stupidest nickname."

That half smile flashes again. "Is it? Because that's exactly what you are. But I'm game. Your turn to deal."

We play in concentrated silence. It's not an easy one. The air is taut between us, and I notice every move he makes. The curl of his hand around his tumbler. The shift of his long legs under the table, one of them brushing my calf.

He doesn't feel like a typical hiker.

Plenty of tells to give him away. His boots are well used

and top-of-the-line. Expensive. But his pants look new, and his leather jacket is absolutely nothing a hiker would choose.

A study in contrasts.

He looks at his cards. "So. Where are you headed?"

"LA."

His eyebrows lift. "LA, huh? Big city compared to this place."

"Yes. Have you ever been?"

His lips quirk. "Once or twice, yeah."

"Me, too, but only for short trips. I'm looking forward to being there longer and actually exploring more of the city. Seeing the sights."

He nods and reaches for another card. "There's lots to do."

"Mm-hmm." We play in silence for another round. This one goes faster than the previous one, and by the end, he's groaning when he busts through 21. I win with just a measly 14.

"I didn't think you'd get that one," he says.

I take a sip out of my wine and meet his gaze. "Don't underestimate me."

His gaze lingers on mine. "I'm learning not to."

The wine is sweet on my tongue, adding to the fiery fuzz already enveloping me. I can taste another adventure.

Judging by his eyes, so can he.

Someone clears their throat. We both look up, the moment broken, to the bartender standing there. "We're closing the bar now, I'm afraid," the bartender says. "I'm really sorry."

"That's a shame." Aiden looks at me, his eyes unreadable. "We've won two games each."

"One left," I breathe, and then we'll know. Best out of five.

"Seems like we'll have to finish this game somewhere else," he says.

My breath comes fast. "It does, doesn't it?"

"Good thing there's a conveniently empty suite down the hall."

CHAPTER 3

CHARLOTTE

"The room does have a minibar."

His smile widens. "And whoever wins the game will end up paying for it. I like the way you think, Chaos."

We head down the hallway in silence, toward the room we both have the keycards to. The gold numbers on the door are glossy, a contrast to the dark wood.

He scans his card and holds the door open for me. I step by him, into the space I had thought was mine for the night.

There's a large bed in the middle of the room.

A desk in one corner. A two-seater sofa and a small armchair, as well as a television. And then the bathroom, off to the right, where we'd... *met* earlier. We both walk right past it.

And a *large bed in the* middle of the room. That fact now feels far harder to ignore. It's giant, with plush white hotel linens and more pillows than could ever be used by the people meant to share it.

Aiden opens the minibar, while I sit down on the sofa. I stroke a hand over the soft fabric and try not to think too far ahead. I want to stay in the moment. Make a dumb decision.

I'm in my in-between state. I could be anyone I want for a night, and then get in the car tomorrow and move on.

Aiden hands me a few small bottles and takes a seat in the chair across from me. He looks larger here somehow. Takes up more space, the armchair disappearing beneath him. He's a sharp contrast against the polished elegance of the room around us.

He deals the cards with strong hands. My gaze lingers over them. The long fingers, the broad backs. "Tell me something about yourself. I know almost nothing," I say.

A smile ghosts across his lips. "You're not one to talk. For a woman I've seen naked, I know nearly nothing about you."

My breath hitches. "And that's not the norm for you then, is it?"

"No," he says and takes another sip of his drink. "It isn't."

This room is spacious. It's a room with a private terrace, an upgrade from the standard room I'd booked. But it suddenly feels very small.

"In my defense," I say, "it has been a very long day."

His look turns wolfish. "I don't think you need an excuse."

I reach for my cards. "Not every place has… great water pressure."

"I can imagine." His eyes feel heavy on mine.

Heat rises through me under his gaze.

"It's a shame I"—he shuffles through his cards before looking back at me—"interrupted you before you could finish."

My fingers tighten around the cards. "It was a bit rude."

"And unfair. As you pointed out earlier. I've seen so much of you, and you've seen nothing of me."

"Not very sportsmanlike," I say.

He shakes his head a little. "Not at all. Almost like we should up the ante a bit."

"Winner still gets the room," I say.

"Yes. Of course." His fingers drum against the armrest,

eyes on mine. "But let's extend it a bit… best of nine rounds. Not five."

I hide my smile. "Seems like you have nowhere else to be, either."

"I do. I just need to win it first, like you." He cocks his head. "Instead of questions… the loser of a round has to remove a piece of clothing."

My heart stutters in my chest and then starts pounding. I cross a leg over the other and do my best to sound unbothered. "Sure. Why not?"

I'm wearing perfectly respectable underwear. I think. Black panties, right? Maybe gray. And the bra is one of my regulars.

It'll have to do.

Both of our movements are faster now. It's an unspoken thing. To speed it up.

He loses the next game. It's harder to play smart the longer we keep drinking. And honestly, I've slipped more than a few times. He's distracting. But I manage to come out on top this time again, and he curses softly when he reaches for his jacket.

"You're good, Chaos."

"Don't sound so surprised."

His lips curve into that half smile, and he shrugs out of the worn leather. He lets it fall to the floor behind him. He's in a gray flannel shirt underneath, the two top buttons are undone. Tan skin and a hint of chest hair peek out from the open collar.

I slowly look down at my cards. He might be the most handsome man I've ever been with… if this night goes as planned.

We play in silence for a minute or two. Our game retains the same speed, our hands coordinated over the small coffee table.

Aiden looks at me as he waits for me to finish my turn. "Do you usually use a showerhead?"

I feel too hot. Too studied. But also like I'd die if he looks away. "No, it's pretty rare. Sometimes my hands. Sometimes… my vibrator."

"Do you have it with you?" His eyes have an almost predatory focus.

Everything I have and lived with in the last four months is in my two giant suitcases, and that includes the slim, black vibrator with a rounded tip. I know that's what he wants to hear.

So I smile at him instead. "Why do you care?"

"Well," he says, and the pause makes my heart stutter. "I find myself very invested in your orgasms."

I have a ten and a five. They bleed together in front of my eyes, but I try to focus on them anyway. Blood rushes into my cheeks. It might not be enough. But drawing another card… would likely bring me over 21. So I don't.

We lay down our cards, and I'm the one who's lost. He's got twenty.

Aiden leans back in his chair, and a small bottle of whiskey dangles from his fingers. It looks tiny in his hand.

"That's very kind of you," I say and reach for the hem of my sweater. I pull it over my head, knowing there's nothing but a bra underneath. I hadn't bothered digging around for a T-shirt or a camisole earlier.

I toss the garment away, letting it land on the bed. I sit back in the chair, bare from the waist up, aside from my plain black bra.

Aiden is very still across from me. Only his eyes roam over my body.

"Damn," he mutters, and there's wry amusement in his voice. "What a shame you lost."

I swallow hard and reach for my cards. He's handsome. Maybe not my usual type. Those guys are usually a bit younger, with messy lives and messier cars. Sharp tongues and nothing going for them.

This isn't a guy. He's a man, and he's hardened and tall and broad in a way that I'm not used to. Speaks with command of both himself and others.

"Don't be nervous," he says and lifts his own cards. "I'll make sure to lose and even the playing field."

My eyes snap to his. "I'm not nervous, and you're not throwing the game!"

His smile widens. "I knew I liked you, Chaos. All right, I won't."

But he loses anyway. I know it's fair and square, though, because I play well. And he rolls his eyes as he reaches for the buttons of his flannel. He undoes them quickly, efficiently, and shrugs out of that piece of clothing, too.

I try my best not to ogle him.

I don't succeed.

There's an expanse of broad chest, hair in the center, and the outline of muscle in his pecs and stomach. Thick muscle, the kind that amplifies a man and speaks of years, if not decades, of good health. No vanity abs, but the hint of them, of true strength beneath.

He's tan, too, and it's only spring. This man likes to spend time outdoors. Expensive watch, though. Expensive taste in whiskey. And a penchant for poker.

"Hey," he says. "My eyes are up here."

I look away immediately, my cheeks burning.

Aiden chuckles darkly, and I roll my eyes. He's got me. "Only fair," he repeats and reaches for his cards. "Now we're even."

"We're nowhere near even," I grumble.

He chuckles again. This time, the deep rumble of his voice sends shivers down my spine. "That can be arranged."

By the end of the next two games, neither of us has won two in a row. The room is still unclaimed, and both of us are in significantly less clothes. I opted for shimmying out of my pants, revealing my black panties. He watched me do it.

I've never been particularly shy about my body. Not for the last few years, anyway. I'd accepted my flaws and my strengths, and that it was my home, one worth taking care of.

But I still feel a frisson of unease, standing in nothing but my bra and panties in front of a man and knowing nothing other than his first name. Fear… and something else.

Excitement.

Aiden's eyes move over me, his gaze darkening. For a few moments, neither of us speaks. The air has drawn tighter around us until it feels like it can be cut with a knife.

He looks at me for a long time and then, slowly, demonstratively, puts his cards down. I sink back onto the sofa across from him. There's so much skin now. Less on him than on me, and I need to win another round to get him out of those pants.

"Charlotte," he says.

I straighten. "Yeah?"

There's a smile in his eyes, one that makes my stomach tighten. He leans in like he's about to tell me a secret. "Let me make it up to you by helping you finish."

CHAPTER 4
CHARLOTTE

He says it so casually, like we're just talking about the weather. Like he's offering to hold the door open or to carry my bags to the car.

A hot flush creeps up my body. It makes me feel too warm, too under scrutiny. I look down at my hands. At the tiny bottle of alcohol, and wonder if I'm brave enough to do this. "And how would you do it?"

"Help you come?" he asks in that casual, deep voice again. "Depends on your preference. Maybe with my face between your thighs. Or I could sit us down in front of the large mirror over there—you in my lap, your legs spread. And I'd touch you while we both watch, and you tell me what feels good."

My breath hitches. "Do you usually go around… offering this service to women?"

Aiden runs a hand along his jaw. I see the hint of a smile behind it. "No," he says. "You're a pretty big exception."

My legs are locked tight together, and despite wearing almost nothing, I feel warm. Very warm.

"Okay," I breathe. "But… you first."

His eyes light up, and he reaches for the cards. Shuffles them *all* together.

"We're going to play a very simple game," he says and turns up a single card. It's a seven. "Higher or lower, Chaos."

"What do I get if I'm right?"

"You get to ask me to do something. I have the right to refuse. But it's… a good start."

"Higher."

He flips, and the next card is a four of spades. I draw in a breath. Shit.

Aiden taps his knuckles against the lowly four. "Oh, damn. That doesn't bode well."

I can barely breathe. "Why?"

"I'm afraid that bra of yours, it's going to have to come off." His eyes rest on mine, and while there's demand there, there is also a playfulness. "If you want. Anything and everything with me is always on your terms, Charlotte."

Right there is when I know I'll go through with this. Wherever this night takes me.

I reach for the clasp and undo it. Slowly, I let the straps fall down my arms, and the cups drop away.

His hands tighten around the cards, and for a long moment, he is still as a statue. He looks, though. And I've never been so looked at in my life.

Sitting in an armchair, late at night, in a hotel room, in nothing but my panties.

I lean forward and reach for the deck of cards. His eyes track the movement, and there's an audible sound when he swallows. "Fuck, you're pretty," he says.

I take the cards out of his unresponsive hands. "Your turn." I flip up an eight, but he's still watching me. "Aiden," I tell him.

He looks down at the card and clears his throat. "Lower."

I turn up the next one, and it's a queen of hearts.

He's lost. I tap my finger against the card. "I want you to take your pants off."

He shakes his head a little, but there's no hesitation in his movements. He stands and undoes the button and the zipper on his pants, and pulls them down. Steps out of them, and then folds them over the back of the armchair, like he's not standing there in just his black boxer briefs.

There's a thick outline through the fabric that I can't look away from. The room isn't warm. But it suddenly feels blazing hot, and I reach for my wine.

As if it will cool me down.

Aiden sits back down on his chair, arms draped along the armrests. Legs spread and his body on full display. "Your turn."

"What do you want this time? If I lose?"

He shuffles the cards a little and then lets his hand hover over the top card. "I want to see the vibrator."

The air feels thick, and I look down at his hand, fingers curled around the edges of the deck.

"All right." I lean forward and revel in the way his gaze drops down to my bare chest. "Turn the card."

It's a three. I look at it for a long moment and then shrug lightly. "Lower."

He chuckles. "I see how it is."

He flips the card, and it's an eight. Naturally.

"What a shame," I say and rise from my seat. I can sense him watching me as I walk to my suitcase, and I feel like someone else, someone I rarely am. Nighttime Charlotte, who drinks wine and indulges in handsome men, and who travels from city to city. Who has no insecurities, no hang-ups. Who knows what she wants and takes what she deserves.

"Damn," he mutters behind me.

I smile and rummage through my bag. The vibrator is in its usual silk bag, and I turn to find Aiden watching me.

"Catch."

He does, easily, and pulls out the thick black vibrator. "Ah," he says. "Interesting."

"It's watertight, so I could have used that instead of the

showerhead." I don't return to my spot on the sofa. I sit down on the bed instead and lean back with my hands on the comforter.

Aiden turns the vibrator over in his hands. "It's a good size, I think."

"Are you an expert?"

"Mm-hmm. Of some things." He looks from the vibrator to me. "How do you usually use it?"

A thread of nerves slithers through me. I don't usually talk about this sort of thing with guys I sleep with. It's never this drawn out, foreplay rarely consists of conversations like this.

"On my clit."

He lifts an eyebrow, and the look he gives me is so full of heat that I have to swallow. "I see." He reaches for the cards and flips up a jack. "I want to kiss you, Chaos. Higher or lower?"

"Lower," I whisper.

It's a queen. "Damn," he says and rises from the chair. He feels big, standing when I'm seated, and another thread of nerves punches through me.

His hand brushes my cheek, coming to cup my face. His skin is warm and just a bit rough, and my eyes flutter closed. He waits another delicious moment and then he presses his lips to mine.

Shivers race through me at the faint touch. His lips are warm and taste like whiskey at first, and then just him.

I reach for him and rest my hands against his chest. His bare chest. Warm, firm skin against my fingers. I slide my hand up over his broad shoulders.

He groans against my mouth and then deepens the kiss. His free hand finds my own exposed skin, curving over my waist, and he kisses me like he could do it all night. Like it's his favorite thing.

I've never been kissed like this before.

Heat floods through me with every touch of his lips. Makes me feel lightheaded and loose-limbed.

"Chaos," he murmurs, and his mouth moves down my cheek. To my neck.

I use my newfound freedom to breathe in deep. His hair tickles my skin, and his lips brush the sensitive skin at the hollow of my throat.

He kisses down my body. His lips close around a nipple, and there's a punch of hot pleasure through me. It races downward, setting off a throbbing.

He runs a hand down my thigh, and then up the inside. Tremors roll over my skin at the light pressure of his fingers. And then, without missing a beat, his touch ghosts between my legs.

My breath hitches. I didn't realize I was this sensitive, but hours of playing, of undressing, of anticipation have set me off.

And I didn't come earlier.

I'm still in my panties. But he caresses through the fabric with casual, careful strokes. "So rude of me," he mutters, kissing across my breastbone, "to have interrupted you earlier."

CHAPTER 5
CHARLOTTE

I arch into his kisses, wanting him back to tease my other nipple in the same way. "You can make it up to me now."

He finds my hand and pulls it down my stomach. Lifts the waistband of my panties and pushes my palm between my legs.

"Touch yourself," he demands.

My fingers are already there, and I start circling. Even as I feel another hot pang of embarrassment. No one had ever seen me touch myself before, and now this man had seen it twice in one day.

"I thought you were going to make it up to me," I say.

He's beside me on the bed—large, tanned. Thick hair, mussed. The outline of his erection is a thick club beneath his boxer briefs.

He looks me over, and there's such sharp appreciation there that my embarrassment disappears. "I will."

He reaches for the vibrator he'd thrown on the bed. And then, he goes to stand at the end of the bed and grips my ankles. Pulling me closer to the edge, he runs his hands down my legs, my thighs, teasing me several times along the waistline of my underwear before gripping the material.

I stop circling my clit.

Aiden tuts. "Keep going," he says and tugs my panties down my legs.

So I continue, and feel scorched by his eyes, locked on the skin between my legs he's revealing. And my fingers, pressing down right where I always touch myself.

"Fuck," he mutters. My panties make it to my ankles, resting against his chest. "Fuck, Chaos. You don't know how turned on I am."

"I haven't touched you yet," I whisper.

"Just as well." He throws my panties away without looking where they land. When they're fully off, he touches me. Fingers on my clit, slipping down through my folds.

It's intimate, and vulnerable, to have all his focus resting between my splayed legs. "Kiss me again," I whisper.

Aiden's eyes gleam, and he bends down, pressing his lips to mine. Somewhere during our makeout session, he finds the vibrator again. He rearranges us, pulling me up against his chest while he leans against the headboard. I sit between his legs. My back to his front.

One of his hands is playing with my nipple. The other settles the vibrator between my open legs. He props it against my clit. It's at the lowest setting, a rumbling that stimulates my sensitive skin. When I'm breathing hard, he slides his thick finger inside me.

A gasp escapes me. I drop my head back, resting it against his shoulder. He kisses my neck, and the combination of sensations is so strong that pleasure quickly swells through me.

"Look at yourself," he tells me.

I look in the mirror through half-lidded eyes. It's catching almost all of us. Him, large behind me. Me, splayed out and naked in his tan arms.

And his hand between my legs, another gripping my small breast in his hand. My boobs have always been tiny.

Another insecurity I don't usually have time to think about during quick hookups like this.

"Can you come for me?"

"Kiss my neck again," I whisper.

He chuckles, but does just that. Touches me. He's everywhere. A finger curls inside me, and then those vibrations against my clit. Low enough that I can't *quite* come. It's not *quite* enough, and I'm so close.

I tell him.

He starts pumping his finger. "Relax," he tells me. "You'll get there. Relax, sweetheart, let me hold you through it."

I do. And somehow, the combination of sensations and the painfully low rhythmic pulses against my clit, push me over the edge. I come.

My climax takes me by surprise.

Aiden keeps his finger inside me and his mouth at my neck throughout my orgasm. When I finally come back down to earth, his erection feels like a steel rod against my back.

I squirm against him—once, twice—until I turn in his arms.

He groans when I stroke him through the fabric of his boxer briefs. "I want to see you, too," I whisper into his neck.

He pulls me up until I straddle him. "I'm yours."

It doesn't take long to get his underwear off him. And then I have him in hand, and he groans against my cheek. "Fuck," he mutters. "I have a condom somewhere."

"So do I," I say.

There's a brief pause, and he groans again. "I'm starting to think that you getting caught in the shower wasn't a mistake."

I slap him lightly on the shoulder. "Absolutely not. I still can't believe the hotel messed up that badly."

"Me, neither."

It takes him less than a minute to find the condom in his

bag. Afterwards he sits back down against the headboard and motions for me.

"You want me to be on top?"

"Don't you?" He rolls on the condom, and I watch him as he does it. His muscled forearms, the girthy cock, the swollen head. When it's fully on, he strokes himself with one hand and reaches for me with the other. "Come here."

I straddle him, and he holds himself upright while I slowly sink down on his length. I grip his shoulders for support, taking inch after inch. He's thick and it's been a while and the stretch is everything.

This feels more intimate than a typical one-night stand. Having his face so close to mine, I'm momentarily frozen. But Aiden's features are tight with pleasure, and his hands slide down to grip my thighs. He rolls me forward, and I fall into a rhythm that's slow and intense.

He kisses me as I ride him. Watches me whenever we pull away to draw a breath. Looks down at where we're connected. And when my pleasure starts to rise again, he reaches for the vibrator and sets it between our bodies.

I come again.

Gripping his shoulders, falling forward, head to his chest. He chuckles into my ear when I finally come down from my high.

"Good, Chaos?"

"Very good," I whisper.

"Think you can handle a bit more?"

I don't even have to think about it. "Yes."

He lifts me, drawing me close, and lays me down on my back.

And then he thrusts hard and deep, sitting up on his knees. It's so forceful that it rocks the bed, and I'm there for every single moment of it. My hands grip the comforter.

This is the best possible celebration I could ever have for finishing my last ghostwriting project.

He grabs my hips for leverage, and when he comes, his face tightens with pleasure that makes him look like he's in pain. It's perfect. I feel like a sex goddess again, Charlotte of the Night.

"Charlotte," he says later, when the condom is discarded and our breathing is under control. "I live in LA."

My brain feels shot. A jumble of pleasure, awash in sensations.

Slowly, his words pierce through. "What?"

"I live in LA. Let me show you around when you arrive."

The pleasure inside me spikes. He hadn't mentioned that earlier when I said where I was headed. I look at Aiden across the bed. The sheets are messed up. We've fallen on either side of the California king. Only one hotel room... and the smartest thing is for us to just share.

I raise my eyebrows. "Are you asking for my number?"

"Yes," he says simply. "I am."

I twist, wanting a better look at him. His eyes are so unusual. A light-green color I've never seen before. They meet mine without any hesitation. He's not embarrassed to have asked, not worried about my response. He's not backtracking.

He's going to be different from everyone I've been with before.

I push off the mattress and slip out of bed. I'm fully naked and terrifyingly aware of it. Aiden watches me walk over to the desk.

I reach for a notepad and pen. *Red Rock Resort* is printed at the top in gold letters. I write my number quickly, feeling his gaze on my exposed body.

When I'm done, I turn to glance at Aiden. He's lounging in the bed. Fully naked. An arm bent behind his neck. And his eyes searing me.

"Call me," I say.

CHAPTER 6

CHARLOTTE

Two weeks later, I'm in Los Angeles, and Aiden has not called.

Not the day after our hook-up. Not the week after. I've stopped hoping for a text.

The small apartment that has been rented for me is in the Westwood area, in a condominium filled with short-term rentals, mostly occupied by students. A small living room, an even smaller bedroom, and a minuscule kitchen. It's clean, though, with only nominal wear and tear from the people who had lived here previously.

I pause, running my hand over the the small wooden table. There's a fake bouquet of tulips in a vase.

This place reminds me of the cast accommodations during the LA press junket ahead of the release of *The Gamble*. Small, impersonal, clean.

I hate that.

It's been almost ten years since *The Gamble*. Ten years since I was a naive nineteen-year-old and too-hopeful to know what I was getting into when I signed onto the reality show.

Nearly a decade since I've been back in LA.

I grab the fake tulips and shove them into the back of a kitchen cabinet. Tomorrow I'll go buy fresh flowers or a potted plant. A throw blanket for the couch. Anything to make this space feel just a little bit less generic.

The round dining room table is covered with a stack of papers for this job. The job I *still* know almost nothing about. Not even the name of the subject. All I know is that it's a man and that he runs a big company. But that's it.

I signed the contract today, and Vera told me that she would send over the packet with the information ASAP. That was hours ago, and she still hasn't. My editor at Polar Publishing is usually on top of things. We've worked together for almost five years at this point, ever since she scouted me as a young, independent, freelancing ghostwriter. Jointly, we've produced almost a dozen memoirs and biographies over the years.

She promised me that if I hit this next book out of the park, we'd talk about getting me on a contract for a non-fiction book under my very own name. Investigative journalism on a topic that we'll brainstorm together. Not someone else's story; but, a tightly woven narrative about the lives of many.

The carrot—dangled.

The stick? This memoir. It has a hard deadline and is shrouded in secrecy. Two months, that's all I have before I need to submit the first draft.

I've worked on short deadlines before. But nothing quite like this. Three signed NDAs and no information about the subject.

As night falls, I crawl into bed in my tiny, impersonal, Westwood apartment. A place that's likely seen a student living here before.

My cracked window is humming with sounds. Cars driving by, cicadas chirping, distant voices. And the heat. It's comfortable here right now, but we're heading into a hotter season. I lie on my side and listen to it all. Breathing through my unsettled nerves, I contemplate murdering Vera for not emailing me as she should.

I never get the chance to.

Morning comes, and so does an email from Vera, sent somewhere around one a.m. I'm bleary-eyed but excited until I read: *I've been stuck at JFK since last night. The flights were delayed because of the storm and now I won't make it in time. Heading back into the City now. So sorry!!! I've told my coworker Jesse to email you the packet. You got this. Hope it goes well!*

No email in the inbox from Jesse. I call the office and get put on hold. Great. Just freaking great.

I'm outside my small condo building at the time Vera's car is supposed to pick me up. The car arrives, sans Vera, and I get in.

We eventually pull to a stop at the entrance to a large office building in Culver City. It's not that far from my tiny rental, but the LA traffic ensures that it takes plenty of time to get there. The exterior of the building is all glass. Elegant, expensive, and entirely anonymous. This entire assignment is shrouded in so much secrecy, it's unreal. I've never experienced so much hush-hush in my life.

I'm supposed to call up from the lobby. Give my name and be escorted up. It's rare that my editor isn't there for the initial meeting, but I guess rescheduling with this businessman wasn't a possibility, either.

It takes ten minutes for someone to come down to get me.

Into the lobby walks a thin man with Southeast Asian features, including black hair slicked back from his forehead. He's wearing red-framed wire glasses and in an impeccably tailored navy suit.

His gaze lands on me immediately. "Ah. Charlotte. You're here."

"I sure am." I extend a hand. "You're Eric Yuwachit?"

"Yes, that's me," he says and gives my hand a quick shake. "Mr. Hartman's executive assistant."

Hartman. My brain whirls, trying to think of the famous corporate leaders I know. Hartman... *Hartman...* It rings a faint bell.

"Come with me," Eric says. His voice is brisk. He looks like a man who runs an impeccable digital calendar and brokers no-nonsense. "A shame your editor from Polar couldn't be here."

"Yes, I know she wishes she was here, too. But with a storm that intense..." I give a light shrug and smile at him. He might not be my subject, but the charming starts here.

I've collaborated with subjects who had assistants before. Eric here is the gatekeeper.

"No, of course." He calls for an elevator, clicking his heels together. "Have you been briefed this morning?"

A thread of unease rushes through me, there and gone again. That's what Vera or Jesse should have done. I've been waiting for that packet email with the brief on the client since I woke up at seven this morning.

But it never arrived.

"No, not quite," I say. "I've been kept out of the loop on the finer details of this project. I only signed all the documents yesterday."

Eric nods again, and we step into the elevator. "That's right. There are certain... sensitivities in this matter that require discretion. Mr. Hartman will explain further."

"He's the subject," I say. It's a guess, but I phrase it like I'm certain.

The elevator starts to move. Up and up, toward the top floor.

"Yes, he is," Eric says. The doors slide open. "He's the CEO of Titan Media."

I falter. "Sorry?"

Eric looks over his shoulder at me, a faint furrow between his brows. "Titan Media. It's one of the largest production companies in the country."

"I know of it." It takes effort to start walking again. To keep my face pleasantly neutral. The hallway is long, and the white walls stark.

Eric nods at a few people as we pass. He walks like a man on a mission, and I have no choice but to follow him. My mouth feels dry.

Titan Media CEO.

They have no idea who I am. And how could they, based on reading my resume? I switched to my mother's maiden name eight years ago. Charlotte Richards, the blonde who stepped off the set of *The Gamble,* is gone. Charlotte Gray is a brunette with a mission.

Titan Media was in charge of producing *The Gamble*, the reality show I was on when I was young and dumb, and I've spent almost a decade running from.

And I've already signed the paperwork. Vera had told me this would be a challenging assignment. *But it has a huge potential, Charlotte,* she'd said. *Huge potential.*

I repeat the words in my mind as I follow Eric. There have been plenty of formidable subjects throughout my career.

Breathe in. Breathe out.

I'll have to strategize later.

We stop at the large door made from frosted glass; bright natural light shines through it. "He's through here," Eric says.

The door swings open.

I'm faced with a large, brightly lit office where the floor-to-ceiling windows let in the bright Los Angeles sun.

There's a wide desk at the center of the office.

And behind it stands a man. He's in a pair of black slacks and a neatly tucked gray button-down, the fabric starched and wrinkle-free. No tie. The top two buttons are undone. He's broad-shouldered, and his arms are crossed over his chest.

Thick, black hair pushed back from his square forehead in a controlled mass. Tanned skin. Sharp eyes.

He's clean-shaven this time. It makes him look much younger, and also harsher somehow, his jaw is square and his eyes that unusual green.

And he's staring straight at me.

"This is Aiden Hartman," Eric says beside me. He makes a small urging sound, and only then do I realize that I've come to a dead stop at the threshold of the office. "The CEO of Titan Media, and the subject of the memoir."

He looks almost like a stranger, silhouetted by the LA sunlight. But he's not a stranger. No, he's not a stranger at all… he's someone I slept with and gave my number to.

And then he never called me.

He smiles. "Come on in, Ms. Gray."

CHAPTER 7

CHARLOTTE

I take a few steps into the office on wooden legs. My pulse is high; it's audible to my ears. A dull pounding and a sense of fight or flight make my legs shake.

What are the *odds*?

The man I met two weeks ago in Utah belongs to a different time. To a different me. To an evening of adrenaline, bad decisions, and fun.

He doesn't belong here.

But he is here. Standing tall behind the desk like he owns it, like he owns everything else around us. His face is so neutral, it could be cut from stone. Gone is the messy hair and beard.

He looks like a complete stranger.

Which is exactly what he is.

And the CEO of Titan Media.

Eric sits down in the chair across from Aiden's desk, and motions for me to take a seat beside him. I do. My eyes never leave Aiden.

He still hasn't shown an outward sign of recognition… but it's there, glinting in his eyes.

"Ms. Gray is the writer hired to pen your memoir. Polar's editor-in-chief, Vera Tran, was delayed by the storm over the

Eastern seaboard, or she would be here for this meeting, too," Eric says. He looks at me, and it's clear in the faint frown on his face that he is wondering why I'm silent. Why I haven't said a single word.

I clear my throat.

"Hello," I say.

Aiden's lips curl a tiny fraction. "Hi."

"It's a... pleasure to meet you," I say, and clear my throat. "I'm the writer connected to Polar Publishing. The one your company vetted and hired for this project. The book, I mean."

"Yes. I've read your profile, Ms. Gray. You've ghostwritten memoirs for several high-profile individuals. Including a former member of *The Real Housewives*."

There's a faint note in his voice, and I wonder if it's judgment. *As if I haven't heard it before.* Anger flares to life inside me, chasing away some of my nerves. This company produces copious amounts of reality TV.

I would know.

"I did, yes. Frankie Swan's book, just before her sentencing."

"I can't say I've read it."

"I'd be surprised if you had."

He lifts an eyebrow. "The CV I read mentioned the memoir by Matthew Bennett, the former US champion in cross-country skiing."

"Yes. I spent a summer living near him and his family in Minnesota, and the result was a beautiful story about winning and the costs that come along with it."

"I haven't read that one, either." Aiden won't look away from me. Is he challenging me? Taunting me?

"Well, maybe you're not a big reader," I say.

There's a small intake of breath from the assistant sitting beside me. *Oh.* Eric.

But Aiden doesn't spare him a glance. "Maybe I'm not. Which book of yours should I pick up first?"

"Whichever interests you the most," I say. *I'm not intimidated,* I think, and will that to be true. "Considering the scope of this project, perhaps the book I co-wrote with William Young about the rise and fall of his tech company. I think that would be most… relevant."

"I know William. I asked him about his experience with you after I received your resume."

My mouth dries out. I had provided references, of course, but had not expected the subject himself to be the one to vet them. Not with a team around him, and so much secrecy that I hadn't even known his name until this very day.

I take another long breath. When in doubt, I've learned to use silence to buy myself time. "Well, since I'm here today, I assume the conversation went well."

His lip curves. "Indeed it had. He said you were agreeable to work with, a quick writer, and amenable to making edits."

Yes. *Edits.* William had certainly required more than his fair share—combing through chapter after chapter I'd written about him to polish away any shred of humanity until all that was left was a superhuman beacon of intelligence and character.

But that was the job sometimes.

"I'm glad he recommended me," I say. But the main question still swirls. How the hell are we going to work together?

Are we just going to pretend like nothing happened between us?

He runs a hand along his jaw, and all I can see is when it was between my legs. I look down at my notes instead. I can't believe he's the CEO of Titan Media and I never knew.

The silence feels heavy.

Eric is the one to break it. "All the paperwork is signed, including the NDAs, and we're set to begin." He holds up a tablet and clicks open what looks like a schedule. "We've worked in blocks of time every week for you to have access to Mr. Hartman."

I look at the schedule. Most of the weeks are blocked out with black squares, but there are a few slots of green with text in them.

Car ride to office. 20 mins.

Lunch break in office. 15 mins.

There's a whole lot of black and very little green.

I look over at Aiden. My thoughts must have been clear on my face because he shrugs. "I'm a busy man, Ms. Gray."

"Charlotte, please," I say. "And I understand that you're busy. You run a company, after all. But with the intense time-line we're under with this memoir, you and I might need to work a bit more closely than this. At least in the beginning."

"This is what we have to work with," Eric says decisively. "If you have any questions, want more material, pictures, or background information—please reach out to me. My office will put together dossiers for you to refer to. This schedule has been forwarded to your email address, and the shared calendar will be continually updated."

I look back down at the schedule. The little ten, fifteen, or sometimes twenty-minute intervals will have me running around the city.

This will be a far cry from spending a summer living in Minnesota right next door to the former athlete and his family who opened their doors to me and gave me access to every aspect: the bad, the beautiful, and the ugly.

"All right," I say. "We're just going to have to make it work."

"We will," Aiden says. His words are confident, but there's a furrow between his brow. I wonder how involved he's really been in this entire process.

He wants a memoir?

He's only thirtysomething.

But Titan Media has been in a storm of bad publicity recently. News broke that the former CEO had been charged with embezzlement and fraud. The company had nearly gone bankrupt.

Along with my family, I'd cheered for it to go belly-up.

The realization that I don't even know the basics about this man, didn't know his *name* until this morning, makes me want to scowl. I need access to make this work.

And I don't even know if I *want* access.

"I believe that's everything. All communication will go through me," Eric says. "You have my number, and I'm only a text away."

I look from the poised man next to me to the man in a suit across the desk. He's staring back at me with an inscrutable look in his eyes.

I can't tell what he's thinking.

"I won't have your number?" I ask.

Aiden blinks once but doesn't look away. Doesn't answer right away, either. Humiliation rests heavily on my shoulders, adding to the maelstrom already raging inside me, but I don't look away. I gave him *my* number. He said he'd call.

But he never did.

"Mr. Hartman has decided that—"

Aiden cuts Eric off with a raised hand. "May I have a few words with Ms. Gray alone, please, Eric?"

Eric's eyebrows fly skyward. For a passing moment there's a tense look on his face, and like he's worried about having done something wrong. It seems that Aiden inspires loyalty in the people around him, or at the very least, respect and fear.

I wonder how he does that.

"Of course. You have… four minutes until your next meeting."

Eric leaves, and the door closes behind him with a sharp sound that rings out ominously loud in the quiet space.

Aiden runs a hand over his jaw again, and there's a spark

in his eye. My breath catches in my throat. I have no idea what's going to come next.

What *I'm* going to say next. Can I write this memoir?

"So *you're* the ghostwriter?" he asks.

"I am."

"Impossible." His voice deepens with something like frustration.

"I can't believe we…" I shake my head. "You know, the proper thing to do would be for me to walk out of here. To rip up the contract because I can't be unbiased."

"Do you have to be unbiased to write a memoir commissioned by the person it's about?" Aiden asks drily. "It won't be presented in front of a panel of impartial judges. No one needs to know about Utah."

"Let's hope they won't." *Vera can never find out,* I think. This memoir is supposed to prove just how far my writing has come. She had told me it would be a sensitive piece of work. *A challenging one.* "You're the CEO of Titan Media," I say. It comes out like an accusation.

Aiden nods. "Yes. Have been for almost two years."

Two years. But it has been over nine years since I was on that first, explosive season of *The Gamble.* The show has been airing ever since. It's one of the highest-watched on the network.

His network.

"You want a memoir," I say. My mind is spinning.

Aiden's hand keeps running over his jaw, a tension in his expression. "The company wants a memoir, yes. There's a packet prepared for you, with background information. Eric will give it to you after this."

I wet my lips. They really *don't* know about me, or my history. It's not on my resume… and I don't look the same. Not that I have my picture on my CV or anything.

Can I do this?

Aiden's eyes are burning through me. For all of his

strangeness, the missing beard, the suit, the commanding air, his gaze is the same as it had been at that resort in Utah.

"What do you say, Charlotte?" he asks. There's a challenge in his voice, a dangerous one. "I can stay professional these months. Can you?"

I've spent years chasing my curiosity. Throwing myself into new challenges. New memoirs, new cities, new subjects.

This will be the hardest one yet.

But I have become tough. I've had to be.

I extend a hand across the desk. His palm meets mine, and warm dry fingers close in a tight grip. We shake.

"You bet," I say.

CHAPTER 8
AIDEN

The fucking memoir.

I rub a hand over my face. The stubble feels rough to the touch, and I know I need to shave again tonight before having dinner with the investors.

I should never have agreed to it.

But what choice did I have? Either appease the Board… or lose the opportunity to expand Titan Media in the direction it needs to go. The direction we all need to go in.

Modernization, technology. *Streaming*. Every day that passes we lose another chance at creating something lasting. The train has already left the station, and we need to get on it.

It's the only way to get this company *truly* back on its feet and ready to face the future. And to prove myself to everyone who would love to see me fail.

There are nine members on the Board, including two who were old friends of my dad. The only ones I haven't been able to replace, yet. But they're heading for retirement soon enough, even if I have to push them there by force.

The Board is younger now than it was when my father or my grandfather ran the company. Partly because of sheer necessity. When my dad's fraudulent activity was exposed, the Board was almost as much to blame as my father. Corporate oversight is sort of their job, after all.

And there had been very little oversight.

Now, the new Board wants a new image for Titan Media.

I turn in my chair and look out at the city. I would rather be anywhere else than right here, right now. The rolling hills of Utah. Joshua Tree National Park. A stretch of beach at an exotic destination.

The memoir isn't about *me*. Not truly. I know it, the Board knows it, and, soon enough, so will Charlotte. The story will be about my father—my relationship with him, his court case, and the time he's currently serving. And it will conclude with a beautiful triumph about how I helmed the company and turned it around in the nick of time.

It's a memoir about *my life*, part of it anyway, but really it's about Titan Media. It will be picked apart by tabloids and business media alike for nuggets they could splash across web pages, newspapers, or turn into a high-profile documentary in a few years.

The Board wants a bestseller that will cleanse us all with holy fire. Use the lemons my father left us with and make lemonade. Apply whatever metaphor you want, and the result is the same.

They want to control the narrative.

But it's my family's story that will be presented like a sacrificial lamb on a pretty little platter for the public to tear apart.

Well.

I had agreed to a first draft in two months. A hard deadline for the deliverable in exchange for the Board's approval of my new investment. They'll sign off on the finalized negotiations once that initial draft is in their inboxes.

But I never intended to make it easy for the memoirist.

They'd want my secrets? My personality, my demons, the scoop on my family? They'd have to drag it out of me. It was a *fuck you* to the Board, with the poor memoir writer as a civilian casualty.

But yesterday the door opened and she walked in... Charlotte. I received the information about the ghostwriter before the meeting. The first name had been the same, sure. But what were the chances? There was no photograph. No other identifying traits.

The writer enjoys solo road trips across our country's great national parks.

None of that.

But there she was.

Charlotte Gray.

Standing in my office in a pair of dark-blue jeans, a gray blouse, and with her long light-brown hair wavy around her elfin face. Bright-blue eyes and a plump mouth.

Staring at me like she just walked into a nightmare.

The odds of us meeting again were astronomical. So fucking slim that, had she been a lottery ticket, I would have won millions.

Millions.

There was a flash of panic in her eyes. I'd been ready to send Eric away, to let her know that if she wanted out of the contract, she could leave. But then she'd steeled herself. Rolled her shoulders back, met my gaze, and delivered her sentences with deliberate professionalism.

It was too damned intriguing. All of her is so damn interesting. Just like she'd been in Utah. Competence and vulnerability living side by side in her dazzling, intelligent gaze.

A complication.

Made worse by the fact that she had given me a goddamned fake phone number. She had brushed me off, and we both knew it.

But we still have to work together for two whole months.

My gaze lands on a helicopter in the distance. Sweeping over Los Angeles, a sprawling city that sometimes makes me feel like a king, and other times claustrophobic. It's where I grew up, where I have my base.

My pride can take it.

It should be able to. What's a snub, after all? So she didn't want more than just one night. There have been times in my life when I haven't, either. Nothing personal.

Except, as first times go, the sex had been fucking amazing. I had a feeling that it would only get better if we got to know each other more. Had seen in her eyes that there were secrets to uncover...

Okay. Maybe my pride was stung.

And the effects have continued for weeks since the night in Utah. My thoughts had returned to her regularly, and more than once with a tinge of bitterness. Clearly, I'd played my cards damn wrong if she felt the need to give me a fake number.

And now I'll have to spend time with her every single week.

It was spiteful of me to tell her I preferred communication via email. But I'd been pissed, sitting there and seeing her looking at me—notebook in hand, eyes serious and wide on mine—like she was fully throwing herself into this *professional* conduct.

She wouldn't give me her number... I wouldn't give her mine.

Spite. Pride. They are emotions I hate in myself. Emotions that had been my father's downfall. But here I am, prone to them anyway.

My childhood had been idyllic, by all conventional standards. Privileged. A multimillion-dollar house in Brentwood, and later in Malibu. Two dogs, private school, plenty of friends, sports. A little sister.

It was almost embarrassing how good it was, looking back.

Even with the cracks that were there. Barely visible to a

child, but obvious to an adult in hindsight. Raised voices behind a bedroom door. Arguments that were brushed under the rug. Holidays where Dad showed up late. Where Mom put on a brave face. My grandmother's harsh words about my father.

I was twenty-nine when the news first hit. Front page. The company my grandparents had built and that my father took over, was in the news. And not in the best of ways.

Under the worst of circumstances, to be honest.

And I was too stupid and too ambition-driven to let it be sold to the highest bidder. I'd stepped in as the CEO two years ago, after the majority of the company's Board was forcibly changed, and everyone thought I was about to fail.

Including me.

A company with perfect financial books was now in ruins. Parts had to be sold off. People let go. At the same time, my father was in custody and awaiting trial.

The fall of the golden family.

That had been one headline, published in a small magazine read by a cultural elite, but I'd never been able to shake the accuracy of that statement.

It's been two years since that day, and I don't want to relive that time. But Charlotte is going to force me to.

There's a sharp knock on my door. I turn in my chair, but the door opens before I have a chance to speak a single word.

Ah.

A blonde woman comes waltzing in. She has honey highlights in her hair, new since the last time I saw her, and a wide smile on her face.

She practically bounces through the space.

"You look happy," I tell her. "And you should have called first."

Mandy waves that away. "Of course not, I'm always welcome. You were the one who told me that."

"Can I rescind it?"

"No." She bends to swiftly kiss my cheek, her red bag bumping against some papers on my desk. It just barely misses the coffee mug. "You look like you're in a mood. What's happened?"

"What hasn't happened?" I ask. "Every day, another fire."

"Yes, yes, being the CEO is very hard," she says and sinks onto the chair facing my desk. "But this is more than that. Did you get smacked in the head by your surfboard this morning?"

I level my sister with a withering glare. "I don't have time to surf anymore."

"Okay, so what's up then?" She leans back in the chair, a wide smile on her face. "Let me play therapist."

She's six years younger than me, and that had been abundantly obvious when we were growing up. When I was sixteen and she was only ten, when our interests were worlds apart, when I felt like an adult and she was just a kid. But that was then, and now is now, and over the years... we'd grown closer. Learned how to be adult siblings.

"I told you about the memoir. Right?"

"You're going through with it?"

"I have to."

Mandy's eyebrows pinch together. "You don't have to do anything."

"The Board demands it in exchange for approving my expansion plans." I tap my fingers against the desk. "So, I kind of do."

"Who's writing it? You?"

"No. The Board approved the executive team to vet and hire a ghostwriter. I met her yesterday."

"I'm not sure I like this," Mandy says.

I sigh. "Yeah. Me, neither. Ergo, mood."

"I mean, memoirs are usually written about people who have *done* a ton of things. Like, incredible athletes, war veterans, or former presidents. What have you done?"

I give her another withering glare. "Mandy."

She continues, her voice tinged with amusement. "You inherited a company in distress, sure, but so have a lot of other people. You're not particularly athletic *anymore*, even if you surf every now and then. You're not a president of anything, and you certainly haven't—"

"I get it, I get it. I'm an incredibly unimpressive person."

She shrugs. "Well, you're not, but you know it's my job to keep you grounded. Are your feet firmly on the ground?"

"We're on the thirteenth floor."

"So that's a no. I will keep going." She lifts her hand, like she's about to count on her fingers. "You've got no sense of—"

"You're ridiculous."

"And you're in a better mood than when I arrived," she says smugly. "So what's bothering you? That the Board wants you to... relive things?"

"They want the memoir to be a clickbait. An excuse for me to be invited to interviews, profiled in magazines. It's an attempt to dredge up the past while controlling the narrative."

"They've said that?"

"They didn't have to. It's clear."

She digs her teeth into her lower lip. "That sounds... Aiden, I don't think I want that."

"I know. I don't, either."

"How will you avoid it?"

The look in her eyes is exactly why I need to thread this needle. My family has come a long way in the past year. Healing has been an odd process, coming in sudden lurches and then long periods of standstill. But we've somehow gotten there. Into a new reality, a fragile truce with the past, and a father we seldom mention.

"I've given the Board my word to help with the memoir process. That's it. That's as far as I've committed. I'll play the rest by ear. And the memoirist can't write about Dad if I don't give them everything, now can they?"

Mandy nods, but there's a furrow between her brows. "Yes. That's true. Besides, maybe there is a point to... acknowledging it publicly. We never really did. Well, *you* never really did."

No. I took over a company that was on the brink of bankruptcy, a company that was my grandparents' crowning achievement, a company that employed thousands of people.

I shouldered a mess when I had expected to inherit a legacy.

And I've worked day and night to make everyone forget that *Hartman* or *Titan Media* means scandal.

"Don't worry," I tell Mandy as I push away the memory of Charlotte sitting in the same chair. Her hand shaking mine. The intrigue I feel despite my intention to give the ghostwriter next to nothing. "I know what I'm doing."

CHAPTER 9
CHARLOTTE

The Los Angeles air is the perfect temperature. It's mid-April, and spring is here. At least this early in the day. By lunchtime, it'll be the kind of heat I'm used to in summer.

But now it's only seven, and I'm waiting outside the house where Aiden lives, just barely visible behind a giant gate outside his Bel Air estate. I'm so nervous, it's hard to focus on anything but my nerves.

Car ride to office. 20 mins.

That's on my planner, one of the few little windows of time when I've been granted access to him. I've worked with very busy people before. This won't be any different in that regard.

Only that it's *him*.

And it's Titan Media.

And *this* is why I shouldn't sleep with random strangers. Why I spent years trying to move away from making bad decisions. I'm a smart person who makes smart, considered, tactical decisions. I never get emotionally invested, and I definitely don't sleep with my subjects.

I was up late last night, reading through the info packet I received from Eric. It includes pages and pages of details about the company. On the other hand, significantly fewer pages about Aiden. It read more like a résumé. His schooling, notable achievements, and the date he took over Titan Media.

The rest I googled. His father. The fraud investigation. The heavily publicized court case and the sentencing hearing. Pictures of Aiden from when he attended the courtroom and sat in the back row. His clean-shaven face was carved in stone, his hair a bit longer back then.

His eyes were unreadable as he stared up at the judge.

And then he'd taken over the control of Titan Media, the company that produced *The Gamble*, and allowed the cesspool that it is to flourish.

I don't think about *The Gamble* or that time in my life much these days.

It hardened me. The public ridicule. The comments. The looks. Simply being the topic of so many conversations.

On the whole, I know it was just a flash in the pan. Fifteen minutes of fame I never wanted, but inadvertently invited into my life. And afterwards, my life continued. So had everyone else's. Except I came out scarred by the experience.

Heart, broken.

Pride, shattered.

Trust, betrayed.

I rarely get recognized these days. That had taken time to achieve. But I'd gotten here, after a bit of growing up. I stopped adding the bleached highlights to my hair and let it return to its natural brown. I stopped straightening it to death and embraced the natural wave. I learned how to exercise and eat healthy in a way that allowed my body to fill out organically and settle into its own feminine shape that I'd been fighting against as a teenager.

Changed my last name.

I hit rock bottom when I walked off the production set of *The Gamble* at nineteen, having made a fool of myself and barely understanding how I ended up in that situation in the first place.

But when you're on rock bottom, the only way is up.

Yet here I am. With Aiden Hartman, Titan Media, and the contract I signed before I knew who the subject was. That had seemed intriguing at the time. I had fun fantasizing about who it might be before learning the truth.

This will be a big one, Vera had said. *Career-defining, possibly.*

Like a fish, I'd been baited and hooked. I wanted this deal so badly because of what I stand to get after. An entire year to spend investigating and writing a story of my choosing.

Writing memoirs has been great. A way to hone my craft and a stellar means to pay the bills while flitting from town to town and story to story. But the old dream hadn't died… and even now, when I should run, it's what I'm clinging to.

Vera had promised. Impress her entire team with this sensitive project, and they'd trust me with a story of my own. I'd be a published author, with a book under my own name.

My fingers tighten around the notepad I'm holding. It's not my only instrument. In my pocket, I have my phone with an easily accessible voice recording app. But I don't know if Aiden will allow me to use it. Not all subjects do, at least not in the beginning.

Establish rapport.

Build trust.

Sketch out the basics of the story and identify areas of interest for a deeper dive. Create a list of other people for me to talk to—friends, siblings, parents, coaches, coworkers.

I have my process, and I need to lean on it to make it through these next two months in one piece. Bury the rest. *The Gamble.* My hatred for Titan. That night in Utah.

How safe I felt with his body around mine.

I take a deep breath. Release it. Repeat it several more times until I feel like I'm back in reality, in the moment I'm in. It's one of many tricks I've learned to handle my anxiety.

I look at the palm trees across the street intensely, I think about nothing else than how pretty they are.

The sizable gate behind me rumbles, and I startle at the sound. I step aside to let a large Jeep drive out.

Aiden's behind the wheel, and he's rolled down the window beside him.

The fragile calm I've built wavers, but it doesn't snap.

I look over at him. "Mr. Hartman."

Aiden is in a navy suit, which fits him so well it must be tailored. His black hair looks even darker... slightly damp? Like he'd just gotten out of the shower. Brows drawn low, his eyes meet mine. "Have you been standing here waiting for me?"

"I like to come early," I say. "Your time is valuable."

"Professionalism in action," he replies. It echoes the words we'd spoken in his office... and the unspoken vow that we'd leave Utah in the past.

"Yes."

"How'd you get here?"

"I took a rideshare," I say. "I assumed it would be easiest."

He frowns, but then gives a nod. "Right. Get in, then."

"Thank you."

Once I'm settled in the car, he pulls out onto the quiet, curved street that runs beside his house, and we wait for the gate to close fully before he drives away.

I turn toward him in the comfort of the leather seat, my notepad in hand. I don't look at it. This is the first interview, and setting the tone is key.

Only, it's never been *quite* this nerve-racking before.

There's a small smile to Aiden's lips. I hate that I *still* like that expression. It reminds me of the resort lobby and the conversation we had. Of the moment when it felt as if I met someone who *understood* what I meant beyond the spoken words...

I squash the feeling. Remind myself that he runs Titan.

Remember that I have a job to do.

"Charlotte," he says. "Where are you staying?"

"At a short-term rental in Westwood."

He makes a thoughtful sound. "Right. It would be better if I picked you up. When we do one of these drives next time."

"That would rob me of about ten minutes or so of your time. Right?"

A smile flashes across his face, there and gone again. "Yes, I guess it would. I don't think you've lived in Los Angeles before, right? If I remember correctly."

"No, I haven't. Just been here a few times." I give him a professional smile. The allusion to our previous conversation won't throw me off. "But you're born and raised here. Partly in Brentwood, just down here, and then in Malibu. Is that true?"

He gives a single nod. "It is."

"Do you still have a house out there? In Malibu?"

"Yes." His hands tighten around the wheel. "Would you like coffee, Charlotte? We can stop on the way to the office."

"Oh, I don't need—"

"I do." Judging by the faint shadow along his jaw, he hasn't shaved today. "Let's make this little meeting more interesting."

"Coffee makes things more interesting to you," I say. My voice comes out dry, and damn it, I don't mean to be bantering here. I'm supposed to be forming a working relationship.

Aiden chuckles. "I'll think more clearly after I have some, yes."

"Mm-hmm," I say. So, he's fielding questions about where he grew up. Something I already *have* information about in my papers.

Lovely.

Time for a different tactic.

I look past him, out the window. "Do you take the same route to work most days?"

"I do, yeah," he says. "I often stop on the way at a cafe in Westwood on the way and pick up coffee. Best coffee in this area of town."

"A daily ritual?"

"I suppose you could say that," he says. "How do you take yours?"

"My coffee?"

His eyes flit to mine, like he's the interviewer. I've lost control of this conversation. "Yes."

"I don't drink coffee."

"Never?" There's a faint thread of amusement in his voice. "One might think you're a sober-living kind of person, but I know you drink alcohol."

Another mention of that night.

"I've just never learned to enjoy the taste. I like the smell, though," I say like an absolute idiot. *Establish rapport, Charlotte.*

"What other state-altering substances have you tried, Ms. Gray?" His voice is a steady drawl, his head back against the headrest.

"I didn't know I was the one having a memoir written about me," I tell him.

His lips curve. "Maybe I want to get to know my memoirist a bit better."

"Worried about my professionalism?" I ask. "Don't worry, your team is welcome to drug test me any day. Aside from the occasional glass or two of wine, I'm not even a drinker."

"Not even a drinker," he repeats, the small smile still there on his face.

"How about you? Any substances you regularly abuse?" I let my little notepad slide down behind my outer thigh, trapping it against the door. For whatever reason, he wants this conversation to be a game.

Very well. I can play.

"I abuse a lot of substances," he says easily. "Most of them legal."

"Coffee," I supply.

"That's one of them, yes."

I don't let my eyes waver from his. "Are you going to make me guess the others?"

"Is any of this great material for a corporate memoir?"

"We're building a working relationship," I say. "Anything could be useful as background information."

"Alcohol," he says. "Preferably scotch; bourbon if that's not around. A good whiskey works, too. Cold beer on a warm day. If needed, I might even share a bottle of wine with a beautiful woman while playing poker. All perfectly legal."

My eyebrows lift. "*If needed*? It was your idea."

His grin flashes again, followed by a brief chuckle. It lights him up. Makes the handsome features almost painful to look at, and reminds me of the challenging, infuriating, carefree man I'd met at the resort.

I shake my head and try to get a grip on the situation. "Any of the illegal substances?"

"You just won't let this go, will you?" he asks lightly. "Like a dog with a bone. I saw on your CV that you studied journalism in college after a gap year. Did they teach you this? To pin your subjects against a wall and never let them go."

That makes me scoff, it's so untrue. "You're incredibly unpinned, Mr. Hartman."

"Aiden," he corrects me. "Call me Aiden."

I try not to let the deep timbre of his voice throw me off. "Aiden. Tell me about your drug habit or don't, that's entirely up to you."

"Fine," he says. "You have wrung it out of me. I give up."

His grandiosity makes me roll my eyes, even as a reluctant smile tugs at my lips. "What is it? A little weed smoking?"

"I dabbled in other things when I was young and dumb, with friends. We were high on adrenaline and testosterone, but apparently not high enough." He shrugs, a casual movement. "There are some worlds where cocaine is served like dessert. Brought out on a tray like crème brûlée."

For all of his casual drawl, he sounds faintly annoyed. *Served like dessert.* I repeat the words to myself. If only I'd been recording this! This is exactly what I want to know.

About the man who was raised in the lap of luxury, in one of America's wealthiest families, whose grandparents were early Hollywood elite, and whose father nearly destroyed their entire legacy.

"It sounds less tasty than crème brûlée," I say. Another stupid comment from my end.

But Aiden just snorts. "Yeah, these days, I'd rather have the sugar. It's just as sinful." He nods at me, and there's a wryness in his voice now. "I saw how your eyes lit up at that, Chaos."

"I'm a writer," I say. Which is why I'm here. Doing this. To get my own book with my own name on the cover and explore a topic of my own choosing.

I have a feeling I'm going to have to remind myself of the goal a lot.

"Yes, you are." There's a trace of bitterness in his voice, so faint that I don't know if I've imagined it. "Tell me you didn't try anything illegal, and I won't believe it."

These interviews are not usually about me. Sure, my subjects often want to get to know me a bit in return. Build trust. Establish rapport. But it has never gone very deep.

Somehow, I fear this time will be different.

"I've dabbled," I echo his words. Lean my head against the headrest, too. Our eyes meet over the black leather console. "But after a few bad incidents with alcohol when I was young, I don't like losing control."

It's an honest answer. A *very* honest answer, if only he

knew. But he doesn't. The gap year he referred to earlier is just that. *A gap year.* The only part on my CV I deliberately gloss over.

He raises an eyebrow. "Like being in control, do you?"

"Yes," I say honestly. "Don't you?"

"Oh, Chaos." His deep voice turns wry once more. "Nowadays, it's the only thing I've got left."

CHAPTER 10

AIDEN

I have a headache. It's not uncommon these days, but it's fucking annoying. Just like that strategy session I just held. The streaming service I want Titan to purchase doesn't want to get sold. The sibling owners have been toying with selling for months, and I've entertained them, played their game, for *months*.

Even with the failing financials, with the lack of capital keeping their enterprise afloat, they're resistant. They want more money. More influence. They're on the same page, and then suddenly, they're not.

I've met every shade of person in this business. But everything hinges on this purchase. *Everything.* And my patience is wearing thin.

The future of Titan Media as a production company and media network is in streaming. And it's in *owning* the means of getting our content out to people.

I down the water bottle I keep on my desk. Reach into the top drawer for an Advil and look at my watch.

It's only a little after noon.

Which means there's still too many hours left of meetings.

It had taken me time to get used to people's eyes resting on me with expectations. Waiting for orders, for speeches, for encouragement or reprimands. Now those gazes have gotten familiar enough that I can feel them even inside this office.

I click open my calendar. There's a twenty-minute lunch break scheduled soon, and it's marked green. Charlotte's name is on it.

She's coming to my office for our second interview.

The sight of her name on my agenda is... thrilling. As inconvenient as it is, as *she* is... there's no denying that talking to her was the most fun I had yesterday, and it was all before eight in the morning. In a car. Stuck in traffic.

She's fierce. Takes everything I give her and responds in kind. Often in surprising ways. It's dangerously sweet. Something I could easily become addicted to.

Sunlight streams through my full-pane windows. It's a bright spring day, and I want air. Los Angeles air, sure. It won't be particularly fresh. But I spend far too much time inside these four walls.

I grab my suit jacket and phone, and head out of the office. Pass Eric on the way.

"Tell Ms. Gray that our meeting location has changed. I'll meet her in the lobby instead."

He's up and out of his chair so fast that the wheels make a scraping noise against the tiled floor. "You will?"

"Yes."

"Do you need me to come, too?"

I'm already walking toward the elevator. "No thanks, Eric," I call over my shoulder. "Man the fort while I'm gone!"

His response of *will do* reaches me just as the elevator doors shut. I hit the button for the ground floor and look at my watch again. She should be here in five minutes. Which means, I'm taking my lunch a bit ahead of schedule.

What a rebel.

I run a hand through my hair. The headache hasn't abated, not one bit. Maybe sunlight will help. Maybe Chaos will help more.

She's already in the lobby.

Standing by the reception, talking to the man behind the desk. It isn't until I'm right next to her that I can make out the conversation.

"Ah... yes, here you are," the receptionist says. His eyes are glued to his screen. "You're on the approved visitor list. Let me grab your ID and make a copy."

"Every time?" I ask. "She needs to do this every time?" She should have gotten an access card the very first day she was here.

"It's protocol." The receptionist looks up from his screen. His lips part, and there's a slow beat of silence. "Oh. I'm sorry, sir. She's your guest?"

"She is. Issue her a permanent visitor card."

His mouth works once, but no sound comes out. Like he's about to protest. But then he just nods briskly. "Absolutely. I can have it done in a few minutes."

"We'll pick it up in twenty. Thank you." My hand finds Charlotte's elbow, and I steer her away from the reception.

There's a confused furrow between her brows. "You're not having lunch in your office?"

"The weather is too nice. Have lunch with me outside."

"I like the sound of that," she says and falls into easy step beside me. "That wasn't necessary, by the way. Intimidating the receptionist like that."

"I didn't intimidate anyone."

"Sure you didn't," she retorts. "Just like every head isn't turned in the lobby right now?"

I glance over her shoulder. Perhaps a few people are looking at us, yes. But that's nothing unusual. Irritation makes my headache pulse.

"Maybe we are attracting a few glances." I push open the glass door for her. "I usually ignore them."

"I bet you have to, to make it through a workday," she says. Her shoulder-length hair sways with every step, gleaming caramel under the bright spring sunlight. "So, where are we going?"

I point across the trafficked LA road to the food trucks. "There."

"We're having street food?" There's a trace of excitement in her voice. "I have to say, I didn't expect that."

We cross the street along with a group of business-clad people. It's midday and plenty of people are out hunting for lunch.

"Do you usually eat here?" she asks me. "Is this another favorite place of yours, like that coffee shop?"

"I'm almost never here." I order tacos and a large bottle of water from the guy in the food truck. I motion for Charlotte to make her selection at the same time and she steps up to the plate.

I pay for both of our meals, and we head with our food to a sunny bench.

I should do this more often. Escape the four-walled prison that's become more familiar to me than my own house.

Charlotte crosses her legs and turns toward me on the bench. There's a glow on her cheeks, mirrored in her eyes.

She's distractingly cute.

"We spoke about everything and nothing yesterday," she says. "That's good, as a starting point for me to get to know you."

"Mm-hmm." I take a large bite of my beef taco and look away from her bright blue eyes. My determination to give her almost nothing hasn't wavered.

"But I'm curious, what are you looking to get out of this? What parts of yourself do you think are key that we need to highlight during this process?"

"You never stop working," I say.

She makes a small sound of surprise. "Well, I'm hired to work for *you*, Aiden. And I have far too little access to you as it is."

I appreciate her diligence. It's just damned inconvenient at the moment. "Why did you start writing memoirs?" I ask instead. "What is it *you* get out of it? Only fair I learn stuff about you, too."

Charlotte takes a bite out of her fish taco. Chews slowly, her head slightly cocked. "I studied journalism in college, with a minor in creative writing. I've always enjoyed people's stories, you know? Just understanding what makes them tick, why they make the choices they make... I grew up loving both fictional storytelling and documentaries. There's just something about *real* stories, though. Real people don't follow scripts.

"They're not created by trained writers to evoke certain emotions. They're messy and complicated, and full of conflicting emotions." She shrugs a bit, and looks at me with a strong gaze. Like she's daring me to object or find it silly. "That's why I love writing memoirs. It's fascinating to tell a real person's story."

Well.

Damn.

I run my free hand along my jaw and look back out at the people milling about on their lunch hour.

"That's a very good answer."

She gives a surprised little chuckle. "Well... thank you. What about you? Why do you enjoy doing what you do?"

It's an innocuous enough question. But *enjoy*?

I meet her blue gaze. "It's a family company. I have a responsibility to my employees, to my family, and to my grandparents' legacy to ensure it operates to the best of its ability."

Her eyebrows draw together. "That's a powerful motivation."

"It's a life sentence," I say.

CHAPTER 11
AIDEN

"A life sentence," she repeats. The sunlight glints off her wavy hair. "Do you see it like that?"

She looks at me like I'm a puzzle piece she needs to make fit. A problem to be solved and a mystery to be unraveled. It's been a long time since anyone looked at me like that.

I want to talk to her, stupid as it is.

"Not always in a negative way. But it's not like I can do something else, no. This is it for me."

"What part of your workday do you enjoy the most?" she asks.

I look away from Charlotte to the crowd of people. The line to the food trucks grow ever longer.

"Strategy meetings," I say.

It's the truth, even if the one today had been frustrating. And I do have to give her something, just not enough *somethings* to string together the kind of salacious memoir the Board wants from me.

"Strategy meetings," she echoes. "Is that where you plan programming for the next year or two?"

"Yes, among other things. Expansions. New hires. Upcoming projects. Financials. Strategy is at the core of most of our decisions."

"You like making those long-term decisions."

"I do."

She blows out a soft sigh, and my gaze is drawn back to hers. To the slight narrowing of her eyes. "How involved are you with... the various shows you produce?"

"It depends. Most often, I'm not involved at all in the storytelling or production. Only in the big-picture decisions. Which shows to continue, which to ax, which to invest in more." But I'd rather talk about her. "How do you decide what to keep and what to toss when writing a memoir? You must get more information than you know what to do with."

"I get a lot, yes. All too often." She shrugs lightly. "It depends on the story the subject and I want to tell."

That word makes my lips curve. "The *story*."

"Yes."

"Aren't memoirs meant to be true?"

"Ah, but whose truth?" she asks. "That's for one of our future meetings. I'll give you a few narrative options, and you can choose which one you want me to go with."

"Narrative options?"

"The hero's journey, for example. An antihero perspective. The David and Goliath story." She inclines her head to me, a wry smile on her face. "My guess is you want a hero's journey. But we'll see."

"My journey isn't heroic," I mutter. My hand closes around the paper and napkin still in my hand, bundling it all up into a tight ball.

For years, the only thing I've fought for is privacy. For me, my mother, and my little sister. Privacy that my dad didn't afford us when he blew up our entire lives and left us behind.

And here I am, going against just that so I can expand Titan Media. The painful irony of that isn't lost on me.

I don't have time for anything else. No space for anything else. Even if the woman by my side is making me want to rethink that.

"Oh?" Charlotte asks. "I would have thought that's the narrative you wanted. You know, with... the company's history."

Yeah.

That's the narrative the Board wants. They want me to expose my father's lies and secrets, tell a sob story of how I rescued a business in dire straits, and cleanse the public image of both the studio and the founding family.

The sun is warm on my face. The sounds of the city are loud, and I wish I could ignore them. That there would be the blessed silence of my childhood instead, or of evenings by the ocean and hikes in the mountains.

Charlotte breaks the silence first. "We don't have to talk about that right away. If you don't want to."

I look at her. "Would you want to talk about the greatest shame of your life?"

Her gaze turns flinty. She swallows hard before replying. "No. I don't usually talk about mine. Even if I'm not the one writing a memoir about myself. You must have had goals with this, right? Rehabilitating your public image? Focus on that, and we'll get through the hard parts."

My goal is to get the Board to approve my billion-dollar purchase. The memoir is a painful means to an end.

I nod down to her half-eaten food instead. "We're almost out of time. You should finish your taco."

She glances down at it. "You can be pretty demanding sometimes, you know. And good at evading questions."

The words slip out of her, a trace of annoyance in her tone. I don't think these are words she wanted to say. They don't belong in her normally composed, professional dialogue of interviewee and interviewer.

A smile tugs at my lips. "This isn't my first interview."

"I'm on *your* side," she says. "We both want a truly great book out of this."

"What's next on our schedule together?"

She blinks. "Next Monday, during your workout. I'll be in your home gym."

That makes me smile. "You'll be watching me work out?"

"I'll be asking you questions and taking notes," she answers sharply.

"Work out with me," I say with a shrug. "There's space for two."

"Why does it feel like you're less interested in *actually* letting me get work done?"

"I don't know, Charlotte. Why does it?"

She narrows her eyes at me, and damn it, I love getting her annoyed. "We shook on being professional."

"I'm nothing if not professional," I say. "I haven't mentioned Utah once."

"You just did!"

"Oh, did I?"

She rolls her eyes. "I'm going to show up with a giant list of questions, and I'm not going to take any diversions or misdirections."

"Not even if I work out shirtless?" I ask her, grinning. My headache is gone. It might be the Advil, but I think it's her.

"You're impossible. Do you conduct other business meetings like this?"

"No. Why don't you sit in on a few, for your notes?"

Her mouth parts. "Really? You'd be okay with that?"

"Sure. Your NDAs prohibit you from reporting on anything business sensitive, and the Board will have final approval." I hold out a hand. "You're not going to finish your taco. You didn't like it."

Her eyes flash down to her food, and then back to me. "What makes you think that?"

"You frowned after your first bite."

"It's got too many chili peppers," she admits, her voice a bit sheepish. "I forgot to tell him not to add them, and then it was too late."

"You could have asked for another one." My hand is still extended. "Come on, give it to me and I'll buy you another one."

"You definitely don't need to do that. You have to head back inside, you have another meeting—"

"I can be late."

"Eric said that you're never late." She makes her voice deeper, an imitation. "'Mr. Hartman values punctuality above all else.'"

I chuckle. "Mr. Hartman also takes the lunches of his employees very seriously."

"I'm not your employee."

"Hired freelancer, then. Now here, hand it over."

"I don't remember you being this bossy."

I raise an eyebrow. "Don't you?"

She blinks rapidly a few times and then puts the taco in my hand. "Fine. Here. And I do have a question... Do I need to contact Eric every time I want to ask you something?" she asks. "I might have questions throughout this process."

"You want my number?" I ask. The question comes out dry, and just a bit bitter. Damn it.

Charlotte's eyes widen and then a fierce color races up her cheeks. She looks down. Is she embarrassed about giving me a fake number?

I clear my throat a bit harshly. "You don't have to contact Eric every time. Here." I dig into my pocket. Find my wallet and one of my business cards there. It doesn't have my phone number on it.

But it does have my direct email address.

I hand it to her. "Make sure you write *Charlotte* in the subject line."

She looks down at the smooth paper, gripped between her fingers. Maybe I shouldn't have mentioned the phone number thing. Women blow men off all the time. She must have had her reasons. The desire to ask her about it, to invite more pain in, is on the tip of my tongue.

I bite down on it. We shook on remaining professional.

And as intriguing as she is, I still don't have time for a relationship. That was the whole reason my last one ended.

She runs a finger over the logo at the top. "CEO of Titan Media," she murmurs.

There's something in her voice that I can't place. She doesn't sound happy. Like this simple fact is somehow a problem. I open my mouth to ask her something—anything—when my phone rings. Eric. *Time's up.*

But despite it all, I wish it wasn't.

CHAPTER 12
CHARLOTTE

Ten million.

No. That can't be enough. I know how expensive this area is, and the kind of houses I'm surrounded by. What I don't know is who lives in them, but I bet I'd recognize some of their names.

Twenty million? Maybe. I've seen those reality shows where they sell houses, and in LA, they're not cheap. The one I'm standing in front of at 5:50 a.m. on Monday morning is enormous. It's hidden behind large Bel Air hedges, high on the mountain behind Westwood.

The weather is warm, but there's a tiny chill that makes my jean jacket entirely worth it. I did *not* come dressed in workout clothes.

There has to be a limit somewhere, and that's mine.

It's been a week since I was first introduced to Aiden as the subject, and I have almost nothing. No direction for this memoir, no list of people in his life I'll be able to speak to. The man is a vault.

A frustratingly charming, evasive vault.

Ignoring the night in Utah has been easier than ignoring that I'm writing something *in favor* of Titan Media. Something to clear its name and help rehabilitate its reputation.

That makes me feel dirty.

It's a profit-driven corporation that produces, among other things, reality shows without any safeguards to protect the young men and women who participate. Anything for the drama. Anything for a good show.

Anything for viewers and money in the bank.

But Vera's promise is driving me. The promise of *if* this memoir does well, *if* I impress her and her team, I'll get a contract to write something of my own choosing.

Not to mention the contract I signed.

That chafes most of all. Since *The Gamble*, I've made it a priority to always go over every contract with a magnifying glass.

I never want to be trapped by *contractual obligations* again.

Yet here I am. Standing in front of the black wrought iron gate and peering at a giant, white house. Perfectly manicured gardens. Sharp, modern angles and glass.

Twenty-five million, maybe.

I roll my neck. Push my shoulders back. Take another deep breath and remind myself that I've survived far more difficult things than Aiden Hartman. I can handle this. The first week is over. Only one month and three weeks left to go.

I don't have the code to his gate. It's too large to scale, and no doubt, I'd be instantly shot down by the security snipers stationed on the roof. For twenty-five million plus, I bet that's included.

Aiden comes into view.

He's walking from the side of the house. Black shorts, gray T-shirt. His dark hair is pushed back messily, and the sight sends a jolt through me. I've never seen him like that. Here, in his home.

"Hello. Fancy seeing you here." He pulls the gate open.

"I parked on the street. Is that okay?" I've heard how the residents in areas like this one hate when people do that. But Aiden just nods.

"Yes." He walks over to the large garage beside his house. Two cars are parked outside it, and I add a few more million to my estimate. One's his Jeep, the one made for off-roading. The other looks smaller and faster, and even more expensive. I haven't seen that one before.

"In here," he says and opens yet another door. "I'll get you a key card for the gate for next time."

That's a fairly big step for people with his level of privacy concerns. But he doesn't seem bothered, walking straight across the large home gym to the bench. It has a weightlifting bar resting above it, and he settles down to start chest presses.

Like I'm not even here.

There's a lot of him on display. Golden skin, and thick calves, and his arms are bulging as he lifts the barbell. Once. Twice. Damn him for being handsome, too, on top of everything else.

I've read all about him these past few days. Combed through the dossier I was given—every word, every number. Read every page on Titan Media's website. Online articles. The web has been my constant companion these past few days, outside of my twenty-minute meetings with him.

The rubber sole of my shoe makes a screech against the hardwood floor, and I look around for a place to sit. The space is fully stacked. A set of free weights, resistance machines, a treadmill, and a stationary bike. There's a wall-mounted TV that plays the morning news at a low volume.

"This is fully equipped," I say.

"Yeah, it's a good home gym." His eyes dip down, travel over my body. "You decided not to join me, I see."

"I'm here to work."

"Right." There's a smile in his voice. "And what's the plan today? Twenty questions?"

"Would you really answer twenty questions in a row? Because I'd love that, if you're willing to play ball," I say.

He motions to one of the benches. "Have a seat. Make yourself at home."

"So that's a no," I say and shrug out of my jean jacket. Hang it on the back of a machine. "You know, I've read almost all the interviews you've ever given, which haven't been many. Did you put those interviewers through the ringer, too?"

"Maybe I just test everyone," he says.

"Maybe you do." I sit down on a Pilates ball and instantly regret the decision. It's hard to feel dignified when you're gently bobbing up and down. "Do you usually get up this early?"

"When I'm working, yeah."

That makes me perk up. "What do you usually do when you're not?"

"I travel. With family or with friends." He pushes off the bench and walks over to where a huge row of dumbbells is perched. He grabs some of the heaviest and starts slow, methodical biceps curls.

I do my best to ignore the display of testosterone.

"Family and friends. Who would you say your closest friends are?" I ask.

He glances at me, wry amusement in his gaze. "We're doing twenty questions regardless?"

I meet his gaze head-on. "Yes. I was given a thirty-page dossier on you and Titan Media by your assistant, but those are just facts on paper. I want to hear it in your voice."

"Sure are," he mutters. His arms are still moving in slow, deliberate bicep curls.

"Do you think there's any chance I could talk to them, also? Your friends?"

His eyes are on mine. Heavy, as always. "Why?"

"Because they likely have a different perspective on you.

We don't always see ourselves so clearly, you know. But our friends and family usually do." I shrug, making sure to keep my voice light. "It's a normal part of the memoir writing process."

"Hmm," he hums. There's a faint sheen along his forehead, and his arm muscles bulge with the movements. "Right. Well, most are busy and working a lot."

"I know how to work a video call," I say with a bright smile. "Where do you usually travel when you're not in the city?"

"Need addresses for the book?"

"No." I feel like one of his dumbbells. Lifted up and down, up and down. "But your habits are part of you, and you're the focus of it, after all."

"I go out of town as often as I can," he says. "To the ocean, or the mountains. I'm in Europe a few times a year, sometimes on business and sometimes for pleasure."

"And Utah." I regret the comment immediately.

He raises an eyebrow, glancing in my direction. "And Utah, yes." Something in his voice makes the word sound salacious. As if it's an event rather than just the name of a state.

I look down at my hands instead. "You played a lot of sports in school."

"I did," he confirms. "Was that in your dossier?"

"Yeah. You were on the football team in college. That's not an easy spot to get."

"I was mostly on the sidelines," he says. "It was a fun pastime. The other guys played on scholarships, for future careers. Not me."

My hand itches, wanting to reach for the notepad in my back pocket. But his confessions seem far and few between, and I don't want to remind him about the process more than I have to.

If only I had his permission to record!

"Because you were always set on this as your career? The family company?"

He lets the silence hang for a moment before responding. "Yes."

"My guess is the timeline was moved up a fair bit, though. With the succession coming earlier than planned."

Flashing lights. His father's trial. The prison sentence.

"Yes," he grits out. The dumbbells look heavy, and he's been doing countless reps. "You could say that."

"Hard times in your life. But you've managed to turn things around. Titan Media did record numbers last year." And *The Gamble* is still one of their most popular shows. "Do you miss college?"

"It was all right," he says and sets back the dumbbells. Moves to a machine in the corner instead and notches up the weights while I watch. He notices my gaze and looks back at me. "It was fun. I was a kid in college, legal drinking age. Of course, they were fun years."

I clear my throat and the Pilates ball bobs gently beneath me. Still such an undignified choice, but now that I've made it, I gotta stick with it. "You have one sister, right?"

"Yes."

"Are you two close?"

"Close enough," he says. "As most siblings."

"Many would say that you were raised wealthy. The Business Digest interview you gave a year ago described your family as 'golden.'" They also proclaimed *the golden family's fall from grace,* but I'm not mentioning that. "Is that a description that resonates with you?"

He pauses. "You read the interview."

"I've done a lot of research over the past week, yes."

"Not everything the papers print is true."

"I'm sure it isn't," I say, trying hard not to sound annoyed. "That's why I'm asking you about it."

"I was raised rich, yeah," he says simply, pushing off the

weight machine and moves toward another machine with handles. Must be arms and back day today.

A glance at my watch tells me I'm almost running out of time. Only five minutes left, and there's almost *nothing* I've gotten out of this. Infuriating man. No one I've ever worked with until now has proven to be this hard to get information out of.

Most people who have memoirs written about themselves are *eager* to tell me as much as possible.

They'll show up to meetings with lists and lists of anecdotes they want me to include. Family trees. Pictures.

Aiden starts using the machine. His black T-shirt, shorts, and shoes blend in with the gym gear, somehow highlighting the vast expanse of muscle and exposed skin on display.

"What values do you think you got from home? That your parents really fostered in you and your sister?"

The weight plates in the machine drop in a loud crash, the cables and pulleys stopping in their tracks. Aiden leans forward, bracing his arms against his thighs. There's a challenge in his eyes. "You want to know if they taught me to say my please and thank yous?"

I want to throw my hands up. God, this *fucking* man. When he's like this, it's hard to remember what I had found so irresistibly charming about him out at that resort.

"I want to get to know *you*, yes. What shaped you. The material I have right now would hardly fill two entire chapters."

"We've only worked together for a week."

I narrow my eyes at him. "Can I give you homework?"

"Homework." He does another pull-down. "What is it?"

"Think of an anecdote. Just one, that illustrates something about you or your past that you think is relevant."

"I don't spend much time sitting and just thinking about myself."

I push off the Pilates ball as gracefully as possible. "First of all, I don't think that's true for a *second*. And even if it is… just try. Running a company *cannot* be easier than sharing a little info about yourself."

A curved smile stretches across his face. "You're angry."

"No," I say, but my clipped voice betrays me. "I'm being professional. Which means that I care about delivering a comprehensive and moving first draft of your story."

Aiden rises off the bench, and I lose my height advantage. He runs a hand through his mussed hair, and I hate that he looks so much more like the man I met weeks ago and not the tailored suit-clad CEO I've been faced with lately.

"The next time slot on our schedule is a car drive tomorrow evening to the fundraising event," he says in another stunning display of changing the subject.

I want to cross my arms over my chest.

I want to tell him that he's being obstinate.

"Yes, we have about forty minutes."

"The invitation includes a plus-one," he says and takes a step closer. His eyes are locked on mine, and there's that glint in them again, like he's setting me up for a challenge. Like he wants to see if I'll back down. "Come to the event with me."

It will give me more time with him. And time to observe him in his natural habitat. My teeth dig into my lower lip. Right now, I don't want to spend any more time with him than I absolutely have to.

But I have a book to finish. And the sooner I get the details I can from him, the sooner I can retreat to my writing cave and just focus on creating output.

"I'll go."

His mouth curves. "Need a dress? My assistant can take you to the stores. It's on me."

That makes my eyes narrow. "I have dresses. Thank you. And I'm not sure that would be a good use of Eric's time."

"Just asking," he says, still smiling. He walks over to grab his water bottle and runs a white towel over his face. "And Eric wouldn't be going. It would be my personal assistant."

"Eric isn't your personal assistant?"

"He's my executive assistant, and handles my work engagements." Aiden hangs the towel around his neck, and the room feels too small, with so much masculinity on display. "Elena is my personal assistant. She takes care of personal travel, household maintenance, that sort of thing."

Right.

He's as close to American royalty as they come. This is just another reminder of everything that makes his world different from mine—the helpful hands and money and redirected responsibilities.

I open my mouth to ask if he can get Eric to send me the details for the event.

But Aiden speaks first. "And no, I don't think Elena or Eric would be good interview subjects."

My mouth clamps shut. They would be *excellent* interview subjects.

Why does it feel like he's sabotaging his own memoir?

CHAPTER 13

CHARLOTTE

I lied.

I don't have a dress. Not one fit for a gala, anyway, in the suitcases I brought to Los Angeles. The nomadic lifestyle has its downside sometimes.

But the smug look on Aiden's face when he suggested I buy a dress on his dime... No, thank you. I can't forget even for a moment just what company he's the CEO of.

So I bought one, a floor-length strapless gown that doesn't look *too* cheap, even if it's more of an off-the-rack prom dress than haute couture. I can't imagine needing to go to many more events like this in the future.

It's funny, thinking of how many *costumes* I've worn in the past few years. When I lived up in Alaska, interviewing the national female champion in dog mushing, working on her memoir, I was in thermals and braids and not a stitch of makeup.

When I worked together with William Young on his memoir, it was all slacks and white button-downs to fit in with his slick Silicon Valley vibe.

And now I'm in heels and a long dress, waiting on the sidewalk outside my rental unit, with my hair softly curled and smokey eyeshadow highlighting my eyes.

Being a chameleon has been an asset in this job.

The Los Angeles evening air is pleasantly warm. Cicadas sing in the background, and I look down at my shoes on the beige concrete. They're old block heels I've used too often. But they'll have to do.

A black car pulls to a stop right beside me. Aiden gets out of the back, leaving the door open. He's in a tux without a bowtie, clean-shaven. No mussed hair. No sweat. He's back to the neat, dashing celebrity he so often resembles.

"Charlotte," he says. His eyes look over the deep emerald of my dress. "You look…" His voice trails off.

"I pulled something together," I say quickly.

His lips curve. "You certainly did." His eyes travel from me to the nondescript condo building behind me. "This is where you live."

I square my shoulders. "This is where your company arranged for an apartment for me through the contract with Polar Publishing, yes."

"These are student accommodations." His smile is gone now.

"Mm-hmm, but I imagine it was affordable." I walk past him and slide onto the plush backseat. The last thing I need is for him to be patronizing, too.

Aiden climbs into the car after me, and the driver pulls away from the curb. *Game time.* I open my clutch and take out the three neatly folded documents I prepared.

Because come hell or high water, I *will* write the best memoir about him. The deepest, most emotional, interesting portrait of a man who's overcoming the difficulties of his father's indictment and turning his family company around.

I have too much riding on this *not* to hit it out of the park.

"You brought… what is this?" he asks.

I unfold the first page and clear my throat. He won't throw me off. "This is a list of questions that will greatly help me. I understand that you're not a big fan of interviews, but for a successful memoir, I need some answers. It might be hard to tell me outright, in person. And that's fine." I push the paper into his hands. "I'll also email a copy of this directly to you. Feel free to answer in an email form or through voice notes. I'm flexible."

"Homework," he says, his eyes scanning over the list. "You want to know about my first girlfriend? If I had a child-hood pet?"

"Yes."

He gives a low chuckle. "My reaction to my father's arrest. Well, you've really gone high and low with this list."

"I'm building the character sketch for you."

"I'm not a character."

"Of course not," I say, and my voice stays calm. Neutral. *Professional.* I unfold the next piece of paper and hand it to him, too. "This is the rough outline I've laid out for your memoir. All of it is changeable, and I'll probably have to move the chapters around when I gain more information. Please look it over when you have the time and see if it's acceptable to you."

It's a neat little document, with a two-column table. Chapter by chapter headings, with descriptions of what I'll need for each.

"You've decided what narrative you're going for, then," he says. There's a faint frown on his lips, his head bent slightly to look at the documents in his hands. Outside the car windows, the city passes by in a blur.

"A classic hero's journey," I say.

His eyes skim the list. "The Start. The Legacy…" he mutters, reading the working chapter titles. "The Crash, the Trial, the Rebuild, the Strategy, the Comeback, the Philoso-phy… You have it all figured out."

"It's a preliminary sketch," I say. "Something to work

with. I'd love your thoughts about this narrative, your input on what you think is important to be covered in each section. We can start with these bulleted points and expand upon them in order."

"Methodical," he says.

I don't know if his tone is one of admiration or admonition.

But it doesn't matter much. I try to let it roll off me and reach for the final piece of paper.

Hand it to him.

There's a punch of silence, accentuated by the sound of traffic outside us and the rumbling engine.

"This is a list of people," he says, voice quiet in a way that makes him suddenly feel dangerous.

I force my voice to be strong. "Yes. These are people who either know you well or know the various aspects of you. Facets. Talking with them would greatly help me form a more holistic view of you."

He turns to look at me, his fingers tightening around the paper. "This list includes over twenty people."

"Yes."

"Eric and Elena are both on it. My driver. Board members. Old friends from college. My mother. My sister." He doesn't add the final person, but it hangs in the air.

His father.

It had been a crazy streak of defiance when I added his father's name to the list. His father—the man who made this entire project necessary, and who is serving time for fraud in a prison upstate.

"I need to get to know you, and that requires access," I say briskly. "Think about it. You don't have to agree to all of them, and not everyone will likely agree to participate. But if they do, they may speak on or off the record. I'm open to just having their views as background info." I reach over and tap the paper still in his grip. "I'll also be sending this directly to your email and will include Eric in the cc."

Aiden's handsome features are so blank, it looks like I've shocked him. I wonder how often that happens.

Then his eyes narrow. "You're good at your job, Charlotte."

It sounds like an accusation.

"Yes, and I take pride in a job well done. Just like you do, it seems," I say. "We both want this memoir to be a bestseller. I'm willing to do my part. Are you?"

He doesn't look away from my glare.

I don't avert my eyes, either. Let him give me the CEO stare, the one that's probably won him negotiations and intimidated lesser people. I won't be one of them.

I've faced worse than Aiden Hartman in my day.

There's a sharp clearing of a throat from the front seat, and it breaks the standoff between us. Aiden looks at his driver.

"We're here, sir," the chauffeur says. "I'll be on standby. Five, maybe ten minutes away, tops."

"Thanks," Aiden says. He looks back down at the papers in his lap for a second before folding them up in precise squares. He slides the bundle into his inside pocket, out of sight.

Out of mind?

He still hasn't answered me.

"Aiden?" I ask.

He looks at me then, his green eyes appearing nearly black in the dim lighting. "Time to go, Charlotte. You can ask more of your questions inside."

"I can be an observer tonight," I say. Seeing how he interacts with other people, hearing their conversations, is a great way to gain information. A fly on the wall.

He lifts an eyebrow. "Can you? Well... let's see."

There's a crowd of people, attendants, guests, and security. And a gold carpet rolled out from the event hall.

Aiden extends his arm.

I hesitate, looking at his hand and the hint of a watch peeking out from beneath his sleeve.

"There are photographers here," I say. Why hadn't I thought about this? I'd thought about everything else.

"There are," he says.

"They might think we're dating. That I'm like... your date."

There's a tug to his lips. "You are my date."

"I'm your plus-one."

"Semantics."

"I can't be involved with my subject," I say. My voice comes out prim, and I hate that, hate how his lips curve further.

"You're not involved with your subject," he says. "Unless you want a repeat of Utah, which—"

"I don't," I hiss and look over at where the carpet beckons. The CEO of Titan Media. In pictures. *With me.*

He's a public figure. I've tried to stay out of the spotlight in the last few years. Fought for my privacy, and it *worked,* damn it. It worked, but all it'll take is a bored internet sleuth for things to come crashing down again.

"At this point," he says in a drawl, "I'm taking this a bit personal, Chaos. Is it really that offensive if a stranger or two think we're here as a couple?"

I take a deep breath.

"I see. It is." He lowers his voice. "There's a boyfriend in the picture, then. Someone who doesn't... know about Utah."

I shake my head. "No, of course not. No. There isn't."

"Right," he says, but I'm not sure he believes me. His arm is still outstretched my way. "If you want to avoid photographers, I can make that happen."

It's not a big deal. Not weighed against the enormity of what I'm doing already.

I put my arm through his and ignore the faint energy that

runs through me at the touch. He's an enemy. A means to an end. A good memory.

Nothing more.

"Just as long as you know," Aiden says in a low, deep voice as we start walking up the golden carpet and past the red ropes, "that the other guests will still think we're dating."

SOCIAL MEDIA

@midnightmusings: A new season of The Gamble just started!! Did you hear Samuel and Heather calling each other Sugar Puff? I love how they never let that joke die, lol. Who remembers Charlotte from Season One?

@starbuzz: Star Buzz Weekly just compiled a new list: 10 most memorable moments in reality TV history, and they're based on YOUR votes. And of course you all voted the Sugar Puff girl as the number one most memorable!

@Zenith3000: Hey, this blonde girl from the meme? Anyone know what she's doing now? She's kinda hot, not gonna lie.

@TheGambleOfficial: Check out this reel of the TOP MOMENTS you'd thought you'd forgotten from The Gamble's early seasons! Who remembers the showdown between Charlotte and Blake?

CHAPTER 14
CHARLOTTE

It takes exactly six minutes before the first person asks Aiden to introduce me. "Is this your date?" the interloper asks. He's in his mid-fifties, and was one of the first to come up to Aiden.

I want to glare at the man beside me. But it's my own fault for not realizing how things would look. Of course people here would spot a woman on Aiden's arm. Even though there are plenty of glamorous women here, gliding around in dresses that must cost tenfold of what I'm wearing.

Aiden seems perfectly at ease amid it all, meeting the man's curious gaze with an almost lazy look of his own. "Unfortunately not. Charlotte here is writing a piece on me and is here for research purposes."

"Writing a piece? What kind of piece?" The newcomer looks at me with appraising eyes, and damn it, I've signed an NDA.

I look over at Aiden. His eyes hold the same spark as earlier. He's going to let me answer this.

Thread the needle.

I smile at the curious man. "It's in the early stages so far, and we'll have to see what it evolves into."

The man chuckles. "All right, I know evasiveness when I see it. Neither of you have drinks yet—here, let's fix that." He raises a hand and motions for one of the neatly clad waiters carrying a tray to approach. "How's it going then, Hartman? The financial reports your company published back in March looked stellar."

Aiden smiles. It's not all together friendly. "Still keeping tabs on us, I see."

"You know how it is," the man says. "Everything good at home? The family?"

"Everything's great," Aiden says. He looks as unbothered as before, but… his voice sounds harder somehow. The change is barely noticeable.

"Good, good. Well, I know you have plenty of people to chat with before your speech. And hey, don't forget the fundraising part, yeah?"

"How could I," Aiden says dryly, and the man—whose name I still don't know—laughs again. "I'm well aware of the part I need to play."

"Good man." He claps Aiden on the shoulder and then moves on toward the next group of people. The waiter he waved over earlier finally makes her way to us with an apologetic smile.

Aiden takes two champagne flutes and hands me one. I grip it tightly and thank the server.

"Although I shouldn't drink," I say after she leaves. "I'm on the job."

Aiden makes a small sound of amusement. "Right. A really demanding job, too."

Is he being patronizing? I can't tell, and I meet his serene gaze with one of my own. "Who was that man we just spoke with?"

"Maurice Brown."

"And he is?"

"He runs an investment firm."

"He asked about your family," I say. "You seem well acquainted."

The tightness around Aiden's mouth returns. "He knew my father well."

"Ah. And he... remains a close friend today?"

Aiden's eyes harden. "He is not someone you're adding to your list of people to interview."

"So that's a no."

"People are turncoats." He takes a sip of his champagne and then shakes his head sharply. "We're not talking about this."

"Not here," I say. The conversation in the car still has me revved up. "But we will have to eventually. Won't we, Aiden?"

His eyes meet mine, and the question hangs in the air between us. For a second, I think he's going to reply.

And the answer in his eyes is *no*.

But then he puts his hand on the small of my back and ushers us toward the seats. "We're definitely not having it *here*. Not even hints of it."

I look around. There are people everywhere, dressed in beautiful chiffon and tuxes. The soft melody of a string quartet plays in the background. A flash goes off, and my gaze lands on a photographer bending to get a good shot of a group posing nearby.

"There are photographers everywhere," I admit. And I need to make sure not a single one gets a good shot of me.

"It's not the photographers I'm worried about," Aiden mutters.

"It's the people?" I ask him. We've stopped by a row of seats labeled as *VIP* and *Speaker*. Maurice had mentioned that Aiden was going to give a speech.

I hadn't known that.

Aiden blows out a breath. "What did I just say? We're not having this conversation here, Chaos."

"I'm not asking about the past. Just about the present." I look over his shoulder, at the crowds of people attending the event. There are so many of them.

I haven't liked being in crowds for years.

There's often *one* person who looks at me for a little too long. Who racks their brain, and sometimes it clicks. Who I am. They nudge their friends. *Remember that girl who had a freakout on TV? Remember the meme?*

Aiden seems so at ease here. He always does, everywhere he goes. But I wonder… He has a reputation, too.

A past.

I did anticipate that being in LA would be hard. This is the epicenter of film and movie production, including a lot of reality TV. There's probably a higher chance of being recognized here than in Minnesota or in the Alaskan wilderness. But so far, no one at this venue seems to be staring.

I'd forgotten that in a city with so many famous people, my own blip fades in comparison. I'm a speck of dust when matched against the real stars.

The thought is very comforting.

"Do you know many of the people here?" I ask him.

He takes another sip of his champagne. "A fair number. Not all."

"But they know you," I guess.

His eyes narrow. "Know *of* me, most likely. Yes."

"How does that make you feel?"

"You really are on the job." He touches his champagne flute to mine. "Take a sip. It'll help you relax."

"I am relaxed."

"Mm-hmm," he says dryly. "So am I."

It takes me a moment to realize he's being sarcastic. *So, he's not relaxed in these environments.*

But he's very good at acting like he is.

Another nugget of information I file away, like an archaeologist unearthing a new find. "Why do you go to these events?" I ask instead. "If you don't like them?"

"Means to an end," he says.

"What speech are you giving?"

"I'm donating the largest sum tonight to the charity. That buys you a certain level of visibility."

"What charity is it?"

"Dementia research," he says. "Playing twenty questions?"

"Would you rather play ball with me or network with someone out there?" I incline my head toward the masses. A few people are looking his way and it's likely only a matter of time before he's approached again. "Why dementia?"

"I don't know," he says. "You'd have to ask Maurice about that. He's on the Board for the event."

"Why are you donating such a large amount, then?"

His mouth tightens again. But then he shrugs, and his voice is all charm. "For the same reason the Board hired you."

"Good PR."

"The very same," he says.

I hesitate only a second before I ask the next thing. "Does it feel like you've been doing damage control since you took over the company? And do you think it'll ever end?"

"That," he says sharply, "belongs to the list of things we are not discussing."

CHAPTER 15

CHARLOTTE

"Here," I challenge. Again.

"Yes, fine. *Here*," he mutters and looks over his shoulder. A group of people are approaching us.

Approaching him.

His shoulders relax, and his mouth softens. The furrow between his eyebrows smooths out, but his gaze sharpens.

He looks powerful and casual all at once.

The all-American CEO, with his thick hair and square jaw.

And I realize that I don't know where to place him. It's easy, when I'm sparring with him and his eyes on mine, to forget that he is the one who runs the company that produces exploitative reality TV.

That Titan Media made millions, and I had my life ruined.

But he isn't innocent. He runs the company and *may* have known about his father's fraudulence, if what I read in some of the articles is true.

He's also my ticket to a year-long contract with my editor to write a non-fiction book of my own. So really, Aiden could be good or bad.

Doesn't matter.

Even if I can't figure out why he agreed to the memoir if he's going to hinder its progress. There's being hesitant, even nervous, and then there's being obstinate. And Aiden is falling into the latter camp.

I follow at Aiden's side for the next half an hour. People talk to him, ask him questions, exchange business cards. He navigates all of it with the casual ease of someone who has done it many times before.

No one else asks about his father or his family.

And there are definitely some individuals who don't approach him. I notice a group of them, standing off to the side, looking out of the corners of their eyes.

I want to take notes.

But if there's one thing that would be out of place in this fancy place, it's that. Whipping out a notebook and a pen would be quite indiscreet. But I know I won't forget this. *Not everyone has accepted Aiden after what his father did.*

After all, in the circles of the rich and truly wealthy, is there a more hated crime than defrauding shareholders? His father had taken a sledgehammer to people's fortunes, and people aren't quick to forget the dents.

There's the sound of a bell ringing, like we're about to enter an opera or a theater. Aiden's hand lands on my lower back again. It's the second time he has put it there, and I hate how aware I am of the faint touch.

"If you'll excuse us," he says smoothly to the couple we're talking to.

He leads us toward the front row of chairs by the stage.

"You're about to speak," I say. "Right?"

"Yes."

"Do you have notes?"

"No," he says. "I'm going to wing it."

"Really?"

"Your confidence is inspiring," he says dryly.

"Sorry, I didn't mean to imply… You're probably a great public speaker."

"Oh, the flattery. It's too much," he drawls.

"I don't think you need flattery," I say with a smile. "You have a driver, two assistants, and an entire building filled with employees."

"Don't sound so jealous, Chaos."

That makes me blink. "I'm not jealous of your life."

We reach our chairs, and he motions for me to take a seat. He sits down beside me with a glass of champagne still in his hand, eyes on the man waiting on the stage for people to simmer down.

"Well, then I need to step it up as a memoir subject," he says. His profile is strong, his mouth quirked. "You need to do what I do, right? How about we sky jump tomorrow?"

"Aiden," I protest.

"Afraid of heights? That's too bad, Chaos. Who knows what deep, dark secrets I might spill while I'm airborne and hurtling toward the ground."

"Probably not a single one," I say. "How about a simple, quiet lunch where you actually answer my questions?"

"I've answered all of your questions."

My hand reaches out, gripping his wrist through the fabric. "You've answered *none*, Aiden. None."

He blows out a breath, his eyes boring into mine. "You're too pretty to be this damn inconvenient."

My eyes widen. "Excuse me?"

"I know you have questions. But you're not getting access to any of my family members, and not to my friends, either. Possibly to my staff, but I'm still undecided." A hush falls over the crowd, but he's still talking, his voice deep and low. "It's nothing personal, Chaos."

"Nothing *personal*," I repeat in a hiss. "This is my job! How else am I supposed to take it?"

"You just said it. It's a job," he says. "Just do yours."

"I'm *trying*, but *you* are my job." My hand tightens around his wrist. "You're saying that you—"

"Aiden Hartman!" a loud voice says. It sounds strained. "Do we have him in the audience?"

I release Aiden's arm immediately.

He curses under his breath—a tiny, muttered thing that only I hear. Then he stands and gives a wave out to the gathered crowd, a wide smile on his face. Takes the stairs to the stage with brisk steps and accepts the microphone from the host.

Aiden gives the audience a moment of silence before he speaks. There's a large arch of flowers behind him, along the charity's logo. "Sorry about that, folks. My beautiful date is more than a little distracting."

I glare at him. He really isn't planning on helping me, not even a little bit. And he doesn't even have the courtesy to tell me why.

Irritation is a firebrand beneath my skin.

Why did he invite me here tonight, then? Does he find it fun to toy with me? Am I nothing but entertainment?

I was hired to do a job, and he's making it impossible for me to do it.

Aiden waits a second for the chuckles to die down, one hand gripping the mic and the other braced on the podium. He looks relaxed, broad-shouldered, and totally at home up on that stage.

Unbothered by me, by our argument.

Maybe this is all just sport to him. Like asking for my number and then never calling. Like running a giant media conglomerate that makes millions on other people's drama.

He starts talking, but his husky voice just washes over me. I can't make out his words. Something about philanthropy and the importance of Los Angeles coming together as a community, and empty platitudes that say nothing about who he actually is.

Just like he's done with me.

I take a deep breath, and then another, forcing down the

irritation. Searching for the calm and professionalism that have been mine for years. Regardless of how challenging the subject is.

But I can't find it.

It's out of reach.

I twist, turning to look for the nearest restroom, and that's when I feel it. A sharp rip, and then the tight grip of fabric around my chest loosens.

Falls.

I wrap my arms around myself just in time and feel the bare skin on my side where the zipper has come undone.

Fuck.

Fuck.

I glance around at the darkened room, but no one is looking at me. They're focused on Aiden up on stage.

I find the zipper and try to wriggle it about. It doesn't work. I need better lighting and I need to turn the dress around. I also need to *not* be in a room with two hundred and fifty of Los Angeles's elite where I risk showing them my A-cups.

I glance at the stage again and then slip out of my chair. I duck to stay out of sight, my arms still wrapped tightly around my chest and the traitorous green fabric.

As quickly and quietly as I can, I hurry in the direction of the back room, the one where we came from. I pass a few loitering waiters and damn it, where's the bathroom?

It takes me almost a minute to find it by the coat check alcove. I feel too hot and just a bit sweaty. Clutching my small bag in hand *and* the two sides of my dress that refuse to stick together.

Why did I think strapless was a good idea? And why did I think it was a bright notion to skip the bulky strapless bra?

Built-in corset dress, sure. Only works if the damn thing stays up.

Quick, hard steps follow behind me. "You're leaving?" Aiden asks, his voice rough.

I falter next to the startled coat check clerk and turn to meet Aiden's narrowed eyes. My anger flares to life when faced with his.

"So what if I am? It's not like you'll give me any answers if I stay."

His eyes burn. "Walking off during my speech is a bit much though, don't you think?"

"Your ego really is that fragile," I spit back.

"If my ego was fragile," he says, "don't you think I'd want you to write a puff piece like the memoir you did for William?"

"That wasn't a puff piece," I tell him, and take a step back. My hip bumps into the coat check counter. It's also a lie. William's book was a total puff piece, and I hated working with him.

"Sure it wasn't," Aiden says, his voice dripping with sarcasm. "I read your memoir about the Olympic swimmer. That's the kind of writing you want to do, Chaos. Intimate and emotional."

My eyes widen. "You've read it?"

"You recommended I do."

"Yes, but I didn't think you would."

"I am literate, you know, despite what you seem to think about me and my ego, or my ability to do things for myself." His voice is frustrated. "If you're going to *leave* in the middle of the night, at least tell me about it."

"Not that it's any of your business, but I wasn't leaving," I say. My arms are still tightly wrapped around me, but all it takes is a loose finger and my dress will come undone. "*I* don't just leave when things get tough."

The implication is there. That *he* does.

His eyes narrow again. "Neither do I. And why are you holding yourself like you've been hurt?"

"I'm not hurt."

"Sure you're not." A frown mars his lips, and he inspects my chest with terrifying scrutiny. "What... Fucking hell, Chaos, your dress is falling off."

"I *know* that," I hiss, "which is why I left. I'm trying to fix it but it's not going great."

He looks over his shoulder, at the large room we just departed. We're standing right by the exit, and there's a good chance people will soon pass through here again.

He looks at the coat check clerk. "We just need a moment," he says with complete confidence. "Thank you."

Dropping his hand on my lower back again, Aiden walks us behind the counter and in between the mostly-empty rows of hangers. It's warm enough that few people brought anything to check.

"I'll help you fix it," he says in a dark voice, "and you're welcome to keep ranting at me while I do."

CHAPTER 16
AIDEN

"I'm not *ranting* at you," she says. "I'm just trying to understand. Why even invite me here if you're not going to answer my questions? What game are you playing?"

"I'm not playing any games." A few stray coats surround us, the fabric rustling when I brush past a rack. Charlotte's soft waves kiss the tops of her shoulders, leaving her upper back bare. It's an expanse of silky-looking skin.

And then there's that green dress and the sides she's still holding together as tightly as she can.

God, she's frustrating.

Frustrating because I hadn't planned on it being *her* when I agreed to this stupid fucking scheme. It should have been some prim English Literature major—a man perhaps—who primarily reports on business. Not someone with an interest in getting to the heart of issues and finding the real person within.

And definitely not Charlotte.

Her anger is justified. But I'm not about to sell out my family and my private thoughts and feelings just to appease her, so angry she'll have to remain.

"Yes, you are." She comes to a stop at the far side of the room and turns to face me. Her cheeks are flushed with color.

"You invited me here, insisted I come when I was only supposed to interview you in the car, and for what? To show off your donation? To jerk me around and play these... these... games?"

"I said I'm not playing games." My voice comes out hoarse. "Now turn around and let me see the zipper."

She does as I've asked, lifting her arm to show me a stretch of bare skin from below her armpit down to her waist.

She's not wearing a bra.

I guess she wouldn't have to with that tight-looking corset of a dress. Despite her clutching the front of the dress to her chest, the faintest hint of a curve is visible. And fuck if I don't perfectly remember the weight and feel of her small tits.

"If you're ogling me, I swear to god, Aiden—"

"I'm not," I say gruffly and reach for the slider. It looks fine, but... it's on the wrong side of the fastener. Like the teeth of the zipper itself had just burst.

"This is humiliating enough as it is," she continues, and I can see the quick expansion of her ribs beneath my fingers. She really is angry. "We've only danced around the topics that actually matter. I'm starting to think you don't want this memoir written at all. You give me *nothing*!"

My fingers brush over her skin on their way to the base of the zipper, and damn it, she's just as soft as I recall.

"Of course I don't want this fucking memoir written," I grind out. The pull tab is tiny and the lighting isn't great, and she's so distractingly close and warm.

"*What*?" She turns her head to glare at me.

I focus on the zipper and try to get it closed. "Would you want an entire book dedicated to the worst fucking time of your life? Revisiting the things you've spent *years* trying to bury?"

A faint sound escapes her. It sounds almost like shock, and a bit sympathetic, and I don't want that. Never that.

But then she shakes her head sharply, and the light-brown

waves brush along her shoulders. "Then why did you agree to it? Why sign the contract, and why hire me? Why am I here, Aiden?"

To drive me mad, I think. The zipper catches, and I pull it closed and snug up the side of her dress. But for every inch it draws together, it comes undone again below the slider.

"The zipper is broken," I say. "The teeth won't stay shut."

She twists in an effort to see, and her dress gapes open even more. I catch the solid swell of her breast and look away, toward a gray peacoat hanging right next to my face.

"No way. It can't be," she hisses. "This is my only formal gown."

I look back at her. "I offered to buy you a dress."

"Which would have been completely unprofessional. But thanks," she adds, so clearly as a polite afterthought she doesn't truly mean, it makes me smile.

She narrows her eyes at my expression. "Why did you agree to this, then? The whole memoir if you're determined to sabotage it?"

"I'm not determined to sabotage it. I'm determined to make it bland and boring," I say.

She looks like she wants to throw her hands up, but doing that would make her dress fall. She glares at me instead. "That's the same thing as sabotage! I have a career riding on writing good, well-received, bestselling memoirs. We have to tear up the contract."

"No," I say immediately. "We can't do that."

Her eyes are so angry they burn. "Oh my god, and why *not*? Why are you putting both of us through this if you don't even want a memoir? Why drag me into this?"

"You are an unfortunate casualty," I say.

"You did not just say that."

I blow out a breath. This isn't what I wanted to talk about tonight, not what I wanted to admit. "The memoir is a trade with the Board. They want a good PR opportunity and a new narrative for the company."

"And you don't?" she asks, her eyebrows furrowed. She's even pretty when she's fuming.

"No. But in return for my agreement, the Board will green-light a new acquisition and the project they've been dragging their feet on for years."

"This is a calculated move on your part," she says. Her arms are still wrapped around her chest.

"Yes, of course it is," I say gruffly. What else would it be? I'm running a company that employs thousands of people, and it needs to recapture stability. It needs profits, and it needs to get back on track moving forward.

"Well, you're going to have to find another memoirist." She looks left and right, and then shakes her head. "Damn it. I should get out of here."

A hum of voices reaches us from the lobby. The speeches must have wrapped up.

I wrapped up my own as soon as I saw Charlotte leaving her seat.

Not planned. But I saw her hurry through the space with quick steps like she was fleeing, and the remaining platitudes slipped out of my mind. The only thing that mattered was her.

No one's ever gotten under my skin like she has.

"I can call the car."

"No need," she says and pushes past me. She stumbles on her heels in the dimness, and I reach out to steady her.

My hand lands on the bare skin of her back, exposed by the gaping dress.

"Charlotte," I say.

"I read the contract thoroughly beforehand," she says sharply. Her eyes meet mine, and damn if a shiver of arousal doesn't rush down my spine, right alongside my frustration. "I am allowed to break it if the interview subject substantially hinders my efforts. It's just in the fine print, but it states that if I'm not given adequate resources, I can break it."

"What qualifies as adequate resources?" I ask. "Want us to battle that out in the courts?"

Her eyes narrow. "You'd do that?"

"I don't think I'd have to. Don't you think your editor will just replace you with another memoirist? Your publishing house wants this memoir just as much as my Board does."

"Because they think they're getting the scoop!" she says. "When what they're *actually* getting is a noncooperative, evasive, frustrating, occasionally rude CEO with no interest in sharing even his favorite color."

"Blue," I say.

Her mouth tightens, like she's trying to hold back an expletive. But then it bursts open. "Damn it."

I shrug out of my suit jacket and hold it up for her.

She stares at it as if it's a weapon.

"Until we get to the car," I say.

"I can't walk around in your suit jacket."

"Do we have much of a choice?" I ask dryly and look down at her dress, still only held up by her hands. "Or do you want to risk flashing all the good men and women out there?"

She turns with a muttered curse. "Don't look," she instructs me, and I look away. I feel her slip into the arms of my jacket but keep my gaze firmly on one of the beige walls.

"Don't call your editor."

"I can't work like this," she says. "I refuse."

"You never struck me as someone who backs down from a challenge, Chaos."

She turns so quickly that her hair hits my still hovering hand from when I held the jacket out to her. "I don't," she says. "I just know a losing battle when I see one."

"That sounds like giving up." I'm being an ass. An ass in a way I rarely am. At least not since I was a bored and rich teenager. Needling and needling and not saying the right thing like I always have to otherwise.

I've never watched my tongue around Charlotte the way I should.

She's a dangerous creature, standing there with my suit jacket wrapped tightly around her chest. It's too large on her, the sleeves covering her hands.

She looks delicious.

"You," she says, her eyes blazing, "are playing games. Even if you're calling them something else. And I don't like that. So if you think I'm giving up? That's fine. But I know what I deserve, and it's not this."

Charlotte is going to walk away.

And I know I don't want this memoir written. I don't want secrets exposed. I don't want family trauma reexamined and read by thousands of people. I don't want new Business Digest articles with clickbait titles.

But I know I don't want her to walk out, either.

She's fascinating. Complicated. Intelligent. Our little sparring matches have been the most fun I've had in months.

"You don't like games, then. But how about a deal?" I ask.

She crosses her arms over her chest. "What kind of deal?"

"You want me to answer all of your questions," I say. "Then, you'll have to respond to the same ones."

Her eyes widen. "What?"

"For every answer I give, you give me one, too. It's only fair that I get to know you just as thoroughly as you'll be getting to know me."

"You can't be serious. I'm not the one who is being written about, and I bet you're not even interested."

I lean closer. "Is that a bet you're *really* willing to make?"

Her teeth dig into her lower lip for a second. "Why?"

"Why not?" I ask. "Maybe I don't want to be the only one baring my life to scrutiny."

She shakes her head slowly, a humorless smile on her lips. "Right. An eye for an eye and a tooth for a tooth?"

"That's right."

"I think I'm willing to go deep," she says, her voice holding a warning. "This memoir is important to my career."

"There's one caveat, of course."

Her eyes narrow. "Of course there is. What?"

"I get final approval before you deliver the first draft to the Board."

"You'll ax everything I'll write."

"No. I promise to be fair. Convince me that you can write this and do it justice. Make me *want* to expose all the personal stuff and send it to my Board and publication."

I see it in her eyes. A spark of defiance, hidden amid the frustration. From the start, she's seemed like a woman who likes to be challenged. Who likes people with a bit of a bite.

"I have a counter caveat," she says.

The voices out in the lobby are growing louder. "Tell me."

"If you don't approve the memoir, you'll need to explain it to my editor. I want it noted why you're not satisfied, and for *you* to directly admit that it's too personal."

She's hedging her bets. A grin flashes across my lips, there and gone again. "Clever."

"Don't patronize me."

"I would never." It's the honest truth. I hold out my hand. "Do we have a deal, Charlotte Gray?"

Her eyes meet mine with obvious vehemence. But then she slips her slim hand in mine, her skin warm.

We shake once.

"We have a deal," she says. "And I'll hold you to it, Hartman."

My lips curve, and it's not entirely with joy. "I'm counting on it. Oh, and one more thing."

"What's that?"

"You want more access?" I lean in closer. "You'll move into my guest room."

CHAPTER 17

CHARLOTTE

It makes a reluctant kind of sense. That's the only reason I pack up my clothes and belongings into the two giant suitcases I lug around, the ones that have become home as much as the tiny rental spaces I move between. Shove everything into my old but trusty Honda.

The apartment remains available to me.

That had been one of my conditions. I need to be able to go back there if needed, and Aiden had agreed without protest.

I drive the winding road from my Westwood condo past UCLA, across Sunset, and enter the storied Bel Air. Up the curving streets, past lush trees and ornate estate gates.

This time, I edge my car to the gate and hit the call button. I'm meant to get a key card today, if the information in the email I received is correct.

A woman answers after a few rings. She lets me in, and I park my little Honda next to Aiden's Jeep. It makes my car look rather sad, and most definitely not clean. I should give it a wash.

The smiling woman introduces herself as Elena, Aiden's personal assistant. She's in her mid-fifties, wearing a strict black dress and her red hair in a low bun. She's the one who handles his private affairs. I still don't fully understand how he can have enough work for both Elena *and* Eric, but I suppose I'm about to find out.

"It's a pleasure to meet you," she tells me. "Mr. Hartman has a large guest room. He's not home much, either, depending on his work schedule."

"Yes, Eric has provided me with the schedule. Hopefully this will give me more opportunities to spend time with Aiden." I shrug a little, and feel compelled to add, "For research."

She nods and pulls the giant front door to the modern house open. "Of course. Let's get you settled in."

The place is huge.

That's my first impression. I'm awed by the sheer scope of it. There's a large foyer and a staircase that leads upstairs. Art that hangs on the walls has a distinctive *expensive* look. Big pieces, in modern frames. Lots of colors and patterns that I know next to nothing about but can surely identify as investment pieces.

There's a large wine cellar built off the kitchen; a temperature-controlled room with a glass door. Shelves upon shelves are filled with bottles, and in the middle, a small table made from an old wine barrel.

"That's Mr. Hartman's collection." Elena is warm but brisk, and soon sweeps me onwards to my room.

It's on the second floor, at the far end of the corridor, and has a window that looks out over the backyard and the infinity pool that tops it off. Inside, there are gray wainscoted walls and a ceiling light fixture that looks like a cloud. There's a small desk in the corner, and a large queen bed with white bed linens takes center stage.

It's such an upgrade from my small rental.

"Mr. Hartman's rooms are down the hall and past the TV on the landing. You'll have your privacy here," Elena assures me. "The en suite is just through that door there."

"Thank you," I breathe. My suitcases look obscenely massive next to the sleek black dresser, and more banged-up than usual against the pristine space.

"I'll leave you to it," she says. On the desk, she leaves me a set of keys and a small guide that has my name on the top and includes the Wi-Fi password and instructions on everything from how to work the window latches to how often the laundry is done. Then she departs, leaving me to myself.

I lie down on the giant bed and stare up at the cloud lamp. It's pretty. Prettier than anything in other rooms I've stayed in over the last few years. All I've been doing is moving with my suitcases from place to place, never staying long in one spot. Never settling down. Just the way I like it.

But just in case I ever have a home of my own, I take a picture of the overhead cloud light. If it's not obscenely expensive, I want one just like it.

My clothes fit into the dresser and the walk-in closet with plenty of space to spare. I have boxes of stuff stored at my parents' house, labeled *Charlotte's future home* in my dad's blocky handwriting.

I work for a few hours. Expand the narrative framework for Aiden's memoir, the one I'll run through with him more in-depth now that he's agreed to work with me and not against me.

I add longer summaries of each chapter, and what details I'd like to include. *Anecdotes from your school years. A description of you by your sister and mother. Recount three of the hardest decisions you've had to make for Titan Media since you became CEO.*

When my neck starts to hurt and the time gets late, I venture out of my room with a book under my arm. I walk on quiet feet. It almost feels like I'm trespassing.

The upper floor has a few rooms. The doors of several of them are open.

There's a small office that looks mostly unused. One side

is filled with books across the entire wall, while the other features a large framed photograph. The image is of a beach, with lots of surfers in a row, out on the waves. It's grainy, like it was taken in the seventies.

I check the next half-open door. It's another guest room, but far smaller than mine. It's tastefully decorated in green colors.

Up by the staircase, separating the two sides of the large hallway, is an open-concept TV room. An oversized L-shaped cloud sectional sits snugly against the wall, along with a TV projector. I stare at it for a solid few minutes before deciding that I *have* to try it out one day when Aiden is not home.

At the far end of the corridor is a door that's completely shut. It must be what Elena had gestured to hours ago. Aiden's bedroom. I look at it for another moment before heading downstairs.

There's another guest bathroom—how many guests does he plan on having?—and then, that beautiful wine cellar. I open the fridge. Find it mostly empty except for some preprepared meals. Packaged beautifully, with names of the contents written on them. *Expires Wednesday* is written in a sprawling hand. The sticker is from a restaurant I vaguely remember passing earlier.

So, he doesn't cook.

I walk into a dimmed corner of the downstairs, past the large sitting room. The space is darker than all the other rooms I've seen, like the blinds have been closed here. And inside, there's a large dining table in the middle. No, that's not a table for meals. It's a pool table. On the wall is a large blackboard, but I can barely make out the names at the top. *Aiden.* The second name is written in an even more sprawling hand, and it starts with an *M*.

"Are you snooping?" a voice asks.

CHAPTER 18
CHARLOTTE

I jump. "Oh my god."

He chuckles, standing there behind me, leaning against the entryway jamb. "Nice to see you're making yourself at home."

"I didn't hear you arrive."

"You were clearly busy." He lifts an eyebrow. "Like what you've found?"

"You do have a beautiful home," I admit.

"You say that like it's an unfortunate thing."

"Did you decorate it?"

"Mandy did most of it," he says.

Oh. His sister. I look past his shoulder at the white and navy colors of the living room. The large painting on a wall featuring a beach. "She knows you well."

He crosses his arms over his chest. "Yeah, she does. Have you settled in all right?"

"Your PA showed me around. Elena."

"Mm-hmm. Good." He steps closer and stretches out a hand. "What are you reading?"

I hesitate only a moment before I hand over the book I'd planned to read on one of his large couches. It's well-read, and the color of the pages is just a bit yellowed. "It's by one of my favorite authors."

"Grace Ellington," he reads. "*Invisible Threads. The unseen connections that shape our everyday lives.*"

I feel oddly exposed, seeing his head bent and eyes reading the synopsis on the back cover. "Yes."

"Is this the kind of book you want to write?"

"I'd be so lucky. She's fantastic." I reach out and take the book from him gently, tucking it back under my arm. "But it's the genre I want to write, yes. Non-fiction that captures the reader immediately, and leaves them… thinking. Entertained. As much investigative journalism as it is psychology, anthropology."

Aiden's still in a suit, like he just got back from work. Outside the windows, the pool is glittering softly under the outdoor lighting. The sun has already set. It had gotten late somewhere between my work and unpacking.

"You told me that you might get a deal to write a novel of your own after this memoir."

"Yes."

"What will you write about if you do?" He walks over to the minibar in the corner and pours himself a glass of scotch. Looks over at me. "Want one?"

I sit down on his large, white couch. My jeans and sweater feel very casual all of a sudden, but this is a golden opportunity. I need all I can get with him.

"Yes, please."

He hands me a tumbler and sits down across from me. His long legs, clad in dress pants, stretch out beneath the beautifully decorated coffee table. His left arm drapes along the back of his couch. He looks so at home sitting there—casually wealthy, handsomely bored, sporting a five-o'clock shadow—among the interior that screams riches. "Tell me," he says.

My cheeks heat up. I hate that they do, but this isn't something I talk about often. "I'm not sure yet. I think I want to investigate online culture. Something about fame, but I haven't really settled on the entry point."

"Fame?"

He had asked to get to know me in response. It'll have to be a careful dance, this whole thing. This bargain. To open myself up to his scrutiny so that he will do the same. "Yes. What it costs people, and what it grants them."

His eyebrows rise. "That's unexpected."

"I really enjoy investigative books like that," I say, "But I have to work on the framing of it, and pull the loose threads I have into some kind of narrative."

He holds my gaze. "I think that's a fantastic idea. Can't wait to read it."

"If I ever get around to properly writing it. Hopefully I'll be able to sell it to Vera after your memoir."

"If you impress her," he says, "by what, exactly? How riveting my memoir will be? That seems like too high a bar."

I give him a wry smile. "You have a juicy life. She wants me to get emotional with it, to deliver on the brief."

"Mm-hmm." He looks down at his glass of whiskey, his face unreadable. "Did Eric send you an updated schedule for the coming week?"

I nod. "Yes, I have your times and everything. There are a few evenings where you have nothing planned?"

"We'll have dinner here. You can ask me anything. Unless," he says and tips his head in my direction, "you have a lot of dates planned in your spare time. I know you said you wanted to see the city."

I look down at my own drink. I had said that. Weeks ago, at the resort in Utah. "This is my job. It's what's most important."

"What do you want to see most?" he asks.

"The usual tourist things," I say. "I'd like to see the beach while I'm here. Maybe go to Hollywood Boulevard. I know it's cliché, but I've never been."

He nods like he's taking mental notes. "Okay. All very doable."

"I'll figure it out."

"I'll get Elena on it."

"Your staff shouldn't have to cater to me. I promise I'll be out of their hair," I say. "There was something about laundry in the papers Elena gave me. But I can do my own."

"I'm sure you can," Aiden says with the tone of someone who doesn't add *but you don't have to*. It's implied.

I shake my head and look beyond his large windows. It's dark, but I can make out the confines of his large backyard. Despite it all, a small smile spreads across my lips. "I've never lived like this before. You're so surrounded by... luxury."

Aiden is quiet for a moment. "Yes. I haven't reflected on it in a while."

"Just look at my beat-up Honda parked next to your cars," I say with a widening smile. "It'll make you appreciate them in a second."

"Beat-up?" he asks. "It's safe, though?"

"It's perfectly safe. It's just not particularly beautiful." I shrug a little and look from him to the room we're in. "Do you hang out here often?"

"No," he says.

"That's a shame. Your couches are very comfortable." I look back at him, seeing a hint of amusement on his face. "What do you usually watch on that large projector upstairs? Your own shows?"

"No," he says again, and his lips curve. "Is this you changing the subject?"

"It's me getting to know you better."

"Right. Well, by all means."

I look down at my knee and pick at a frayed seam on my jeans. "Why not your own shows? Titan produces so much."

"Most of it is trash," he says, so casually. "A few of the critically acclaimed shows are good. The one about the gangsters we produced a few years ago, for instance. I watched that."

I look at him. "Trash, huh?"

"Don't quote me on that," he says, still with that easy amusement on his face. "The shareholders or the Board wouldn't like it."

"But it's how you feel?"

"They're reality shows. Dating, drinking, all of that. It's not my favorite part of the business. You don't strike me as someone who watches them, either."

I look back down at the gently sloshing amber liquid and the elaborate crystal pattern across the glass. The words feel hard to say. "I don't watch them, either."

"What do—"

A loud signal rings out in the house. Aiden sighs and pushes up from the couch. "Perfect timing," he mutters and walks through the large archway toward the foyer.

Uncertainty has me frozen in place on the couch. Do I follow? Do I stay?

I hear the door open, and curiosity propels me forward on quiet feet. I have to pass through the archway to get to the stairs leading up to my room anyway. Perfectly legitimate.

"Aiden," a high, feminine voice says. "I asked Eric, and he said you'd be home."

"Did he now?" Aiden's voice is dry.

"I thought I'd stop by," she says.

I peek through the archway. The woman is beautiful, with long blonde hair and an easy smile. She has a hand on Aiden's upper arm. "I brought the documents you wanted."

"Good," he says. "I'll fix it for you."

"Thank you. I appreciate it, as always." Her voice softens. "You know, the business is doing *really* well."

"I saw the latest numbers you sent over. They look great."

"You sure you don't mind reading the reports? I know you're busy."

I'm intruding on something. They're clearly not just friends, and not a boss and an employee. "Of course not. It's my job to take care of you."

I've never heard him say that sort of thing before.

The pang beneath my breastbone isn't just embarrassment. It's something else, something that feels a lot like sour jealousy. She's beautiful, he's handsome; he's worried about her safety.

I knew he had to be dating or involved with someone.

There're a few feet of open space for me to pass through, in full view of the two of them, before I make it to the staircase. And they haven't noticed me yet.

I glance one extra time at the pair, take a deep breath, and then walk briskly past the open archway.

I'm nearly safe when her voice sounds again. "You have a guest?"

"I do," Aiden says. "And I would have mentioned that if you'd called me instead of Eric."

"You don't always answer your phone, but Eric or Elena always do." The woman's voice is intrigued now and... *damn it*. I turn on my heel and quickly smooth out my expression. Seconds later, they've both rounded the corner.

She looks at me with curious eyes. "Hi."

"Hello," I say.

"This is Charlotte," Aiden says. He leans against the wall and has the expression of someone long-suffering. "She is working on the book I told you about, and is staying here to ensure we get enough time together."

The woman glances at him for a few seconds too long before turning back to me. A guarded glint is in her eyes now. Her green-colored eyes... Just like Aiden's.

"You're the ghostwriter," she says.

"Yes, I am."

"This is Mandy," Aiden says. "My sister, who is not entirely convinced that a memoir is a good idea."

She shoots him another annoyed look, before facing me again. The ground beneath me shakes, just a little, the way it does when I find myself on uncertain terrain.

"You're writing about our family," she says.

"As it relates to Aiden, yes, and the company," I say. "Aiden will have complete control over the contents of the first draft. Anything he doesn't want in there, and by extension you, can be cut."

She nods slowly. "Oh. That's good."

"I understand that your family has been through a lot," I say. It's risky, bringing it up like this. Dancing around the topic of their father and his lengthy jail sentence. A topic Aiden and I have still not delved into. "I don't want to be another negative piece in that puzzle. Quite the opposite."

"I like the sound of that," Mandy says. She's still looking at me with anxious eyes. "The idea of a book is… scary."

"I understand that," I say. "Everyone I've worked with—from the world poker champion to a tech investor, even a Real Housewife—they were all scared. And nervous. Even if a book was their idea and they're used to sharing their lives."

"You've worked with a Real Housewife?" Mandy's eyes widen. "Which one? And can you tell me everything?"

I chuckle. "Probably not everything, but a lot, yeah."

Aiden pushes off the wall. "Let's not badger Charlotte as the first thing we do."

"I'm making conversation," Mandy says primly, and I like her immediately. "But yeah, I should get going. I've got a dinner reservation. Aiden, I've left the documents on the table over there."

"Thank you," Aiden says. "I'll have the lawyers look through them."

"Thank you!" She kisses him on the cheek and waves goodbye to me, and then the front door closes.

I walk toward the stairs. Aiden trails after me, step in step.

"So, now you've met Mandy," he says.

"Can I interview her?"

"How did I know you would ask that?" He sighs. "Maybe. It'll be on her terms, if at all."

"Thanks. I meant what I said—anything she doesn't like can be cut out. Same as for you."

"Good."

We reach the top of the landing. His bedroom is in one direction, mine in the other. I reach out and grip the railing. The iron is cool under my fingers and feels nice against my warm skin.

"I have to say, for a second there, I thought…" I shrug and let the words die. I shouldn't speak them.

Aiden lifts an eyebrow. "You thought what?"

I force myself to smile. "That she was your date or a girl-friend coming over. I was trying to sneak up here without interrupting you."

"Chaos." He shakes his head. "You think I'd bring women over while you're living here?"

"Why wouldn't you?" I ask back. "I'm just your ghost-writer. You're just my subject. It's your house. There's nothing stopping you."

"Right. And we're just professionals," he echoes, but he's closer now than he was a few moments ago. "I remember."

"We shook on it."

"We sure did."

He doesn't look away. Neither do I, determined not to be the first to waver. On the railing, his hand is close to mine. Only inches away. "I won't bring dates here," he says, "and neither will you."

That's easy for me to agree to. I haven't thought about dating since I arrived in LA. There's been no free space in my mind for it.

He takes up all of it.

"Celibacy it is," I say and extend my hand.

Aiden looks at it for a long moment before shaking his

head with wry amusement. "That's the last thing I would want to shake hands with you on, Chaos." But he fits his large hand to mine, and a rush of heat races through me at the contact. "To not dating anyone else."

"That's not what I said," I whisper. But our hands bob, intertwined.

His lips curve. "Isn't it?"

CHAPTER 19

AIDEN

I cross my arms over my chest. "Not going to happen."

Charlotte's eyes are defiant. She's sitting at my kitchen table, the remnants of the takeout I ordered for our dinner between us. "We have to go into those topics in the book. They're crucial for understanding your story."

"I have worked very hard to *get away* from that narrative."

"This narrative will help you."

"It'll put the conviction right back into the public spotlight," I say. It had taken months—*years*—to have news headlines about Titan Media that were not just negative.

"I understand that," Charlotte says. Her intelligent, blue eyes hold the same frustration I feel. Her notepad, the one she loves to scribble in during our conversations, is beside her laptop. "It will have to be done tactfully. Just listen to me for a second, okay?"

"I am listening."

Her lips quirk slightly, a clear indication that she doesn't think I'm paying attention at all. I lean back in my chair and fold my arms across my chest.

"The people who'll buy this book... Will they already know about the conviction? The trial and your father's sentencing?"

I grind out the word. "Yes."

"Okay. So by mentioning it in your memoir, you're not telling them anything they don't already know."

"You're speaking to me like I'm five, Chaos."

She rolls her eyes. "Yes, but that might be necessary sometimes."

"Oh?" I raise my eyebrows. Reluctant amusement pricks through the frustration. "By all means, continue then."

"Okay, so, we won't be telling them something they don't know. Instead, you'll be reframing their views. Have you read the studies on memory? That we can actively change how we remember certain events over time?" She holds up her notepad. "With this book, you can do that to the minds of thousands of people!"

"Have *you* read the studies on memory?" I ask. "Because, it's also said that the more you repeat something, the more it sticks."

Her smile falters. "Yes, well, I prefer my point."

"And I prefer mine."

"It's what the Board wants from you," she says. "It'll be an odd memoir if we don't go into the... troubling stuff."

"We can mention it. Gloss over it."

"Glossing over things doesn't fill a book that needs to be at least two hundred pages."

"It's a corporate fluff piece," I say.

"It's a chance for you to become *more* than your father's son," she shoots back.

My teeth grind together on instinct, and my gaze lingers on the wine cellar. Two of the few things my dad imparted was a love of the ocean and an appreciation for high-quality wine.

And Titan Media, of course, and the media storm.

"Aiden," she says. Her voice is softer, and I roll my neck, trying to shake off the unease. I can't handle her pity.

Showing weakness isn't something the Hartman household is good at.

"People will see it as a strength if you own the narrative," she says, and my eyes snap back to hers. It's like she heard me. "Not to mention it'll make it a more compelling book, leave them with a sense that you had something to overcome."

I narrow my eyes at that. It makes sense. Of course it does. "We'll need to go through it with a fine-tooth comb," I tell her. "I don't want a single misplaced sentence that can be pulled out and turned into sensationalized headlines."

"Got it." She leans forward, a smile hiding in the corners of her lips. "We'll triple-check every phrase. I can easily work together with the editor on that."

"Okay. Good." I sigh and look at her laptop again. On the back of it, she has a tiny sticker with a sunset and the name of a national park I've never heard of. "We could make a deal about this, too."

Her hand pauses over her notepad. "We already have a deal."

"Yes, we sure do. Which means," I say and meet her gaze, "if we're discussing what it was like to walk into a courtroom filled with thirty photographers and my father in custody, we'll be talking about your most shameful moments, too."

She takes a deep breath, like that rattles her. But then she nods and there's steel in her eyes. "I know."

Curiosity burns through me. What can she possibly have in her life that she doesn't want to talk about in return?

"How about this," I say. "You can bypass that requirement by doing something else for me."

Her eyes narrow. "And what's that?"

"Let me read the newly written chapters of your book. The one you want to publish after my memoir."

"Oh." Her mouth remains open, and then she chuckles. "Really?"

"Yes. You can't be spending all your time every day working on just my book, can you?"

"That's what I'm hired to do," she says carefully.

I want her to work on herself, too. It's not right that she has to spend these weeks focusing only on me and my story when this memoir won't come close to how good a writer she truly is. I've read her other stuff.

"But you can do more than that," I say. "Send me a few chapters of your new book, and I'll give you a free pass for a hard question. No need to answer it back."

"Will you read the chapters?"

I raise an eyebrow. "Of course."

She leans back in her chair, too, and I love this. Squaring off like we're negotiating. "Okay," she says slowly. "But you need to remember that they're just draft chapters."

"I won't judge."

"Mm-hmm." She sounds like she's not entirely sure of that.

That makes me chuckle. "Don't believe me? I've read most of the books you've ghostwritten in the past few weeks. You're a good writer."

Her eyes widen. "*Most*? I've ghostwritten almost a dozen."

"I think I've read seven or so."

"You're joking."

"I'm not."

"Which one was your favorite?"

I smile at her attempt to trap me. "The Alaskan musher, Alice Copeland. But I quite like the one about the Olympic swimmer, too, like I mentioned."

"When do you have the time to read?"

"Audiobooks are a great invention, Chaos."

She blows out a breath. "You're always surrounded by people. By me, this past week or so."

"Not always," I say. Sleeping isn't something I'm great at, at least not when I'm focused on business. Or distracted by other things, or… individuals.

Her audiobooks have kept me company during the dark nights. Even if the stories are about other people, and the narrator is someone unknown, the words are hers.

She shakes her head and looks down at her laptop. "Okay. So… you're okay with this narrative? The chapter structure I laid out?"

It makes sense. Of course it does, and I don't have to like it to see the commerciality of what she's organized. It's a good story. I just don't know if I want it told about myself and my family.

But I swallow my apprehension. "Yes. But fine-tooth comb, Chaos."

"Fine-tooth comb," she agrees. Then she starts putting her things together and reaching for her empty takeout box. I watch her throw it in the trash.

It's late. So far, she's spent most of her time in her room, staying out of the way, except for the times we have scheduled to work on the book together.

I push off the chair and walk over to the neatly stacked pile of her things. That damn notepad that she scribbles in all the time is on the top.

I grab it and sit back on the chair, flipping it open. "What kind of notes do you take in this thing, anyway?"

"Just observations. Anecdotes. Things I might use in my writing."

Her handwriting is slanted, just faintly cursive. She writes in black ink. The last few days' notes are neatly scribed here, with the dates written at the top.

Meeting with his team about the purchase of BingeBox. A is direct, firm, and makes harsh demands while smiling. Easy to see how he gets his way.

"A?" I ask. "Is Aiden too long to write?"

"It's code," she says, her voice sarcastic.

"Hard to crack. I see that I'm both potentially jealous and fragile of ego." I flip another few pages and find the day she came to the gym. She had her notepad with her then, too.

"'Working out with A,'" I read out loud. "'He gets up ridiculously early. Probably cold plunges and listens to an audiobook at 6x speed. Obnoxious in the gym. He has white shoes with black shoelaces. Seems to enjoy bicep curls. Muscles and vanity are clearly important. What a scoop! God, he's such a dick.'" I look up at her. "I'm a dick?"

"You were being a dick at that moment," she says and snatches the book from me. She closes it with an audible snap. "That was then, and I was annoyed at your evasiveness. I've gotten much better information since then."

"That's what worries me."

She shakes her head, but she's smiling. "Right."

"And," I add, leaning in, "maybe work on the recordkeeping, too. The date we met up in the gym was the nineteenth, not the fourteenth."

"My records are always stellar," she says, and her hand lands on my chest. It's a firm, warm weight through the thin fabric of my button-down. "I know how to do my job. Maybe you should go to bed so you can do yours properly tomorrow."

"It's not that late."

"It's late enough," she says and slides off the kitchen chair. I watch her walk toward the staircase with her notepad and laptop clutched to her chest. "Good night, Aiden," she says over her shoulder.

"Good night, Chaos."

It isn't until I've closed my own bedroom door that I realize the implication of what she'd just said, and of her handwriting on those pages.

I dig into my back pocket for my wallet. I pull out the small piece of paper from Red Rock Resort with a phone number written on it in slanted handwriting. If her fours look like nines... well, there's a possibility she gave me her real number all along.

CHAPTER 20

CHARLOTTE

I'm in bed, face washed and mind exhausted, when I see the notification on my phone.

UNKNOWN NUMBER

> Hey. It's Aiden from Red Rock Resort. Had a great time that night. Sorry it took me a while to text, your fours look kind of like nines. Hope that corporate guy in LA you went to work for isn't too much of a dick.

I read it again, the shock settling into a dull sense of panic.

He had tried to call. But he must have gotten someone else or a number that wasn't in service.

He had tried to call!

Had he thought I brushed him off? Given him a fake number?

I think back to our interaction over the tacos lunch. *Are you asking for my number?* he'd said in a low voice, almost sarcastic. I thought he was being an asshole. Reminding me of our previous interaction and how he asked for mine, only to never call. Never text.

Until now.

Your fours look kind of like nines.

They don't.

Well, maybe a little. Especially if I'm writing quickly and looping my numbers together.

I turn onto my side and scan the message again.

This changes everything, and it changes absolutely nothing. I feel like I'm on needles. Energy sparks through me and makes my stomach clench.

That night we shared… It can never happen again. We both know that, and I know it more than him. He runs Titan Media, and knowingly or not, his family company orchestrated the destruction of my life. I'm never sleeping with Aiden again.

Even if the attraction is still there. I try to bury it with professionalism, covering it with shovels of distance. It certainly helps that he's a master of being annoying. But it's still there. At moments when his eyes spark or we're arguing, I might as well be back in that resort restaurant.

Who's the real Aiden?

The scruffy one next to the fireplace, with a leather jacket and a beard. Or the five-o'clock shadowed man in a suit who argues like it's his job because it is.

My fingers type out a shaky response. I shouldn't. I should delete his text and pretend it never arrived, pretend it didn't reach me.

But we're in this boat together. This memoir needs to be great, and there's only a month and a half left.

> He is a bit of a dick, I'm afraid. Don't worry.
> I'm persevering. He has this giant house I get
> to stay at, so that's a plus. Fabulous pool.

I hit send and let the phone fall from my hand, disappearing among the pillows and the fluffy comforter on this comfortable bed. The space smells faintly like citrus from a built-in scent diffuser, and even though I'm bone-tired, I lie awake waiting for the buzz of my phone.

It only takes a few minutes.

> And now you're writing a memoir to inflate his ego even further? Doesn't sound like a good idea, Chaos. You should get out of the big city. Being in the outback looked really good on you.

It takes only a second before another message appears beneath.

> I tried calling several times.

Oh.

My heart pounds, and my fingers fly over the phone.

> Funny, a big ego is something else you have in common with the corporate dick I'm working with. I've told him off about it before, but he just seems to laugh it off.

> Maybe I just want you to tell me off more often. Maybe I enjoy it.

> Enjoying conflict feels like such a masculine thing.

> Conflict? We're not fighting, Chaos. We're arguing. Consider it foreplay.

> It's absolutely not foreplay.

> No, I suppose it's not, considering I didn't contact you until after we started working together. That's a shame.

> It's for the best. It's not like we're each other's types, anyway.

> What is your type?

> I'll tell you my type if you tell me yours.

I hit send before considering my decision. The room is perfectly quiet, save for the soft sound of a working AC; the only light is the soft bluish shine of my phone screen.

I wonder if Aiden's in his bed, too. Just down the hall. Or maybe he's working. Laptop open, always available.

The first time I was in LA, it was for Titan Media's premier party for *The Gamble*. This time, I'm with Titan Media's CEO.

The irony is not lost on me.

> My type? Smart, funny, ambitious. Doesn't matter if she's a hiker out in Utah or a bestselling author.

> A woman's career is unimportant to you?

> That's not what I said. As long as she's passionate about it, I can get on board. So. Your type?

I dig my teeth into my lower lip. This entire conversation feels too close to flirting and yet... He's giving me something. I haven't asked him about his dating habits yet, but it's a key puzzle piece to explain the man himself. And, I know I'll need to broach the subject eventually.

He's giving me a way in.

But for every nugget of information I get, I'll have to volunteer something personal in exchange.

> I don't really have a type. But yeah, I like men with unusual jobs or passions. It's attractive if they work with their hands. Most of all, they have to be interesting.

> Course they do. You like puzzles. And you wouldn't respect a pushover.

I close my eyes and take a deep breath. This is what he does. He gets under my skin, perceives all the things I don't say out loud and rarely even think about. I know it's wrong to not like the good guys. The kind guys. The ones with soft voices and softer touches.

But in the decade since Blake, since my humiliation and losing my virginity in a public spectacle, I've only been on a few first dates with the good guys. Those with the kind eyes that speak of a long-term relationship and commitment and safety.

And none of them got a second date.

I'm a moth, and I've been drawn to all kinds of flames in the last few years. Most of those have burned me, eventually.

I have no doubt he will too.

> I think you're talking about yourself, Hartman. Maybe it's a good thing I was the one hired to write your memoir. Anyone else, and you would have driven them out the door during week one.

> Also, did you just imply that you are a puzzle?

> Aren't I?

> You really are insufferable sometimes.

> Can't be boring, or you'll lose interest.

I stare at the seven little words lighting up my screen. *Or you'll lose interest.* The realization that we were only a slanted digit off from spending another night together in Utah, from whatever that may have resulted in…

It hangs over the entire conversation.

> Who says I'm interested in the first place?

I hit send and then turn over in bed, closing my eyes and welcoming the blackness behind the lids. It doesn't stop my mind from spinning. I don't know if anything can.

I shouldn't have sent that.

Shouldn't have responded to his first message tonight, but here I am—I have, and I don't think it will be the last time we'll engage like this.

For the book, I remind myself. Writing compelling stories about a person is always easier when I actually know the subject. Just like the would-be pilots need flight hours to get their wings, I need interaction hours with whoever's story I'm meant to tell.

That's all this is.

It's interaction. Another data point. Lord knows I have enough to fill a chapter just on his personality.

Tenacious. Persistent. Charming. Well-spoken. Determined. Unwilling to take no for an answer. Really fucking annoying.

There's a low buzz from my phone. I should turn it off, hit airplane mode, throw it across the room.

I look at it instead.

> You might be studying me, Chaos, but I'm studying you in return.

> Would you have picked up? If my call had gone through?

My hand is shaking when I type the response.

> You're not supposed to ask me that.

> I can't help myself, Chaos. I never can around you.

I turn my phone off and push it to the edge of the

mattress. It hits the carpeted floor with a dull thud, and I blink up at the dark ceiling.

He's still my subject for this memoir and my ticket to a new contract with my publisher. He is still the CEO and the heir of a company that I dislike with a burning passion.

My parents would *hate* that I'm doing this job. My best friend back home, my cousins, my grandmother. They would all question my sanity.

But he *had* tried to call me after Utah.

And I hate that that matters to me.

Like a moth, I think.

CHAPTER 21
AIDEN

I'm back in the glass and steel cage that's my home during business hours. The headquarters of Titan Media aren't bad, but the place's got nothing to being outside. On my screen are the latest financials for BingeBox, and I'm trying to find a new in before our next negotiations meeting.

There's a knock at the door, and then Eric's head pops in. "Hey. Do you have five?"

"I do, yes. What's happening?"

"Wanted to update you on the memoirist." He closes the door behind him and crosses his arms over his chest. He looks like a herald of old come to inform the court. Voice professional, face neutral.

"The memoirist," I repeat. At this point, Eric knows her name and her CV by heart.

"Yes. I've set her up with a space down the hall, the small conference room that hardly ever gets used."

"Cynthia uses it sometimes." Our COO is invaluable.

"She approved," Eric says. "We spoke about it earlier today. Ms. Gray will be hosting informal drop-in sessions for people here if they want to come in and chat."

"About what?" My voice comes out sharper than I intended, and I run a hand through my hair. Charlotte and I haven't spoken in person since the text conversation last night. The knowledge has changed things.

How could it not?

"The book. If they want to talk about what Titan means to them, their history here at the company... about you." Eric's lips quirk just a bit. He knows how much I dislike the whole memoir notion. "We give her what she needs... About the company."

And not about me.

"That's not a bad idea."

His smile widens. "Yes. Well, if she's nearby, she also has more access to you. I know that's a problem for you. So I've stressed that she only gets the room today and tomorrow for the explicit reason of interviewing staff, but—"

"No, that's not a problem."

Eric's eyebrows rise. "I've limited her accessibility to you until a few days ago when you changed that. Does this mean you want to give her unrestricted access?"

I don't know what it means.

I'm in over my head. She's a beautiful distraction, a nuisance with her memoir, and an intriguing problem to solve. It means I'm winging it.

"I'll handle my availability to her," I say.

Eric gives a smooth nod, his face returning to its professional mask. "I see. Let me know if you need any changes to the protocol."

"Will do."

He turns to leave, but I stop him. "She wants to interview you. Have you visited the room?"

He gives a tiny chuckle. "Not yet. But I heard she brought fresh donuts for everyone who goes in there. So I probably will."

"Donuts," I repeat. "That's the price of your loyalty?"

He pulls the door open wide with a smile. "I'll only have good things to say."

I run a hand through my hair again. She's right down the hall, is she? And bribing my staff with baked goods to get them to spill all my secrets.

It's nearly four in the afternoon when I have the time to leave my office and head down the hallway. The glass door—layered with frosted window film that makes it opaque—to the conference room is closed.

Is she with a visitor?

I put my hands in my pockets and stare at the door. My employees could be telling her what they think about me, either on or off the record.

There are plenty of workers here who are from the "before" times. When the CEO was still named Hartman, but his first name was Alfred. Charlotte is asking them about that period.

Unease ripples through me. This is what I didn't want.

I can control what I say to her, but damn if I can control anyone else. There's a part of me that wants to interrupt.

But I don't get the chance to decide, because the door opens, and out steps Cynthia. She's a tall, Black woman with razor-sharp intellect and a penchant for pantsuits. She's worked for the company for as long as I've been alive. She was a junior executive when I took over, but I'd quickly promoted her to the COO position.

When she sees me, she pauses. "Waiting for your turn?"

"Did you get a donut?"

"I had two."

Cynthia pushes the door open wider, revealing Charlotte as she's scribbling at the conference table. Her light-brown hair is pushed back behind her ears, the sleeves of her button-down folded back, and that familiar notepad is in front of her.

There's an open box half-filled with powdered donuts.

"Good luck," Cynthia says and breezes past me. There's amusement in her voice that I know is completely at my expense.

I push the door fully open. Charlotte looks up. A smudge of sugar dusting is beside her mouth, and she's wearing reading glasses. I haven't seen her in glasses before.

"Aiden," she says. Her voice carries a thread of apprehension, a frisson of tension, and I feel the same thing reverberating through me.

"Chaos," I say and shut the door behind me. "You're bribing my staff with baked goods?"

"I'm encouraging them," she says. Her notepad falls shut with a dull thud. "Have you come for an interview?"

I sit in the chair across from her. "What have you been asking my staff?"

"Most of it was off the record," she says. "A few have given me fantastic quotes, though. Eric arranged for me to use the space tomorrow, too."

"What are the quotes?"

There's a curve to her lips. "And you claim you're not driven by ego." She flips open her laptop. "Okay, let's see... I'm already working on this chapter, so..." Her hesitant glance lands on me for just a moment. "This is paraphrased slightly." She draws a deep breath as if she's steeling herself. "Okay.

"'He came in here when the company was at its weakest. People were quitting left and right. There were bets placed on whether or not we'd file for bankruptcy this week, or the next, or the one after that. He must have heard the talk. But he never once acknowledged it. From the first day, he acted as if this company was strong, and was only going to get stronger. With an attitude like that, he could easily have been mistaken for being naive. But he managed to communicate strength instead. Like if he wasn't afraid, we shouldn't be either.'"

The words ring false.

I hadn't been strong. Nor had I been in any way sure that

Titan wasn't heading toward bankruptcy. But if I'd hidden it well… that's good, I suppose.

"You're frowning," Charlotte says. She closes her laptop and clasps her hands together on its silvery shell. "That doesn't sound like you?"

I force my face to smooth out into a neutral expression. "I knew they were taking bets. Cynthia was wrong about that."

"What makes you think that quote is from Cynthia?"

"Isn't it?"

"No," she says, "it isn't. And no, I won't tell you who said it. It's off the record. I've had to tell every single person who walked in here today that in no way, shape, or form you would trace what was said back to the speaker."

That makes me scoff. "As if I'd fire them if they said something negative?"

"Yes," she says. "That's a real concern for plenty of mere mortals who don't happen to be the CEO and also the majority shareholder of a company."

Her voice is a tad snarky, her eyes sharp behind her reading glasses.

My lips twitch, a smile is threatening to break out. "Like freelancing memoirists?"

"I'm not afraid of being fired," she says. "Not from this job. Especially since you're not the one who hired me."

I brace my hands on the table, interlacing my fingers together. Mirroring her stance. "Want to play a game?"

Her eyes narrow. "What game?"

"You can talk to people about what I'm like. But they don't know what it's like to be me."

"No," she says. "Which is why I'm also interviewing you."

I reach for one of the donuts. "On Thursday, why don't you live exactly like me?"

CHAPTER 22

CHARLOTTE

Doing what Aiden does for an entire day should be easy.

But it's not.

It starts in the gym. I'm wearing an old tank top with Idaho State's logo on it and a pair of leggings that I use to run in. I haven't tried that here yet. Running the hills of Bel Air. I should, but the roads here have sharp twists and turns, and the cars whip about at high speeds. It's also hot as hell most days. And I haven't found where the designated running trails are.

Frankly, all of these are excuses. But they still work.

I watch Aiden load weights onto the barbell I've seen him use several times before. One. Then two. Three weights. It's almost as heavy as when he does chest presses.

"Okay, I know we said I would do exactly what you're doing, but I'm not lifting that."

Aiden steps back and gives the weights a considering look. Like he's thinking about adding more plates to the barbell.

"You're not even listening," I say. "You're just packing on the weights. Have you seen my arms? They're not like yours. I'm not made out of pure muscle."

He actually cracks a small smile at that. "Right. Well, do you want to be?"

I think for a moment. "Not particularly. But given the way you work out, you clearly want to. So I guess today, yes. I want to look like I could be the movie star, not the movie company owner."

"My company makes very few movies."

"Very few is not none." I take a few steps closer and look at the intimidating bar. "All right. Let's do this. And why is the news not on? I'm Aiden Hartman. I need to be informed of the latest headlines at all times. Especially when I'm working on my already perfect physique." I sit down on the bench. My words come faster than usual, and it's partly fueled by nerves. I haven't lifted weights in a long time.

I don't know if I can do this.

Not with him watching me. In all his six-three, tanned, broad glory. He's not flexing. Hasn't even crossed his arms over his chest, and they're still broad.

Annoying.

I lie down on the bench and reach up to grip the bar. He walks behind me and takes up a position like he's going to spot me. Jesus. He never has a spotter.

"I haven't overloaded," he says, voice even. "You can get eight reps done. Then you could stop if you want. But I know you can do eight more afterward."

"You know, do you?"

"I know. Let's go."

I do the eight. He lets me rest for a bit, and then, somehow, I do eight more. By the time I finish, my chest is burning. It's definitely much heavier than I usually lift, and he's been watching all of it.

He puts me through the remainder of his usual routine. Some weight loads are half of his, most are a third. It's humbling to realize how quickly I get tired. Toward the end, I'm sweaty, I haven't asked a single question that I need for his book, and Aiden has barely gotten winded. Despite doing most of his exercises right alongside me.

I'm slouching, seated on the floor after completing my last sit-up. "Why," I ask and reach for my water bottle, "do you do this *every* single morning?"

He does another biceps curl. "I don't. Only four times a week."

I roll my eyes. "Right. Only four times a week. How come?"

"Why not? Why do you read books or write in your spare time?" He does another curl. His dark hair is damper at the temples, and there's a flush along his high cheekbones now. It's starting to get to him. Now, at the very end. "It's good for me. The mind stays sharp by keeping the body healthy."

"Is this just another aspect you like to control? You know, you can't control what other people do, but you can control what you do?" I ask. It's a frequent characteristic I've seen as a memoirist. People who do great things, truly amazing things, often require significant personal sacrifices.

They are usually control freaks.

Aiden's lips twitch. "Mm-hmm. You're stalling, Chaos. Finish the last set and then you're done for real."

I lean back and start the slow, painful sit-ups again. My entire body feels like it's on fire. "You missed your calling," I say in between heavy breaths. "Clearly you want to be a personal trainer."

He reaches for a neatly wrapped towel and runs it across his face. Wiping away sweat that's barely there. Just a faint sheen that somehow makes him look healthier and *more* attractive. "A shame indeed. Two more, then we're done."

"Done," I mutter. "Your day has only just begun."

A true smile spreads across his face. It's so wide and so genuine that it transforms his features. His visage morphs from the sometimes intimidating handsomeness into something real.

"I don't know what I like best, Chaos. You when you're all chirpy and positive, or when you're grumbling. Now come on. You're done, and we need to get ready if we're going to make it." He extends a hand and pulls me up to stand.

"What about breakfast?" I ask.

"There should be premade shakes in the fridge. We'll grab some on our way out."

I can only get half of mine down, sitting in the passenger seat of his giant jeep and driving down the winding roads of Bel Air. It tastes like equal parts protein powder and vegetables. Aiden finishes his before we even cross Sunset Boulevard.

He only has one hand on the steering wheel. The sleeve of his suit jacket has ridden up a bit, showing a thick watch. "You know," I say. "I should be the one driving, if we're truly doing this right and all."

"Nice try."

"If I'm to live as you."

"Want to go on a joyride, Chaos? We can do that after work."

I play with the hem of my dress. "How will this work today? Am I pretending to be you on the phone? Answering emails like you, ordering Eric around like you?"

"I don't order Eric around."

"No, you're right about that, actually," I say. "He orders you around."

Aiden chuckles at that.

I tilt my head, looking at his profile. The furrow between his brow is entirely smoothed out. "You're in a good mood today."

His eyes slide to mine briefly, there and gone again. "Yes. I suppose I am."

"Torturing me in the gym lifts your spirits? I don't know what that says about you, but okay."

He chuckles again. "Drink your shake, Chaos."

I look down at the thick contents. "I think I prefer mine with lots of strawberries, bananas, and no powder at all."

"Of course you do. We all do. But this one is better for you."

"Are you a machine? Or a man?"

He shakes his head, but the smile stays in place. Even as we pull into the line of traffic backing up through Westwood, heading to cross Wilshire Boulevard. Only a few blocks left to his office in Culver City. "You wanted to live a day like me."

"I have a feeling I'm going to live to regret that."

"Think I'll go hard on you?"

I glare at him. He sees it out of the corner of his eye, and his lips tip up again. "Yes."

Los Angeles is barely awake outside the windows. Cars are out, yes, but the small shops we pass are still closed. The strip mall is still dark.

He pulls into the parking lot of Titan Media and the spot reserved for him right by the front doors. I follow him into the building. The executive floor is still dark. He's the one who turns on the lights.

I walk past him to his office. What compels someone to work this hard? I've tried to understand it. But it's still hard to wrap my mind around. This drive—his desire—to restore his family company, even if he needs to sacrifice his own free time, health, and happiness.

Not that he probably sees it as such.

Inside his large office, he heads straight to the spare chair on the other side of his desk. He lifts and moves it to set it right beside his.

"I was joking, by the way," I say. "About answering emails like you."

"Mm-hmm." He's already sat down in his chair and fired up his computer. "But it's too late. I took you seriously. Now come over here, Chaos, and get immersed."

I grab my notepad and walk around to his screen. "You sure?"

"Yeah. If you're shadowing me today, we might as well do it properly," he says. Then he shakes his head and a rueful expression crosses his face. "It's a humbling thing, Chaos... I've realized that the people you've worked with previously have taken you mushing across the Alaskan tundra and to the World Poker Tournament."

My eyes slowly widen. "Oh no. You're feeling competitive."

"Sure am. So yes. We'll work in the office. Half a day, or so."

"What are we doing later?"

His smile widens. "There's a movie premiere tonight, and you're coming with me."

CHAPTER 23
CHARLOTTE

"This is the plan for tonight," Eric says. He's already sent me an itinerary, but now he's walking through it with me. Just as if I'm Aiden.

I'm a tired mess. I've tried to stay sharp for every back-to-back meeting Aiden has had. He's stayed true to his word and included me in everything. More than he had to.

"All right," I say. "And this premiere is for... *Echoes*. Right?"

"Yes," Eric says. His small frown makes it clear that I'm not paying enough attention. Aiden is on the other side of the table, being briefed simultaneously, but his eyes are on me.

"*Echoes* is the sequel to the blockbuster sci-fi movie that came out two years ago," Aiden adds. "The World Premiere is today."

I remember the first film. My parents loved it. I thought it was fun, but too long. This event is an absolutely enormous deal. "How did you get tickets on such short notice?"

"I've had them for a while."

I narrow my eyes at him. "You planned on this when you suggested *today* be the day I live like you."

He lifts an eyebrow. "Doesn't sound like me."

"It sounds exactly like you."

Eric looks between us a few times and then sighs. It's a very elegant, annoyed little sound. "Mr. Hartman will leave his car here to be taken back to his house. Joe will transport both of you tonight. First to Rodeo Drive, where I've set up two appointments for Ms. Gray—"

"Rodeo *Drive*?"

Aiden crosses his arms over his chest. "Yes. We're getting you a dress."

"I have a dre—"

"You said that last time," he says.

A fierce flush climbs up my cheeks. The zipper. Yes, I had said that last time, and it hadn't gotten me very far.

"Fine. We'll go to get a dress."

Aiden's lip curves. "And shoes."

"I didn't know you were such a shopaholic," I say. Then I realize Eric is here, and my words could come across as rude. Or ungrateful. There's just something about Aiden that gets to me. "Sorry. Thank you, that's very kind of you."

Aiden's smile just widens, like he knows I'm saying it for the audience. "You're very welcome, Charlotte."

Across the table, Eric looks back down at his notes. "Right. The salon next door has also been booked. I've scheduled a phone meeting for you at the same time. You wanted an update on your sister's security."

He nods. "Good."

"Then the car will take you to the Dolby Theatre. I've made it clear that neither of you will walk the red carpet."

The words are so outlandish that I almost want to laugh. Except, that's his life, isn't it? He goes to things like that. Because in his field, being seen is important.

I've spent so many years trying *not* to be noticed.

"We won't stay long," Aiden says. As if reading my thoughts. "We'll see the movie, talk to some famous people, and then head out. I just need to make an appearance."

"No, no, that sounds…" Amazing. Unreal. Something that happens to other people. "Fun."

His lips quirk again. "Good."

———

The stores on Rodeo Drive are legendary. So are their prices. Which is why I've never bought a single thing from any of the designers whose names grace the street and its surrounding neighborhood.

We're in the middle of Beverly Hills, and the people who pass us are either drop-dead-gorgeous or tourists. There seems to be no in-between. No normies just out for a little walk. No regular person popping into a luxury boutique for an afternoon purchase.

The palms that line the street are huge and so straight that it all feels like a feat of engineering.

Joe finds a parking spot outside a store I recognize far too well. It's a brand I've known all my life. A household name. It's just not for normal people.

"Here?" I ask. My voice comes out high. "We're going *there* to shop for a dress?"

Aiden shuts the car door behind me. "Yes. Or would you rather go somewhere else?"

As if it wasn't good enough. Not up to my standards.

"No," I say faintly. "This will… do."

"Great," he says.

"This is not something you'd normally do during your day." But then I think about it, my step faltering. Eric had made the reservations awfully fast. "Or maybe it is. Did you… Do you often bring dates here before heading out?" He'd be able to impress half the country with these kinds of tactics.

He pulls the heavy glass door open for me. "Are you wondering about my dating habits again, Chaos?"

"No."

"Yes, you are." He comes up beside me, dips his head until his mouth is right by my ear. "I have done things like this before."

My stomach sinks, and the glamorous setting around us feels just a bit off. *Oh.* This is routine, then. A small sigh escapes me before I can stop it.

His voice drops. "With my mother, when I was too young to escape. Sometimes with Mandy, when she drags me along. No one else, Chaos."

I look up at him. He's watching me closely. He has seen my disappointment, the flare of jealousy. Saw all of it.

I narrow my eyes at him. "Aiden…"

"Mr. Hartman and Ms. Gray!" A beautifully clad woman comes toward us. Behind her are two other attendants; one carrying a tray of champagne and water. "Welcome, welcome. Let's start the fitting—movie premiere at short notice. Is that correct?"

Aiden puts a hand on my lower back. "Yes. I doubt you have anything as beautiful as Charlotte, but I'd like you to try."

Fifteen minutes later, there's a dazzling array of dresses hung on a clothing rack by the elaborate dressing rooms. "I only need one," I say, but my hand is gliding over the fabrics. Some are soft as silk, others are elaborately woven gems.

Aiden is sitting on a plush sofa right by the changing rooms.

"How much time do we have?" I ask him.

"Don't worry about it." He's got a glass of champagne in his hand, and his long legs are spread out in front of him. Suit pants. Brown shows. I look at his outfit with a faint frown. "You're still in your suit from work."

"Indeed I am."

The attendant pulls the curtain aside to the dressing room behind me, and I step inside. "Will you wear it later?" I call.

"No." There's an amused lilt to his voice. "I'll go home and change when you go to the place next door."

"What place next door?" I wriggle out of my cardigan and the dress I'd worn today. Even the lighting is amazing in this store. I look good in the floor-length mirror, and I rarely do in fitting rooms.

My hair is a mess, brushed back into a low ponytail. Maybe I can throw it up into a ballerina bun?

"It's a salon. They'll do your hair and makeup, Chaos." There's a brief pause. "If you want it. God knows you don't fucking need it."

"Oh." I step into a dress. It's a slinky, sexy thing, with a fully open back. It doesn't feel like me in the least. But the attendant had insisted I try it on.

There's no price tag on it.

There's no price tag on any of the other dresses, either.

I recall the game I'd played with his house and start a similar one here. Two thousand dollars? Three? *Maybe four*, I think when I see the built-in hidden zipper.

A salon. Despite the nerves, excitement swells within me at the thought. I've never been to a movie premiere. There'll be a ton of people there, and while they're all industry figures, there's one guarantee—every single one of them is more famous than my brief fifteen minutes in the spotlight.

"Chaos." His voice is closer, right by the edge of the curtain.

"Yes?"

"Do you want my opinion on these dresses? If not, I'll run back home to get a tux right away. Beat the traffic. The store already has my card—I've told them to put anything you want on it."

I pull back the curtain. "No, that's smart. I can choose one of these. Meet you outside the salon later?"

His gaze drifts over my body. There's a widening of his eyes. I look down, too.

Oh. Right. This dress has the skimpiest of top parts, a deep V-neck that disappears between my tits. It's worth a fortune, but is hardly more than a drape of expensive silk, leaving me bare on the top and pooling on the ground.

"I don't think this one is a winner," I say.

Aiden shakes his head slowly. "No, neither do I," he mutters. "Because I won't be able to concentrate if you're on my arm looking like that."

"On your arm?" I ask. "I'm meant to be shadowing you."

His lips curve, and there's a sinful look there that makes my stomach drop. "Yes, Chaos. Be my shadow. As long as you stay close to me, I'll be happy."

I reach for the curtain. My heart is beating too fast, and I like it far too much. "Come back when I'm finished."

"Not even LA traffic could stop me."

I settle on a long, amber-colored dress and a pair of strappy heels. The dress is asymmetrical at the top—draping over one shoulder and leaving my other bare.

I stress-test the zipper twice in the dressing room. It holds.

The attendants are very, very nice. The kind of nice you might only encounter when you're spending an outrageous amount of money. They add a small purse to the pile, saying that Mr. Hartman had insisted.

A tiny part of me is whispering that all this is too much.

The larger part lets me be swept up in the fantasy. That just for tonight, maybe I can have this experience. One I'll remember forever.

Similarly, the salon next door takes good care of me. My hair is washed and blowdried until it's long and gleaming. And when the makeup artist asks me what I'd like, I look at my bare face in the mirror and think of my fear of being recognized.

"Make me look different," I tell her. "A lot of dark eye shadow, maybe?"

She leans back and assesses me. "We could do a smokey

look. Dark red lip and exaggerated smokiness. I think that would look really good on you."

"Let's do it."

When I'm done, I barely recognize my reflection—smokey eyes and soft gleaming hair. I look taller than I truly am, thanks to the heels, and have a dress that makes me feel like a goddess. The salon had given me a glass of champagne, my second already, and I'm feeling like Nighttime Charlotte again. Stepping into a different version of myself.

Aiden is waiting outside the salon. He's leaning against the car in a tux, talking to someone on the phone. He looks tall, handsome, and rich.

And then he sees me.

He stops talking, and slowly lowers his phone from his ear. His eyes look me over, and I bathe in his languid gaze, in the way it lingers. For the first time since I met him, I feel like I match him. Like, I could stand beside him while he's in his tux and it would look like we belong together.

"Holy shit," he says.

CHAPTER 24

AIDEN

I can't stop staring.

Charlotte is a vision in a long, amber dress that accentu-
ates her hair. It hugs her narrow waist, and then a single piece
of draped fabric crosses her shoulder. Her arms are bare. And
when she takes a step forward, the dress reveals a high slit in
the flaring skirt, and a flash of a long, lean leg.

Fucking hell.

Some kind of magic happened with her hair. The light-
brown waves are glossy, falling around her face and down
her back like a waterfall. She's wearing red lipstick and
there's darkness around her eyes.

"Thanks," she says.

Her voice brings me back to the here and now. She is
made up like a goddess, but she's still my Charlotte. Charlotte of the late nights on the couch, of the sparring matches
in my office, of the banter and quick-witted comebacks.

My eyes snag on her shoes. They're black and strappy, and
fuck, those heels. They look deadly.

"You're not saying anything," she says. She grips a clutch
in front of her. Good. I'm glad they persuaded her on the full
getup. I'm just sorry I wasn't able to convince her to treat
herself to even more.

"You look…"

"It's too much. Isn't it?"

I close the distance between us. There's no resisting it. I put my hand on her waist and rub a thumb over the silky chiffon. "You're a vision. A dream, Chaos."

She smiles a little. There's hopeful excitement in her eyes that robs me of breath all over again. "Really?"

"Yes. I'd kiss you right now if it wouldn't ruin your lipstick."

Her gaze widens, and I realize what I just said.

But I don't take it back.

"Oh." Her smile is soft and gentle, and she looks down at my tux. "Good thing I'm wearing lipstick, then."

"Mm-hmm. What did those people in the salon do to your eyes?"

"My eyes?"

"They're… I'm… I don't have the words." My hand is still on her waist, tracing little circles.

She reaches up and smoothes the lapels of my dinner jacket. "It's a smokey eye. I wanted to look different. Unlike myself."

"You do."

"In a good way?"

"That's a trick question," I say, and her red, glossy lips tip up into a smile that is still familiar. My favorite expression of hers. "You're just as beautiful with as without all of this, Chaos. I've always thought that."

Her fingers tighten around my lapel. "You're a charmer."

"I'm honest. There's a difference." I reach down and find her hand. The need to touch her is always strong. Right now, it's invincible. "Come on. Let's get you to the premiere. You'll outshine all the movie stars."

The car drive to Hollywood Boulevard is surprisingly fast. Distance-wise we're not far, but distance has little to do with travel time in LA. One of the cardinal rules of traffic.

We bypass the red carpet, arriving instead behind the Dolby Theatre directly at the VIP reception. It's held in a secluded area set up like a garden terrace, away from the prying eyes of the press and the public alike. I show my invitation to the man at the entrance, and then he eagerly waves me through.

Charlotte gives a low whistle at my side. "It's that easy, is it? To be Aiden Hartman?"

It's not easy at all, I think. All these people wouldn't take the Hartman name in their mouth two years ago. It's only by relentlessly clawing our way back to the top of this industry, and ensuring I can offer them something they covet, that I have this kind of access again. There is no genuine friendliness in Hollywood. It's all fake smiles and trading favors. And always, *always*, the neverending game of fame.

It's the currency everyone is aware of. It hangs over people's heads like a counter. Of the followers, the gross revenue stats. I've seen plenty of people who let that consume them.

But that's not what Charlotte asked. So I put my hand on the small of her back, feeling the faint shiver that races through her at the touch. "Sometimes," I say. "When I have something they want."

"Leverage," she murmurs. "That's what this industry runs on. Right?"

I look at her for a second before answering. "Yes. It is. You catch on quick."

"It's sort of my job," she says with a slight smile.

"No," I say. "I think it's just you."

Her gaze lingers on mine. The makeup emphasizes the blue of her eyes, and I can't seem to look away from her depths.

"Aiden," she murmurs.

Whatever else she meant to say is drowned by the sudden applause. Excitement ripples through the well-heeled crowd around us, and I search the mass of producers, actors, and musicians.

Ah. The lead actors have arrived. They walk into the VIP reception area like conquering heroes—big smiles on their faces. Four of Hollywood's leading young stars.

"Wow," Charlotte breathes beside me. "I can't believe I'm actually seeing this."

"It's real. Believe it."

"They're much smaller than I thought."

I laugh. "Yeah, film people always are. Don't say that to them, though. Logan put on forty pounds of muscle for the role."

Her eyes turn to me. "You don't know them, do you?"

"Not all. Him, I do."

"You're lying."

I raise an eyebrow. "I'd never lie to you, Chaos. Want me to prove it?"

The fire in her eyes is back. I love that expression. The one that tells me she's game, she's down, she wants to play just as much as I do. I've never met anyone like her.

"If you can," she says.

I grip her hand again. It fits easily into my palm this time, her fingers curving over mine. Like they belong together. "Come," I say.

———

Three and a half hours later, Charlotte is smiling by my side. She's also wobbling. The steps from the theater to the after-party aren't many, but for a woman not used to heels, it's a trek.

I wrap my arm firmly around her waist to steady her. "As soon as we get out of here," I say against her temple, "you're taking those shoes off."

She giggles. "But they're so pretty."

"They're also hurting you. Aren't they?"

She shoots me a look. But then she sighs. "Yes. Is it obvious? I wanted to look all ethereal and cool for an evening."

That makes me smile. "If it's any consolation, you do look *very* ethereal and cool."

"It is. Thank you." She leans into me a little.

There's chatter around us. Behind us. In front of us. As the hordes of guests migrate from the theater to the after-party, with the film screening done. There was a Q&A with the actors and then the director, as well. Charlotte had been on the edge of her seat. I watched her more than I watched either of the discussions or the movie.

"Maybe I should just carry you." I move closer, like I'm reaching for her.

She laughs and swats at my arm. "No, you won't. Not in front of these people!"

I've never had this much fun at one of these events before. It's always been work. Networking. You scratch my back, and I'll scratch yours.

We arrive at the after-party. The venue has been decorated like a desert landscape, to make it feel like the scenery in the movie. And I have to give it to them, it's a stellar job. The large room, the DJ's stage, the area for taking photos. It all looks appropriately beige.

Charlotte marvels by my side. Her wide eyes take in the space, and a broad smile lights up her face. She's beautiful.

She always is.

But when she has that look about her...

"Thank you," she says. "Thank you for taking me here. I know I'm just shadowing you today, but... You could have decided to go somewhere else. To Costco, for example, to do a giant grocery run."

I shake my head. "Right. That's on *tomorrow's* agenda, actually."

"Whew, thank god." Her smile widens, and she looks back

out at the people. "I never thought I'd get a chance to speak to Logan Edwards! Or any of them. Even to *see* any of them. This is the sort of thing that—" Her voice dies abruptly, eyes locked on something across the party.

Her body tenses.

On instinct, I take a step closer to Charlotte and look where she's staring. But all I see are other people mingling about. Some are close by. A few individuals are standing in a half circle, chatting. There's a beautiful Hollywood actress I vaguely recognize as an up-and-comer. A reality star that, if I recall correctly, has been on a few of the shows Titan had produced. Not someone I'm going to talk to tonight.

"Chaos. What's wrong?"

She grips my forearms and turns us abruptly, so I'm blocking her view. "Shit. I… nothing. Nothing's wrong."

I push back a tendril of her hair. She's gone white. "Something's wrong. What can I do?"

Her eyes flick from mine to something over my shoulder. *Someone* over my shoulder.

"They're walking past." Her voice is a frantic murmur. "I need to hide."

There's only a split second to make the decision. She's clinging to me, curving into me, like she wants to disappear entirely. And if she doesn't want to be recognized…

I pull her tight and fit her mouth to mine.

CHAPTER 25
CHARLOTTE

Aiden kisses me.

My heart is already pounding out of my chest, and when his lips slant over mine, it skyrockets. His arm wraps around me and pulls me close. Like he can envelop me whole, if he only tries hard enough.

His other hand cups my face. Slides into my hair and musses it up.

What he's doing is brilliant. No one can see my face when his is pressed against it.

He's hiding me.

His lips are warm, and I slowly respond to his kiss, moving gently against his mouth. Languidly, I slide my hands up the luxurious fabric that covers his hard chest. He's always been big, strong, and handsome. I've done my best to ignore that these past few weeks.

But it's impossible to ignore when he's touching me like this.

Each brush of his lips melts away my panic little by little. Like he's searing it off, one stroke at a time, and I'm left bone-less and heated.

I brush my tongue over his bottom lip.

Aiden groans against my mouth, and his tongue comes to

meet mine. The sweet, sugary syrup that has spread through my limbs is replaced by a sudden flash of fire.

It races straight down my body. Makes my stomach tighten and my legs lock together. *Oh.*

His hand is on my lower back, and I feel it slide down, his fingers splaying before coming to a stop right above my ass.

"Fuck," he mutters into my mouth. His lips move to my cheek, and he's breathing hard.

I rest my forehead against his shoulder, hiding my face from view again. My heart is beating so fast, I hear it thundering in my ears.

Aiden locks his arms around my waist. Firm. Strong. A tree to lean on. Somewhere in the distance, music plays. It comes filtering back through the haze I've been in since I saw Blake standing mere feet away.

Right next to some actress who probably brought him as a date.

He's still in the reality show business, after all. The latest season of *Endurance Island* just started airing—produced by Titan Media—and he's one of the stars.

Time had been kind to him, the way it is to most men. The twenty-four-year-old I'd fallen in love with on *The Gamble*, has now been replaced by a thirty-four-year-old Brit with perfect teeth and a permanent Hollywood tan. He'd filled out, gained little lines on his forehead that make men in this business distinguished, and women so often "past their prime."

I didn't expect to see him here.

Had been so sure that no one would recognize me, that I hadn't even thought I would bump into someone I know.

Aiden's hand caresses my back. "Your heart is pounding," he mutters against my ear. "Who did you see? Say the word, and I'll have them killed."

I chuckle weakly into his shoulder. The panic is gone, and it's been replaced with a different kind of excitement.

We hadn't kissed since Utah.

I'd forgotten how he kisses. The slow, steady movement of his lips. There's no rush with Aiden. It's not a race. He takes his time to learn my lips, to spark the fire inside me. No one has ever kissed me like that before him.

It's always been rushed. At a bar, in a hookup situation. Stolen kisses in rare situationships with only one destination. Bed.

Aiden doesn't kiss like that. He kisses me like he could do it forever. For the rest of his life.

"Charlotte," he urges, and that's when I finally hear the concern in his voice. "Tell me what's wrong."

I shake my head a little and pull back. Blake and his party had been moving toward the terrace, passing dangerously close to us. They should be gone now.

But I'm not taking any chances.

"Can you take me home?"

His eyes darken at the words. But he nods, and his hand slides down to grip mine again. He's held it often tonight. Almost like he can't stop himself. "Yes. Come."

I stop him with my palm on his chest. "Wait," I murmur and run a thumb over his lower lip. "You look like you've been mauled."

His eyes dip to my mouth. "Good. So do you."

"We can't walk around like that."

"With your mark on me?" His hand tightens around mine, and he pulls me along to the exit. "Gladly, Chaos."

We make it to the car and I gladly slump against the seat. The evening has been long—the day has been even longer— and I feel wrung out. Stretched too thin, my skin taut. Too aware of Aiden. It's keeping my nerves on a permanent high.

"Who was it?" Aiden asks. His voice comes out low, and, while I think he's concerned, he sounds angry, too.

I blow out a breath. "Not someone I want to talk about."

"You looked scared, Chaos."

My eyes close against the shame. Blake should not have

that power over me. Not anymore. But I hadn't seen him in almost a decade, and I didn't want... couldn't stand it if Aiden had seen us together. If the puzzle pieces slid into place.

If Aiden would have looked at me like the whole world did back then.

"It was someone from my past. Someone I thought I'd never run into again." My voice comes out weaker than I intended, and I clear my throat. "Thank you for... hiding me."

The silence is absolute from the man beside me. I take a few more deep breaths before turning to look at him. His face is drawn tight, jaw tense.

"Aiden," I say. "I know the way you think. Please don't try to analyze or figure out who or what it might be. Please... I'm asking you."

He looks at me for another tense moment before sighing. "All right," he says, and his hand finds mine again. Lying on the empty middle seat between us. "I won't."

No one to see us now. No one to perform for.

"Promise me."

It takes him a moment, and I can see what it costs him. But then he nods. "I promise, Charlotte."

CHAPTER 26

AIDEN

The next night, it's far too late when I finally head home.

The meeting with investors ran late, and there was too much on the line to leave early. Then Eric and Cynthia showed up with an urgent matter.

One that has left me in a sour mood. Not only had I likely missed my chance of spending time with Charlotte tonight, but there is a fire that needs to be doused within the company that could not, under any circumstances, be leaked to the press.

Wonderful.

I drive up the winding, familiar road to my house on autopilot. I've done it day in and day out for more years than I can count. It was one of the first purchases I made after college. Since then, the value of the property has appreciated so much that realtors are regularly hounding me to sell. But I don't need more space.

I live alone, and I've always liked it that way.

Before.

Because I'm increasingly aware of there being a distinct *before* and a resounding *after*. And it all revolves around *her*.

I hate the promise Charlotte made me make in the car last night. It goes against every instinct I have to get to know her better, to make sure she's safe, and that whoever elicited that reaction from her never comes near her again. But she made me swear, and I'll be damned if I'll be the kind of man who doesn't stand by his word.

That was my father, not me.

I pull into my driveway, and park between my sleek Ferrari Spider and Charlotte's beat-up old Honda. I hate the sight of it now just as much as the first time I saw it.

Anyone can practically *see* how unsafe it is with a single glance.

It's a wonder it made it all the way here from Chicago, across hundreds of miles and rough terrain, with a stop at Zion National Park.

I park my car next to Honda and shoot it another look. I don't want Charlotte driving around LA in that thing. Surrounded by giant vehicles that take the narrow hillside roads up here in the mountains far too fast. I should know. One incident, and she'd be…

Maybe I can convince her to let me buy her a new car. Make that a part of her deal. Nothing flashy, just…

From this decade, at the very least.

The house is dark when I unlock the front door. Of course, she's already asleep. Why wouldn't she be? I walk across the space with more force than needed. Usually, it's my work that sustains me. Right now, I feel like it's the one thing that's bringing me down.

I hear soft voices, and then laughter. I head up to the second-floor landing and hear the voices get louder. Yes, it's definitely the TV.

"Charlotte?"

There's no response. Just more of a laugh track.

I see her on the couch. She's lying on her side, curled up, hand beneath her head. The screen is showing an old episode of *Friends*.

Sprawled on the table in front of her are two notepads, a still-opened laptop, and half a bottle of wine.

I lift the bottle. *Langley Wineries.* Along with my mother and my sister, I own this vineyard estate up in Sonoma Valley. She's doing research?

I look down at Charlotte. She's in a tank top and a pair of gray sweatpants, her face smoothed out in sleep. Long eyelashes rest against her freckled cheeks. Her hair is a wavy mess around the pillow. I want to reach out and run my hand through her gentle waves. I want to pull her into my arms and fall asleep right next to her.

I do neither.

Instead, I sit down on the other end of the couch and reach for a blanket. Being careful not to wake her, I spread it over her and then grab one of her notepads.

My name is everywhere.

She's made notes for different chapters of the memoir in her slanted handwriting. There are comments about Mandy and how she's planning to reach out to schedule a lunch with her. Questions that are still unanswered. There's also a little checklist of topics that she's waiting for my answers.

I look at the pen on the coffee table. Back to Charlotte. And then I sit back down and start answering them one by one.

She stirs when I'm halfway down the list. Curls even tighter into a ball before shifting onto her back. Her eyes blink open a few times, and she rolls her neck.

I put her notepad back down. "Hey."

"Hey," she murmurs, a small smile on her lips. Then her eyes widen. "I fell asleep."

"Yes, you sure did." I hold up the bottle of wine. "Raided the wine cellar downstairs, too, I see."

"I bought it myself!" She pushes up onto her elbows. A strap of her tank top has fallen down, leaving one of her shoulders bare. She's too fucking pretty.

"Please tell me you didn't," I say.

"Yes, earlier today. While I was out on a research trip."

"A research trip?"

She nods and pushes firmly into sitting. Pulling her legs beneath herself in a cross-legged position. "Yes. I did…" She looks down at the mess on the coffee room table. "I went to your high school and elementary school."

"You did *what*?"

"I needed to see them to be able to describe them."

"No reader will be interested in my elementary school."

She gives me a prim look. "Yes, they will, Aiden. Because it's part of painting a larger picture."

"I could have taken you there. If you really wanted to go."

"You were at work," she says.

"I could have skipped out for an hour," I say.

It's a complete lie. I didn't even have time to eat dinner today, never mind taking a break to drive around areas I haven't been to in years. Decades.

"I didn't want to bother you." She looks at the bottle in my hands, and a slight blush creeps up her cheeks. "I didn't plan on having so much. It was better than I expected."

"I'm glad you think so. It's my mother's pride and joy."

"Does she live up there now?"

I smile faintly. "You never stop working, do you?"

With her hair mussed from her nap and her eyes warm on mine, it's impossible to look at her and not remember her lips on mine last night.

On the projector screen, laughter erupts again.

"My work is you," she says.

I focus on the bottle in my hand. "Yeah. I don't know what I think about that."

"You don't like being under so much scrutiny. I get it," she says with a small shrug.

That's not it.

But I don't want to go into the nuances of it. I fill up her glass instead. "You don't mind if I have some of this, do you? And never buy it again. I have an entire roomful."

"I didn't want to steal any of it."

"Charlotte."

She meets my glare head-on, and then she shrugs with a small smile. "Okay. I'll raid it completely and sell everything on eBay tomorrow."

"Good," I say without missing a beat. "Use the profits to buy yourself a new car."

"What's wrong with my car?"

"It's a death trap." I take a long sip of the wine and look over at the screen. "*Friends*, huh? After all this time."

"I needed company, but not something that would distract me. I've watched the whole series so many times that I know all the lines." She shrugs again, and the blush is back on her cheeks. "Sorry. Did you just get home?"

"Yeah, I did."

"Did you really get up at five thirty again this morning?"

We got home late last night after the movie premiere. And I lay awake in the bed, unable to sleep despite the exhaustion, just down the hall from her.

"Yes," I say. Working out had been necessary to get the *want* out of my body. Some of it, anyway. The rest I drained down the shower after.

But it's back with a vengeance now.

She shakes her head, a soft smile on her lips. "You're incredible. I've never known anyone who works as hard as you do."

"That's not true. You work hard."

"I drove around LA today, spent four hours at a coffee shop writing, had a delicious but overpriced lunch, and then sat here with wine and TV until I fell asleep." She levels me with a look. "Not the same."

"You can work from here. If you want to. Use the pool, the

gym, anything. All day." I take a sip of the wine and look away. That idea sounds too good. Her, at home. Here.

"Thanks. It's a beautiful place." Her gaze is soft, and she looks back at the screen. There's some kind of subplot about a cat. I dimly remember the episode. It would be so easy, to sink down on the couch beside her, to pull her close, and to shut my eyes, too.

I reach again for her notepad instead. The one with the questions I still haven't answered.

"You've written that I've been avoiding the hard topics."

"You snooped while I was sleeping?"

"The notepads were left open. And is it really snooping if it's all about me?" I tap a knuckle against the piece of paper. She wants to know about my past relationships. Exes. And in that... I see an opportunity. "You remember the deal we made? I'll tell you mine if you'll tell me yours."

CHAPTER 27

CHARLOTTE

The notepad on his lap is filled with my familiar handwriting. The little scribbled notes to myself were not meant to be read by anyone else. *I still know nothing about his relationship history. Ask? And about aspirations?*

But now Aiden is sitting beside me, a notepad in hand, inviting me to do just that.

If I share, too.

I feel too warm, and just a little bit tipsy. The wine was much better than I anticipated, and I didn't mean to fall asleep out *here*, where he would find me in my sweats and camisole.

"I did wonder..." I start and reach for the glass of wine. The same one he'd just stolen from me. Taking a sip, I gather my courage. "When did you have your first girlfriend?"

He smiles. It's a small, wolfish thing that speaks of all the truths I'm going to have to give him in return. Like I've opened the door and invited in an inquisition.

"I was sixteen," he says. "It lasted for about a year. We went to the same high school."

"What kind of boyfriend were you?"

He crosses his arms over his chest. "You'd have to ask her, which you absolutely won't."

"You're still in contact?"

"No, not at all. But to evaluate oneself…?"

"That's the point of a memoir, Hartman."

"Hmm, I like it when you call me that. Means you're getting annoyed at me."

"You shouldn't like me being annoyed at you," I say. "Masochist."

His lips quirk again. "Well, if I'm the one asked… I think I was an okay boyfriend. Too self-absorbed, but so was she, I think, for it to be anything meaningful."

"Did you love her?"

Something sparkles in his eyes. "I'm looking forward to asking you all of this. Was I in love?" He runs a hand along his jaw. "I thought I was, yeah. Sure."

"You thought you were. But you're not sure now." I spin the wine glass around by the stem, slowly.

He clocks the movement. Looks at it, and then holds out his hand.

"That bad?" I ask and hand it to him.

He drains whatever was left. "You're asking hard questions. Now? No, I don't think I was in love. It was infatuation. Puppy love, if anything."

"Have you ever been in love?"

"You're asking an awful lot of questions, Chaos. I think it's only fair if you answer a few before I continue."

I narrow my eyes at him. "Coward."

He just lifts an eyebrow, his face serene. "A deal is a deal. When did you have your first boyfriend?"

I am calm. I am in control. And I need to give up some of my secrets in order to get more of his.

But I fill up the glass of wine first. Across the couch, Aiden's voice is low. "That bad, too?"

"What qualifies as a relationship?"

His eyes feel heavy on mine. "However you want to

qualify your experiences, Chaos, is fine with me. I'm not a judge."

"The first guy I dated… it was very short-lived. I thought we were something real, but we weren't, and it blew up in my face."

Aiden eyes narrow. "He hurt you?"

I shrug. Hurt feels like such an insignificant word for that period of my life. Blake and I were on TV screens across the nation, and my heartbreak and public humiliation played out to an audience of millions.

"He did," Aiden concludes. "What did he do?"

I can't say it.

He made you *millions of dollars and launched a new reality television show franchise.*

"He was my first love. My first… everything." Heat rushes to my cheeks, and I look away from Aiden's eyes. "I thought we were something great. That he cared about me the way I cared about him." I shrug again. So casual, so unbothered. "But he didn't."

"When was this?"

"I was nineteen, at the time."

"Were you in love with him?"

Every instinct is telling me not to talk about this. To keep the memories buried under the years of experiences I've stacked on top. The new identity I've built, the travels, the confidence.

I have to force the words out. "Like you… I thought I was. At the very least, it was a crush."

"Mm-hmm." His jaw is tense, and he looks back down at his wineglass like it has offended him. A furrow appears between his brows. "Are you in contact today?"

"God no. Absolutely not."

I think about yesterday. The man I'd seen. So much more grown-up than the idiot I'd fallen for during the three weeks in front of the cameras. I was head over heels, plied with more compliments than I'd ever received. I'd lost my virginity to him in front of the cameras, too. And then he moved on. I know he's had a string of others since that time. Enough for an entire pearl necklace. And despite my panic last night...

"I'm honestly not even sure he'd remember me if he saw me again."

"Of course he fucking would. You're memorable, Charlotte. Trust me." His voice comes out harsh and just a little bit indignant. "A man can't be with you and then forget."

"Do you wish you could?" I ask. The words slip out before I can stop them. "That would have made this whole... arrangement a bit easier, yes?"

His lips curve slightly, one corner lifting into a crooked smile. "I'm not the type of man who likes easy."

I take a deep breath, but I can't seem to get quite enough air. His undivided focus is a big thing to be on the receiving end of.

"Yeah. I feel the same." This entire conversation is a terrible idea, and, maybe, that's why it makes me feel alive. Just as I had last night. Being around Aiden is like being close to a flame, playing with fire until getting burned. "What was your most recent relationship?" I ask.

"A lot of interest in my love life tonight," he says.

"In the time I've been here, shadowing you at your work, I've never seen you with anyone. Haven't noticed any dates scheduled in your calendar. And you appeared to be... single... in Utah."

"I was single in Utah. I am single now," he says. Just like that—simple words, eyes on mine. I find it suddenly hard to swallow. "My most recent relationship ended a couple of years ago, give or take a few months."

Right when the news broke about this father.

"Why did it end?" I ask.

"I think it's my turn to ask a question."

I lean back against the couch and take a sip of the wine. Pull a knee up and rest my chin on it. "Hit me with it."

"Why are you single, Chaos?"

"Why?"

"Yes."

"What kind of question is that?" I dig my teeth into my bottom lip and look from him to the beautiful people on the screen. "This isn't a therapy session."

He smiles. "No, it most definitely isn't."

"I don't know why I'm single."

He waves a broad, long-fingered hand. "Take your best guess, then."

I stare at the vibrant red wine we've been sharing. Liquid courage, coupled with a bad idea… and yet, I've always been good at making bad decisions. Lord knows it's gotten me in trouble before.

"I move around a lot, you know? Because I follow the subjects of my memoirs. That doesn't really lend itself to long-term relationships."

"Where's home right now?"

"Los Angeles," I say. There is no apartment waiting for me somewhere, no collection of furniture painstakingly put together from the inherited and the new. No paintings I love, no pet curled up on an armchair. And I like it this way. I like my freedom.

"I see," he says. "And you don't think a right man would follow you?"

That makes me chuckle. "No. Would you? I don't think so. No, that's why most of my… relationships, if you can call them that, have been short." I shrug. "It's never serious."

He nods, and there's a speculative glint in his eyes. Like he's fitting this into his own narrative about me, just like I'm doing with him.

I'm being studied in return.

"And you like them like that," he says. "Not serious, so

you don't have to deal with any loose ends when you move on to the next place."

His frank assessment makes me frown. "I guess so, yes."

He reaches for the wine glass. "We're more alike than I initially thought."

"You don't like loose ends, either?"

"No." He takes a long sip of the wine. "And I don't like leading women on. So I don't."

I tilt my head and study him. He's still in a suit from work, but he must have tossed the jacket somewhere on his way up to the second floor. His white shirtsleeves are folded back, and the top two buttons are undone. His skin is just as tanned at his collar as it is on his face. His thick, black hair is messier than usual. And stubble is sharpening along his jaw.

I wish he'd grow it out more. Like he had it in Utah.

"Your work. That's what ends most relationships for you," I guess.

"It's been my primary focus for a decade. Yes. It's hard for a woman to compete with that."

"Why do you work so hard when you don't have to?"

He shakes his head once, a slight smile on his lips. "Only you, Chaos."

"What?"

"When I 'don't have to'? What does that mean?" He tosses back the last of the wine.

"You're incredibly rich," I say. "Right? You could retire tomorrow and spend the rest of your days doing the things you enjoy. Like being out in nature, surfing, hiking, traveling… I've seen the history books you keep in your bookcases downstairs. You could study that to your heart's content."

"And live a life of leisure," he says.

"Yes. Many people would, with your resources. So tell me, why do you work so hard instead? Why did you try to turn Titan around these years? Why didn't you just sell it or let it go bankrupt?"

He shakes his head again. "My family name was being dragged through the mud every day for a year, my sister was getting papped, my mother was forced out of the life she spent decades building, a staff of thousands was threatened with unemployment... and you're suggesting that I should have retired and lived a life of meaningless pursuits instead?"

There he is. I had suspected the answer. But it came out more forcefully than I had expected.

"I hadn't thought about it like that," I say carefully.

"I work hard because there's no other option," he mutters and sets the glass down on the coffee table. "My father made damn sure of that."

"You resent him for it." It's the closest we've ever come to a conversation about his dad.

Aiden's eyes darken. "Wouldn't you?"

"This isn't about me."

"Then let's make it about you." He drapes an arm along the back of the couch, his hand coming to rest close to mine. "Have you thought about the night we slept together?"

CHAPTER 28
CHARLOTTE

I look away, heat racing through my veins. It's the one thing I try to avoid thinking about when I'm around him. But the answer is clear on my face. I feel my skin scorching.

"That's what I thought," he murmurs. "Yesterday, I kissed you to hide you from view."

My gaze flits back to his. "Yes. You did. Thank you for helping me."

"Don't thank me for that, Chaos."

"Why not?"

He leans forward, shifting his balance on the couch. Closing the distance. "Because I wanted to. Because I've wanted to kiss you every day since you moved in here."

I wet my lips. They feel dry, parched, like I haven't been drinking nonstop for the past half hour. "Oh."

"I thought that was obvious, Chaos." He's closer now, his large body stretched out beside me, his button-down shirt indecently rumpled and undone. A thick lock of his black hair breaks formation and falls down his square forehead. "My question, Charlotte. It's a pretty easy one. Do you want me, too?"

My head feels like it's spinning, and I'm not sure if it's the wine or because of Aiden.

"I shouldn't." It's the most honest thing I've said tonight.

"Tell me you haven't thought about the night we shared," he says. His voice is low. "Tell me it meant nothing to you. That you haven't replayed it, longed for it again. Tell me you don't want me. That I'm alone in feeling like this."

The air in this room is too thin, the temperature too high. He's breaching the casual distance we've established. We can flirt, sure. But never more than that. Could never openly acknowledge what's been coursing through my body every time I'm around him.

I shake my head. "I can't tell you that. But neither can I tell you… that it's not true."

He closes his eyes. "It's all I've been able to think about. Even when I believed you'd given me a fake number, and I was trying to rack my brain why you might not have felt what I had. I've tortured myself with thoughts of how I could have pleased you better."

"You pleased me plenty." My cheeks are flaming. "That wasn't… I can't believe you thought that."

"What was I supposed to think, Chaos?" His hand lands on my calf. Long fingers curving, gliding toward the crook of my knee. "I thought of the way you sounded, your little moans. Considered… Did *she fake it? Her orgasm?*"

I shake my head. "Of course I didn't."

His lips lift in the corners. "No. You didn't, sweetheart. I knew it back then and I know it now. It was only that slip of paper of yours that made me have doubts."

"I enjoyed myself," I say. "That was the whole problem, Aiden. I enjoyed myself, and then I *hated* it when you didn't call."

"I did. But it wasn't you who answered."

"What would you have said? If it had been me?"

Aiden's smile turns into something devilish. The sight makes my stomach tighten. "Good morning, Charlotte." Over my sweatpants, his hand starts tracing circles along the outside of my thigh. "Slept well?"

"Yes. Even if someone kept me awake too long."

He chuckles. "That's not nice. I hope you told him off."

"I didn't. I got him off instead," I murmur.

A surprised grin flashes across his face. "Did you? And how about you? Did you... get off?"

"Yes. You were attentive."

"Mm-hmm." His hand slides over my hip, finding the curve of my ass. Brushing over the swell and up toward my lower back in a slow, firm sweep. "Let me pick you up after lunch."

I stretch out my legs. They land across his lap, and his free hand joins his first. It strokes up my hip and rubs small circles along my waist. The touches are light. Innocent. But they make me feel feverish. "Where are we going?"

"A lazy hike. A swim in the gorge. Dinner at the lodge. Another overnight at the resort." Aiden leans in closer, his face only inches from mine. "I want to find out how you taste."

I find his chest. Spread my fingers out over the firm flesh. He's warm, even through the cotton of his button-down. "This is a terrible idea, Aiden."

"Mm-hmm."

"The absolute worst one we've ever had," I say. But my hand slides up his neck, my fingers brushing back and forth over the stubble at his jaw. *He's so handsome.* I've thought that since the first moment I met him. Too handsome for me by far, but somehow he's here, and it's me he wants.

"Is it?" His hand finds the notch at the back of my thigh, right by my knee. He pulls me down so I'm flat on my back on the couch. "I don't think so."

"It's unprofessional," I breathe. He waits, just a second, lips an inch from mine. A pulse of electricity shoots through me at the sweet anticipation.

"I'm so fucking tired," he says, "of being professional."
And then he kisses me.

CHAPTER 29

CHARLOTTE

His lips are firm and solid against mine, and my eyes close on instinct. There's an initial taste of wine, and then it's just him and me, and my thoughts short-circuit.

He kisses me slowly, like he's savoring me. Like he's thought about doing this for a long, long time. With each brush of his lips, warmth spreads through every cell of my body.

That's the problem with Aiden's kisses. They're never enough. They always make me want more—more of him. My hand slides back, and my fingers thread into his hair. I grip on instinct, and he groans against my mouth.

"Chaos," he mutters, one of his hands finding my waist. The contact shoots another bout of electricity through me. "Tell me this is a bad idea again."

"The worst," I breathe. He's leaning over me, his arm bracing against the couch cushion. There's so much of him.

His tongue coaxes my lips to open, and then he's there, too, running it right along my lower lip.

It is a bad idea. We're already horizontal. It's too easy to run my hand over his shoulders. To spread my knees just a little more to make him fit better.

His lips move along my jawline down to my neck. Shivers

rack me. It's always been one of my more sensitive spots. His hot breath, the stubble of his beard…

He chuckles against my skin. "This spot, huh?"

"Mm-hmm. Yes." Despite the couch beneath me, it feels as if I'm floating.

Aiden's hand glides along the outline of my body. Brushes the curve of my breast, my waist, down to the arch of my knee. He pulls my leg up and notches it at his hip.

Oh.

He's now settled more firmly against me, and I widen my other leg on instinct. A delicious weight, one that's warm and heavy, covering me from head to toe.

Lips trace my collarbone. "Damn you, Aiden," I whisper. My fingers tighten in his hair. Damn him for being so intoxicating, damn him for being who he is.

The tip of his tongue traces the swell of my breasts at the edge of my camisole. Goosebumps explode all over my skin. "Damn me indeed," he mutters. Returning to my lips, he ghosts his with featherlight strokes over mine. Once. Twice. Three times.

His left hand rests by my hip. Stroking there, so close to where a fire has started to burn. I lift my hips to meet his stoic ones, sturdy right above mine.

"Tell me what you want," he murmurs. "Talk to me, Chaos."

I shift my hips up again. He's hard. I feel it through the fabric of his pants. What I want is *him.* And I want him more than I'd let myself imagine in the weeks prior. More than I should.

But that's not what I say. "I don't want to start thinking again. I want to… I want…" My hips rise again, and his hand is so close. I know how good he is with it. How good he made me feel in Utah.

"To come?" He presses his lips to mine. He kisses me for a

few head-spinning moments. "Tell me, sweetheart. Do you want to come?"

"Yes. I want you to touch me," I whisper. The words feel decadent, spoken into his hair.

He kisses down my neck again. "I can do that." His mouth lingers on my chest while he pushes down the straps of my camisole and bra. There's already a sliver of skin between the waistline of my sweats and the hem of my camisole, and he plays with it expertly. Strokes back and forth as he kisses the swell of my breast.

My breaths are coming too fast. Dimly, I hear people laughing somewhere. The TV. The wine. *Aiden.*

He pushes up onto his knees, and I reach for him instantly. He notices, and his lips curve again. The skin on his cheekbones is flushed, and his hair is a mess. "I'll be right back," he says and pulls on the waistband of my sweats. "Lift up for me."

I do what he says. He's kneeling between my legs, and he tugs my gray sweatpants down my thighs. They only get as far as my thighs before he groans.

"Fuck." His hand glides to my hip, fingering the light blue lace. "You wear these little thongs everyday?"

"Yes."

"Even to work? In my office?"

"They don't leave panty lines," I whisper.

His gaze is locked on my body, between my legs. He curses again and pulls my sweats completely off, tossing them somewhere behind us. And then he lowers himself back down, his lips finding mine.

"If I'd known, I wouldn't have gotten any work done," he says darkly. He lifts himself on his elbow and reaches his other hand to cup between my legs.

He strokes the length of me through the lace, up and down. So gentle is the friction in contrast to what I need, that I push up and against his hand.

It's hard to breathe. I try to anyway. "I've got you, Chaos," he murmurs.

He pulls my thong to the side. "Fuck," he mutters, his fingers stroking my sensitive skin. Over and over, the pads of his fingers just a bit scratchy, but so gentle it makes me want to scream. "I've been dreaming of this."

I grip his shoulders tight. "You have?"

"Of your pussy? Your quick breaths in my ear? Yes. All the time. You've been distracting as hell." His thumb finds my swollen clit. He pushes down on it, and the air catches in my lungs at the shockwave of sensation.

"That's it," he murmurs. "That's the reaction I've been craving."

His fingers start to circle, and it doesn't take long for my breathing to turn into panting. That would be embarrassing if I could think straight.

I feel like someone else. Both inside my body and firmly outside of it. Lying here on my back, in Aiden's house. My legs bent and splayed, and his large hand moving between them.

The lights are still on. They gild his black hair, and I grip the strands even tighter. It feels like it's the only connection I have to reality. The silky roughness of his hair and the need coursing through me at every revolution of his thumb.

"You're so sweet." He bends to kiss my collarbone again. My chest. His mouth tugs at the neckline of my camisole, pulling it further down the slight rise of my breasts. "Sweet and fierce, and both sides turn me the fuck on."

His hand never stops touching me. He's lavishing my clit with steady pressure, like he just *knows* that's what I need, and my back arches into his touch.

"The way you walked into that movie premiere." His mouth is moving south, across my stomach. He feathers over the bare skin below the edge of my tank top. "The way you give as good as you get."

He continues a downward path.

A sliver of panic races through me. It's a memory that doesn't belong here, but that's chased me for years. I grip his hair so hard it must hurt. "No. Aiden, I don't... Please don't."

He looks up from my hip. His eyes are the darkest I've ever seen them, intensely green.

"You don't want me going down on you?" he asks.

The words are embarrassing. But I nod. "Yeah. I don't... enjoy it."

He kisses my stomach again—once, twice. Starts moving back up. "Don't worry," he murmurs. "I won't."

He stretches out beside me and braces himself with his free arm. Kisses me in languid, deep strokes. My stiff muscles relax again under his lips and the steady, delicious pressure of his hand.

"Can I do... this?" His fingers move down the length of my folds, stroking around my entrance.

"Yes," I whisper.

"And this?" He pushes his index finger in, up to the first knuckle.

A breath escapes me at the teasing tension. "Yes. *Please.*"

He chuckles and shifts his thumb to my clit. "That's good. You're so good for me, Charlotte."

He withdraws his finger and then pushes it back inside, thrusting slowly and at the same tempo as his thumb circling my clit. It's delicious and electric, and I can't recall the last time just being touched felt this good. Knowing it's Aiden, that he's seeing how I respond, and that he's right here with me...

"I'm going to come," I whisper. "If you keep going."

His lips dip down to my neck. That spot he had discovered, and another shiver runs through my body. My feet turn flat on the couch, my hips rise to meet his hand.

"That's it, Chaos." He shifts his weight and smooths his free palm over my hair. "I want you to come."

I arch my back again, and this time, he seems to know what I want. His mouth descends on my nipple through the fabric of my camisole, and I feel the faint scrape of his teeth.

Aiden adds another finger to the one already inside me. The stretch is a pleasant burn, and then there's only the best kind of fullness. He curves the fingers up, caressing that elusive spot within.

"That's right." His voice is deep, and right next to my ear. Indecent. Decadent. His thumb keeps pushing down on my clit. "Let go, sweetheart. I've got you."

I couldn't hold on even if I tried. My eyes drift close, and my chest rises and falls too fast. The pleasure spreading from his touch is almost painful. Almost, but not quite. I reach down to grip his forearm with both of my hands. It doesn't stop his movements.

"Oh my God." The orgasm barrels through me. My back arches off the couch, and my thighs close around his hand.

Aiden holds me through it, rolling onto his side to avoid crushing me. "You're so good," he mutters, his fingers still thrusting inside me. "That's it. You're so pretty, so sweet…"

I turn my face into his shoulder. "Aiden," I whisper. I feel wrung-out and pleasantly loose.

He kisses my forehead. Between my legs, his fingers continue to gently stroke along my folds. "Good girl."

I close my eyes and breathe him in. Cologne and soap and just the faintest hint of *him*—warm skin and man. The world slowly filters back in. The lights and the soft upholstery of the sofa beneath me.

The rigid length pressed against my hip.

I pull my head back, lips just inches from his. "You're hard," I whisper. I reach between our bodies and trace the formidable weight in his pants.

He closes his eyes. "Impossible not to be."

I stroke him awkwardly through the fabric. The idea of

having this inside me again, of him back on top of me... His breath speeds up.

I press a light kiss on his jaw. "Let's take care of that. I'm all warmed up."

He pats my clit one final time and then pulls my thong back into place.

"No," he mutters and lifts my hand off his crotch.

I dig my teeth into my bottom lip. The rejection shouldn't sting, but it does, and I shift onto my elbow. Look away from his gaze.

Aiden won't let me. He wraps his arm around my waist. "Not because I don't *ache* to, Chaos. But this is enough for one night. For our first night doing this again. You've been drinking."

I meet his stare and see the decision there. "I'm not drunk."

"You're influenced." He traces a thumb over my lower lip. "And so am I."

"This is because of what I... because I stopped..."

He shakes his head once, but the confirmation is in his eyes. "Not only that."

"But it made you think that I...?"

"That we don't need to rush things? Yes." He kisses me. His lips are still strong, still warm, but it's a kiss goodbye.

And it's a promise.

"I always want you," he says in a low voice. "Might be damn inconvenient, but it's true. There will be other nights."

CHAPTER 30

AIDEN

On the other side of my desk, Charlotte is all-focus and all-business. With her notepad in her lap, she's intently listening to every word Eric says.

"…which is why these quarter numbers are crucial," he says. "Cynthia sent them to your email earlier?"

She's not as flushed today as she was the other night on my couch. Her skin is back to its natural creamy peach complexion, with freckles sprinkled across her nose. They've spread since she arrived in LA. Nurtured by the sun.

"Mr. Hartman?" Eric asks.

I clear my throat. "Yes. Right. I saw them, and I'll bring the matter up tonight. Did you make the reservations?"

Eric hesitates a moment before nodding in a way that suggests he has indeed said this already. "Yes. Velveteen, at seven. Caleb and Nora Stone will both be there."

I look at Charlotte. "Wanna come?"

Her mouth parts, and then she nods. "Yes. Yes, I'd love to."

Eric looks like he wants to protest. Yes, yes. I know. Negotiations and purchases are singularly confidential. And in particular, our tactics ahead of meetings. Caleb and Nora need to *want* to sell to me. I can offer them a giant sum of money, sure. But in return, they'll lose control of the firm they've built up for years.

Not everyone is willing to make that trade.

But Charlotte has signed an NDA. She's trustworthy.

"Add another person to the reservation," I tell Eric.

He nods, face taut. "Right. Will do. The car will pick you up at six thirty."

"I'll drive us," I say instead.

The word slips out, and fuck, we're not an *us*. But here I am, using it anyway. It's been a very long time since I was a part of an "us." I can't even remember if I ever was, actually. My ex used to complain about how I often made plans without thinking of her.

I didn't mean to be an asshole about it.

I just didn't... think about her.

With Charlotte, it's always a struggle to *stop* thinking about her.

Work has been a sinkhole for me for the past decade. I could always surrender to it, let it drag me down and forget the rest of the world. The only thing that mattered was the next task.

Growth, expansion, consolidation.

Until now.

Eric excuses himself, and Charlotte rises to do the same. There are hours left before dinner. She has chapters to write.

But I find myself unwilling to let her go.

"You haven't sent me any chapters or ideas," I tell her. "For your own book. Have you picked the topic you want to work on?"

She pauses halfway between my desk and the door, and presses her things tight to her chest. "I think so. Internet culture, for sure, and the relationship with the media. I have some loose ideas but... nothing I can pitch, yet." She shakes her head. She sounds frustrated. "Nothing I can use to convince my editor."

"Write a few pitches and let me look them over."

Her eyes widen. "Really?"

"Yes. I'm not an expert, and I know fuck-all about publishing." I shrug a little. "But I know you, and Chaos, I know how to produce things that sell. Why not test it out on me?"

Her lips tip up. "Okay. Yes, I'll do that."

"Work in here," I say and nod toward the couch.

Charlotte's smile remains in place. "I have a small room down the hall that your staff have so kindly allowed me to use."

"The couch is more comfortable."

She retreats a few steps, her smile turning teasing. I lean back in my chair and drink in her expression. "Maybe," she says, "but the last thing we want is for your employees to start gossiping, hmm?"

"They've been doing that about me for years." I might as well give them something I actually care about to discuss.

She shakes her head. "I'll see you later, Aiden. Oh, hey, is what I'm wearing okay or should I head home to change?"

My gaze slides down her body. The white button-down and the cornflower-blue silky skirt. She looks professional, presentable, and delicious.

I lean back in my chair. "I'm not sure. Twirl for me."

Charlotte laughs. "I know that's not needed, but okay. Fine." She spins slowly on the carpet, the fabric dancing around her legs. She's glorious.

"Sorry, just had to make sure," I say.

"Make sure of what?"

"That there were no panty lines." I grin at her. "I know what you wear beneath those respectable outfits now."

She pauses, gaping at my words. Then she reaches for one of the pillows on my couch and chucks it across the space at me.

I catch it with a laugh. "I'm not sorry!"

———

Charlotte is quiet beside me in the car on our way to Velveteen. We run into traffic near Beverly Hills, and she sighs softly. I watch her undo the hair bun at her nape. She spreads the tresses out with her fingers, the light-brown waves glossy and long.

"What role am I playing tonight?" she asks me.

"Yourself."

She shakes her head a little. "No, that's not the one. Who do these people think I am to you?"

Everything. The word flashes through my mind before I can stop it. "You're working with me on a literary project."

"So we're going with the truth tonight."

"When have we not gone with the truth?"

"I've played your date to several events now," she says. Her hands smooth down her thighs, over the blue fabric.

"Not on purpose," I say.

She ignores that and picks at her hem. "Caleb and Nora Stone. How old are they?"

"Mid-thirties, or so."

"Who founded their company?"

"Nora. She brought her younger brother on a few years later. They split the responsibilities of running it after that. He's the head of technical development, and she's been leading content and marketing."

"Huh. Think you could work with your sibling like that?"

That makes me snort. "No."

Mandy is fantastic, but there's no way she'd think the same about me after a week of working together.

"That says a lot about them," Charlotte says thoughtfully. "They must be very good at compromising, and probably also at separating business and pleasure. As siblings, their arguments are likely fierce. I'm guessing they're not afraid of getting a little dirty."

I look at her for a long moment.

"What?" she asks and pushes her hair back. "Don't you think that's true?"

"I think that's a very valuable analysis."

"It might be completely wrong."

"Tell me after dinner," I say, "what you think about them. You're good at observing people. Observe them for me."

We pull up to Velveteen. The restaurant has valet service, and, as much as I'm used to it, it always makes me feel uneasy to hand my keys to someone else. He better be good at parking.

In the passenger seat, Charlotte is unbuckling herself. "So now you're using me to further your business deals. I get it." But she's smiling, and there's excitement in her voice.

"Use all resources available. That's Business 101."

"I thought the prime objective is to always make a profit. That's what you said, weeks ago."

I roll my eyes. "Don't quote me, Chaos."

"But that's my job!" she says and blinks in exaggeration. "I'm already planning on getting a tattoo of one of your sayings."

She's ridiculous. I lean in closer. "Really. Where?"

"I was thinking a tramp stamp."

I laugh. "No, never. Tattoo my words on your ribs, Chaos, so I'll always be close to your heart."

"You think very highly of yourself," she says.

I lean in even closer. "That's the—"

There's a sharp knock on my window. The valet. I lean back with a sigh. "Right. Showtime."

Charlotte reaches for the door handle.

"Do not open that," I tell her.

She rolls her eyes but removes her hand. "Fine."

I hand the keys to the valet and walk around the hood of the car. The air is cool, in the LA kind of way, and I love these spring months. When you can still be outside without dying.

I've been to this restaurant plenty of times. Still, the throng of people waiting in line for a table keeps growing longer. This place has an obvious problem. They've become too popular.

I open Charlotte's car door.

She looks at me with a wry smile in her eyes. It's one of my favorite expressions of hers.

"My savior," she says. "My white knight!"

I roll my eyes. "Get out here."

She bounces a little on the balls of her feet and looks around. Then her eyes clock the line. "Oh, shoot."

I extend an arm to her. "We have a reservation. Come. Let's see what you'll think about the Stones."

She hesitates only a fraction of a second before sliding her arm through mine.

I'd told her she wouldn't be here as my date. But as we walk past the lengthening line and straight into the dimness of Velveteen, I find it very hard to pretend otherwise.

CHAPTER 31

CHARLOTTE

Caleb and Nora Stone are in their mid-thirties. They're East Asian, both tall and slim, and they're already inside when we arrive.

Nora is in a two-piece suit, with no blouse under the jacket. The outfit is beige but covered with brightly embroidered flowers. It looks designer, and with her pixie cut and dark lip, she looks like a model. She smiles warmly and talks fast.

Her brother is a sharp contrast. He's just as tall, but he's sporting a buzz cut. His suit is a size too big. He's a technical engineer at heart, but clearly a social person, talking nearly as much as his sister.

Nora's older than her brother. Maybe holds more decision-making power, I think.

We're halfway through our drinks when she cocks her head to the side and looks at me with a bit too much scrutiny.

"Are you sure we haven't met before, Charlotte?"

I laugh a little. "No, I'm fairly certain we haven't. I would have remembered you."

"You don't work in the TV business," she continues. "Are you sure?"

I look back down at my menu. "No, I'm sure."

She sighs dramatically and elbows her brother. "Does she not seem familiar to you?"

Caleb's voice is smoother. "No. If she was, there'd be no doubt in my mind that we'd met."

I look up in surprise at him. He's smiling at me a little. Is he...flirting?

I smile back at him. "Thanks."

"Just the truth," he says simply and looks back down at his menu. "We should get oysters for the table."

"Oh, good idea," his sister continues. "They also do that steak here, the one four can share. Let's do that as the main."

It's clear to me, after just a few minutes in their presence, that they don't want to discuss business. Not here. Not yet. They want to vet Aiden.

He seems to realize it, too.

Because he just nods and closes his menu. "That sounds great to me. Should we ask for their mocktail menu?"

Nora's eyebrows rise. "You know we don't drink?"

"I didn't," he says smoothly, "but I'm not tonight. I'm driving."

"Good man," Caleb mutters and closes his own menu.

I glance at Aiden out of the corner of my eye. He knew they weren't drinkers. I know it, bone-deep, and he's playing the game. Charming them without making it seem like he's trying.

He's good at that.

The oysters are delicious, and so are the mocktails. The Stones are talented conversationalists. If I had thought they would be technocrats who preferred their books over people, I would have been wrong. Nora is the driving force behind our exchange, but Caleb interjects here and there in the comfortable way of a sibling.

"So, how long," Nora asks as we all reach for strips of the giant medium-rare steak that has been served on a flat stone, "have you two been dating?"

In my peripheral vision, I see Aiden's lips tip up. He lifts his glass and leaves it to me to handle the question. The jerk.

Well then, I'll handle it.

"We're not dating," I say. "I'm writing his memoir."

"His memoir?" Caleb asks. "I didn't know you were working on one."

Aiden nods a little. If he's annoyed that I came right out and admitted something I technically signed an NDA about, he doesn't look it. "It's about the company and its history. Me. Charlotte is a very talented writer, and she's been shadowing me for weeks."

Nora nods slightly. "You must trust her a great deal," she says, and there's shrewdness in her gaze.

"I do," Aiden says.

"Not dating, huh?" Caleb asks me. He chuckles a little and runs a hand over his buzz cut. It makes his face look more angular. He's beautiful, I decide. In almost a model kind of way. "That's good to know. How long are you in LA for?"

Beside me, Aiden tenses.

"I'm here for a few months, to work on Aiden's memoir," I say. "Gather the necessary material and see the places that shaped him."

Caleb nods. "Does he give you any free time?"

"She's pretty busy," Aiden says. He leans back, his shoulder brushing faintly against mine.

"I set my own schedule," I protest. "Besides, you work a lot, so that leaves plenty of time for me to write."

Caleb smiles. "That's good. Wouldn't want you to miss out on seeing the city."

"I've shown her the city," Aiden says. His voice comes out a bit rough, and I turn to look at him.

He reaches for his drink and drains half of it.

For the rest of the meal, we're having two conversations almost simultaneously. Nora and Aiden, and Caleb and I. The discussions sometimes cross and intertwine, but more often than not, we're talking about separate things.

I try to make sure I talk *about* Aiden with Caleb. Tell the younger Stone some of the things I've noticed about Aiden while living here in the city. About his work ethic and fairness to those he works with. Beside me, I hear Nora and Aiden dance around similar topics. It's a business meeting disguised as nothing but a social nicety before potential negotiations start.

Aiden handles the check. He insists, and like a fencing partner sidestepping through a duel, Nora inclines her head and accepts.

"Very gracious," she says.

Money is no object to either party. They're all filthy rich, and if Aiden gets his way with this purchase, Caleb and Nora will go from being comfortable millionaires to near-billionaires in their own right.

"Charlotte," she says again. Her voice is kind, but her eyes... they are still as shrewd as they'd been earlier. I wonder if she collapses in bed when she comes home. Strips off the expensive, gorgeous suit and wipes off her makeup, shedding the confident facade. Or maybe it's who she is, through and through.

I respect her a great deal, I realize.

"Aiden mentioned that you're working on your own book, as well. What will it be about?"

Suddenly, three pairs of eyes are all on me. I want to kick Aiden under the table.

I clear my throat instead. "It's early days. I have a few ideas, but... I think I would like to investigate the relationship between media and the concept of 'fifteen minutes of fame.' What happens to those people, you know? After their time is over? And how are their stories used by the media to further all kinds of narratives that might not be true?" I wave a hand. "Sorry, that's kind of vague. But remember... that girl who was interviewed a few years ago, after the hurricane? What she said?"

"Of course," Caleb says. "The banana girl."

"Yes, exactly. She said one sort of funny, tone-deaf thing in a news report, and then the media turned it into a symbol of that community's unwillingness to evacuate."

"I remember that." Nora's voice is thoughtful. "You should talk to those people, for your book. Get their stories. What happens after they've been a sensation for fifteen minutes."

"That's a good idea, yeah. If they'll talk to me."

"They will," Aiden says. His voice is full of confidence. "And it sounds like a book that would make an excellent documentary series, too."

Nora's eyes move back to him. "Indeed it does. Something perfect for BingeBox."

"If they offer enough," Aiden shoots back with a wide smile. "Charlotte's talent is worth the price."

Across the table, her eyes shift between us, and she smiles, too. "I can see that."

We leave shortly after. I walk next to Caleb, a few feet behind the other two.

"If you ever need someone to show you around LA," he says with a small shrug, "I'm around."

I nudge him. "You sure you have time for that? I get the feeling that you and Nora work pretty hard."

He rubs a hand along the back of his neck. "We do. Too much, really."

"I've said the same to Aiden. When none of you have to, in reality." I nudge his shoulder again, and maybe I'm not subtle at all, but I have to try. "You could cash out. Just spend the days surfing, or volunteering, or whatever else you can dream of."

His lips tip up. "I don't think you do that."

"I don't work as hard as the three of you, that's for sure. Today, I wrote while lounging by the pool."

He closes his eyes with a groan. "Okay, that does sound unreal."

"The life you want is right in front of you," I say grandly. "But thank you for the offer, truly. Don't be a stranger."

"You, too."

We say bye to the Stone siblings, and Aiden asks for his car. It arrives not even a minute later. He tips the valet driver, and we pull away from Velveteen, past the line of would-be diners that is only marginally shorter now.

"That went well!" I say. I've only had mocktails all night, but the ambiance of the place, the food, and the conversation have me feeling tipsy.

"Yeah," Aiden says. He's got one hand on the wheel, and he's driving as fast as the traffic allows. "Caleb was flirting with you all night."

"And you weren't flirting with Nora?" I say with a chuckle.

He looks over at me. "What? Of course not."

"You were talking most of the night. She was flirting with you."

"She was not. She's engaged to her longtime partner, who is *not* a man, by the way. And she's far too smart to let romance influence this deal." He shakes his head a little. "It was like talking to a shark for two hours."

That makes me smile. "Which means, you had a lot of fun."

He's quiet for a moment. And then he taps his fingers against the wheel. "Yeah. I did."

"Caleb wasn't flirting. He is a shark, too. Just… a different kind, I think."

"He was interested in you," Aiden says dryly. "Trust me. I know the look on a man's face when he sees a pretty woman."

"Maybe you're biased," I say.

He glances at me again, for longer than he should, before returning his focus to the road. "Yes, I am. Which is why I noticed."

"He asked if we could hang out sometime," I say thoughtfully.

"He did?" Aiden's voice sharpens. "And you still think I'm wrong about his flirting?"

"It's because I asked him if he even has time with all his work, and he agreed that he does work too much. Maybe that means he wants you to come and save him," I tell Aiden. "Liberate him from his successful company. Help him, Aiden!"

"That's good thinking, Chaos."

"I'll have a more thoughtful analysis of them tomorrow." I then look at the road we're driving on. I haven't been in LA for many weeks, but even I know we're not on the familiar boulevard journeying back toward Bel Air. We're climbing higher up the mountain drive instead.

"Where are we headed?"

Aiden taps his fingers against the wheel again. "There's a place I want to show you."

CHAPTER 32
AIDEN

The winding road climbs up the Santa Monica mountains that ring the Westside, separating Los Angeles from the Valley beyond. Charlotte shifts in the seat beside me, looking out the window.

"We're heading higher?"

"Yes, we are."

There's a smile in her voice. "I feel like I've really seen your LA."

"My LA."

"Yes. Mansion in Bel Air. Your Culver City office, and Rodeo Drive for shopping, and dinner at Velveteen in Beverly Hills."

"There's no reason to ever leave the Westside," I say.

She chuckles. "Yeah. I'm learning that."

I tap my fingers against the wheel again. Something about her characterization doesn't quite ring true. Or maybe it does, and that's why it chafes.

"I like being out of the city more," I hear myself saying.

"Yeah? Where?"

"National parks in Utah, in particular."

She's quiet, and then sighs a little. "Yeah. They're great. I've been wondering about that, actually."

"Wondering about what?"

"You were there to camp and hike. You do that a lot?"

"As often as I can. That, or being out on the water. There are beautiful places around here." It's been weeks since I was last out in the wild. Joshua Tree, Sequoia National Park, the Catalina Islands. They are all within reach.

"There are," she says. "I haven't explored the national parks around here as much."

I glance at her. We could keep driving. Be in Joshua Tree in a few hours. The wild impulse takes me a few seconds to tamp down.

"You will," I tell her instead.

She looks around. The incline is getting even steeper as I drive around curves in the road. "Where are we heading?"

"Mulholland Drive."

"Oh. I've heard of that street."

I turn onto it a few minutes later. It's a curving snake of a road, nestled high up in the mountains, and mostly deserted this time of night. I rarely have cell reception up here. That might be my favorite part of driving out this way.

To the left of us is the sprawling cityscape, peeking out from between a few trees. It's quickly hidden again behind a large estate. But not for long.

I pull into the scenic overlook and turn off the engine.

"Oh," she breathes. "*Oh.*"

She's already out of the car, leaving the door open. I chuckle and exit, too. "What do you think?"

"It's gorgeous." She's looking at the glittering expanse of Los Angeles. It spreads as far as the eye can see, disappearing to the west into a solid blackness of the ocean. "We're higher in elevation than your house."

"Yes. Much higher."

She leans back against the hood of my Jeep. Her eyes are trained on the city far below us.

"This all feels like a fever dream," she says. "This place. That restaurant. Your house. All of it."

"Is it a good dream?"

She wraps her arms around herself, rubbing a hand up and down her arm. "Yes. I never saw LA like this the last time I was here. There's so many things I never did."

"What have you not done?"

"I haven't surfed. I never hiked up these mountains. Um… that observatory? I've never gone over to check it out."

I open the trunk and find the bag of spare hiking clothes I keep in here. "Griffith," I call.

"Yes. That's it. I haven't been there yet."

"We'll go," I promise her and pull out a blue hoodie. "We'll hit the Getty, too. And I'll take you surfing."

I hand her the sweater. She looks at it for a moment before smiling. "Thanks."

"It's cool at this time of night."

"Yup." She pulls it over her head and slides her arms into the sleeves. They're too long, falling to cover her hands completely. Fabric pools around her, and she sighs a little. Like she's content.

The sight is too fucking cute.

"And the ocean. I haven't been out on it," she says softly.

"Well, Chaos, we'll have to solve that, too." The family house in Malibu is mostly empty these days. Mom is there sometimes, but, mostly, she stays up in Sonoma. She's found a new group of friends there. A slower life. I think it's been good for her. "It wouldn't be hard at all."

Her lips curve a little. There's an expression on her face like she doesn't believe me, but is indulging me nonetheless.

I mean every word.

I lean beside her on the Jeep. She looks at me, and then she jumps up onto the hood. She just *barely* makes it, and I'm there immediately, hands on her thighs to push her back up.

"Whoops," she says.

"You good?"

"Yes. It was higher than I thought." She leans back, resting her hands behind her on the windshield. She's now as tall as me. Her face is only an inch or two higher. "Do you come up here a lot?"

"Some months more often than others," I say. There had been days—when my father's court trial was imminent—after spending fifteen hours at the office and with lawyers and accountants, I would buy food and drive up here around midnight. It felt like the only time I could breathe.

The only time I could relax.

"It's a beautiful place," she says. Her voice turns teasing. "You probably take all your girls up here."

"I've never taken anyone up here."

She blushes, that cute beautiful flush across her skin. She's sitting on the hood of my Jeep, and I want her there—always. On my things. In my house. Wearing my sweater.

Caleb might have gotten her smiles down there, but up here, she's mine.

"I'm not sure I believe you," she says.

"Have I ever lied to you?"

She considers the question. Then she shakes her head. "No," she admits. "You haven't."

"You've been right in the past, you know. I have kept things to myself. But I haven't lied."

She braces her hands against the hood. "I can understand that. I've done... the same."

"It's hard."

"What is?"

"Trusting someone new."

She nods, ever so slightly. There's almost no illumination up here. Just enough ambient light from the glittering city and the stars above to see her, spotlit by a million little pinpricks of light.

"Yes. It is. I feel that way, too," she says.

I step closer, my hand on the hood next to hers. "You've been hurt in the past."

Her eyes slide from the view to mine and something sharpens in them. I see it, as she fortifies her walls.

But then she sighs, and she's my Charlotte again, here with me in the midnight air. "Is it that obvious?"

"No, actually. You're good at hiding it."

"But you can see it."

"Yes." There's an edge to her, and a life that lets her pick up and run every few months. Few people could work the way she does.

"It was a long time ago," she says.

I step closer, and her knees widen a bit, as if welcoming me between them. The desire to fill that spot wells up so strongly, that I need to take a deep breath to suppress it.

"So was mine."

"Mm-hmm. But you live with the consequences every day," she says. "It scars you. Experiences like that."

"You're a mystery, Charlotte Gray."

Her lips tip up a little, but the smile is tempered by the sudden shyness in her eyes. "Don't try to figure me out."

"Why not?"

"You might not like what you find."

"That's impossible, Chaos."

She shakes her head. "It's not."

I step in between her thighs and rest my palms on the hood beside her knees. "You haven't run from me, yet. And you know my family's deepest, darkest secrets."

"No, I don't," she says softly. "And what I know is that your *father* made mistakes. I haven't seen or learned of any made by you, yet."

"I love the use of yet in that sentence. Very confidence-inspiring."

She smiles again. Looks down at me, and at herself. Only inches separating us.

"Aiden," she murmurs. "What are we doing here?"

My hands tighten against the warm steel. "I don't know, Chaos. But I know that I like it."

"We work together." But her eyes are on mine, and that delicious color is sneaking up her cheeks again. "I need to finish this memoir to impress Vera."

"Mm-hmm. And I need it in order for the Board to approve my purchase of BingeBox."

"We both have important things riding on this book." She's close enough that I could just lean forward. Fit her lips to mine.

"We do. And we're also both attracted to one another."

Her breath whooshes out of her. It feels like it takes an eon for her to agree. "Yes. But it's nothing more than that." She shakes her head some more, like she's trying to clear it. "You and I, we come from different worlds."

"I know. Nothing serious."

She dips her head in a nod. "Nothing serious. That's rule one. The second things get emotional for either of us…"

"We stop?"

She nods again. "Yes. We can't let it get messy."

"Sounds perfect." My mouth hovers only a few inches from hers. There's an intoxicating air between us, and I want nothing more than to close it. But I also never want this moment to end. "Whatever this is, it won't affect our working relationship. That's rule number two."

"Yes. It can't stand in the way of the memoir." Her hands come to lie flat on my chest. I feel their warmth through the fabric of my shirt, and sway into her touch.

"It won't." I slide my hands up to her thighs.

"Aiden," she whispers. I feel her breath against my lips. "Should we write these two rules down, or do you think you can remember them?"

I pause and struggle not to smile. "Do you want me to kiss you or not?"

Her fingers find the collar of my button-down, tightening around the starched flaps to pull me closer. "Kiss me."

So I do.

CHAPTER 33

AIDEN

I lay awake later that night. It's not my first time since she moved in.

I stare up at the ceiling. My ears are perked up, like if I just concentrate hard enough, I'll be able to hear her breathing through two closed doors and a hallway.

We got back late, and said goodbye in the hall with another lingering kiss. It was past midnight and she looked tired. Tired and happy, and I didn't want to push my luck.

Maybe she's fast asleep now. Curled up on her side, the shape of a small spoon without a large one to hold her. Maybe she's awake like I am. Tossing and turning.

But the thought that haunts me? That she might be using the vibrator I now know she travels with.

I see it in my mind's eye, and can easily picture how she would use it. Slide it between her creamy thighs, fitting it between them, maybe locking them together so that the pulsating head rests firmly against her clit.

How she might bend her legs and nudge it to her entrance. Slowly push it in, her face tightening, her mouth opening in an *O* at being filled.

Fuck, the image haunts me.

It haunts me because it's not a fantasy. It's a memory. The

sweetest goddamned memory I have, and it hasn't faded from so much use. If anything, it's even more vivid now than a mere day after it happened.

My need for her grows every fucking day. It shouldn't, but it does. And I keep thinking there'll be a peak sometime. A point when I won't be able to keep wanting this much, where it'll become physically impossible, but I never reach it.

I'm rock hard.

Stroking lazily, I continue just enough to edge me closer but not push me over the edge. I'm already leaking a bit at the tip, all from the memories of her.

Memories and regrets. Because there are so many things I lament not doing during our night together. I didn't memorize all the little sounds she made, not like I would now. There are positions I want to see her in, and even more ways to make her come that we didn't explore.

I've thrown back the covers. It got too hot beneath them, even with the AC on. My boxer briefs are gone, too. I'd tossed them off the minute I realized I was too fucking horny to sleep and only had one option to drain the longing out of my system. At least enough to be able to fall asleep.

I grip myself tighter and bring myself back to the brink of release. The alarm clock reads 2:37 a.m. and I'm going to have a hell of a day tomorrow on so little rest. I should get this over with, and try to catch some Zs.

I grit my teeth and hold back a groan. *Fuck.* I picture Charlotte in my arms. Charlotte on the bed, naked and knees gently parted, looking at me. Begging me for it. I'm so damn close.

Then I hear it.

The faint sound I've been listening for. The padding of feet, and then… a timid knock on my door.

If I hadn't been awake, if I hadn't been listening for her, it wouldn't have registered.

I stop just shy of release. Intense fire surges through my body, forces a groan out of me.

Another knock. Slightly louder this time.

I push out of bed and reach for a pair of gray sweats from the dresser. "Coming!"

Pulling them over my angry cock, I hesitate just by the door. The best I can hope for is that she won't notice the obvious outline.

"Aiden?" she asks through the door.

Her soft voice is like another shock wave through my too-heated system, and I take a deep breath before opening the door.

She's standing in the still-dark hallway. A too-large T-shirt is over her frame, skimming the tops of her thighs. Her hair is a wavy waterfall around her shoulders.

Her face is clean of makeup. Just soft, lightly freckled skin, and a rueful smile. "Hey," she says. "I'm so sorry. Did I wake you?"

"No." My voice comes out harsher than is warranted, and I clear my throat. "What's the matter?"

"There's an alarm going off."

"Where?"

She walks down the hall, toward the large staircase that's closer to her bedroom than it is to mine. And then I hear it. The beeping of the tripped alarm.

It's not the main security alarm. That one would have been blaring, and the security guys would already have arrived.

"I'm sorry. I figured it might be important and started to head downstairs to investigate. But then, I thought—"

"You didn't."

She shakes her head. "No. I didn't."

"Good. If you ever hear an alarm here, you stay in your room, okay?" My voice is *still* harsher than it needs to be, but

I'm too tightly wound, in too much pain, and the idea of her coming face to face with burglars alone...

Charlotte nods quickly. "Yes. I'll do that."

I pull up my phone and look at the security notifications. It's a faulty battery in one of the outer perimeter sensors, and that has the main security system downstairs alerting the residents to get it fixed as soon as possible. It's designed to be a low, discreet beep. Sufficiently annoying to prompt action, but not enough to ruin someone's eardrums.

I head down the stairs. The house is dark and empty, and despite this being just a minor issue, I feel on edge. Like, there might be things lurking in the shadows that might harm her.

She follows me. I'm attuned to the sound of her bare feet now, padding across the floors of my house.

And my erection still hasn't fully deflated. Luckily it's dark, and Charlotte is distracted, or she would have noticed the fucking tree trunk between my legs.

I head to the security panel in the main hallway. It's hidden behind a painting that's hung on hinges, a construction the previous owner had put in. I tap the code to open the little door and find the override button for the maintenance alarm.

I shut it off.

"There," I say. "I'm sorry it woke you up. There should—"

There's a crash behind me. I turn, eyes scanning.

Charlotte is standing by a side table, her hands over her mouth. A knocked-over sculpture lies on the floor. It's shattered into several pieces. She must have bumped into it in the dark.

"Shit. I'm sorry."

"Leave it," I say.

She ignores me, of course. Turns to the mess instead and bends over to pick up the jagged shards.

My entire world narrows. She's *only* wearing that oversized T-shirt and a black thong. Her creamy skin, the long expanse of her slim legs, and the ass that fits perfectly into my hands, one cheek in each palm, is right there. And between her thighs, the thinnest little sliver of black fabric.

Fuck me.

The erection was painful earlier. In the past few minutes, it had deflated somewhat. Not enough to stop bothering me, but enough that I can think. Focus. Now it surges back to life with a rush that has me stifling a groan.

She can't walk around like this in my house.

I never thought I'd complain about a beautiful woman in underwear, but right now, that's exactly what I'm doing. Charlotte Gray is too damn fine to be wearing so little clothing around a man she had hot sex with only a few weeks ago.

A man she's not meant to have hot sex with again.

She's not looking at me. She's collecting the little ceramic chunks onto her open palm, meticulously organizing them.

I reach down and rearrange my cock. It's hard to hide it, but I do my best. If she looks for longer than a split second, she'll see it. Hard to miss the clear fucking tent in my sweats.

"Leave it," I mutter again.

She glances over her shoulder at me, and almost like she just realized it, bolts upright. Her free hand tugs on the hem of her T-shirt.

"I'm sorry." I don't know if she's apologizing for breaking a random piece of decor I've never thought twice about, or for flashing me.

Neither is necessary.

"It's fine. Leave that for the housekeeper," I say. "You could cut yourself."

"I clean up my own messes."

I want to tell her that my constant hard-on is a mess of her creation, yet she isn't doing a thing to clean that up.

"You don't have to. Not around here."

She takes a step from the small disaster zone on the hardwood floor and places the shards carefully on a side table. "Okay." Her hands clasp together, and then she looks at me far too closely.

Fuck.

I run a hand through my hair and walk away from her. Turn my back entirely, and head into the kitchen. I still hear her soft footfalls as she follows me.

I pour myself a large glass of cold water, add some ice, and then drain it completely.

"What's wrong?" she asks me. Her voice is careful. "Was it very expensive? I'm really sorry."

I glare at her.

"Oh. Right," she says. "Maybe it had sentimental value? I'll replace it if I can, Aiden. I promise."

"I don't care about whatever that fucking thing was. You just helped me declutter." I set the glass back down and I'm grateful for the kitchen island separating us. Hiding my lower half.

Her eyes widen. "Oh. Well, then, what's wrong? Did the security alarm scare you?" She walks around the counter, step by step, and I want to warn her away. Danger lies here.

My entire body tightens at her nearness.

"Chaos," I warn her.

There's a small furrow between her eyebrows. Like she's concerned, and it's such an unwarranted sweetness, that it makes me sigh in frustration. I want her more than my next breath, and she's concerned.

"You're upset," she says softly. Her gaze drops down to my hand, gripping the edge of the counter. And then further down.

Her gaze lingers for a moment and then returns quickly to my face. A flush creeps up her neck, out from the neckline of her scarlet Idaho State T-shirt. Everything is Idaho-themed with her. I find myself wanting to go there. I've never been.

But I want to. Visit the small town she's from. Meet the parents she's mentioned. All of it.

"I'm not upset," I say.

"I'm so sorry," she says again.

I shake my head and grit my teeth. "You have to stop apologizing tonight, Chaos. You haven't done anything wrong."

"How… why…" She stammers as if the words are too hard to get out. Nearly as hard as I am.

"Why am I… affected?"

Charlotte nods. It's a small, breathless movement.

"Remember when I walked in on you at the hotel? When you were in the shower?" I take a step closer, my hand tightening around the edge of the countertop. "You knocked on my door tonight."

"While you were…"

"You can say it." At this point, I'm just taunting her. Against all my better instincts. But I've always loved seeing her reactions.

There's a flicker of shyness in her eyes, and then she pulls her shoulders back. I love that movement. The expression that settles over her face when she decides to push through and go for what she wants.

"While you were jerking off."

I give a hoarse chuckle. "Jerking off. Yes, I suppose you could say that. I was seconds away from coming when you knocked on that door."

"I'm sorry," she breathes.

I lean in closer. "For the love of God, Charlotte, stop apologizing tonight for things that aren't your fault."

Her chest rises and falls quickly beneath that thin T-shirt. "I feel like I'm responsible for a lot tonight."

"You are. But none of them are things you said sorry for." I'm going to hell. I know that. But there's no stopping this, not when her eyes are on me like that, when her body is only a couple of feet away, and my balls are fucking pulsing with need. "My hard-on, Chaos? That's entirely because of you."

There's a spark of delight in her eyes.

I groan at the sight. Fucking hell, it's not fair for her to look pleased at that. Not when I want her more than I've ever wanted anything in my life.

Charlotte takes another step closer, as if I'm not seconds away from snapping.

"You're this turned on by me?"

The question is so shyly asked, like there could be other alternatives. I give a hoarse chuckle and push a hand through my hair. "I thought we established that earlier. And turned on is a mild way of putting it. I need you. I have for weeks. Lately, I haven't been able to sleep for wanting you so fucking much. So yes. I'm very turned on, Chaos, and it's inconvenient as hell, because we only *just* agreed to have fun together."

Her eyes drop down again, lingering briefly on my bare chest, and then focusing on the outline in my sweatpants.

"Can I help?"

CHAPTER 34

CHARLOTTE

It's thrilling.

To see Aiden standing in front of me in his kitchen—tall, broad, half-naked. He hasn't put on a shirt, and there's so much ripped chest on display. Strong arms, corded with muscles, and broad shoulders. He looks so solid. A wide slab of a man.

There's dark hair on his chest, same shade as the hair on his head. And a happy trail from his navel that disappears beneath the waistband of his sweatpants, where the thick outline of his erection is clear.

Because of me.

"Can I help?" I ask. My voice sounds a bit breathless, even to my own ears. He hadn't let me reciprocate the other week. It had just been me, losing control on that couch, and I want to regain some of it.

Put us back on even footing.

"Charlotte," he says, and his eyes drift closed. He's breathing hard. "If you touch me…"

"Yeah?" I close the distance between us and put my hands on his waist. Slide them over the flat of his stomach and the firm muscles beneath.

He exhales hoarsely. "I'm going to explode."

I glide my hand down, trailing my fingers lightly over the soft fabric. God, he's thick. I remember that from Utah. But it had been dark and late at night, and I hadn't been exploring as properly as I would've liked. As I want to do now.

I stroke him through his pants.

A groan escapes him. "You're playing with me, Chaos."

"You like games," I say. Him in these gray sweats should be illegal. They hide nothing, and now I can't believe it wasn't the first thing I saw when he opened his bedroom door, face tense and shirt off.

"Mm-hmm. And you want to explore, do you?" He turns his back to the kitchen island and grips it behind him with both hands. Taking himself out of the equation... and giving me free rein. His eyes are dark, his jaw is tense. "You do whatever you want."

I reach for the waistband. Pull it down an inch, and then two, over his straining hardness. He's not wearing briefs beneath the pants.

His cock emerges, with the domed head and a vein snaking up along the shaft. I grip him.

His breath catches.

He's firm, but the skin is softer than anywhere else on him. I stroke him slowly and look up to see his teeth grind together. He's gripping that counter hard.

"Payback," I say lightly. "For the other night."

"Mm-hmm," he grinds out.

"You made me come so hard when I thought I wouldn't." I reach down and find the heavy weight of his balls. I roll them in my free hand.

"Fuck," he bites out. They're sensitive as hell, I know. And right now, he's in the palm of my hand.

I stroke faster and let my hand curve over the broad head on every pass. He nearly bucks into my hand, and beneath my grip, I feel him twitch. Is he close already?

Bright color spreads across his cheekbones, and he looks at me through narrowed, hooded eyes.

"You're enjoying this," he mutters.

My smile widens. "Not as much as you are, clearly. The big bad billionaire CEO… reduced to a panting mess because of me."

His eyes darken. "You're on a power trip."

"Maybe I am." I tighten my hand around his balls, and his breath turns into a hiss. More wetness pools at the tip of his head. I feel like someone else—a sex goddess—when he looks at me like that. Like I can do anything with him, *be* anyone with him, and he would want me just as I am.

I'm just Charlotte. An alternate version of myself, where the outside world fades away and it's just me and him. And his lust-filled eyes.

"Every night, you said."

"Every night." His voice is hoarse, his entire body taut. His abs flex and relax, and I marvel at that, too. "You've got me hard and aching all the fucking time."

"Yeah?"

He nods, his jaw visibly clenched. He tips his head back, and it's like I'm witnessing him trying to hold on. Trying not to give up control when I'm so clearly the one holding him in my hands.

I feel high on power. I want even more of it. I want him to come apart because of me.

I pause, my hand gripping his cock tight but keeping still.

His eyes fly open. He's breathing hard, chest rising and falling. "Please, for fucks sake," he mutters. His arms are straining against the kitchen counter, like he wants nothing more than to reach out and touch me.

I smile at him. And sink to my knees.

I lick a broad stripe over his head, and he groans again. It's music to my ears.

"Fuck, Chaos, I'm so close."

I look up at him and wrap my lips around him. He curses again, hand sliding into my hair. There's another garbled warning, and I just keep sucking him deeper, my tongue swirling around his head.

He erupts. I hear him groan above me, feel him twitch and empty down my throat. I look up to see his face twisted into an expression that rides the fine line between pleasure and pain.

I'm invincible. I'm ten feet tall and an Amazonian warrior, ready to face any trial that comes my way.

He twitches one final time, and his strained arms relax. I slowly pull my mouth off him and sit back on my heels. He looks ruined. Handsome, tired, and sweaty. And wrecked… by me.

"Is that a good enough apology?" I ask sweetly.

He reaches for my shoulders, pulling me up to stand. "Fuck, Chaos, that was unreal. You're incredible."

"Just proving a point," I say.

He glides his hands down my arms, over my hips. "Prove it any day."

Lifting me up, he puts me on the kitchen island. The marble is cold beneath my bare thighs, and I lean forward, seeking his heat.

"You're incredible." He kisses down my cheek, down to my neck. "Such a good girl."

"I'm not good." Even so, his words send heat down my body.

He chuckles again. "Yes, you are. My sweet writer. Driving me up the fucking walls, sure, but you're so good." His lips move down my neck, while his hands hitch my shirt up, inch by inch. When he cups my small breasts, I close my eyes at the pleasure.

"Chaos," he mutters and leans back to pull my shirt fully off. "Arms up."

I lift them up, and he tugs the shirt off me completely. His eyes are that deep, dark-jade color as he drinks me in.

"It's nothing much," I say, teasingly, because his expression says otherwise.

"You're everything. So fucking perfect, Chaos." His hands grip my hips, and he devours me. With his eyes, with his mouth.

He kisses my neck again and damn, it's my greatest weakness. I moan, and he chuckles against my skin. "I'm going to enjoy this button."

I can't find the words in my scrambled brain. He touches me like I'm made out of glass, and like he also wants to crush me against him. The effect is intoxicating. Hands slide around my lower back, my ribs, cup my breasts with warm palms. And his mouth drifts down.

"So beautiful," he says again. "It's driving me insane, just how pretty you are."

I tunnel my fingers into his hair. "You're biased."

"Mm-hmm. Biased as fuck." He kisses along the swell of my chest, mouths at the skin. "Perfection. These tits, Chaos? *Perfection*."

I smile at the words. They wash over me, adding to the pleasure welling inside. It's always a heady cocktail with Aiden.

His lips close around a nipple, and he sucks on it firmly, alternating with lavish licks of his tongue. I grip his hair tighter and feel like I'm floating away again. This part is so easy with him. So painfully simple. Like slipping into a comfortable pair of shoes, or putting on my favorite pajamas.

His teeth close around the sensitive peak, and I gasp.

Aiden looks up at me and smiles. "Gotta keep you on your toes, Chaos. These sweet, perfect nipples are all mine now."

"Mm-hmm," I say and squirm on the counter. He's touching me everywhere except where I'm burning. I tip my shoulder forward, pushing the breast he hasn't played with into his grasp.

His grin widens. He opens so wide that nearly my entire tit fits into his mouth, and my brain short-circuits.

Aiden's hands are tight around my waist. One of them slides down, drifts between my slightly splayed thighs, and strokes me through the fabric of my thong.

"So sweet," he mutters again and blows gently on my stiff nipple. "The sweetest tits I've ever tasted."

I shake my head a little and feel myself slipping under even further. Being with him is like losing space and time. "I'm not sweet, Aiden."

"You are." His lips kiss over the gentle swell. "I would know, Chaos. I've got my mouth on you. You've got a hard shell sometimes, but beneath it you're sweet. Pure fucking sugar."

My body stiffens, and my mind clears. Sugar. A man is calling me *sugar* again, and it's all I can focus on.

Aiden's finger continues to stroke through the fabric of my thong, and my body is screaming for me to let him keep at it. The release is right on the other side of this. It would be so easy to sink into him. To listen to his words and *believe* them.

But I know what happens at the end of that route.

The alarm goes off again. It dings through the kitchen, so much louder here than it had been upstairs in my bedroom, coming right from that hidden cabinet.

Aiden lifts his head with a groan. "This thing has *terrible* timing."

I smile a little. "Maybe you should change the batteries for real this time."

His eyes are dark, hair mussed. "There is nothing I'd like to do *less*. But for you..."—he presses a quick kiss to my lips—"I will be the hero."

"Thank you!" I call as he disappears into the hallway.

The marble is cold beneath my thighs and ass, so I reach

for my T-shirt. I hadn't noticed the coolness before. I clutch the shirt to my chest and take a few deep, clarifying breaths.

This is supposed to be easy. Something I can walk away from.

But what just happened doesn't feel like it would be easy to walk away from. It feels dangerously close to something real, something emotional. And I'd been far too tempted to actually believe in his words.

I slide off the counter and hurry back to my bedroom. Because that felt perilously close to breaking rule number one.

No emotions.

CHAPTER 35

AIDEN

LA is too hot today. We're in an unusually early heat wave that has temperatures pushing to nearly a hundred. It's a Saturday, but that doesn't matter at all. I've been on the phone with lawyers practically all morning. The press has somehow gotten a hold of the issues we're experiencing concerning some inaccurate tax returns. It's the one thing I didn't want to happen.

A routine error. We're fixing it now with the tax agency and making the necessary changes with our accounting department.

But given Titan's history...

I don't want this in the media.

And now I have this damned brunch. There's a bunch of people milling around on my deck. My pool is open, and I can't wait for all of these people to leave so I can dive under the surface and not come up again for a long, long time.

Charlotte isn't home.

I haven't seen her since the other night. She's been in and out of the house at different times than me, and I've been hounded by trying to solve this problem.

Since she'd slipped away from me. Disappeared upstairs

while the damn alarm kept blaring and wouldn't shut off until I switched the batteries.

The people milling about my backyard are all industry professionals. It's a small brunch, informal, mainly for networking. Building relationships. Isn't it always like that? Especially since some of the people attending today had turned their back on Titan two years ago.

I'm talking to a TV producer who works in Burbank when I hear the sound of my gate opening. Only a few people have the remote for that.

I spot Charlotte's red Honda.

It really does look like a death trap. I should do something about it.

"Aiden?" the executive asks.

I smile. "Sorry. We were talking about the strikes. How did they affect you?"

We talk for a little while longer. Charlotte disappears, and I lose track of her entirely until I spot her later next to my sister. They're chatting with Logan Edwards.

Mandy and the movie star go way back. They went to school together, and I've known him for most of his life. We're in that nebulous land between acquaintances and friends, but now that we're older, we're also in a good position to help one another. It's a beneficial relationship.

He's smiling at Charlotte. She's in a summer dress that has blue and white flowers all over, her hair cascades pretty around her face, and he's *really* fucking smiling at her.

She laughs at something he says.

And why wouldn't she? He's on posters all around the world right now. One of the biggest up-and-comers. He has a jawline that even a model would be envious of.

I knock back a glass of mimosa Elena arranged to be served and move through the crowd. Mandy sees me and halts me before I can get to where Charlotte and Logan are standing.

"Hey," she says. "Thanks for sending over your thoughts on the financials. Gemma and I have looked over everything, and I think we're in good shape for the launch."

I clear my throat. Right. My sister is now a co-owner of an adult toy company. It's focused on female pleasure, on health and wellness, and on fun. I haven't seen her this jazzed about anything in years.

Mom didn't approve at first.

I had to talk to her about that. Told Mom to not make Mandy's life any harder than it has been, and that if this energized Mandy—if this gave her purpose—to let my sister have this. That was a little over a year ago, and since then, I've seen Mandy blossom. She's always been creative. She just didn't have a place to apply that creativity.

"Of course. I'm proud of you."

She blinks a few times and then gives me a beaming smile. "You are?"

"Yes. Of course, Mandy."

"Thank you. I… thanks." She clears her throat. Dad's conviction was hard on all of us, but she took it the most personally. It wasn't just her feelings that were hurt, but she felt his betrayal on behalf of both me and our mother, too.

She never set foot in that courthouse. Not after everything came pouring out at once after Dad was arrested. The affairs, the lying, the fraud, the clear disregard for all of us.

"Hey," I tell her. "I've been thinking. I know it's months away, but how about you, me, and Mom rent a place in Aspen this winter? Get away for a week. Like one of our old ski holidays."

She seems shocked. "Really?"

"Yeah. Why not?"

"I just… Yeah, I'd love that. You haven't had time for that lately."

I run a hand through my hair. "Yeah. Maybe not recently,

but I think we should get back to that tradition. Even if things are different now."

"Okay. Sure. I can start looking at places," she says with a grin.

"Thanks, Mandy."

She drifts away from me shortly after, toward a few producers she knows well, too. Growing up in this town, you realize just how insular it can be. Enormous, yet also very small.

When I finally reach Charlotte, Logan has just left. She's standing by the edge of the infinity pool with a wide smile on her face.

It dims a little when she sees me. "Hey."

"Hi. Having fun?"

"Yeah. I can't believe I just spoke to him. Had a real conversation."

I frown. "Mm-hmm. He's nice."

"He's really funny, and I keep getting the weirdest sense of déjà vu looking at him, you know? I'm so used to seeing his face on screen and not in front of me in living color."

"Right. Well, he's dating someone, I think."

She rolls her eyes at me. "I'm not *interested* in him. He's way too famous for me."

I really hope so. "Where have you been today?"

"I drove around to find the trailheads in this area," she says cheerfully. "I want to start running again."

"I can show you."

She smiles again. "No worries, I found them. You know, it's an incredible thing, coming back here to find the house decorated for an elaborate brunch and full of world-class celebrities."

"Did Elena text you?"

"Yeah, she did, but it's just hard to believe this is your life." She looks from me to the people milling about.

"It's not my real life. It's my job," I say. "My real life is who I am in that park in Utah. Or up on Mulholland Drive at midnight."

Her breath catches, and I watch as her smile falters, just a little. "But it's also this. You're both, at the same time."

I take a step closer. "You disappeared the other night. While I changed the battery."

Her eyes shutter, and she looks down at her goodie bag. "Yeah. I had to leave you wanting more."

"It's not in my nature to leave a woman unsatisfied," I say.

"Who says I was?"

I raise an eyebrow. "I didn't reciprocate."

She looks up at me, and a slow smile spreads across her face. "I know. But maybe I'll give you a chance to." She takes the glass of mimosa out of my hand. She takes a step back, and then another, while sipping it. The smile on her lips is teasing. "We've just begun to play, Hartman."

CHAPTER 36

CHARLOTTE

LA is hot.

I'm compensating by lounging in my bikini on one of the large deck chairs by the infinity pool. I've gone swimming twice already. Now, I'm fascinated by a little lizard that has been braving the afternoon sun by darting out to drink the pool water, and I've watched him make the trek almost half a dozen times since lunch.

What would it be like to live here?

Not this house. I'm now familiar with that, and I know it's most definitely temporary. I'm also trying very hard not to get too used to the fabulous water pressure, the large marble slabs in the kitchen, and the expensive art on the walls.

But to be in one place permanently. To have a garden, maybe. I've never planted anything in my life, but I'd like to try. To drive down to the ocean on the weekends. Maybe find a place to work out. I rarely do that during my assignments. That's why running has become such a good form of exercise for me. But I used to love doing Pilates in college. And it has been years since I attended a class.

Maybe I could even make a few friends. *New* friends. Not friends for a season, but for years. Lifelong friends.

Find a farmers market to frequent every weekend, and

have a garage that slowly accumulates a bunch of the junk that a life lived well inevitably seems to produce.

Sprout roots.

The lizard darts out again, and I watch his feet move at an inhumane speed to the water's edge. I run a hand through my still-damp hair and push my laptop back into the shade.

I've got plenty of core chapters done for Aiden's memoir, even though I had to craftily fill in the blanks on more occasions than I like. The books I bought on corporate fraud have helped with the more challenging passages. I've added some excerpts from the news articles, too, something I'm certain Aiden will want to cut out of the draft. But I will insist they should remain.

Now I'm tapping my pen against the notepad in front of me. Aiden had asked for pitches for my own book. Vera had, too, and she's the one I actually need to impress.

Something from my conversation with Nora Stone over dinner stayed with me. She had said my story idea would make a good documentary series.

It was an unexpected vote of confidence. Maybe… maybe it will work. My idea. It's the first time my work hasn't centered on someone else's life in years.

Fifteen minutes of fame.

The masses forget, but for the person who has experienced it, everything changes.

I scribble down a few notes. *What happens when the camera goes away? Did they get any help with the sudden media attention?* There are plenty of people who experienced momentary global notoriety that I could talk to. I've already compiled a short list.

I tap my pen against the paper. *Do they keep getting recognized? Can they keep working their normal jobs?*

The sound of an engine close by cuts through my thinking. I drop my pen and carefully rise. Shoving my feet into my slides, I circle the pool, heading toward the driveway.

Toward the voices I hear.

Aiden isn't due home until late tonight. No cleaners are scheduled for today, either. *Fuck.* I've heard about these fancy houses getting robbed. And, I left my phone inside, charging.

I look around. There's nothing, the place so painfully minimalistic. Aiden doesn't just leave baseball bats lying around. No clutter. Just large lounge chairs and a grill that's a centerpiece of an outdoor kitchen area finished in natural stone.

But on the patio table lies a large driftwood sculpture. It's probably very expensive.

I grip it tight and hold it up like a club.

Voices get closer. I creep to the perimeter wall and slowly stick my head out. A man I don't recognize walks up to the open car gate. He's medium built, sandy-haired, and is wearing a white polo shirt.

But he had been talking to someone. He's not alone.

I creep around the corner and take a careful step forward…

Aiden stands by a new silver car on the driveaway.

I jump back. "Shit!"

He looks at me. And then he chuckles. "Chaos? Were you going to use that as a weapon?"

"I thought someone was breaking in."

"If someone is breaking in, you call me, and you go hide in your closet. You do *not* go out to meet them in nothing but a bikini, carrying a piece of wood."

I lower the driftwood sculpture. "I didn't think you'd be home."

Aiden walks up the path from the garage. He pulls off his sunglasses, and his eyes rake over me. "You look…"

He's got that gaze. The one he had in the kitchen the other night, like I'm everything he's ever wanted. I like it more than I should. "It's just a bikini."

"There's no 'just' about you."

He looks good. Linen shirt, dark pants. His hair is more mussed than usual, and there's a look in his eyes that makes my stomach tighten.

"You're a charmer. I thought you needed to be at the office today."

"I do. Just took a lunch break." He reaches into his pocket. "Catch."

He tosses something that dangles my way. I react just in time to catch it.

Car keys.

"What's this?"

"I don't think you should drive your little Honda anymore."

I frown. "What do you mean?"

"It's not safe. I've heard how it sounds when you try to get up the hill here. Drive this one instead."

"It's sturdy."

"It's not safe."

"It's perfectly safe. It doesn't become *less* safe just because you repeat those words." I frown and look behind him to see a silver Audi Q3 that's parked right next to his massive Jeep. "This is a you thing. Are you embarrassed that people can see my car parked here next to your thirty-million-dollar house?"

"This house didn't cost thirty million."

"Fine. Thirty-five."

He chuckles and shakes his head. "I'm not ashamed of your car. That's ridiculous, Chaos."

"Did you buy that?" I point to the Audi.

"It's a lease," he says. "Of sorts."

I look down at the keys in my hand. So innocent-looking —a plastic fob with a big button on it. "You didn't discuss this with me."

"Did I need to?"

"I happen to like my car," I say. It's a lie. That car has been dying a slow death for months, but I keep telling myself to hold off for another ghostwriting paycheck before going to buy a new one. My Honda still works, and that's all that matters.

Aiden crosses his arms over his chest. "What do you like about it?"

"Lots of things."

"Name one."

"I don't need to justify it to you. You shouldn't have gotten me a car." The creeping panic comes crawling, squeezing tightly around my chest. "This doesn't have anything to do with... Aiden, it better not."

"With what?" But I can see in his narrowed eyes that he knows exactly what I mean.

"With us. With the thing that we *agreed* would not be emotional and would not interfere with our work."

"I know what we agreed to. This car doesn't violate either of those rules."

I mirror his stance, crossing my arms under my chest. His eyes dip down and linger a second too long. Right. I'm in a bikini, and the triangles of my top leave little to the imagination. Which was *fine* because I was just tanning in the comfort of his backyard and revising chapters.

"Would you do this for another of your employees?"

He forces his eyes up. "Yes. I care about the people I work closely with and their safety."

"What car does Elena drive, your PA?"

"A Toyota Prius."

I narrow my eyes at him. "And Eric?"

"He drives a Honda Civic. A much newer model than yours."

I roll my eyes at him. "You only know that because both of them regularly come here and park just outside of your front door."

"So what? I still know it."

"You're not giving them new cars, though."

"No, because they drive safe cars. You don't."

I shake my head, remembering too late that I have sunglasses pushed up on my head. I catch them right before they fall. "You're just assuming. You don't know. God, Aiden, what am I supposed to do with my car?"

He hesitates for a moment, and in that pause, I know. He wants to say *get rid of it.* Is that truly a lease out there? But then he shrugs. "Let me take it in to get it serviced, and then we'll park it in my garage."

"My dad serviced it six months ago."

"Old cars need regular love."

"Just admit it. You're doing this because you…" I can't say the words, and all of a sudden, they feel silly. Words not meant to be spoken out loud, under the blazing sunlight, in the open air.

"Because of what, Charlotte?" He takes a step forward, and then another. "I remember the rules. This car is yours to use while you're living in LA. It has great AC. It handles the hills here like a champ. Don't be dumb, and just accept it."

"I am *not* dumb."

He rolls his eyes. "Of course you're not. You're the smartest person I know, sometimes terrifyingly so. But you're being stubborn about this."

I push past him and walk on bare feet over the hot stones to the driveaway. The sun is warm on my skin, and I look down to make sure my bikini bottoms are still in place. Ties tied at my sides.

Aiden follows me. "Were you by the pool?"

"Yes." Anger still pulses inside me. I'm not dumb. I've worked very hard not to be, and he doesn't get to lob that at me just because I don't roll over and accept it when he makes decisions without my input.

He mentioned the rules. They're the one thing I've been clinging to, even when he calls me *sugar*. No emotions. No complications.

But here he gets me a car?

The shiny silver Audi Q3 looks enormous next to my old, dull-red Honda. I hate that it looks nice. That I can only imagine how smooth it must be to drive.

Something twists in my chest. I don't know how I should feel or handle this.

"Just drive it," he mutters beside me. "For me. It will make me feel better."

"Are you saying I'll be doing you a favor?"

"Yes, for god's sake, Chaos. Yes."

I look at him out of the corner of my eye. "Remember the deal we made in the coat room at the fundraising gala? Anything I ask of you, you get to ask of me. That goes both ways."

His jaw tenses. "What are you saying?"

"If you ask me to drive this car, I'll ask you to drive mine."

Aiden is silent for a few long moments. Up here in the hills, in this rich neighborhood with only the sun as an onlooker, Los Angeles is quiet. I didn't know a major city could be this quiet.

"You can't be serious."

"Why not?"

He runs a hand along his jaw. "Fuck, you're making this hard."

"I don't think you'd like me if I made things easy," I say. The words feel painfully accurate. I've spent years building myself into a person who can stand up for herself. Who doublechecks every contract, who's whip-smart, always reading between the lines.

"Drive your car," he repeats. His voice is sour. "No, I can't do that, Chaos."

"Would it ruin your image?"

"Yes," he mutters. "Fuck, is that what you want to hear?"

"I want you to be honest. That's not a lease, is it?"

He glares at me. I glare right back at him. The word *dumb* echoes around in my head.

"No, it's not a lease," he says. "They're a drain of money."

"And buying a new car isn't?"

Aiden blows out a breath. "Money isn't an issue."

"You just said you wouldn't get a lease because it's a drain, so clearly, you do care about money."

"God, you're too clever by half, sometimes." He runs a hand over his face. "I thought this would make you happy."

"Yeah. Has it been a success for you with your women in the past?" That's not hard to imagine.

He looks at me with cautious eyes. "I don't know how that is relevant, since per rule number one, I'm doing this for my business associate. Not my woman."

I hate my own logic when it traps me like a lasso. I turn to stare at the car instead. Search my mind for anything to say, anything at all, when in truth, I do want to drive it.

"Why this color?"

He shoves his hands in the pockets of his slacks. "You wear a lot of silver jewelry," he says. "I noticed."

I look at him out of the corner of my eye.

He side-eyes me right back.

Our silent, deadly staring match is interrupted by the ringing of his phone.

I walk toward the car and look through the driver-side window while he answers the call. His voice is low, but I hear Eric's name.

The seats are gray leather. They look comfortable, and there's not a single scratch on the upholstery. Brand new. He'd bought me a brand new car to use in the upcoming weeks.

"...how can that be? Did Francis not— No. I'll be there right away."

Aiden gives me another look after he hangs up. "At least

take it for a test drive," he tells me, striding to his Jeep. "I'll see you later."

I watch him open the gate and back out of the driveway. And only when he's gone do I open the door. It still has that new car smell. I slide into the seat and run my hands over the smooth leather of the steering wheel.

Maybe I should take it for a spin.

CHAPTER 37

AIDEN

Los Angeles gleams outside my windows, a vast expanse stretching into the far distance. Shining like it always does with an artificial kind of prettiness. A poor replica of the night sky only visible far away from light pollution.

I take another sip of my scotch. It's far too good to be wasted on a night like this. But it's a dulling agent against the anger burning inside me.

News stories have been making the rounds since this afternoon. And all of them were like a fucking dagger between the ribs. *Accusations brought against new Titan Media CEO for tax fraud.*

This is the exact headline I've wanted to avoid. Successfully evaded the past two years and was able to find my footing in the business world instead.

I eradicated my father's misdeeds from the public's memory one inch at a time. Replacing his dealings with *it was unfortunate indeed* and *we have no contact* until all they saw was me steering Titan Media on the right course. I worked to prove myself, day in and day out, and to restore some semblance of honor to the Hartman name.

Fraud is the last fucking thing I ever wanted to be connected to.

I've been in crisis mode from the moment Eric told me yesterday. On the phone with lawyers, with my concerned sister, with my executive team. The Board called an emergency meeting.

The negotiations with Caleb and Nora Stone have ground to a halt. We had come so far—me trying to convince them to accept the deal that would make us all legends in this industry, and launch their fun, garage-born small idea into a global success. I had the Board convinced.

We were so close.

And then some fucking bozo in accounting had missed a zero, opened us up to an investigation, and the news outlets have found a delicious story to run with.

This day has been long enough already. The fight with Charlotte this afternoon had taken the last of my patience, and then Eric called to tell me that the story had hit the mainstream.

I've been putting out fires ever since. It's late, too late, and I'm trying to douse the last one with another glass of scotch.

There are traces of Charlotte everywhere. Her shoes are in the hallway, put neatly to the side. Her sweater is thrown over the back of the couch I'm sitting on. I reach out and run my hand over the soft fabric, and it feels like a silky caress on my skin. Like her hair.

Where she is, I don't know.

Probably asleep upstairs.

The car in the driveway had been moved, though. I noticed it when I came home. It's now parked next to her disastrous red Honda. So I know she took the Audi out for a drive.

I take another long sip of the scotch.

The timing couldn't be worse. For the deal. For the memoir. This press release could derail everything I've been working on for years.

Fury rolls through me. At the people across this city in

their little specks of white light, filling up the night sky with so much brightness that we've drowned out all the stars. At my accounting team for creating and not catching this fuckup. At my lawyers and PR people for not getting a handle on the story earlier and killing it before it gained traction. At my father for opening us up to this kind of scrutiny in the first place. At his petty greed, his ego, his wants. His way of handling the trial that made it into a news story of its own.

And at myself, for not being better.

I knock back the last of my drink and brace my head in my hands. Fire races through me. It burns and soothes at the same time. I want to run a lap through the house, but also yearn to lie down on the couch and fall asleep. For a few moments, I consider going to the gym and hitting the sandbag hanging there.

I want, and I want, and I want. And I can't make myself move.

Tomorrow, it all starts over again. More meetings. More fires to put out. And on Friday, the Titan Media's annual gala, where all the eyes will be on me for hours on end.

With this investigation hanging over me.

You build and build, only to have all of it threatened by a split second of bad press.

Soft footsteps sound through the living room. I look up to find Charlotte entering the living room. She's in a pair of pajama shorts and a tank top, her hair loose and wavy.

Her eyes are wide on me. I believed she was already asleep. I got home late.

"Hey," she says. "Are you okay?"

She's so beautiful it hurts to look at her. My want of her flares to life again, and I hate myself for our earlier argument. For having to pretend she's just a business associate. "I'm fine."

"You don't look fine." She walks across the carpet and

looks from me to the tumbler I've just emptied. "I heard about... today."

"Did you, huh? You and everyone else." My words come out angry, but it's not her I'm angry with. Never her.

I shake my head to chase the spite away.

"Aiden," she murmurs, and I close my eyes at the tone in her voice. If she doesn't go away, I'm going to do something stupid. I can feel it growing, the need to reach out and pull her down beside me.

"I spoke to Eric a bit. He said it wasn't true."

"It's not. My lawyers are already fighting it. But that doesn't stop news outlets from running with it."

She stops in front of me, stepping in between my splayed knees. "I know," she says, and there's a fierceness in her voice that takes my breath away. "They'll say anything if it makes them money."

I reach up, fit my hands to her waist. The thin garment she's wearing does nothing to stop the warmth of her skin from seeping into my palms.

"I'm not in a good mood," I tell her. "And we argued earlier."

She runs a hand along my jaw. Her touch is light, sending shivers down my spine. The want is like acid on my tongue. "I can tell," she says. "Do you want to be alone?"

I pull her onto my lap. Her breath hitches, her legs settle on either side of mine. "No."

"Good," she murmurs and slides her arms around my neck.

I kiss her hard. It's more forceful than usual, and I can't stop, can't prevent myself from crushing her against my chest. But Charlotte doesn't seem to mind.

She kisses me back and moans against my lips when I roll her against my erection.

"Just let me make you feel good," I whisper. My hands are

on her shorts, fingers slipping above the waistline and finding the warm skin of her hips. "That's all I need. You ran away the other night before I could make you feel good."

"Aiden." Her voice is a soft breath against my lips, her hands dig into my shoulders. I love it when she clings to me like this. She'd done it on the couch too, when I fingered her, holding on to me like I was her anchor.

I want to wipe away this day.

My hands move up, gliding over her rib cage. Pushing her tank top upward with each movement until her tits are free, their faint swells filling my hands. Energy pulses through me at the sight.

"You're so pretty." I lean forward and catch her nipple with my mouth. Use my teeth. Charlotte's breath hitches on a moan, and I fucking love that, too. Love it just as much as I love her tits in my face. Love everything about her, and maybe the strength of my feelings would scare me if I wasn't half a bottle deep and drunk out of my mind on her.

"No compliments," she whispers. She tugs off her tank top, and it lands somewhere behind us with a muted whoosh.

"Is that a new rule?"

"Mm-hmm."

Getting the pajama shorts off is harder. She's straddling me, and I don't want to let her go, even for a second. I grip the garment at her hips and fist the fabric in my hands.

"Don't you dare rip these," she mutters against my neck.

I groan. "How else am I gonna get at you?"

"I'll take them off." There's a smile in her voice as she slides off me. She barely stands before I reach out and tug her pajama shorts and panties straight down.

She's so pretty. I groan at the sight of her pussy and pull her close, a hand on her hips. I need her on my tongue.

She stops me. "Aiden," she says, and there's a warning in her tone. Fuck. *Right*.

"Sorry, sweetheart." I pull her back down on my lap

instead and kiss her. She's naked in my arms, on top of me, and I let my hands roam. Over the curve of her spine and the dimples at her lower back. She grinds against me, and I encourage the movement. Even if it makes my cock ache while her heat is so close to me. "God, you're beautiful."

That "no compliments" rule is impossible. Might be smart, sure. To keep this from getting too emotional. But I can't help myself.

She moans when I reach between our bodies, my thumb finding her clit. It swells rapidly at my circling, and I fucking love this—how responsive she is, how wild she is. How she's always been game.

Her nipples are taut, and her tits jiggle a little with each sharp inhale.

"I wish I had your vibrator," I mutter. "I'd tuck it against your clit while you ride my hand."

Charlotte shudders in my grasp, another small moan escapes her. "I…. have it with me. It's upstairs."

I curse against her lips. It's so tempting, but I can't let go of her to save my life. It would kill me. "We'll use it later."

"Okay," she whispers.

I move my thumb around her clit, pushing on the little button, circling, alternating. I slide my other hand further down until I find her entrance. She's wet and slick and tight, and I slowly thrust my middle finger inside her.

Charlotte collapses on me, pressing her face to my shoulder. "Oh my God," she breathes. Her hips move, and I spur her on.

"That's it, Chaos. Use me to make yourself feel good." She rolls her hips and sinks down more on my hand.

I press our mouths together again, even as I'm working between her legs, and feel her clench around my finger.

"I want you to show me how you use that vibrator later," I mutter. "I want to see all your orgasms."

She's breathing fast. I flick my thumb back and forth over

her clit, the same as I would have with my tongue if she'd let me, and another deep-body shudder racks through her.

"I just want you inside me," she murmurs.

CHAPTER 38

AIDEN

I want it so much, it's physically painful. My cock is hard as granite beneath us, and I know the second it's freed from behind the zipper, I won't be able to resist sinking into her tight heat.

But we haven't had sex since that one night all those weeks ago.

The self-discipline it takes to not pull down my zipper and thrust into her strips years off my life. *Years.* But right now, I'm too tightly wound and too angry, and I can't be gentle or go easy.

And I'm not fucking Charlotte just once.

It has to be right when it happens. So I slide another finger alongside my first, stretching her tightness. Charlotte shudders again, and her hands on my shoulders morph into a vise-like grip.

"I am inside you, Chaos. Nowhere else I'd rather be."

She tips her head back, a sharp blush rises up her chest. "Aiden," she says, her hips undulating against me. She's a vision, a work of art. Beauty personified, and for an instant, I'm so close to coming myself that white-hot pleasure centers at the base of my spine.

But this is about her.

"That's it, Chaos. You're so pretty. You feel so good around my fingers." I flick her clit back and forth again before giving it a gentle smack. She moans, loudly, her body tightening. "Can you come for me? Let go, sweetheart."

Her back arches further, like she's offering her tits to me. I take them. Kiss across one and then bring her nipple into my mouth, biting down on it.

Slap her clit one more time.

"Oh my God," she says, and then her orgasm overtakes her. I release her hardened tip to watch as her body quivers, listening to the broken mewls spilling out of her lips. Her pussy squeezes tight around my fingers and I damn near pass out from the pleasure of watching her take her own.

She moans again, and her body shudders. Goes limp and falls forward against my chest. I give her clit one final rub before wrapping my arm around her bare waist.

"You did so good," I tell her. She's breathing hard, her face in the crook of my neck and body still shuddering.

"I can't believe that just happened," she whispers.

"I can."

High color spreads across her cheeks. I wait until she's looking at me, eyes locked, before I pull my fingers out of her heat.

I put them in my mouth and slowly lick them clean.

Charlotte's eyes widen, and she stares at me in shock. A furrow appears between her eyebrows and I know she's worried about this.

"Delicious," I say when I'm done. "I always knew you would be."

She digs her teeth into her lower lip but says nothing. Still sitting in my lap, still naked, her chest heaving.

"Wow," she murmurs after a stretched moment. "You mean that?"

"Sweetheart, you've got me so hard, I'm going to come the

second I stroke myself. Yes. I mean it. You've got nothing to worry about."

She looks down at where she's been grinding. My erection is a steel rod, outlined through the black fabric of my suit pants.

Charlotte reaches down and runs her fingers over it. Pain shoots through me, I'm so close.

"Chaos," I say. The whiskey is making my head thick, and despite her being the ultimate mood booster, I know this isn't somewhere we should tread. Not when I'm this on edge. "I'm going to come in zero point five seconds. After all this time, our first time having sex again won't be when I can't fuck you properly, and when I'm pissed off at the world. And not after we argued."

She stands in front of me fully naked. The length of her silky body is cast in beautiful light from the sconces behind her.

My eyes travel over the expanse of her skin. Linger on her tousled hair, bouncing around her shoulders when she cocks her head. "So come then, Hartman."

The words send another jolt of heat through me. "You want to watch, Chaos? Is that it?"

She takes another step back, and reaches for the bottle of whiskey I left abandoned on the table. She pours a knuckle's worth of amber liquid and takes a sip before letting the glass dangle from her fingers.

There's an expectant look in her eyes. "Yes. It's payback. You saw me in the shower... I want to watch you."

"You're going to be the death of me," I tell her and reach for the buckle of my belt. "Before this damn memoir is even finished."

"I guess I'll publish it posthumously." Her eyes burn into mine. Those blue, intelligent eyes that I've been incapable of looking away from ever since our night in Utah. "That will make it a guaranteed success."

When I walked in and saw her standing much like she is right now, under the bright bathroom lights in the hotel shower, with the nozzle between her legs and pleasure on her face.

I knew I shouldn't think about that image again. Knew it was a violation. And couldn't help picturing the scene in my mind anyway.

Pushing down my pants, I grip my cock. Her eyes narrow in on that, and her look alone makes my dick twitch in my grasp. I'm so fucking hard, it hurts.

The need to be inside her pounds through me.

But not tonight. Not when fury is still running through my veins and anger is a vise around my heart.

"This is what you want to see?" I ask and start stroking. My breaths turn wheezing. "How undone you make me?"

She nods, her eyes glued to me. "Yes."

"I think about you day and night, Chaos." I tip my head back against the couch and watch her with half-lidded eyes. Her body, her face. Her mouth. Heat radiates from where I'm stroking, and it won't be long until I spill. "You've invaded every part of my life, and I don't know how to get you out of it."

"Me neither," she breathes.

"Going to bed every night," I say, groaning at the tight grip of my hand, "while knowing you're just down the hall?"

"You think about that?"

"Of course I do. I think about you, and your mouth, and your body. Standing in front of me just like that. Or lying beneath me. I think of how you'd feel beside me in bed." My hand speeds up, and I'm seconds away. "Fuck. You've made my entire life… chaotic."

She takes a step closer, her eyes locked on my cock. And I can't take it anymore. Fire spreads from the base of my spine up through my body. It erupts through my length, and I come in violent spurts.

Charlotte watches all of it. And afterward, she leans her hip on the opposing couch and drains the last of my whiskey.

"Are you in a better mood now?" she asks.

I look at her. Spent, still irate, still wanting. Always wanting when she's around.

"No," I say.

Her lips curve into a smile, and she takes a few retreating steps. Toward the staircase and back up to the room that's hers, the bed that's hers.

"That's a shame," she says. "Because I certainly am."

My gaze follows her naked form the entire way up the stairs, and when she's gone, I close my eyes. I can still see her behind the lids, lighting up the darkness like a brilliant night sky.

CHAPTER 39

CHARLOTTE

"You have another meeting with your PR team at eleven," Eric says. His glasses are red today, wire-framed, and rest perfectly on his slim nose.

"Got it," Aiden says. The composed, competent man is back after the other night. His eyes are sharp and focused on Eric as the two of them go through the rest of the day's schedule.

Me? I'm sitting on the couch in Aiden's office, my laptop balanced on my thighs as I'm sorting through a few chapters. My agenda for today includes shadowing most of Aiden's meetings and attending some kind of gala tonight.

But first, the morning's briefing with Eric.

It's been nearly a week since I was last at Titan. Two days since Aiden had given me the car and I rode his hand on the living room couch. We've barely spoken since then. He's been too busy with the latest round of allegations. I've watched him work himself to the bone to crush them into dust.

"Lunch with your sister," Eric says. "I've booked a table for two at Fork & Flame. You can make a soft exit at one thirty, a hard one at two, if you're meant to be back for your meeting with accounting at two thirty."

"Right. Good."

"I pushed the lobbyist meeting to tomorrow to make room for the PR session. You have the final meeting with the organizers of the gala this afternoon, just prior to being picked up to head home to get ready. The latest you can arrive at the gala is at eight; your keynote is at nine."

"I've got that covered." Aiden looks over at me. "Has Ms. Gray received an invite?"

Eric nods. "I sent her one just this morning."

"I'm also in the room," I say.

Aiden's lips curve. "Yes, you certainly are."

Eric looks over at me. "I'll send a car to pick you up, too. Do you have something to wear?"

These men with all their questions about clothes. It feels like the only thing they want to talk about. "Yes," I say. "I have something to wear. What is this gala exactly?"

"Titan Media's annual event. Actors, news personalities, and reality stars will all be there. Awards are given out, people network," Eric says.

My hands tighten around the thick plastic frame of my computer. "Stars will be there?" I repeat woodenly.

Aiden lifts one shoulder in a shrug. "'Stars' in the loosest possible definition of the word. The higher profile actors don't come to this event. You'll mostly see tons of industry people, newscasters who are full of themselves, and vapid reality personalities hungry for anyone to cast them in the next embarrassing show." His voice is dismissive.

His words land right beneath my breastbone, so sharp it feels more like a knife than a punch.

Of course he feels that way.

Many people do. He just profits from that kind of entertainment—here in his fancy office, with his pedigree, elite schooling, and historic family business. But the actual shows are beneath him.

The people are beneath him.

"Those shows make the company a lot of money," Eric

says. His eyes stay focused on his tablet screen. "The stars are assets."

Aiden looks at his assistant for a long moment. So do I. But Eric is the picture of competent ease. No smile on his face, but no scowl, either.

"Yes. I suppose that's true," Aiden says.

I take a deep breath. This is what I can never forget. The kind of man Aiden is. The same type I'm always drawn to. One who will burn me in the end—too hard, too fast, too consuming. And, definitely, not someone I can open up to or be vulnerable with.

Not like that happens often anyway.

I learned early on what comes about when you give someone everything. They take it and leave, or worse, laugh at the offer. And you get nothing back.

"You'll come tonight?" Aiden asks.

I give him my professional smile. The one I've used too often in the past. *Armor.* "I'll come."

As soon as I'm back in the little conference room I've been using, the panic rises. Every image I see online from past events draws out additional horror. There are people I recognize. Famous reality stars, producers, industry people. In one picture from a few years ago, I see Blake.

I hadn't realized this gala would be… *that* kind of event. I had thought it would be attended by boring investors. A dry shindig, much like the last one I accompanied Aiden to when my zipper broke.

I can't go.

I haven't liked crowds for years. Avoided them as much as I could. And when I couldn't, I wore a cap pulled low on my head.

But tonight wouldn't be safe for me.

I wait until Aiden is at lunch with his sister. Then I quietly pack up my things as if I'm heading out to grab a bite to eat myself. Cough a few times as I walk through the office hallways, and then slip out of the giant building that Titan Media considers its own.

I get back to the house around the time Aiden should be back in the office after having lunch with Mandy. I shoot off an email to Eric, and then one to Aiden.

I'm so sorry, I've come down with a migraine. I don't feel great. Will just work on the book at home. Please cancel my car for tonight.

To Aiden, I add something extra.

Good luck tonight!

He replies within a few minutes.

Do you have everything you need?

It should be easier. Telling this little white lie, just like the others I've said so many times before to hide the year of my life that *The Gamble* had consumed. Glossing over it, avoiding it.

But it's not easy, lying to Aiden.

I do, yes. Thanks for asking.

I order food and work on his book instead. There are plenty

of chapters I could write from my understanding of what happened or from secondary sources.

I spell out his college years and his first years of working at Titan before he took over as the CEO. It's different from writing a climax that everyone who'll read the book will already be aware of—and a climax they'll eagerly buy the book for anyway.

I need to milk it, but not too much, or I'll frustrate the readers rather than entice them.

It's nearly nine in the evening by the time I close my laptop and head to wash my face. I remove my makeup and pull my hair into a bun.

As I'm getting ready for bed, Esmé texts me. She has about fifteen minutes to chat after she's put the kids to sleep and before she needs to start watching the new period drama with Tim as she promised.

Oh, the married life.

I lie on top of my queen bed and tell my best friend all of my latest updates... except for what Aiden and I have done. Or that he's the CEO of Titan. I tell her I'm seeing someone, though. Just an anonymous *someone*.

It still feels too fragile, too new. Maybe it would help me to talk about it. But I can't find the words.

I call my parents after getting off the phone with Esmé. Their excitement on the line makes me close my eyes against a sudden wave of tears. I don't call them enough. I don't go back home enough.

"Is everything okay, honey?" Mom asks. "You sound a bit tired."

"I am tired."

"Oh, I bet you are. Los Angeles is a big city. Are they keeping you busy?"

I think of the deadline looming for the first draft. Of Aiden's unpredictable schedule and my own unpredictable urges where he's concerned. Of Titan Media, the company my parents hate almost as much as I do. Or used to.

Seeing it from the inside, it's… well… It's a company like any other. Profit and loss balanced against corporate goals. It doesn't make it easier that I was a cog in their giant machine. But at least it wasn't personal.

"Yes. The subject is… demanding."

I'm on their speakerphone, likely lying on the living room table between them. "Do you have any chapters I can read, yet?" Dad calls out.

"We still don't know who it's about," Mom adds. "Who's the subject?"

They've both taken such an interest in everything I've done since that summer. Since I couldn't get out of bed for four months straight. I know it took a toll on them, and it feels like whatever I do for the rest of my life will never be enough. I'll never be able to live down *The Gamble*.

"I'm still bound by NDA's," I say. The guilt makes my stomach churn. They'll know after. Everyone will, that I wrote Aiden's memoir. The best I can hope for is that they'll understand when I tell them why I did it.

The chance that my publisher would give me an opportunity to write something else, with an advance that would see me through a solid year of writing.

We say goodbye, and I curl up on the bed with a streaming service on my laptop. It's not the one Aiden is so determined to buy. But it's similar, and as I scroll through the offerings, I quickly bypass all of the reality shows. It's taken me a long time to be able to watch and enjoy the genre again. The more normal the people are, and the less alcohol involved, the better it goes for me.

I settle on rewatching an old comedy series instead. I'm four episodes deep and nearly asleep when my phone rings. It vibrates incessantly against my comforter.

It's almost eleven thirty.

The name on the screen sends a jolt through me. *Aiden*. Catastrophic scenarios race through my mind. People he might have spoken to tonight, clips he might have seen. The last thing I want is for him to think of me as yet another *vapid reality star*.

But that may only be a matter of time. Despite my new hair color and the changed last name, the past always catches up to me anyway.

I answer on the last possible ring. "Hello," I say cautiously.

"Hey." His deep voice is familiar. "I'm almost home. Wanted to check if you're still awake."

"I'm awake."

"I can tell," he says. "I'm unlocking the front door in a second, and I've got food and painkillers for you. Come down, Chaos."

CHAPTER 40

CHARLOTTE

I quickly undo the messy bun and run a hand through my hair, and stop by the mirror in my en suite.

I don't look sick. But I do look sleepy, I suppose, and definitely unkempt. No makeup and my hair is a mess. It'll have to do.

I hurry down the stairs.

Aiden is in his large kitchen. His phone in one hand and a brown paper bag in the other. "There you are," he says and sounds altogether too pleased about it. I wonder how much he had to drink tonight. "How are you feeling?"

He's in a tux. It's immaculately done up, the bowtie at his neck, all the scruff on his lower jaw gone. Clean-shaven. The consummate professional. The handsome CEO who saved the entire company from near-ruin.

Except for the lines on his forehead. I bet he's had to do a lot of convincing tonight to truly put new rumors to rest.

"Better." I lean against the kitchen island. "Did you go shopping?"

He starts rummaging through the paper bag and pulls out two white containers. "Soup," he says. Then he pulls out a small bottle that rattles with the sound of pills.

"Did you raid a pharmacy?"

"Yes." He also pulls out two large bottles of mineral water, a bag of chips, and over a dozen chocolate bars. "I got every kind. Didn't know which one was your favorite."

I dig my teeth into my bottom lip and watch him set it all up on the island like it's an offering. I don't like lying. Never have. But here I am, doing it anyway.

"Maybe I don't even like chocolate."

He looks at me. "No one dislikes chocolate."

I reach for the one with a tiny galaxy on the packaging. "This one. It's my favorite."

His lips curve. "Good choice."

"Thank you for all of this."

"Anytime, Chaos." He pushes the container of warm soup into my hands. "Eat that before your dessert," he says and lifts his free hand to untie the knot at his bowtie.

"You're bossy tonight."

"I'm bossy all the time," he says. "That's my job."

I sit down on a bar stool across from him and open the lid to the soup. It smells delicious. "How did the night go?"

He ignores my question. "How do you feel? Do you get migraines often?"

I stir the soup with a spoon. "Sometimes."

He frowns. "I don't like that. Have you been checked out for them?"

"It's not that serious. I just had a massive headache and knew it would have gotten worse with so much stimulus." I look at him. "Now tell me about your night."

He waits a moment, his fingers drumming against the kitchen island. "Great. A roaring, fan-fucking-tastic success."

I narrow my eyes at him. "That sounds like sarcasm."

"No. It's true. It went great." He reaches up and undoes the top two buttons of his shirt with sharp movements. I see his Adam's apple bob when he swallows. "I've charmed and convinced and told them all that there is nothing to the

rumors about our tax filings. I've been the picture of ease."
Then he shakes his head. "Fuck, I hate these events."

"You go to a lot of them," I say carefully. "Do you hate
them all?"

"Yes," he mutters. "All performance, all charm. That's
what's needed of me. I'd much rather be out on the ocean, in
a forest, on a motorcycle. Working at the office, even."

I set my soup down. "Really? I thought you enjoyed them.
You always seem so... confident in front of people."

"I have to seem confident. If I let them smell the faintest
trace of weakness, I'll be eaten alive."

"You're speaking as if they're predators and you're prey."

His lip curves in a humorless smile. "That's the game,
Chaos. I learned early on to turn myself into a predator of my
own."

He'd taken over the company on the brink of bankruptcy,
dealt with despondent shareholders, confronted a Board that
had failed in its functions, and handled staff who feared being
let go.

And faced the Hartman family name in the news, taunted
as one of the biggest corporate frauds in modern history.

"It's all been one big confidence game," I murmur. "Since
you took over Titan Media. Hasn't it?"

He looks at me for a long moment. And then, gently, "Yes.
Eat your soup, Charlotte."

"My head hurt. Not my throat." Still, I reach for the
container. The soup is delicious. There's even a small piece of
freshly baked bread wrapped in thermo foil.

I wonder where he found that this late at night.

He watches me eat. I watch him watch me. The moment
stretches, extends like a rubberband.

Aiden blows out a breath. "I've been thinking. I should
apologize."

"For what?"

"Our fight. The other day."

"About the car." I look down at the soup and stir it again. It's hot. "I've driven it every day since then."

"I've noticed. Do you like it?"

"I do, yes. And I think I should apologize as well. I got defensive."

He runs a hand along the back of his neck. "I'm used to making decisions. Not... compromising or negotiating. I should have spoken to you about it first."

"Asked," I say softly.

"Asked," he repeats. "Yes. Some of the things you said, Charlotte..."

I put the spoon down. "I know. I reacted too strongly. The rules we set up? I guess I just felt like they were maybe... shaking a little."

"Mm-hmm. I get that."

"You do?"

His facial expression is serious. "Yes. The parameters are important to you. No emotions involved in our extracurricular activities."

I smile a little. "Yeah. That's nice phrasing."

"Thank you. And those activities can't affect our working relationships. I remember the rules, Chaos. Including the new one you threw in the other night."

I have to look away at the memory. Me, riding his hand in the next room over. "I just think that the compliments, they might... affect rule number one. You know?"

He's quiet for so long that I have to look at him again. His hands are braced on the kitchen island, and his eyes are ablaze. "Yes. I understand. But I want you to know that, while I'll try to refrain, it doesn't mean I don't think you're beautiful, intelligent, and so fucking hot that it's regularly hard for me to think straight around you."

A flush races up my cheeks. "You're doing it again."

"I know. And now I won't. Promise."

"You're hot, too. Which makes it kind of hard to believe

you're calling *me* hot, but you know." I shrug and swallow another spoonful of soup. I'm not insecure about my looks. I like my appearance, even. It's one of the few things I don't feel vulnerable about. But it's hard to dismiss the clear difference between us.

"Don't do that," he says, "or you're going to make it impossible for me to keep my compliments to myself."

"Fine. I'm very hot. It's entirely believable that I seduced a successful, attractive, extremely rich Los Angeles executive."

His eyebrows rise. "Did I just reverse psychology you into breaking the 'no compliments' rule yourself?"

"I guess you did. Shoot."

"Don't worry. You're a good opponent."

"Mm-hmm. So are you." Annoyingly, sometimes. His eyes are warm, and I don't want to look away. He takes off his tuxedo jacket, and it's like he's slowly coming unbound, standing here in his home again, returning to the man I know.

I wonder if he's been drinking tonight. If lots of beautiful celebrities and reality stars hung on his arm, trying to charm and impress him.

But he came home to me instead. Bearing gifts.

He walks around the island. "Feel better?"

I nod. He cups my chin and tilts my face up. "I'm sorry you couldn't come tonight, for purely selfish reasons."

"You are?" I turn toward him, and he steps closer. I have to tip my head back to meet his gaze.

"I would have enjoyed myself a lot more with you by my side." His thumb glides over my lower lip, his stare is bottomless. "I don't like people who aren't who they say they are. That's what I like about you, Chaos." He bends closer, his mouth hovering over mine in an almost kiss. "You've always been honest with me, even if you're hard to figure out. I've had to learn to read between the lines."

His lips brush against mine in the faintest of kisses. Once. Twice.

"You can kiss me like you mean it," I whisper.

"You're sick," he says.

I wrap my arms around his neck. "Not that sick."

He kisses me slowly. Deeply. When he lifts his head, I feel faint, and it's definitely not because of my imaginary illness. I want him to hold me closer.

He's a drug, and I'm getting more and more addicted.

"You should be sleeping by now," he says.

"You're not a nurse. Or a doctor."

"I know the basic science of health."

I smile against his lips. "Yeah? And what's that? Sleep equals good?"

"Yes. It's the most fundamental health advice there is."

"You never sleep."

"That's not true."

I pull back, hands still around his neck. "I've seen you. You're up late, working. Your light is always on."

He shakes his head a little. "You're stalking me."

"We sleep down the hall from one another."

"Terrifying, to think I've invited a stalker into my home. I'll end up on one of those documentaries that Titan produces. *He liked his roommate. She liked him dead.*"

I feel warm inside. The soup, most likely. "I wrote more chapters about you tonight."

His smile turns into a frown, and his hands tighten around my hips. "Tell me you didn't, Chaos."

"Why not?"

"You had a headache."

Right. "I mostly revised, after my Advil kicked in."

His thumb moves in a slow circle. "Still. I don't want you to kill yourself over this book."

"I'm not killing myself. I'm actually excited to show you some of my new content."

"You need to stop working."

I rake my nails down his cheek, and his eyes darken. "Are

you gonna take your own advice? Because I've never seen someone work more hours than you."

He kisses me again. It's another one of those languid, leisurely kisses, and I feel like it's all too close to encroaching on rule number one. But it's also too good to turn down.

"Come on. You can show me your writing in bed."

I slip off the stool and push the empty soup container away. I grab my favorite chocolate bar. "Mine or yours?"

CHAPTER 41
CHARLOTTE

Whenever I'm alone with him, it's like he occupies all the space in the room. I can't see past him or the muscles of his forearms, the handsomeness of his face, or the eyes that rarely leave me.

Like I take up just as much space in return.

Aiden is standing by my bed. It's still made but rumpled from when I was lying on it.

I look down at my laptop. "I wrote the prologue and a chapter about your college years. I also spoke to one of the Board members and now I'm trying to outline that chapter."

"Damn." He sets down one of the giant bottles of mineral water on my nightstand and takes off his shoes. This whole thing feels far more intimate than I initially intended.

I sit down on my bed with my back to the large headboard. He does the same, climbing on beside me.

"Okay," I say.

"Okay," echoes. His voice sounds amused, his hand resting between us on top of the covers. "Hit me with it."

"I can't believe you're not sleepy. You've been working since… Did you work out this morning, too?"

"Yes."

"You're a machine."

"I'm not," he says, and when he says it, I know that he's tired. He could have picked up the banter baton but he chose not to.

I hesitate, my laptop slightly turned toward him. "We don't have to do this, Aiden."

He shakes his head. "I won't be able to sleep anyway. What have you written?"

"This is an attempt at a gripping first chapter." I'm nervous about it. It's prologue-style, opening with what the audience knows well. The day his father was arrested by the FBI, and the lens of an entire business world turned on Aiden and on Titan. When speculations ran through newsreels. "It's short, and compelling. But it cuts right before you enter the… the courthouse. The next chapter flips back to your early life."

"Gripping," he mutters. "All right."

He shifts my laptop, and I look on as he reads, worrying my lower lip between my teeth.

I can't take it for long. "Which one are you starting with?"

"Reading early life now," he says. "This part is… interesting."

"What part?"

"This part." He moves the cursor over the third paragraph. Lingers over the sentence where I've written about how he attended great schools but didn't necessarily enjoy his studies. That he is someone who sees merit in knowledge but only if there is a clear purpose to it.

"We've never spoken about this," he says.

"Maybe not. But it's true. Isn't it?"

"Yes," he mutters. He scrolls down, cursor resting over another sentence. "'*The family structure was ordinary only at surface level.*' We haven't spoken much about my family."

"No, but I can't leave them out, can I?" My voice doesn't waver. It's confident, calm, and I meet his gaze.

He doesn't look away. "You're forcing my hand."

"If you won't tell me anything," I say, "I'm going to have to make things up. Form my narrative based on inferences, clues, and what I've gleaned from the media. The way everyone else has."

"The way everyone loves to," he mutters.

I pat the comforter between us. "That's the thing, Hartman. This book will let *you* control the narrative for once."

"It will invite strangers into my life. Into the part I don't like thinking much about myself."

He's close, resting on his elbow. My hand flattens against the comforter. "It can be scary."

"You're using a therapy voice, Chaos. That's what's scary."

I roll my eyes. "I'm trying to be supportive."

"Mm-hmm." His eyes glance back down again, at the screen. They linger there. "It's well written," he says. It's almost begrudging, his praise. "I like your voice. This might work better as a biography than a memoir."

"I'm good at my job," I say, "just like you're good at yours."

"Clearly, considering you've gotten much further in this process than I ever planned to allow."

I reach for a pillow and fluff it beneath my head. "Were you *really* planning on just stringing the poor ghostwriter along for months and then nixing the entire project at the final stage?"

The curve of his lips is entirely unashamed.

"Aiden!"

"All is fair," he says with a one-shouldered shrug. "I didn't expect the ghostwriter to be an infuriatingly persistent, interesting, distractingly pretty woman I'd already met."

"Distractingly pretty?"

He runs his free hand through his hair. "You know exactly

how beautiful you are, Charlotte. And you wield it like a sword."

It takes my brain a few moments to process it. Heat races up my neck and makes my chest too tight. He really does think I'm beautiful.

"That's a compliment," I whisper.

Him, with the body shaped like an athlete's, and with a magnetism that draws everyone in a room to his side.

"Yes. But I won't apologize." He closes the lid of the laptop between us. "Tell me about *your* childhood. Your parents. And I'll tell you all about mine later."

He's surrendering. I can tell. And so I scoot down and turn to face him. It feels like I'm sinking through the mattress, being enveloped by softness on all sides.

"Okay," I say softly. "My parents are... old school. They're from a small town outside of Cleveland. My mom is a journalist for the local news station, and my dad teaches high school biology."

"You're an only child?"

I nod. "Yes. My parents struggled to have kids. It took them almost six years before I came along."

"I'm sorry," he says.

"I was surrounded by good friends in my hometown, instead. We all grew up playing together in our cul-de-sac. That part was pretty idyllic, actually." My eyelids feel heavy, but I'm not about to stop looking at him. At those light-green eyes resting on me.

"Were you a tomboy?" he asks. "Did you prefer to read, to play indoors?"

"I wanted to be where the action was. My curiosity has always been my downfall."

"Do you miss your hometown?"

I pick at the edge of the comforter. *I miss that it used to be a safe place.* It's not anymore. Everyone knows me, knows of *The*

Gamble. Everyone followed the show when it aired. Little Charlotte Richards on TV.

It's the one place I've permanently lost my anonymity. No change of hair color in the world will save me.

"Charlotte." Aiden's voice is quiet. "Did something happen?"

"Yes," I whisper. "And it makes it hard to go back. Even if I miss seeing my parents and my best friend, Esmé. But a gulf opened up between us, and I can't seem to bridge it."

His hand settles on top of mine, resting on the bed in the narrow space between us. Warm skin covers mine entirely. He has a firm grip, and I look at that instead of facing him. Focus on the long fingers and slightly rough knuckles.

"What happened?"

"I'd… rather not talk about that." I avoid his eyes. It would be his right to remind me of our bargain. To force my hand, and tell me that without revealing my shame, he won't talk about his.

But he doesn't do that.

"What are your parents like?" he asks instead.

He's a better person than I am.

A yawn escapes me. I smother it, curling up closer. "My dad makes the most amazing chocolate chip cookies. When I was a kid, the scent would waft out onto our street, and all my friends would line up at the kitchen window. The batch lasted an hour or two tops."

"That sounds lovely." His thumb circles over the back of my wrist.

"Did either of your parents bake?"

"No," he says quietly. "They didn't."

"My mom wasn't very good at it. But she's always been a fantastic storyteller." My eyes drift closed. "In the summers, we would… have BBQs in the backyard. Invite my cousins. And Mom would tell stories while we all roasted marshmallows at the firepit."

"Like you," he murmurs.

"Hmm?" I can't keep my eyes open. He's warm and smells good, and I feel like I'm floating.

"You're a storyteller." His hand is comforting around mine. "Sleep, Chaos. I've got you."

CHAPTER 42

AIDEN

There's a faint buzzing. It cuts through my head like an arrow. A particularly annoying one, even if it's familiar. I keep my eyes closed and reach for the nightstand. Grip my phone and press down on the button that will shut it the hell off.

I was having such a good dream.

I'm also lying on my back in a bed that's far too soft. I feel like I'm drowning in it, cocooned like in a hammock, it's swallowing me whole. There's also a warm weight draped over me. My left arm is around someone.

Someone.

Charlotte.

Her leg is on top of mine, and I reach down with my free hand to find the crook of her knee. Her head is a weight on my chest, lifting gently with each one of my breaths. I hear the soft wafts of her own exhales.

I look down at the top of Charlotte's head, and her silky hair spread out over me. She'd fallen asleep first last night. I remember that. Her eyelids shutting, her hand wrapped in mine. I moved her laptop off the bed and then settled beside her with a book.

I hadn't planned on falling asleep, too.

But I must have... and here she is, clinging to me like I'm her favorite pillow.

She smells good. Draped over me, her body soft in sleep.

And I'm hard.

It's been a while since I've woken up hard. It's usually not much of a problem. A quick cold shower solved it; or a longer, warmer one and the aid of my right hand.

Now there's a dull, throbbing weight between my legs, rising up beneath the waistband of my boxer briefs. The zipper of the slacks is uncomfortable.

I'd much, much rather have slept in the same bed as her without our clothes. Under the comforter.

Rubbing circles over her knee, I take a few deep breaths. I need to get back to work. The rumors haven't died down yet, and I've scheduled several interviews today with news outlets. Somehow, I have to be coherent for them.

She mumbles something against my chest. Her hand tightens by my waist, as if I'm a body pillow she's hugging.

I run a hand down her back. "You're talking?"

"Mm-hmm." She nuzzles against my chest, her nose brushing the open V where several of my shirt buttons are undone. "Good."

I smile. "Good?"

"So... annoying," she mumbles and then sighs deeply.

I smile. That can only be about one person.

I didn't know she spoke in her sleep.

My phone rings again. It's an alarm in the form of Eric, and I reach over to shut it the hell off. It's a Saturday. But that's never stopped him or me before.

This time, Charlotte stirs against me. Her arm tightens, and her leg shifts. Her knee brushes over my erection and I bite out a hiss. Fuck, that is not abating.

She blinks at me. Her skin is rosy with sleep, her lips parted. "Aiden?"

"Good morning."

Her eyes close briefly. "Ugh. It's too early."

"Yeah, we didn't get many hours."

"Not enough." She rests her forehead against my chest, and a weak laugh escapes her. "I can't believe we fell asleep."

My hand keeps moving in long sweeps over her back. "You were tired."

"I'm sorry. I've... well." She looks down at my exposed skin rather than my eyes. "Used you as a pillow."

"Does it seem like it bothers me?" I ask.

She smiles. It's a small, almost shy expression, so different from the fierce Charlotte who negotiates, and who doesn't take any crap.

The sight makes my chest tighten.

"No," she whispers.

I lean my head back against the pillow. Desire still pulses through my body, driven by her presence and my dream. A memory, really.

Her body beneath mine on the couch.

"I like it too much," I mutter.

"What do you— *Oh.*" She shifts again, and this time, it's her forearm that brushes over my stomach and against my erection.

"Ignore it. It'll pass," I say tightly.

Charlotte doesn't do that, of course. Because she is nothing if not curious.

Her hand traces my lower stomach until she brushes over my head. My cock twitches, and I close my eyes.

"Do you wake up hard often?" she asks.

"Sometimes. It doesn't help when a pretty woman is draped over me."

"Oh." There's a smile in her voice, and her fingers dance lightly along my length. The touch is tantalizingly light and not nearly enough. I grind my teeth together. "Maybe I'll use this opportunity to ask you some... questions." On the last word, her hand wraps around my balls, and a hissing breath escapes me.

"Like what?"

"Like... if you give me good answers, I'll keep going. Stonewall me, and I'll stop."

"That's extortion." But my hand keeps moving up her back, slowly. I feel her warm skin beneath the fabric of her tank top.

She slides her hand up, flattening it against my stomach. "What was the worst part of the trial?"

I groan. "Talk like that will get me further from the finish line, Chaos."

But then she moves her hand under the waistband. It takes every ounce of restraint I possess to lie still on my back and let her torture me.

Nimble fingers undo my button and pull down the zipper of my pants. She folds down the two parts, and I hold my breath. Waiting.

Then she takes my cock fully in hand. Skin against skin.

Heat surges through me. But she just holds her hand there, gripping me tight, like the sweetest kind of torment. *Fuck.*

"Okay," I grind out. "What I hated the most? The media. Being picked apart every day for some minute expression. Having people place bets on whether I knew about Dad's fraud or not, based on nothing but what color my fucking shirt was."

I close my eyes and throw my head back. She's stroking me now, base to tip, slowly and skillfully.

"That's good. That's great, actually."

I look at her with half-slitted eyes. "I feel like I'm getting my ego stroked."

"Not the only thing I'm stroking." She looks glorious—all messy hair and soft sleepy eyes, lit up with excitement at the new game. "Okay. Do you still talk to him?"

I grip the comforter beneath me with both hands. Focus on breathing in. Breathing out. "I have almost no contact with him these days."

She speeds up, just a little. "Oh?"

"He writes from prison like clockwork. To me, to Mandy, and to my mother. But I haven't responded to a letter in a long time." I reach up and pillow my head with my arms. I need a better view. "The last time I did, it was intercepted by someone who leaked it to the press."

Her mouth opens, and her hand falters. Almost without her realizing it. "What? Really?"

"Yes. I killed the story. Had to pay a hell of a lot of money to do it, too."

"Shoot. I'm so sorry."

"Saves me the trouble of needing to have a relationship with him, I suppose. Chaos, your hand."

"Oh. Right." She looks down, at where I'm hard and aching, and smiles softly. Her hand speeds up, and her grip tightens.

"It was right before Zion," I volunteer.

Her movements falter. "When your letter was… intercepted?"

"Yes." This room is too hot. "I had to… get out of LA for a bit. Clear my head. But I found you instead."

"I didn't help?"

"You helped," I say darkly. "But my head hasn't been clear since."

Her other hand reaches below to grip my balls.

"Fuck," I bite out. They're sensitive as hell, and here she is, fondling them. A steady electric pulse pounds through me. Every firm stroke of her hand sends a jolt through my limbs.

"Do you miss having a relationship with your dad?"

"This is the weirdest hand job I've ever received."

The grip on my balls tightens, but her hand on my cock

stills. I nearly buck into her palm, needing her to keep stroking. Fuck if I'm not turned on like hell.

"I like giving you weird," she says.

"Uh-huh. Right. It's complicated." I look at her hand wrapped around my dick. Long fingers, short nails, no nail polish. I don't know why I like that. The no-nail-polish thing. But I do. "I'm angry with him. Have been for years. Since before the FBI came to pick him up, to be honest." My voice comes out between harsh breaths. "He was not a very present father or husband."

"I'm sorry about that." Her hand curves over my head on an upturn, and it's almost painful with how hard I am and how desperately I want even more. Her naked again, beneath me, against me. Her tight, wet heat surrounding me.

"There are moments I miss that I shouldn't. All of us at the house during the summers. Rare times when he would fire up the grill, and I would help him. Hearing him bark orders on the boat. But those are just moments, I suppose… and not the total sum of a person. So, no. I don't miss *him*."

"He saddled you with an awful lot of things when he did what he did." Her voice is soft, but her grip isn't. She rolls my balls in her hand and grips my head tightly, and the only thing I can do is nod. My jaw is clenched while I try not to explode all over her pretty fingers.

"Yes, he did. And he lied throughout all of it. To investors, to the Board members. To me." I force my head back against the pillow. "Fuck, Chaos, I'm going to come if you keep doing that."

"I think you've earned it. You've given me more in the last ten minutes than over the previous weeks." She starts to lean down, her lips dangerously close to the leaking head of my cock. I know how good it would feel. Her hot lips stretched over me, wet heat—

But I put my hand on her shoulder. "No."

Her eyes flick to mine. "What?"

"Our deal. What you do to me, I do to you, remember? And you don't want me going down on you. So no blow jobs."

It's fucking agony to say the words.

But it's worth it for the widening of her eyes. "You're unbelievable."

"Tell me why you don't like it, and I'll rescind the rule."

"No man has ever said *no* to having his dick sucked."

"Maybe asshole men who don't care about reciprocating. But I do." The pleasure-pain dances through my system so fiercely, it's difficult to form words.

Her reaction when I wanted to eat her out has haunted me. Seeing her, touching her, fingering her... but not tasting her. She'd stiffened up all over—a fear response if I ever saw one.

I want to find out why she had responded that way... and killing, maiming, or torturing whoever is responsible for it. Because it's not hard to believe that there's a man out there who once made her feel a certain way about it.

Charlotte stretches out beside me. Her hands increase their tempo, gripping me so tightly that I momentarily black out. Her mouth comes to rest by my ear. Lips brush the side of my cheek, and I'm so, so close to exploding.

"Why are you allowed to use your mouth on me, while I'm not allowed to do the same, hmm?" I ask. My voice is barely audible.

She turns her face into my shoulder. "I didn't think you would mind."

"I'm close." I touch my lips to her silky hair. It smells floral and sun-warm. "I've imagined eating your pussy too many times to count."

"That's very unprofessional," she says.

"Yes. It is. But that's not why you don't like the idea of my mouth between your thighs." I'm breathing too hard. "Someone made you feel bad about it once. Didn't they?"

Her hand curves over my head, and I groan. "Maybe they did. But going down on your memoirist would be *decidedly* unprofessional."

"And jerking off the subject of your memoir isn't?"

"Maybe neither of us are good at remaining professional." Her hand squeezes, and that sends me over the edge. Heat erupts through my body and my balls tighten in her hand.

Heavy spurts land on my stomach and my chest, ruining the crumbled button-down. I buck into Charlotte's hand on the last reflex. The room fades away, the whole world— there's only pleasure. And her. Her touch. Her eyes.

Afterwards, I press my lips to her head again. "With you, Chaos, it's the last thing I want to be."

CHAPTER 43

CHARLOTTE

Aiden turns to kiss my neck. I feel languid and more than a little proud of myself. He'd just told me things I can use to build entire chapters around. Sure, I'll need to ask follow-up questions, but still…

"Mm-hmm," Aiden says. "I feel you glowing with triumph."

I slide my hand into his hair. I love it when it's messy like this. "Will all our interviews have to be conducted like this?"

"I should say *no* to that, or you'll get everything out of me." His hands circle my waist, inching up the fabric of my camisole. "What questions can I get you to answer?"

I chuckle. "I'm not so easily manipulated."

He pulls back and lifts his brow. "Oh? Wanna bet?"

A loud sound rings out through the house. A doorbell. Aiden groans and buries his face between my breasts.

"No," he mutters.

I run my nails lightly over his scalp. "You're expecting someone?"

"No. At least not this early. But it seems like she's here anyway, and she will let herself in if I don't open in four seconds."

I sit up straight. "Mandy?"

"The very one." He releases me with another groan and falls back on the bed, running a hand over his face. "I need a shower before I can talk to her."

I slide off the bed. The last thing I want is for Aiden's sister to find me in bed with her brother. To her, I'm still just his memoirist. The one reopening old wounds. "I need to get dressed."

"Yes," he says and doesn't make a move to get off my bed.

I smack one of his feet. "Come on! You need to get your butt down the hall and into the shower!"

He chuckles and rolls out of my bed, rising to stand tall in yesterday's rumpled and ruined tuxedo. He carefully tucks himself back into his pants, pulls up the zipper, and gives me a mock-serious look.

"If you get downstairs first, tell her I'll be out soon."

"I can't tell her that! I'll let her know that you might be sleeping in, which you normally don't."

He looks down at his watch, and then his face goes slack. "It's after nine."

"Go. Go!"

He cracks open the door just as another ring of his thunderous doorbell echoes across the house.

I hurry to get ready. It takes me a few minutes to brush my teeth, pull my hair into a braid, and change my clothes. I quickly spritz some perfume and pause by the mirror.

The last time I saw Mandy, she was glamorous. In a bohemian, richly nonchalant kind of way. She's the type of woman who could get expensive laser treatments and facials, but is happy to wear a pair of oversized jeans and no makeup at all... just a pair of designer sunglasses. Like Frankie Swan, *The Real Housewife* I wrote the memoir for a while ago. I know the type.

I don't look bad. But I look ordinary, and a little tired. It'll have to do. Because Mandy's perspective is missing from Aiden's book, and I'm determined to get it.

I head downstairs. The doorbell has stopped ringing, but based on Aiden's earlier comment, it might just mean that his sister has let herself in.

I find her at his large kitchen island. Her blonde hair has a load of highlights I hadn't noticed last time, and she looks more tanned than previously. She starts talking without turning around. "It's not like you to sleep in. You're not sick?"

"Sorry. He's not up yet, I think. Or at least his door wasn't open." I am the worst liar. "Hi, Mandy."

She twists to face me. Her eyes, too shrewd and too like Aiden's, look me up and down. "Hi, Charlotte. I was hoping you'd be in, too."

"You were?"

"Yes." Her face softens with a slight smile. "I was wondering... I know you've been wanting to talk to me. For the book."

I need to play this cool.

"Yes, but only if you're comfortable. Would you like something to drink?" I walk past her to the giant side-by-side fridge and grab some orange juice. "You decide the parameters, too."

"Right. Like whether or not I'll be directly quoted?"

"Yes. Your input could just be used as the background."

"Which means I won't be mentioned at all."

I pour myself a large glass of OJ, and after seeing her nod, a second one for her. "Yup. It'll help inform my chapters, but no one needs to know the info came from you. You know that Aiden will have full control over the manuscript, too. I'm sure he'll let you read it. You can nix anything you don't like."

She taps her nails on the marble counter. Short, oval-shaped, with blood-red polish on them. She's in a well-fitted tank top today and a pair of oversized white jeans. Her hair is loose, and she's wearing what I suspect is that "no-makeup" makeup look that's so hard to achieve for us mere mortals.

"Okay. I like the sound of that. Because I've... well I've been thinking."

"Yeah?"

She pulls her eyebrows together tightly. "This could be a good thing. It might not be. But... it could be. Like, a chance for Aiden to get some vindication."

I nod. "Yes, it's an opportunity to tell his story. *Your* story, in some ways."

"I hate the way the media..." She shakes her head a little. "It's just so raw, you know?"

I can't even imagine. Having your father dragged away in handcuffs, having to see him in the courtroom every day, embroiled in a case so widely publicized that it got its own hashtag on Twitter at the time.

"Yes. People consume it like entertainment, but for you... it's your life. It's *your* family." My voice comes out fierce.

Mandy taps her fingers against the marble again. "Yes. Exactly! It's infuriating. The public got *so* many things wrong!"

"Like what?"

She opens her mouth, but then she shakes her head with a smile. "I know what you're doing. You're getting the interview already."

"I'm just getting to know you."

"Uh-huh." She sets a large paper bag on the kitchen counter. "I was hoping you'd be here because... I actually want to invite you to something tonight."

"Oh?"

"Yes. It's a tiny bit self-serving." Her smile turns winsome. "I'm a part-owner of a company, and we're launching our next line this evening."

"Really?"

"Yes, at a launch party over in the Hills. Restricted guest list, and there's a no phones policy."

I like the sound of that. "What company?"

Her smile widens. "I think I'll let you figure that out when you arrive. Is that terribly presumptuous of me? I just like the idea of giving you a challenge."

I laugh. "Honestly, you sound a lot like your brother right now."

"I do?"

"Yes. He loves a game, and never wants to submit to an interview question unless he gets something in return." As soon as the words are out of my mouth, I feel heat racing up my cheeks.

Like an orgasm.

I take a long sip of the cold juice and try to look innocent.

Mandy starts to chuckle. "Well, we were raised in the same household, after all. He's coming tonight, too. I've badgered him into it."

"That'll be fun."

"Yes. And I was wondering if, maybe, you'd want to write a little piece on it?" She's looking at me with wide eyes, and I know I'm being manipulated. But I also know this might be a necessity to gain the interview.

I've done far weirder things in the past to get an "in" with the memoir subjects.

"I can do my best, yeah. Where would it be published?"

"Online," she says, like that explains everything. Her face is all smiles again. "You're a very talented writer, or so my brother says. I'd love to read a few of your draft chapters."

"I can show you. We could meet for lunch tomorrow or the day after," I suggest. "You can then see the article I write about your company's product launch, and read some of the chapters about your brother. And we could chat."

When in doubt, formalize the agreement.

Mandy looks at me across the kitchen island. She hears the bargain just as clearly as I do.

But then she nods. "Yes. We'll do that. I'll book us a table."

"How about working here? I can order in, and we'll sit out

on Aiden's patio." I give her a friendly smile. "Less noise. We can focus better."

"All right, that makes sense. But," she says and holds up a finger in my direction, "don't become a hermit like Aiden."

"A hermit?"

"He doesn't do *anything* since he had to take over Titan. He doesn't go out, doesn't meet up with friends, barely goes up to visit Mom in Sonoma."

"Mandy," a deep voice says. Aiden strolls into the kitchen. His hair is damp, and he's in a button-down and slacks again. But he hasn't had time to shave, so there's a rugged shadow covering his jaw.

I look away, or the memory of what happened not even an hour ago will show on my face.

"Don't fill Charlotte's head with lies," he says.

"They aren't lies. You don't do anything social!"

Aiden shakes his head and comes to stand beside her at the kitchen island. "I work."

"Balance, Aiden. There needs to be balance." But she's smiling as she says it, and I get the sense this is a conversation they've had many times before.

Judging from his face, it's also one he's tired of. Doesn't surprise me. There's a reason he's working so hard, and it's to restore something their dad nearly ruined. It's easy to see that Aiden is annoyed at his sister for not realizing that. Or maybe just for ignoring it altogether.

I fill a glass with juice for him. He accepts it with a warm look cast my way.

"You're still coming tonight, right?" Mandy asks him.

"About that," he says.

Mandy turns from a glamorous, smiling blonde to annoyed little sister in a heartbeat. "Don't say it. You *are* coming. You promised."

There's tiredness etched into every bone of his being. I can *feel* it, standing across from him. For just a day, I'd like to give him space to be nothing but himself. With no one tugging him in a million directions—for interviews, for meetings, for decisions.

Not even me.

"Please come, even for just an hour or two. Several of my single friends will be there, and they'll bring single friends, too."

"Mandy," he says. "It's weird for me to come."

"Of course it's not. I asked Charlotte to come, too, and she just said yes! She's going to write an article about it."

Aiden's gaze slides to mine. "You're going?"

"Yes."

His eyes darken, and then he looks back at his sister. "Charlotte has enough work on her plate without being forced to write an article about your business start-up."

"I didn't force her!"

"I don't feel forced."

Aiden runs a hand through his hair, mussing it again. It looks even better now. "Fuck. Fine. I'll go tonight, but Charlotte..." His eyes slide back to mine, and he takes a deep breath. "You have no idea what party you've just committed yourself to."

Mandy pushes the bag in my direction. "Dress code is lingerie. I brought you a few choice outfits from our latest collection, just in case you don't have anything that fits the occasion." Her smile is so wide, it's blinding. Like looking at the sun. "Can't wait to see you there!"

CHAPTER 44

AIDEN

I arrive later than planned at Mandy's party. The entire day had been spent with Eric and my COO Cynthia, working through the press strategy to combat the tax investigation.

"Make sure the biographer includes these baseless allegations in the book," Cynthia had told me, hunched over her laptop during a quick lunch. "Make it a part of the narrative, like the bloodthirsty jerks just won't stop taking potshots at us."

It's a good idea.

More and more, I'm starting to realize that letting this memoir be published might actually be... beneficial.

Painful. But advantageous.

Mandy's company has rented a large mansion high up in the Hills for the launch event. It's all square angles and white plaster walls, like one out of a dozen. The driver drops me off at the gate and disappears down the narrow, curved road. As I approach the building, I hear the music drifting from the inside.

Charlotte will already be there. I texted her earlier, and she said that she'd take a rideshare here.

Security is on either side of the entrance. I give my name, and I'm waved inside. After surrendering my phone.

I fucking hate having to part with it.

But it's the whole vibe they are going for here: the security protocol, the secrecy. I'm forced to trust that adequate procedures are in place and that my phone won't get stolen or broken into. Hacked and misused.

The venue smells thickly of incense and something else, like a heavy fragrance. I walk past a group of women sporting high heels, lingerie, and long wavy hair.

Mandy and her business partners have gone full-out.

I can only imagine what Charlotte will say about this place.

Entering the main living space, I spot a waiter in a floor-length silk robe, walking around with a tray of drinks. He's paradoxically the most dressed person here.

Him and me both, because I'm still in my suit from work.

I recognize a slew of people. Some are from Mandy's circle of friends, others are minor celebrities. One or two are fairly famous. Seems like all the stops have been pulled out for this party.

But nowhere is a five foot seven woman, with a lean body and long light-brown waves that fall past her shoulders. No blue eyes that sparkle with excitement.

I wander outside. Dulcet tones play from a DJ's booth set up by the short side of the pool. Several people are in the water, their hair drenched. Giant inflatables decorate the pool. I flag down a waiter and grab a drink off the tray. It looks like a martini, and I drain half of it in one go.

That's when I see her.

Standing on the other side of the pool, her back to me. Long legs stuck in a pair of strappy heels that look like the ones she'd gotten for the movie premiere.

Those endless legs are entirely bare. All the way up to the very tops of her thighs, where they're kissed by the hem of a dress. If it can be called that. It's more of a lingerie than anything—virtually sheer and hemmed in lace. It flares from her narrow waistline, creating an *A* shape from what looks like a bra with thin straps that hug her bare shoulders.

The only thing I can do is stare.

It's Charlotte, but as a cream puff. A tantalizing sweet delicacy in black lace.

I move before I remember giving my legs the command. There's a group of chatting guys in the way, and I push past them, barely registering the huff of annoyance.

Only when I make it past the crowd do I realize she's chatting with someone. A man. I see his face clearly, and, *fuck*, it's Logan Edwards. Like the other week. He had been too interested in her then, too.

I drain the other half of the martini. There are no ties between Charlotte and me, not officially. Those two fucking rules govern everything between us.

They're good rules. Sane rules. Very pragmatic, utterly respectable, very useful. Relationships take time. They can cost you, too. Nothing hurts like being betrayed. I should know. So, very good rules. It was great of Charlotte to establish them.

Even if I want to break them every single time I see her.

I walk up to her side. Logan catches my gaze first, and he smiles widely.

"Hey, man. Figured you'd be here."

I stand closer to Charlotte than a mere friend would and reach out to shake his hand. "Hey. Glad you made it. I know it means a lot to Mandy."

He shrugs a little. "It's a cool party. I got a goodie bag." He holds up the purple silk bag, and his face reminds me of a kid in the candy store. It's the sort of endearing, boyish look that has gotten him so far in movies. A flush is lingering on his cheeks, either from the alcohol or the thrill of being at the "no phones" party.

Things were different a few years ago. Now, the room changes when he walks into it. People on the street turn around. I know what that's like, to a lesser degree, and would empathize with him on a normal evening. An evening where he *isn't* chatting up Charlotte.

Again.

I look at Chaos, and then nearly black out.

Whatever top she's wearing is practically see-through. Her nipples are hard, and they're poking out through the thin, sheer fabric of her barely there dress.

She smiles at me. Freckles dot her nose, and the tops of her shoulders look a bit red. She's gotten more sun.

"Hello, Aiden," she says. She's holding a goodie bag of her own and a half-finished glass of bubbly.

A dull pulse starts to throb at my temples. The desire to pull her close is so overwhelming that I have to fist my hand at my side.

Jealousy is not an emotion I'm familiar with.

I can't remember the last time I felt it around anyone but Charlotte. It's irrational. Like most emotions, it serves no purpose. But it's damn impossible to evade.

"Logan was telling me—"

Charlotte's interrupted by a group of people joining us. Mandy's business partner is among them, and she immediately puts a hand on Logan's arm.

It's a chance for an escape.

I wrap my arm around Charlotte's waist. "We'll be right back. Gotta top up her glass," I tell everyone and steer Charlotte away from the pool.

"My glass is half-full," she tells me. "Or are you a half-empty kind of guy?"

"Very funny." I look around us, but no one is staring at her tits. "What are you wearing, Chaos?"

"Apparently, it's part of the new launch," she says. "Your sister gave me this babydoll dress."

"It's see-through."

"I know. Isn't it crazy?" She laughs. "But I'm wearing underwear."

There's a quiet alcove, further away from the action. I lead her toward it. "Your tits are out."

"What tits?" she says and chuckles again. "I barely have any. It's fine, Aiden."

She pulls away and twirls slightly in front of me. The skirt splays out, rising high up. I see the swell of her ass cheeks and the matching thong she's wearing underneath.

"Do you like it?"

There could be a raging wildfire behind me, and I wouldn't be able to look away from her.

"Yes," I say, "but I *don't* like that everyone here can see so much of you."

She laughs again. There's an air about her—like she's a little drunk, a little happy. It washes away the jealousy that has gripped me like a vise.

"It doesn't bother me. There are no phones here. I love that rule."

"Someone might break it."

"Don't be like that." She pauses her spinning, and her hair falls back into the soft waves. A smile plays on her lips. "I feel like I'm playing another role. Nighttime Charlotte goes to sex parties, gets goodie bags, and talks to famous movie stars."

She looks up at the sky above us. It's dark, barely any stars are visible. But she smiles up at it like the entire Milky Way is on bright display just for her.

It wouldn't surprise me if it was.

"I feel alive tonight, Aiden."

"You look it. You look beautiful."

She looks at me over her shoulder. The playfulness is still there, lurking in the corner of her smile. "No compliments, my dear sir."

"How much have you had to drink?"

"Not much. Just some champagne."

I sit down on the low settee across from where she's swaying to the music the DJ is playing. Every song feels like an erotic remix of the originals. Deep bass, slowed-down beats.

"I've spoken to your sister a ton. And her friends." She shakes her head, moving her hips from side to side. "I didn't know she ran a sex toy company."

"Technically, it's a female sexual health and pleasure empowerment collective."

"Right. Sorry." She reaches into the goodie bag and digs around for a bit. Then she pulls out a silicon circle and rotates it a few times around her finger. "Like this. I think this is a... cock ring?"

"Put that away."

She giggles again. It's not a sound I'm used to hearing from Charlotte, and damn if it doesn't run like an arrow through me. "Okay, fine. I guess you're not interested in wearing it..."

"Not here, I'm not." I thrust a hand through my hair. "It's a pretty new venture. She's always been curious to try, but it was in the past year that she... well. Decided to go for it."

There's something liberating about the demise of our family's good name, my sister had told me. She had nothing left to prove. She could simply be Mandy Hartman *and* work in a business that designs sex toys.

"It's inspiring. She's such a character."

"That she is." I lean back on the sofa and just watch Charlotte. Arousal is simmering beneath my skin, just from the sight of her being this unbound.

We're far enough away from the others that her transparent dress is for me and me alone. But the jealousy hasn't gone away completely. It's there, threatening to break out. I shrug out of my suit jacket and keep it ready to hand to Chaos if someone comes our way.

She sits down beside me on the settee. The tops of her

shoulders are rosy. "You've been tanning today, as well," I tell her.

"I went for a run today on the trails," she says. "I like the sun out here."

I stroke my thumb over the redness. "It doesn't like you back."

"Aiden," she says. "Everyone here has a tan. You're tanned as hell, even if you have an olive complexion. It's not fair."

"An olive complexion," I repeat slowly. "What does that mean?"

She rolls her eyes. "Nevermind. I'll wear more sunscreen tomorrow. Will that please you?"

I bend to press a kiss on her shoulder. "Your pale skin is beautiful. Don't change it."

Her breath catches at the brief contact. "So... your sister," she says. "She said earlier that there are single women here she wants to introduce you to."

I groan. "Ignore that."

"Does she often play matchmaker?"

"No, and never successfully."

"Because the important Titan CEO doesn't have time to date." Her hand lands on my shoulder, fingers curving over the muscle. It doesn't seem like she realizes that she's touching me. She's drunk and happy. My chest expands, warmth flooding through it.

Fuck, this woman.

She's going to end me.

"Not usually, no. Like you."

"Like me," she agrees. "But when you do... I've been thinking. There's a bingo card in the goodie bag. I haven't looked at it closely, yet. But it's this list of positions."

"You're asking me about my sexual preferences," I say. "That's very invasive. You're going to make that a part of the book?"

"Of course not!"

I put a hand on her knee. "Sure you are. You're asking me what turns me on the most."

"Is it quarterly reports? When your profit margins increase?"

I close my eyes and pretend to shudder. "Don't make me hard, Chaos."

Her laughter is sweet. It fills the warm air, and she reaches for her goodie bag. "You're such an idiot."

With her, of course I am. There's nothing but *her* when she's around. It's been that way for weeks. My hand slides further up her bare thigh. "What turns me on, is someone else's pleasure. Your pleasure."

The breath seeps out of her. "Oh."

"Do you know why?"

"No," she whispers.

"Because you can't fake it." I lean in and touch my lips to her cheek. I glance past her to the party and the throng of people. No one is watching us. "Some women think they can. But they can't. They are real, your orgasms. And they have to be earned."

"Oh, wow."

"I love it when you come, Chaos. Nothing else gives me more pleasure."

She leans back a little, her eyes wide. "You were jealous earlier. Out there. Right?"

"I'm still jealous."

"Of what? I'm here with you."

I slide my hand up and grip her hip, and look pointedly down at the see-through lacy triangles that form the top of her babydoll dress, or whatever she'd called it.

"That thing must have come with a proper bra."

"No. It didn't. And other people here are in skimpier things than me."

I look at the crowd again. People are dancing in far more revealing things than Charlotte is wearing. It's true.

But she's *her*.

My hand drifts upward, and I brush the bottom swell of her small, firm tit. "Everyone can see these."

"They're just breasts. Tiny ones."

I groan, low in my throat, as her nipples harden into peaks. I move my thumb up and trace the outline of one through the delicate lace.

"Anyone could see," she whispers. But she doesn't pull away, either.

"You're blocking everyone's view." I meet her gaze with a glare. "Don't go out there showing anyone else these."

Her smile widens. "How else am I going to enjoy myself at this party?

"Wear my jacket."

"That would be a little suspicious, wouldn't it?"

She stands suddenly, the hem of the dress fluttering against her bare thighs. She grabs her goodie bag. "I know there are sex toys in here. Maybe I'll just have to go and find someone I can use them with."

"Charlotte," I say darkly.

She takes another step back, her smile widening. "I'm about to turn around. In three, two, one..."

"Don't you dare."

"Catch me," she says and dances off into the night and the throng of people.

CHAPTER 45

CHARLOTTE

I float through the crowd of people. Everywhere there's exposed skin and beautiful silk or lace. Some people are in full pjs, others in little negligees. Mandy herself is in a fabulous red silk robe. I spent the earlier part of the night with her, chatting with her and her friends about their company.

I hadn't realized how much more at ease I'd be with the "no-phone" rule.

But here, there is no risk of someone looking at me a little too long and then snapping a picture. Or pulling up Google and searching for me, finding out in a heartbeat everything I've tried to run away from for a decade.

There's anonymity in that. Plus, there are far more famous people here. Logan? Again? I can't believe this is their world.

I look over my shoulder, and another electric current passes through me. Despite the cool evening and my state of dress, I feel warm.

Aiden pushes through the crowd to get to me. His eyes are dark, eyebrows lowered. He looks angry. He's also the only one in a suit.

Far too dressed, compared to everyone else in silk and lace. Shorts and T-shirts.

He catches my eye and mouths a single word. *Stop.*

I grin at him and turn back. This place is huge. A sprawling estate. And I wonder, do people actually live here, or is it one of those houses that's always rented out—used for music videos, celebrities' vacations, and parties?

I pass by the bar. There are small wooden trays of tequila shots lined up, ready for people to grab them. On impulse, I snatch one. The ornamental board is engraved with text on the side and holds four little shot glasses, a plate of cut lime, and a tiny pouch of sea salt.

Aiden is closer now. A glance back tells me he's almost caught up to me.

I rush to the side, to where the dancefloor lies. Mandy is out there. I see her, blonde hair and red silk robe, and I wonder if it would be safer for me to be right next to her. Aiden wouldn't dare then.

But maybe… I want to get caught.

I head inside, walking straight into the living room. The giant glass walls must have been pushed aside, allowing the party to spill easily from outside to the interior of the mansion. On the massive table at the center of the room is an array of products on display. Mandy showed them to me earlier.

Pocket vibrators.

G-spot stimulators.

Edible underwear.

A few are already in my goodie bag, slung over my shoulder.

"Chaos," a voice says beside me.

I keep going, past a group of men with grins on their faces who are all collectively examining a set of beads.

An arm wraps around my waist, and then I'm pulled back against Aiden's body. His voice is gravelly in my ear. "Charlotte," he says. "Are you trying to drive me insane?"

I close my eyes. "Maybe."

"It's a dangerous game you're playing."

"Maybe I'm just conducting some research."

"Here? Where everyone can see?" His mouth moves lower, lips feathering over my neck. My brain short-circuits. It always does when he kisses me there. "You're very close to everyone seeing *just* what kind of professional relationship we have."

"I thought," I murmur, "you wanted to hide me away. My clothing is indecent, after all."

He mutters something against my neck. It sounds like a curse. Then his mouth drags back up, lips against the shell of my ear. "You won't wear my jacket, so stealing you away is my only choice."

He pulls me down the hall. I almost spill the tequila, and he shakes his head, taking the tray from me.

"Get in here," he says and pushes open a random door. It leads into an elegantly decorated bedroom that looks sparingly used. He shuts the door and stands with his back to it.

His eyes drag over me. "That dress is going to be the end of me, Chaos. I was ready to fight all the men out there."

I feel ten feet tall. Eternal, ageless, and in complete control when he looks at me like that. Intoxicated by the magic that happens when we're together.

"I didn't think you were the jealous type."

He sets the little tray of tequila down on a nightstand. "I am when it comes to you and the see-through dress," he says darkly.

Aiden looks from me to the tequila shots. There's a little engraving on the side of the wood that says *body shots encouraged*. I see him reading it.

I take another step back, excitement racing through my system. "What are you going to do?"

He looks at me. "I'm going to take a shot, and if you insist on walking around dressed like *that*, it's going to be off you."

"Oh." My knees hit the edge of the bed, and I sink backward on the soft duvet.

Aiden grabs the tray, and suddenly it feels very real, here in this house, with the door closed and locked, and him standing in front of me.

I let my palms glide over the fabric. Velvet, maybe? Something soft and decadent.

"Lie back," he says, "and be a good table for me."

I smile and do what he says. "I'm just an object to you."

He shakes his head and reaches for a shot. "You're far, far more than that, but for the sake of rule one... sure." He runs his free hand lightly over my body. Across my bare upper chest, between my breasts, down the center of my stomach.

He pauses at the hem of my dress. Grips it, and tugs it up to expose my midriff.

I'm breathing fast.

"Calm," he murmurs and slides his hand over my waistline before pouring the cold tequila into my belly button.

His fingers glide upward, coming to rest by my jaw. "Open," he murmurs and fits a slice of lime between my lips. I grip it gently with my teeth and watch him grab a pinch of salt. He deliberates for a single breath before leaning down and licking a stripe across my left nipple. It dampens the thin, sheer fabric, making it stick to my skin.

"There." He sprinkles the salt on the spot.

Keeping his eyes on mine, he leans down again and kisses my lower stomach.

A shiver races through me. I feel like I'm holding my breath.

He kisses up another inch, and then he's by the tequila. His lips are warm and so is his tongue as he drinks off my skin.

Aiden moves up, and then he's only inches from my mouth. He tilts closer, our lips almost touching as he takes the lime from between my lips. He sucks for a second and then tosses it away.

Finally, he lowers his head to my left breast and fits his

mouth around it. He sucks and then licks the nipple with a twirl of his tongue that sends warmth through me.

He looks up at me with eyes that are nearly black.

"I think that was the wrong order." My voice comes out a little breathless. It's usually salt first, tequila, then lime.

But Aiden just shakes his head and straightens. "No, this is the right order. There's no way I was not finishing at your tits."

He reaches for the other shot and repeats the process. Pouring, licking, salting.

There's a dull ache at the apex of my thighs, and I press them together to try to soothe it.

Aiden runs his hand up my inner thigh, and when he bends to my belly button again, his hand slides up to press between my legs. He runs his finger down my seam, over the fabric of my thong.

My breath catches. It's hard to draw air with another slice of lime between my lips.

"I know," he murmurs, kissing his way up from my stomach to my lips. His thumb keeps moving, stroking me up and down. "You're not meant to lie still."

His lips close around the lime, just barely touching mine in a brief kiss before he lifts his mouth. He removes the citrus with his free hand and then bends to my right nipple.

He pauses, an inch from the wet, salty peak. Between my legs, his fingers start to circle my clit.

"This right here," he says, eyes dark, "is what I can't wait to taste. You're soaking through the lace, and I want you to know just how badly I want to have you on my tongue."

My stomach tightens at his words, and my hands dig into the comforter. "Aiden."

"I know. All in good time, sweetheart." He looks down at my nipples, like they are everything he's ever wanted. Like I don't have tiny breasts, barely A-cups that have taken me years to be okay with. "These sweet tits need my attention now. But Charlotte... I want you to imagine it's your clit I'm sucking on instead."

He licks the salt off me and presses his thumb down on my clit at the same time. My back lifts off the bed at the sensation. His mouth sucks my entire left breast into my mouth, and I can't think around the pleasure.

He slides his hand beneath the rim of my thong, and then it's all him, cupping me. He pushes a thick finger inside and keeps pressing down on my clit.

His tongue laves my nipple.

How would that feel? On my clit?

"I'm close," I whisper, my hand raking through his thick hair.

He uses his teeth. Bites down around my stiff nipple, and my orgasm sweeps through me like a soft summer rain. Trickles through my body. My toes curl inside the painful high heels, and I drop to the bed, panting.

I slowly come back to myself. To Aiden's head resting against my breastbone, his heavy breathing. His middle finger, still inside me, and the rigid set of his shoulders.

His delicious weight.

"Fuck," he mutters and pushes onto his elbow. There's a fire in his eyes that makes me feel ready all over again. "I need to be inside you. And when I do, Chaos... this won't be a one time thing. Once we start, I'll need you all the fucking time."

I reach for his suit jacket. "What makes you think I'll only need you once?"

CHAPTER 46

AIDEN

She tears off one of my shirt buttons.

"You're feral," I mutter against her temple. But I'm just as eager. She's hot beneath my hand, and it hurts, physically *hurts*, to pull my finger out of her heat. My hands shake slightly when I grip the sides of her thong and drag it down her long legs.

I pause when it's at her ankles. She looks at me from her recline on the bed. The sheer fabric of her dress is now soaked and clinging to the outline of her small tits, and the *V* between her legs laid fully bare.

I kiss her ankle and find the straps to her heels. "You're wearing the shoes I bought you."

"They're my only good heels," she says.

"They're also not the kind of shoes you can walk in." I unclasp one, and then the other. "Don't wear them again."

She lifts herself onto her elbows. "I like them."

"They hurt you."

"I look good in them."

I groan and toss the shoes to the carpeted floor, along with her black thong. "You look good in everything." I reach for the silk bag she's left on the bed and turn it upside down. All the contents fall out. "But you look even better naked, and definitely when you're not in pain."

Her eyes roam over the contents I've dumped on the bed. But I'm only looking for one thing—the foil packet that must have been included.

There's a small bottle of lube. A pocket vibrator and, *fuck*, the fun we can have with that.

I reach for the buckle of my belt and undo it. Charlotte lies back, the skimpy see-through dress pooled around her waist. Her long legs are bare and bent, slightly splayed, just enough to show me the glistening pink of her pussy.

I pull down my zipper, and chuck off my pants.

Charlotte's eyes fall to my hard cock. Just having her look at me makes it twitch.

I need her skin against mine, and I need to bury myself inside her heat. I need that more than my next fucking breath.

I roll on the condom while she watches my every move, until the latex sheathes down to my base.

"Aiden," she whispers. "Could anyone walk in?"

I shake my head. "I locked the door. Do you think I'll let anyone but me see you naked? See you like this?"

Her face softens, and her lips part on an exhale. She looks so beautiful like that, with her light-brown hair spread around her head, it squeezes my heart to look at her. I want to swallow her whole, wrap myself around her, be inside of her.

My hands find her ankles again, and I pull her down so her ass is by the end of the bed. She giggles again, that soft, beautiful sound, and fuck if I don't want to make her do that again with me. All the time.

I glide my hands down her thighs, parting them. Step in between and let the head of my cock rub up and down her slit, coating myself.

As I reach for the array of toys on display beside her, her eyes track mine. "What are you— Oh."

I squirt some lube and then slide the cock ring on. It's a

snug fit. I've used one before, but it was years ago. It fits to the base of my cock, and I look up, amused, to find Charlotte watching with intense fascination. Her curiosity is never far.

"What will it do?" she asks.

I use my index finger to trace the silicon until I find the small button. Turn it on, and the faint vibration makes a humming sound.

"Oh," she breathes. "*Oh*."

"You said you wanted me to use it."

"It was a joke."

"No," I say and nudge the head of my cock to her entrance, "it wasn't."

She looks down between her legs. We both watch as I disappear an inch at a time inside her. When I'm buried to the hilt, the ring comes to rest against her clit.

I stay still, unmoving.

Charlotte's breath catches. "Oh. *Oh*."

"You feel that?"

"Yes," she murmurs and grips the comforter. "I do."

I thrust into her, a slow roll of my hips. She feels fucking incredible. Better than I remember, too good for me to last as long as I want to.

And each time I bottom out, I stay there for a heartbeat. Let the vibrations hit her where she needs them most.

Beautiful color spreads across her skin. She's so pale, it's easy to see her flush with pleasure. Standing like I am, with her sprawled before me on the bed, I see everything.

I never want to look away.

Her eyes are heavy-lidded, her hair mussed. There will be no hiding what we've done after this, and fuck, I'm at my sister's party with her friends. I'll figure out a way out the back. Carry Charlotte in my arms and get straight into a car.

She arches beneath me, and I fuck her faster. All the built-up need makes it hard to think about anything else but being inside her, getting closer to her.

I already knew she liked vibrations. Seeing her now, I'm reminded of just how much. She moans every single time I hit deep inside her.

Fuck sliced bread or electricity. This cock ring is the best thing ever invented.

Gripping her thighs, I use them as leverage to drive into her harder. Her moans get louder, and I'm dimly aware that could be a bad thing, that this is a party, but the thought dies as soon as it hatches. There's no space for it.

She's so pretty it hurts to look. I want to fuck her harder, and I want to stroke my hands over her skin and take care of her. I want both at the same time. Consume her, but also cherish her.

Her breathing ratchets up, and I know she's close. I've learned the signs. On the next thrust, I stay seated inside her. My dick protests with a throbbing ache at the sudden lack of movement.

I groan and look down at where the silicon of the ring presses against her clit.

"Oh my god," she whimpers, her back arching. "Oh my god, Aiden, that's...."

I reach down and increase the vibration speed by a setting or two. And then I start to feel her tighten around me with the first tremors of her orgasm.

Every muscle in my body tenses with the effort not to thrust. To stay inside her, ring to clit, and just ride out her waves. I nearly growl.

Charlotte arches higher off the bed. She moans and comes beneath me, around me; her muscles squeeze me tight enough that my vision fogs at the edges.

It sends me over the edge.

I come with a groan. It feels like I'm dying, electricity zapping down my spine, straight to my cock. Not moving, not thrusting, just letting it race through me. It's a different kind of pain I've never experienced before.

It's so fucking intense that I have to close my eyes, my hands gripping Charlotte's thighs tightly.

"Aiden," she moans, and my control snaps. I grind into her—once, twice—with the last spurts of my own climax.

When I finally open my eyes, it's to a sweaty, happy, gorgeous Charlotte lying in front of me on the bed. I'm still standing. Somehow. It's a miracle.

Slowly, I pull out, and she winces a bit as the vibrations cease against her clit. I stroke my thumb over her pussy. "Sensitive?"

"Incredibly," she says. "That was... I've never experienced that before."

I tie off the condom. "Me, neither. Fuck."

"That ring might be the best thing I've ever been given," she says.

I toss the condom and return to her, still splayed on the bed in this random guest room. I gather her into my arms, and she turns to me immediately. Loose and willing, warm and smiling.

"This isn't how I imagined fucking you again after all this time," I confess against her temple.

She chuckles. "At a party? With merch gifted by your sister?"

I groan. "Don't mention that part, ever."

"I didn't imagine this, either." She leans back in my arms, her light-brown hair spread out around her. Her eyes sparkle in the dim lighting, with a smudge of mascara under the lid. She looks sweaty, and happy, and alive. "But nothing with you has ever been how I've imagined it."

CHAPTER 47

CHARLOTTE

"Okay," I say. "I think we might need to… talk."

Aiden is lying on the other couch across from me. We've been working for the last hour in his giant living room. It's Tuesday evening, and for the past few days, we've been in and out of bed. In and out of his large en suite shower. On and off these large couches.

With a few short breaks for him to take calls from the office, or for me to chat with Vera about the book's progress. We swam in his pool this morning, where he cornered me in the deep end and then slowly peeled off my bikini top like he was unwrapping a present. Then he'd made me come around his fingers beneath the surface of the water.

It's been… a very good few days.

At my words, Aiden looks up from his sprawl of papers. His hair is messy, and the scruff on his jaw is thicker now. A dark shadow that more and more resembles the short beard he'd had at Zion National Park all those months ago.

I had told him the other day that I liked him with facial hair.

He hasn't shaved since.

"Sure," he says. "Do you have the pitches ready for me?"

"Almost," I say. The document is open on my computer,

the idea I've increasingly become enamored with. But showing it to him... I don't think I could handle it if he didn't think it was good enough. "But that's not it."

He leans forward, elbows resting on his knees. "What do you want to talk about, Charlotte?"

Nerves make it momentarily hard to speak. But I've done harder things. This shouldn't be so complicated. "About what we've been doing."

A slow smile spreads across his face. "I'm happy to talk about that."

Despite us having done virtually *everything,* a flush still creeps up my cheeks. We'd put the things in that little goodie bag to good use. He's so free in bed, comfortable in ways I've never experienced before. Like nothing is off the table.

"I just want to touch base about the rules again."

He lifts an eyebrow. "Right. The rules."

"Yes, the rules. They're good for both of us. We only have a few weeks left now until the deadline."

"I'm aware."

"Right. Well, I don't want to *stop* doing what we're doing... I just want to doublecheck that you didn't spend Sunday here instead of at the office because of me. Or that your sister suspects anything after the party. Or that you had a thing tonight that you might... have canceled."

He nods a little. "Right. Because that would violate rule number two. This—us—might then affect the memoir. Our professional deal."

"Yes, exactly." His sister and I had lunch out by the pool yesterday. It was fantastic. I'd gotten so much good material that I had to write all day today just to get the ideas down.

Aiden leans back on his couch and motions for me to join him. "Come here. If you wanna talk about this, do it while sitting with me."

"I think that'll make the conversation even harder." But I've already pushed my laptop away. He opens his arms for me, and I sink onto his lap. The pull to touch him, to be near, has strengthened over the last days of intimacy until it feels like a cord. Stretched taut between us.

"No. Touching you makes everything easier." He settles his hands on my hips and rests his head on the back of the couch. "Now, talk to me."

"I just did."

"Tell me what's really bothering you."

I wrap my hands around his neck. His skin is warm to the touch. "I'm feeling a bit scared about what we're doing," I say. There's enough truth to my words to make the nerves in my stomach tighten

He just nods once, like that's to be expected. "Yeah. I get that."

"You do?"

"Yes."

I breathe out a long-held breath. "Good. And we have the rules."

"We have the rules," he agrees. "We're also both adults. You can tell me what you need, Chaos. Anytime."

"Even if it'll make you upset," I say, smiling a little. "You know what? I really like the car now."

A smile curves on his lips. "Good. I like you driving it."

"I really like living here, too. More than I thought I would."

"There's more comfort than you're used to on your trips," he says. "I just finished listening to the audiobook of your memoir on the Alaskan dog musher. The one who nearly got you killed."

"A blizzard hit! We had to take shelter."

"You spent a night in freezing temperatures, huddled under a tarp." His voice is low. "None of that was safe."

"Only until the storm passed. It was an adventure." I lean forward. "It was a *fantastic* adventure."

"Mm-hmm. And you like adventures."

"I do. Why do you insist on listening to all of my books?"

"Why wouldn't I? I'm doing research."

I look at him skeptically. "Research on me? I'm here. You can just ask me things."

"Right. Because you're always so forthcoming."

"I promised you I would be. Weeks ago, and you promised me the same thing."

"Do you feel like I've lived up to my side of the bargain?" he asks.

I look at him. This man, who was a mystery to me. Who still is, in so many ways, but one that is slowly unraveling in front of me like a spool of yarn. Inch by inch, and surprise after surprise.

He's so much more than I thought he was. So much more than the story I expected to tell. I just had to learn how to read between the lines.

"Yes. I'm getting to know you more and more."

"I'll take you to where I grew up. The family house," he says. "We can go later in the week."

"Really?"

"Yeah."

I stroke my thumb along his jaw. "Thank you. And... me? Do you feel like I've kept my part of the deal?"

His mouth widens into a wry smile. "Mostly, sweetheart. But there are still plenty of questions left. Things about your past I don't know."

"You know most of it. You're reading every single one of the assignments I've done over the past few years."

"Those are professional dealings. They don't tell me what you felt. What your hopes and dreams have been." He lifts both of his eyebrows. "You won't tell me why you won't let me go down on you."

I roll my eyes. "That's what you're stuck on?"

"I feel like there's something I'm missing there."

"You're such a man."

His hands tighten on my waist. "Yes. Maybe. But tell me, and then you can ask me a sexual question. About anything, and I'll answer."

"Anything at all?"

"Yes."

I consider that for a moment. It's a very good offer. "Okay. But I'm warning you, it's such a stupid story."

"I doubt that, Chaos."

It's not very flattering, either. But Aiden's done nothing to make me believe he may feel the same way Blake did. "Remember what I told you about my ex?"

"I do."

"Well, he was the first guy to ever... you know."

"Go down on you," Aiden fills in.

That's another of his traits. He's so comfortable talking about this, speaking things out loud that I rarely have. I've had my fair share of casual sexual relationships, but part of that kind of intimacy is rarely talking openly about what we're doing.

This is different.

"Yeah. Exactly. And later, I heard him talking to some people about it. He said that..." I shrug. Like this is nothing to me. "He said that it was part of the job, but not something he enjoyed. Just a way to butter me up for sex. And that next time, he'd make sure I showered right before."

Aiden's face goes blank, and then he closes his eyes. The hands at my sides tighten into fists. "What?"

"He was young and dumb. I know he's likely not repre-sentative of *all* men, but it's just gotten into my head, you know? And now I can't get it out."

"Makes perfect sense," he grinds out the words.

"You okay?"

"Yeah. Just angry."

"Oh," I say. "At him, I hope."

"Of course it's at him." He releases a long breath, like he's forcing his limbs to relax. The fingers on my hips spread wide, warming my skin through the tank top. "Did you believe him?"

"Believe him? I mean, it was very clear he was telling the truth."

"His truth," Aiden says. "Not *the* truth. Because trust me, Charlotte, there's nothing wrong with you. Going down on you would not be *part of the job*. It would be a fucking privilege. Has anyone but him done it?"

I hesitate only a moment before shaking my head. "No. I never let anyone else after that. It was easier just... to avoid that bit of sex."

"He was the problem, Chaos. Not you."

"You can't know that for sure," I say. It's such a vulnerable thing to admit. It makes me feel like running. Opening up like this to Aiden.

But it also feels scary-good. And it's been a long time since I've done things that feel scary-good.

His eyes are warm on mine. "Do you trust me?"

It takes me a moment to answer. "Yes. More than I should."

"Then trust me when I say he was an asshole. There's nothing wrong with you... and I can't wait to prove you wrong."

I play with the collar of his shirt. "My question to you, then."

"Ah, yes. Hit me with it."

"What's the best sex of your life?"

His eyebrows lift, and a slow smile spreads across his face. "Really? That's your question?"

"Yes. Don't insult the question."

He chuckles. "I won't. All right, Chaos, if you're sure you want to hear about it..."

Suddenly I'm not so sure. I didn't think this through. But

this is emotionless. I *should* be able to hear him talk about a woman from his past.

And besides, I'm here with him now, aren't I?

That should be the only thing that matters.

"It was pretty unexpected," he says and uses his thumbs to stroke circles over my hips, down to my lower stomach. "She was funny and direct. Beautiful, of course, but more than that. Intriguing."

My stomach is tight. But I just nod. "Oh."

"It was at a hotel, and we went back to her room."

"Right."

He leans forward, and his smile widens. "We played poker, and it turned into strip poker. She had a vibrator, and I got to use it between her legs while watching her in the mirror, and feeling her come around my fingers."

My mouth falls open.

Aiden laughs and pulls me even closer. "You really thought I was talking about someone else? Never, Chaos. You're the best sex of my life. Every fucking time."

CHAPTER 48

AIDEN

Producers shuffle into the conference room.

Some I recognize, some I don't. There are assistants there and some reality stars. They rarely attend, but a few of the bigger ones came to pitch their own shows.

I haven't spent much time overseeing the reality TV department in the last few years. It's become a successful juggernaut and our least prestigious offering. But the profits subsidize our larger ventures in news and network shows, not to mention the deal I almost closed for the streaming service.

The costs of producing reality TV are low, and the appeal for that type of entertainment is high.

A necessary evil.

Everyone files into the conference room, and a low chatter soon fills the room. Allison, our head of internal programming, walks in with a large binder in hand. "We've got some great new program suggestions," she tells me and moves to sit down beside me.

I glance over my shoulder at Charlotte. She's in a chair in the corner of the room, ready to sit in like she often does. Her laptop is propped open on her lap, and her fingers rest casually on the keyboard. I like having her near.

But her eyes are locked on the group of people taking a seat. There's an odd expression on her face, like she's a million miles away.

I head her way. "Hey. You okay?"

Her nail starts tapping against her computer. "Um, what kind of meeting is this? It said internal programming on the schedule."

"Yes, it is, for the reality TV division. Producers will give updates and pitch new shows." Being here is more of a formality for me. The content team will do most of the work. But Charlotte wanted to come along to see how internal programming worked at Titan, and I was happy to indulge her. "You're shaking. Charlotte?"

"I'm going to sit this one out," she mumbles and pushes past me, laptop tucked under her arm.

She beelines toward the door. Past the group of people.

That's when someone stops her. "Hey—Is that you?"

It's Jeff. One of the senior producers who's been at the company for over fifteen years. He now spearheads several of our trashiest shows, ones with ratings high enough to justify his large bonuses.

I watched one episode of his, years ago, and never watched another.

He looks at Charlotte. "What are you doing here?"

Charlotte is frozen in place. I push around the table, trying to reach them. There's a guy around my age standing next to Jeff who looks vaguely familiar. Deep tan, thick sandy-colored hair. He's handsome in a Hollywood kind of way, which is always less striking in person.

"I'm... I'm... working here," she says.

"You're *working* here?" Jeff asks. There's a sharp incredulity in his voice that makes my teeth clench. "As what?"

I reach her side. "She's working with me."

The man by Jeff's side smiles at her. "I haven't seen you in forever," he tells her. He's got a British accent. "Man, it's been an age! Look at you."

Charlotte looks between them, but her gaze keeps snapping back to the blond guy. "Blake?"

"Yeah, that's me," he says again. He snaps his fingers in the air, like he's trying to remember something. "Sugar Puff!"

She makes a small, pained sound that makes me want to punch someone. Jeff turns to look at me. His eyes are wide, true confusion in them. "Mr. Hartman? Charlotte Richards is working with you?"

"Charlotte Gray," I correct him.

"*Charlotte*. That's it!" Blake says. "How've you been? You're looking good."

Jeff looks back at Charlotte, and his bushy eyebrows scrunch together. "Charlotte here was on the first season of *The Gamble*. Helped the show's ratings soar after her dramatic exit," he says.

"You were good," Blake says, his smile widening. "I remember that."

I hate him.

"You changed your name?" Jeff asks her. "How come? You got famous off that season. We made you a star."

Her face is so still, so carefully blank that it looks like she's wearing a mask. Her eyes flicker to me only for a moment before she nods at both men. "I have to go." She shifts on a heel and darts out of the room.

I stare at Jeff. "What do you mean, she was on your show?"

"She was on *The Gamble*. Remember the whole media storm during the first season? The sky-high ratings? That was all her." He inclines his head toward the door she just escaped through. "'*But I'm your little Sugar Puff,*' and all that."

"That was legendary," Blake says, still smiling wide. He's got a slightly dopey look on his face that he probably thinks is charming, and I dislike him intensely. He'd forgotten her name? I can't see how anyone who meets Charlotte could ever forget her.

"You're not making sense," I say. "Either of you."

Jeff lifts his hands up as if he's saying *you do you, but...* "She was blonde back then. Just google Sugar Puff and *The Gamble*, and you'll find her."

I walk to the door. Behind me, I hear Allison calling my name.

"Start the meeting without me!" I yell.

The hallway outside is deserted. Damn it. I shouldn't have lingered.

I stride down to the other side of the executive floor. But she's not in the small conference room that's become her office, and her bag is gone, too. *Fuck.* Eric is not at his desk, and there's no one I can ask if they'd seen her.

I hit the elevator button so many times it's a wonder it doesn't break. Charlotte's not in the lobby, either, but I find her outside the building.

She's on her phone, standing at the curb. Trying to get a rideshare? We'd driven to the office together, and her car is back at the house.

Her shoulders are rising and falling rapidly. I take her forearm. "Charlotte."

There's horror on her face, her eyes distraught. She's breathing fast. Her eyes flick from me to the building behind me.

"Are you okay?"

"I need to leave." Her breaths are shallow and rapid. Is she about to have a panic attack?

I pull her along to the parking lot, toward the row of executives' cars. There is a small bench flanked by a few trees. "Come. Have a seat."

She walks woodenly beside me, her breathing increasing in speed. I put a hand on her lower back. "Breathe in. Breathe out. Can you do that for me, Chaos? Whatever is happening, I promise we'll fix it. Breathe in. That's it… breathe out." I pull her down next to me on the bench. There's no one in sight in the parking lot, and my car is just a few feet away.

She's shaking her head quickly, tears pooling in her eyes. *Fuck!* Anxiety rises inside me. I've only heard about panic attacks, never helped someone through one.

I know Mandy struggled with them. What did she use to say…?

"Breathe in deeply… that's it. Breathe out. You've got this."

Charlotte buries her face in her hands and just inhales. Her breathing is still rapid, but it's steady. I hope.

I rub large circles over her back with my palm. "You're okay. You're okay."

Through her hands, I hear a faint sob. Is she crying? The anxiety squeezes tighter around my heart. Should I call someone? An expert? A doctor?

I wrap my arm around her instead and tuck her head under my chin. "You're okay, Charlotte. Just breathe."

Her hands grip my shirt, and her shoulders shake. I've never seen her this rattled before. Even when her zipper broke in a ballroom, she handled it like a champ. She gives as good as she gets every single moment.

What's this?

I press my lips to her hair. We're in the shade, and maybe that's why a shiver races through her. I tighten my arms. "Breathe, sweetheart," I murmur. "That's it."

She shudders again, her shoulders slowing. Over the top of her head, I catch sight of my marketing executive with a cigarette in hand and a phone pressed to his ear.

He notices us, though he looks away quickly when I glare at him. A few seconds later he leaves the parking lot entirely.

Good.

Charlotte leans back, and my arms fall to her waist. Her eyes are red and her cheeks are wet. Her gaze meets mine, but then close all together. Her breathing is heavier now, and I take solace in the steady sounds, so different from the quick, ragged ones of earlier.

"Are you okay?"

"This is embarrassing," she whispers.

"No, it's not." Charlotte takes another deep breath, and I rest my hand on her shoulder. "What happened?" I ask.

She shakes her head in small little movements. "I'm sorry, Aiden."

"Don't apologize."

"I didn't know what the meeting would be about," she whispers. "If I did, I wouldn't have been there."

Her words drop like heavy stones through clear water. Sinking to the bottom. *If I did, I wouldn't have been there.*

"So it's true?" I ask quietly. "You were on one of Titan's shows?"

Her gaze meets mine, and there's a heartbreaking hesitation there. Like she wants to say *no* but can't. Like a comfortable lie has broken.

"Yes," she whispers. "And it ruined my life."

The words hit right below the breastbone. "Why haven't you told me?"

"I couldn't," she says. She shakes her head again, and it's more frantic now. "Aiden. I can't, I can't think about you knowing, seeing it…" Her hand reaches out and grips mine, tight enough to hurt.

"It's okay. It's in the past," I say.

Her eyes fill with tears. "That's the thing. It's not. It's *never* behind me."

"It was years ago. You're not—"

"Promise me you won't watch it," she says. Her words are frantic. "Promise me. Okay? You won't watch the show. Please don't look up any clips. *Please,* Aiden, I just need… I can't imagine…"

"I promise. Hey, look at me. I promise, okay? I won't watch a single minute of your season."

She nods and seems to center herself. Like she's drawing strengths and rebuilding her armor. "Okay. Good. I just need…" Her phone dings and she seems to take it as a signal. "I have to go." She pushes away from me. "I ordered a rideshare."

I want to pull her back against me.

"Charlotte," I say.

But she's already taking a step back, jitters burning through her. I can see the urge to run, and I recognize it. She wants to be alone.

"Get home safe. Take as much time as you need."

She nods and heads toward the waiting car at the curb. It's painful to stay where I am, rooted to the bench in this tiny excuse of a green space, surrounded by concrete and steel and an endless sea of cars.

The Gamble.

I know the show. It's not one I like, not one I'm proud of. It's a big earner, though. Has been since the very first season. I remember being in the office when Jeff pitched it to Dad and the other content producers. People weren't convinced. Weren't sold. But it had a low enough budget and ended up getting a green light for one season and one season only.

I watched the first episode, I remember that. But I shut it off. *Trash.* That's what I thought, and my dad along with me, even as he pocketed the profits. Like I've continued to do.

Because the show blew up. It's now the grandest reality TV hit that Titan produces.

Jeff had said Charlotte was responsible for that success.

I quickly google her name, with the name that Jeff had mentioned. Charlotte Richards.

It gives me to a slew of results. And images.

There she is. A younger Charlotte. Slightly thinner, her face still elfin and heart-shaped. Sharp eyeliner and bleached hair. It falls, straight and light-blonde around her frame. She's smiling into the camera with bright, hopeful eyes. Beneath the image is the text: *Charlotte Richards, a 19-year-old contestant, eliminated after seven dramatic episodes.*

She was only nineteen when she was on the show.

We cast teenagers for these shows? Why had I never reflected on that before?

The Gamble is by far one of the wettest and most lascivious shows in our programming. Twenty singles at one Mexican resort… with an open bar. The entire premise of the show is stupid. People need to couple up and compete in challenges that vary from the athletic to the downright idiotic.

And all the while, they're gambling on the other person keeping them in the game. Continuing to choose *them.*

People need to be paired up by the end of the posed challenge or risk getting voted off.

My thumb scrolls through the results. She's listed under *Ten of the most memorable reality contestants of all time.*

Below is a meme that I vaguely recognize. I still have a social media account, even if I considered shutting it down the same week my father's sentencing hearing was held.

I cleansed it entirely. Kept it private. I only go on every now and then to keep up with a few surfers I know.

But I *have* seen that photo used in memes. Her in a purple dress, blonde hair and blonde bangs, standing by a pool with angry tears down her face.

Fuck. I hadn't recognized her at all. Today, she looks nothing like that young girl. The Charlotte I know is a brunette with fierce eyes and scathing comebacks. She's someone who works hard, has solidly erected walls, and is only soft sometimes. When you *earn* her softness and her quiet confessions.

She must hate me.

That's the only thing that makes sense. She said it herself. The show *ruined* her *life.*

Yet she chose to write the memoir and stay with me.

Then I remember the NDAs.

Fuck. She hadn't known who I was before signing. That was the blank look of shock on her face when she walked into my office. Sure, it was also recognition from Utah, but it couldn't have been only from that.

I run a hand over my face. The sun is warm, but I feel none of it. Only the cold grip of dread. I put my phone back in my pocket before I accidentally see more than she wants me to.

My chances with Charlotte might have been blown before I ever met her.

CHAPTER 49
CHARLOTTE

After yesterday's disaster, I consider staying home. Maybe I could just email Eric to say that I won't be able to interview Mr. Hartman during his lunch break because of an acute and sudden illness.

I could lie in bed with the door locked, pretending that there's no world outside of these walls. Just stare up at the cloud lamp and dream I could float away much the same.

I consider booking a flight out of Los Angeles and never coming back.

And I ponder asking Vera to be let out of the contract. I've even written the email, apologizing for my unprofessionalism and promising to relay everything I have to the next ghost-writer she would hire.

Anything to avoid talking to Aiden again.

My thumb hovers over the *Send* button in my email app.

The loud car horn outside breaks me out of my reverie. It's a familiar sound on these narrow, curving streets.

Doing any of the things I'm planning would be "running."

I am very good at running.

But there's a reason I agreed to this job in the first place... And I'm not a quitter. I've followed through on every single one of my memoir assignments in the past. No matter how early I had to get up to meet with the subjects, be it to train in an Olympic-sized swimming pool, dog sledding in the polar darkness, or trudging through security to reach the prison's visiting room.

Quitting because of what happened at Titan would be pathetic, and I'm so tired of being pathetic. Even if fear makes my stomach churn all through the morning.

So I get ready, put on some makeup, and slide into the beautiful Audi Q3 that I'll only be able to drive for a few more weeks.

When I arrive at Titan Media's headquarters in Culver City, the corporation's logo on the building is the only thing I see.

Funny, how in the past few weeks, I'd somehow forgotten just what company Aiden is running. Had managed to bury that knowledge deep down where it didn't bother me anymore. I'd gotten cocky. Naive. *Again.* Imagined myself safe. Fooled myself into thinking that since no one recognized me *yet*, no one ever would...

Now, the glowing *Titan Media* letters are staring me in the face.

He will see me differently after this.

Which is exactly how it should be. We should never have gotten entangled in the first place, never crossing those lines. Maybe a reminder of just what company he runs is a good thing. It'll help me keep those boundaries.

I walk through the executive floor with my keycard hung around my neck and my head held high. I'm prepared for Aiden being reserved. A bit cold, even.

He'll resent me for hiding a secret. He won't have kept his promise to me, of course. I'm sure he's now seen clips of the show online. Maybe even watched a whole episode.

Everyone does.

It's good. We'll return to the rules, and whatever *this* was between us, whatever *it* has become, it'll stop. As it had to anyway.

I roll my neck, a fighter ready to head into the ring.

Eric's sees me first, at his desk outside of Aiden's office. I have a fifteen-minute meeting scheduled with Aiden in a few, sandwiched between two of his phone meetings. I sent Aiden more chapters to review a few days ago, and he's supposed to have feedback for me today.

"Good morning," Eric tells me. His eyes linger, as if he knows, too. Of course he does. He knows everything about his boss.

I pause by his desk. "Is Mr. Hartman ready for me?"

"Yes," Eric says. He taps his pen against the desk a few times. "For what it's worth, you were my favorite during that season. And Blake is an asshole."

I blink at him. "I was?"

"By a long shot," Eric says. His voice is just as professional. His glasses today aren't red, but a bright turquoise, matching the handkerchief tucked into the pocket of his suit jacket.

"Have you known? Since the beginning?" I ask.

The door in front of me swings open, a soundless invitation into the giant corner office that belongs to Aiden. But I can't go in just yet.

"Yes," Eric says.

I incline my head toward the office. "You didn't tell him?"

"I understand wanting to keep some things hidden."

I want to hug Eric. But that would wrinkle his immaculate suit and ruin the professional relationship we have. So I just smile at him instead.

"Thank you for that. Truly."

Eric smiles and looks back at his screen. I take a deep breath before stepping into Aiden's office.

He's standing by his desk.

His eyes track me as I cross the threshold into his office

and the door closes behind me with an audible snick. Locking us in together.

I meet Aiden's gaze and work hard at keeping my face neutral and shoulders back.

"Charlotte," he says.

"Let's review some chapters," I say.

"We're not going to pretend like yesterday never happened."

"Why not? We're great at pretending things between us don't happen." My voice is confident and doesn't waver at any time. I should get a medal for that. "Rule number two, and all."

"I've never pretended," he says. "Are you feeling better?"

"I feel great."

"We don't have to meet here if it's painful for you. We can go for a drive. Or back to my house, or your rental apartment. There are options."

"You don't need to make adjustments for me," I say.

He can't be kind to me. That would truly break me.

Aiden takes a step closer. "The Titan Media gala. You had a migraine. That wasn't true, was it?"

I look past his shoulder at the view of Los Angeles. "No."

"You could have told me the truth."

"Could I?" My voice turns acerbic. It's a defense mechanism, and I hate that I'm aware of it, and still can't stop it happening. "You have been very clear with your opinion on the reality shows, and the reality TV stars, in particular."

"You're not a reality star," he says. But then he curses, shaking his head.

"Right. I am, you know. Technically speaking. As much as I hate myself for it, too."

"You shouldn't hate yourself."

I cross my arms over my chest. "We should review your chapters."

"We should talk about this."

"Because we're so good at talking about hard things?" I ask dryly. "Because we have wonderful little hearts-to-hearts?"

Aiden narrows his eyes, and he crosses his arms over his chest, too. Mirroring my stance. "I see," he says, and it sounds like he truly does. "Let me ask you something, then. When you realized I was the memoir subject you had to write about... When you realized it was Titan Media... Why didn't you back out of the contract?"

"I would have had to pay back the advance."

He shakes his head slowly. "Not good enough."

"Because I have another contract with my editor riding on this," I say. "Perform well, and I get to pitch my own non-fiction book. You know that."

His eyes are burning on mine. Like he won't let me get away with fortifying my walls, or with running. Maybe I am a fool to think he ever would.

His presence scorches, and I've become addicted to the burn.

"The real reason," he says and takes a step closer, "you didn't walk away is because you love a challenge. You love the fight, you love the adventure. You didn't walk away because you didn't *want* to."

My breathing speeds up. I hate that he sees that. Sees what my parents and best friend would call *self-destructive*, if they knew, and knows that it's a part of me. Has become in the last few years.

"Just like you working eighty-hour weeks," I say. "You don't have to. Your family is fine. Your family *name* is even fine, Aiden, if a bit tattered. I've seen how people still look up to you. Some are curious, but they don't condemn you for what your dad did." I take a step closer, too, until only a few feet separate us. "You do it because *you* like the challenge. Because it fuels you, and because you like the idea of punishing yourself. You've decided this is your cross to bear, and you would never put it down. You love it too much."

He leans in. His green eyes have darkened with something that looks like relish. "I guess," he says, "*like* recognizes *like*."

My lips press together. I don't *like* the cross I have to bear. Being recognized for the stupidest thing I've ever done.

He sees the denial in my eyes, and his lips curve without humor. He hasn't shaved today, and there are tired lines around his eyes. As if he didn't sleep well last night, either.

"How much have you hated yourself," he says, "for sleeping with me? The CEO of the company that, in your own words, has *ruined* your *life*?"

I don't answer him. I put a hand on his chest instead, meeting his gaze. "How much of my season did you watch last night?"

He leans his head down. "None of it. I only googled your old name."

"Fuck you," I say softly.

"It's the truth," he says. "I promised you. I also fired Jeff yesterday."

My lips are so close to his. "You did *what*?"

"His time with this company is over. So is Blake's, soon enough." He brushes his lips against mine, and my hand on his chest turns, fingers gripping the collar of his shirt instead.

I feel too hot. Like I'm standing next to a furnace.

"If you've been worried," I murmur, "that it might get out that your ghostwriter was once on reality TV, it's never happened in the past."

"I wasn't."

I pull him closer. "I go by my mother's maiden name now."

"It's a good name." His hands close around my waist, large and firm and trapping me entirely. "I want to hear the story from you."

"I never want to talk about it."

"Too bad," he says, voice soft. His lips trail along my cheek. "We both have to talk about things we don't like to get this memoir finished."

A shiver races down my spine. "You bastard."

"Yes," he mutters, mouth returning to mine. "Since I met you, I can't help myself. But I would never hurt you."

He presses his lips to my own. They're bruising in their intensity, and I kiss him back just as strongly. It doesn't make any sense. This never has, but it's the only thing in all of this that feels easy.

I cling to him in much the same way as I should be pushing him away. He knows about the show. Has likely seen the meme. The laughter and the comments and the—

I bite his lower lip.

Aiden chuckles against my lips, and his hands slide down to grip my ass. He's a pillar against me. Immovable. His tongue brushes over my lower lip, and I groan into his mouth. He turns us around, and then he lifts me, puts me on the edge of his desk. Something digs into my hip, and I know I'm sitting on his stuff and he doesn't seem to care about it.

Aiden tips my head back and kisses my neck. I shiver in his embrace, my knees splay so he can step in between them.

Something falls to the floor.

He chuckles against the column of my throat. "You bleached your hair blonde before," he says.

I run my nails along his scalp, and he hisses out a breath. "Yes."

"This is your natural color?"

"Mm-hmm."

He kisses across my collarbone, lowering the strap to my tank top with every touch. "I like it. It suits you."

I reach for the buttons of his shirt. I get the top two undone so I can slide my hands under the fabric, across the warm, taut skin of his upper chest. I've seen what he does in the gym to maintain this kind of body.

Aiden kisses me again. It's more forceful this time, and I fall backwards. He catches me, arms twining tightly around my waist.

"Fuck," he mutters. He's breathing hard, his hair mussed from my hands. "I want you, and this is the wrong moment." He kisses me again, hands sliding up my sides. Brushing past the swell of my breasts. I want the clothes off—*now.*

But his kisses slow into teasing, heated touches. "Let me take you out to dinner later."

I work on more of the buttons of his shirt. Something about feeling his skin is making everything clearer for me. Like I can only focus when I touch him. "Take me out?"

His hot breath washes over my ear, his hands find the hem of my shirt. He runs his large palm up my lower back. Warm, so warm against my skin. "Yes. Let me take you out tonight. Take your mind off everything. We'll do something fun."

"You have a meeting with investors."

"I'll cancel it," he says.

"Where?"

"Anywhere. I'll think of something." His fingers toy with the clasp to my bra, but he doesn't undo it. His entire arm is underneath my shirt, warm and firm against my back.

Just holding me.

"Like a date?" I regret the question as soon as it's out. It would violate rules one and two. And he's the owner of this company, and he doesn't *date* people like me. He doesn't date at all, really. But his memoirist? Who made a fool of herself on national TV? The question is naive.

A testament to how stupid I can *still* be.

But Aiden just kisses me again.

I melt under his touch, caught between his chest and his arm pressed to my bare back.

"Chaos," he says. //"If you want it to be? Then yes, it's a date."

CHAPTER 50

AIDEN

"Where are we going?" Charlotte asks. She's sitting beside me in the car, wearing a black dress and with a short jacket thrown over her bare arms.

She's beautiful.

And was waiting for me when I came home. I saw her sitting cross-legged on the sun lounger and enjoying the view of LA. The small smile on her face when she saw me...

"We're going out to dinner. It's a disgrace that I've only treated you to takeouts so far or to meals with my business associates."

She glances at me out of the corner of her eye. "You're taking me out to a restaurant?"

I put a hand on her thigh. "Yes. Don't overthink it, Chaos."

"Okay. I won't," she murmurs. "What restaurant?"

"You once said you loved Chinese."

"Really? Are we getting dim sum?"

"We're going to the best damn dim sum restaurant in the city."

The restaurant is upscale and trendy. Covers of popular songs play loud enough through the speakers that there's no doubt the crowd is young. The food is spectacular, and the place was awarded a Michelin Star last year.

I pulled some strings to get a reservation.

Charlotte smiles all through our first round of drinks. I love seeing that expression. I want to make her smile more.

I want to let her know what I'm doing to Blake. That he's being cut from every show, and will never be allowed on Titan Media's property again. That I'm taking care of her in all the ways I can think of.

But not yet.

I don't want his name here, in this small oasis of calm we've created after the turmoil of the last twenty-four hours. I never again want to see her like she was yesterday. Panicked outside my office, with the instinct to flee stamped all over her face. It rattled something in me.

Her happiness feels like the most important thing.

Her foot rests next to mine beneath the table, and she smiles down into her drink.

"What are you smiling about?" I ask.

She looks up at me through her lashes. "Nothing. I was just thinking... you remembered that I said dim sum was one of my all-time favorites."

"Of course I remembered."

"I just didn't think you would, that's all."

"I remember everything you've told me, Chaos."

She raises an eyebrow. "Everything?"

"Everything."

I move my leg closer to hers and grab a hold of my chopsticks. "After you're done with this memoir," I say. "Where will you go? To write your new book? I'm still looking forward to hearing your full pitch for it, by the way."

She looks down at her dumplings. "You're assuming I'll get the deal."

"You will. You're working on the first few chapters, and you're writing a killer memoir."

She shakes her head. "Sometimes, I think you see more in me than what's really there."

"Impossible."

"Thank you," she says, but doesn't meet my eyes. She's looking down at her dim sum.

"For what?"

"For acting like yesterday didn't happen. For not asking me about it."

I put my hand on hers. "You'll tell me when you're ready."

She nods—a tiny movement—and blows out a breath. "I'm not sure I'll ever be ready."

"You will. You're stronger than you give yourself credit for."

"You're saying that, but you haven't seen my season," she says. She cocks her head and meets my gaze again. "Can I say something? And please don't read too much into it?"

I fight to hide a smile. "Yes."

"Well, it's not *that* serious. But I've been thinking. You once said that you don't do relationships because you work too much."

I reach for my drink. "Yeah, I did say that."

"I've seen you work a lot."

"Mm-hmm. I think we both work a lot," I say. "I've seen you stay up late writing... almost every day."

"Yeah. Maybe that's a bad habit we both share."

"It definitely is."

"I don't know how I would fit a relationship in, either." She holds her glass of wine. Her third tonight, and there's something honest in the air. I put down my chopsticks. "With all the work."

"Work is important," I say.

She nods. "Yes. It is."

"That's the reason I haven't pursued anything serious in years. There hasn't been time." I reach for my glass and look at her over the rim. "But I'm starting to think that work shouldn't be the *most* important thing in my life."

"Yeah." She smiles a little. "I've been thinking about that, too."

After dinner, Charlotte leans into me as we wait for the elevator. She smells good, and I nuzzle her temple. It feels painfully easy to get used to having her beside me. To watch her chase her dreams and have her sleep in my arms.

It's the easiest thing I've ever done, surrendering to my feelings for her. At every turn where it should terrify me, I find myself... excited instead.

Falling is easy.

We're standing outside the upscale restaurant, waiting for our driver. People walk by us, line up, or head on out. A group of fashionably dressed twentysomethings get out of a car. Two women in high heels and a lone man.

One of the women locks eyes on Charlotte.

Not surprising. She's gorgeous.

But the woman's gaze lingers. She nudges her friend, and they both giggle.

"Hi," one of them says to us. She's dark-blonde with eyes rimmed with black make-up.

Charlotte is tense beside me, and I keep my hand on her waist. "Hello," I say.

"I'm so sorry to bother you both," the blonde continues. "But you look a lot like... Are you Charlotte? From *The Gamble*?"

Chaos is silent for a long beat. The two women exchange a look, and one of them giggles again. "Yes," Charlotte finally says.

"Oh my god, that's *so* cool. It's been years! What are you up to now?" She smiles like they're friends.

The other woman doesn't wait for Charlotte to reply. "No way. That song you made up, the 'Sugar Puff' one? We played it that whole summer. It's still on our nostalgia playlist"

"I didn't make up that song." Charlotte's voice is small.

The blonde pulls out her phone. "Do you mind if we take a selfie together? I *have* to tell my sister I met you. We were obsessed with your season! Like, watch-party-level obsessed."

"Do you like, get paid when your meme is used?" the guy behind the women asks. "No, right? Because that's wild."

Charlotte takes a small step back, into the curve of my body. I wrap my arm more firmly around her.

"We're just heading out." I make my voice deep and unfriendly. It's worked wonders with journalists over the years. "Enjoy the rest of your night."

They blink at me. "Oh. Right."

"If you'll excuse us," I say and lead us past them. Charlotte's steps are quick beside mine.

"That hasn't happened in… a while," she says once we're in the car.

"Are you okay?"

She nods and looks out the window. But I can sense her withdrawing into herself, pulling away from me. Tightening the hatches and bracing for a storm.

I don't want her pulling away.

Her hand rests on her lap. I reach out and thread our fingers together without saying a word. Her breath hitches, and her hand squeezes mine.

Once we're back home, she walks ahead of me into the house. Still silent.

Damn it. This wasn't the ending to the night I'd hoped for. I wanted a break from the panic attack, from Jeff and Blake, and the story she doesn't want to tell.

I shut the door behind us. "Charlotte."

She shakes her head softly and walks with quick steps toward the kitchen. I follow her at a slower pace, shoving my hands into my pockets.

They ache to reach for her.

"That hasn't happened in a while," she says again, dejection in her voice. She pours herself a glass of water and leans against the kitchen counter, hands gripping the glass to her chest.

"I'm sorry about that."

She shakes her head again. Her eyes look glossy, and *fuck*, are those unshed tears? My chest tightens with shame—potent and thick—that I've been a part of causing her this anguish.

I never wanted this.

"I'm sorry you had to see that." Her voice is thin, her hand tight around the glass of water.

"Don't apologize to me. Please."

She takes a deep breath, and her eyes move from mine to the window. It's the Charlotte I saw in the parking lot. The woman who's reeling from something she thought she'd conquered long ago.

"That was embarrassing. It doesn't usually... well. It happens. God, I'm so ashamed."

I take a step closer. The distance between us feels ocean-wide. "Chaos, stop."

Her shoulders lift in a shrug. "Mistakes truly do live forever. Especially if they're online."

"You didn't make a mistake."

"You haven't seen it yet," she whispers. "When you do, you'll know. And you'll never look at me the same way again."

CHAPTER 51
AIDEN

"Then tell me about it. Tell me your version of it. That's the only one I'm interested in." I want to hold her. But she's wrapped her arms over her chest like she's trying to keep herself together. "In your own words."

"I can't... if we're doing this..." She fills her water glass back up and walks past me to the living room and the large couches within.

I sit down next to her. "There's no rush," I say. "I'm here."

She pulls her knees up and circles her arms around them. "I had just graduated from high school when I saw the ad online. A friend sent it to me, actually. I'd already gotten into college, but I was so... excited about life, you know? Finally getting out of my hometown. I had never really traveled further than the Midwestern states. So my friend and I decided to apply together."

There's an odd strain to her voice. Like it might break at any moment. "It was going to be shot in Mexico, at a beach resort. It was going to involve games. *Games.* But that's how they sold *The Gamble.* A show with lots of young people, focused on team-building, with challenges to compete in order to make it through each episode."

Something sinks in my chest. It's painfully easy to imagine

a casting call that does just that. Letting all the superfluous details slip between the lines, counting on most people getting the drift on their own.

"No mention of dating, then."

"Some," she admits. "But I was eighteen, about to turn nineteen. Why not a few dating elements? That sounded fun. It didn't seem like that was the... *entire* premise."

"I'm sorry."

"Don't," she warns me. "Don't start apologizing or saying that you feel sorry for me, or I won't make it through the whole story. And you said you wanted to know, and I want you to hear it from me, and not... not... off the internet."

"I'll hear it from you," I say. There's a heaviness to the air, and I know without needing to consider it that this is a make-it-or-break-it moment. How I react to this is going to dictate everything between us going forward.

She curves inward, and it hurts like fucking hell to see her like this. To sit here and not close the distance between us.

"So my friend and I applied on a whim. At the time, I was also looking at volunteering overseas or becoming a camp counselor. Anything I could think of. I was just hungry, you know? For adventure.

"And then... I got the call. So I went in for an interview. I realize now that I gave all the wrong answers to make the producers think I was right for it." She sighs. "They saw someone naive, excited, young. Someone idealistic and easily manipulated. Of course they cast me. I fit into one of the... predetermined narratives.

"My friend got called in for the interview, too, but she didn't end up going to it. It was just me. And I got offered the spot.

"So, I deferred college for a year. I packed my bags with cute new bikinis. Bleached my hair to make sure it was up to the task. And then I left for Mexico." She hides her face behind her hands. "I look back on it now, and know just how stupid I was.

"I showed up and tried to make friends with the other girls. Shared way too much about myself, took the first challenge way too seriously. And... and... there was a guy there, who said all the right things."

I don't move a muscle. I don't frown, don't groan. And yet, I suspect what's coming, and can feel the adrenaline starting to pump.

"It was a dating show." She puts her hands down. "I realized that, even as naive and thick as I was. And he, well... he made it seem like that part was easy.

"We would stick together throughout the entire show. In between the shoots, in those rare moments when we didn't have the cameras around, he told me that we'd date after the show, too. That he couldn't wait to meet my parents, and we could live together out in LA."

"He didn't mean a word he said," I say slowly.

"No. Of course he didn't. But that's the thing, right? I didn't get to see all the things the viewers saw. I just saw... *him*, right? And he was this gorgeous, twenty-four-year-old Brit, saying all these wonderful things." There's an edge of bitterness in her voice. "He started calling me... God, I can't believe I'm telling you all of this..."

I can't hold back any longer. I reach across and fit my hands to her waist. "Come here."

She lets me pull her beside me. I remember hearing somewhere that talking about hard things is easier side-by-side than face-to-face. So I settle her against my side, my arm around her.

Charlotte rests her head against my shoulder. "Thanks," she says. "I didn't think this would be so hard to talk about. It was years ago."

I stroke up and down her back. "Why wouldn't it be? Time doesn't heal all wounds."

"I've been avoiding it, too." She leans her forehead against my chest and takes a deep breath. "Fine. All right. He started calling me Sugar Puff."

"Sugar Puff?"

She groans a little. "Yes. And I will kill you if you ever call me that, just for your information."

"I won't. I prefer Chaos. Or sweetheart."

"At the time, I thought it was cute. He told me that it was this fun, common endearment in England. It's some kind of cereal, or was, at least. Puffed rice."

I frown. "Oh."

"Yeah. *Oh*. But I was young, and I thought it was... I thought I was in love. We sailed through the first few challenges on the show. I saw the others getting into drama, and how some of the girls were looking at Blake, but I thought we were golden. We were in love."

I press my lips to her forehead. "I'm sorry."

"You don't know what's going to come."

"No. But I think I could guess."

"There was a producer on set." Charlotte lies back, her head resting right next to mine. She looks straight up at the ceiling. "There were many, but there was one who was assigned to me. You know, to help... *massage* my storyline. But really, to influence me."

I run a hand over my face. "Fuck. Was it Jeff?"

"It was," she says. "Production knows everything, you know. They know what all the cast is saying—but we don't. I didn't. He asked me all these questions in the confessionals. Got me to say these *silly* little fantasies on camera, about how Blake and I wanted to get married one day."

I close my eyes. "I'm sure they did."

"I was a virgin when I went on the show." Her voice wavers, just a little. But she keeps going with the force I've come to expect from her, and my hands clench into tight fists. "I was in love with Blake, of course. Or I thought I was. Now,

I think I was just... blinded. Like someone who looked at the sun. Dazzled."

"Charlotte," I murmur.

She shakes her head a little. "I have to keep going. Or I won't... The cameras were always rolling. We were promised that nothing would be salacious."

I grit my teeth. *The Gamble* is known for being deeply salacious. In the seasons since Charlotte was on, it's built a reputation for being just that.

Sure. It's never porn. But it's hints of sex, the sounds of it, movements under covers or behind opaque shower doors.

"We had to share beds, right? You know the premise. One night, he... went down on me."

I turn to look at her. She smiles faintly, but it doesn't look happy. "Yeah. *That.* Everyone spoke about it the next day, but not in front of me. I saw it later when I watched the aired episodes. And the next night, we had sex."

I feel myself going rigid. Every muscle in my body coils, entirely without my control. "Fucking Blake."

"I was into it," she says, and her voice is almost thoughtful. *Almost.* If the undercurrent of shame wasn't there, too. "I thought I was in love, and experiencing this wonderful thing... Of course, it was under the covers, but all of it was filmed."

A coldness sweeps through me. "They didn't air it."

"Of course they did. Not all of it. But enough." She looks up at the ceiling, her jaw clenched. "I don't think I'll ever live down that shame. Of knowing that my parents, my friends, people I went to high school with, teachers, and parents of friends..."

"I'm so sorry."

She closes her eyes. "The production team assured me that things would be cut. But they didn't put it on paper, of course. And I wasn't knowledgeable enough about the contracts to realize what I'd signed. They told me this would be fun and wholesome, but the whole time alcohol was flowing. I was nineteen, but we were in Mexico, you know? And Blake made it seem so fun. I got swept up in the whole thing."

"Fuck. Nothing about that is okay."

She sits up and looks away from me, to the large windows overlooking the yard. "Oh, we haven't even gotten to the worst part, yet."

CHAPTER 52

AIDEN

"The next episode they shot, things started to fall apart for me. I hadn't known, of course, but Blake was being lured by another girl. Turns out he wasn't hard to poach. And those challenges to stay in the game?" She shrugs. "The real way to stay alive was to couple up. End up getting dumped, and... well, you're off the show."

I watch her shoulders fold inwards. "That's what happened."

"Yes. And when I found out, I was so hurt." She wipes her cheek. Is she crying again? The idea makes my chest constrict. "I made a fool out of myself. I tried to mimic his accent, saying... God, have you not heard this?"

I sit up too, and brush her shoulder with my own. "No. I haven't."

"It was everywhere at the time. I should just show you the video... but I'll never live it down." She takes a deep breath. "I tried to say it in a British accent, the... *But I'm your little Sugar Puff.*' Except it was awful. I had been drinking and was clearly pretty drunk, and Blake just laughed. I had to be escorted off the set by the production team.

"That moment, though... it became legendary online. People made it into a meme. 'But I'm your Sugar Puff' was remixed into a song, and it made the rounds at the clubs that summer. It ended up charting, actually."

"What the fuck?"

She shoots me a look that's equal part wry and equal part sad. "*The Gamble* still uses the term. It's become part of the lore. I've even seen people with *Sugar Puff* T-shirts."

"Fucking hell." How could anyone have let that happen? "But when the show aired, surely people saw? You were the victim in all of it."

"Not the way the show was edited. I came out looking pretty sanctimonious in my innocence, and my attempts at making friends were chopped up and rearranged. I looked smug and petty beside Blake, and my love was entirely naive."

"You were *nineteen*."

"Yeah. Maybe it would be different if the season aired today, but it was a decade ago." Her words are wooden. "When the show aired, I finally saw *everything*. I saw Blake chatting with the other guys. Telling them he called me Sugar Puff because that's what my *tiny* tits reminded him of."

Her words are a bucket of cold water over my head. "He did *what*?"

"He did it all with a smile. The kind of fuckboy that people can't help but love, you know. Remember what I told you… about my experience with oral sex?"

"I remember," I say darkly. "He said that on TV, too?"

"Yes. He did."

I push off the couch and start pacing in front of it. My hands squeeze again into fists. I need to do *something*. Anything. But I can't, because this was ten years ago, and the pain is already there. The damage is already done.

Her shoulders slump, like she knows what's coming and is bracing for it. She doesn't look like the woman I've grown to know, and for a second, I want the floor to open up and swallow me whole. Drag me down where my own shame can drown me.

This is a fucking show that I still keep on air.

"And now you'll think of me the same way the viewers did," she says. Her voice sounds hollow. "The way everyone still does."

"Of course I won't."

"How could you not?" She buries her head in her hands, and I ache, seeing her sitting there. "I was a laughing stock. People yelled 'Sugar Puff' after me on the streets. And I knew it was because of him, because I'm flat chested. My god-awful British accent made into a soundbite, and I was reminded of it *everywhere*."

There will be time for anger later.

I sit down beside her and wrap my arms around her body. For a moment, she struggles. Sits stiff and tense. But then she sags, falling into me as if her strength has left her. Her face is still hidden behind her hands.

"I'm so embarrassed," she murmurs.

I rest my chin on the top of her head. "Don't be"

"I hate it. I hate that it's out there, I hate that the dumbest thing I've ever done is entertainment… And I *hate* that you know about it now."

"Charlotte…"

"Do you think less of me for it?" She pulls back, her voice fierce despite the question. There are tears sliding down her cheeks, and I feel like I've been stabbed, seeing them.

I wipe one of the wet trails off with my thumb, dragging the pad across her silky smooth skin. She's crying silently, but her eyes are defiant. "Of course I don't think less of you."

"Most people do."

"Most people are fucking idiots," I say.

She blinks twice, rapidly. "It was such a stupid thing of me to have done."

"You were young."

"Other young people go to war or… or… release amazing music. I did this." More tears track down her face, and I pull her tightly against me. We end up in the middle of the couch, with her lying on my chest and my arms wrapped around her.

I feel the wetness of her tears through my shirt. "I'm sorry," I mutter against her temple. "I'm going to make it right."

"It's not your fault," she whispers.

"Yes, it is." I kiss away the saltiness of her tears. "That show should never have aired."

"The editing made me look like such an idiot. And Blake? He came out on top."

"I know."

"There was so much more that wasn't shown, you know?" She presses her forehead to my collarbone, her hands still fist the fabric of my shirt. "I got the villain edit, the bad edit, whatever you want to call it."

"You couldn't have known," I say. "Don't beat yourself up for decisions you made at nineteen."

She pushes up on her elbow, and her tear-stained eyes are lit with fire. "How can I not? It's all that will ever come up when people search for my name. Even if I get my editor to approve my plans for the book, even if I somehow get it published… This will always haunt me. And I could have avoided all of it if I had just been *smarter*."

I sweep back a tendril of her hair. The frustration in her gaze spears me, and I know I'm unworthy of holding her. Of being the man she chooses to spend her nights with when I'm responsible for the pain she's living with.

"You *are* smart," I tell her. "You're funny, witty, and well-read. You're a beautiful writer. And you have a past that makes you interesting and complicated. I know how it's like to live with regrets. But Chaos, who makes it through life without a single one?"

"People smarter than me," she murmurs. Her hand glides to my neck, and her short nails scrape the scruff under my jaw.

"If you're going to be mad at anyone," I say, "it should be me. Not yourself."

She traces a finger down my Adam's apple. "I know," she murmurs. "But that's getting harder and harder to do."

SOCIAL MEDIA

Ten years ago

@PurpleGirl3000: OMG, that scene was hilarious. I was waiting for her to figure out she wasn't all that. The way Sugar Puff was lording her relationship over the others. As if Blake was a catch!

@ Caffeinated4ever: Is it bad that my boyfriend and I have started calling each other Sugar Puff now? It started as a joke but now we legit can't stop. Embarrassing LOL.

@T-Rexoperator: I'm SO glad Sugar P is gone. The high horse she was on was getting old! Becky knows how to have fun. Glad she and Blake finally coupled up.

@Inkedvoyage: HAHAHA, I can't stop laughing. That British accent was SO BAD. Wouldn't want to be her today. Or tomorrow, to be honest.

CHAPTER 53
CHARLOTTE

The too-big house is empty when I wake up the next morning. My steps echo on the hardwood floors, and I lean against his kitchen island as I drink my morning coffee, watching the city beyond the floor-to-ceiling windows.

He slept in my bed with me last night. Just slept. Held me even after my tears dried. He was gone when I woke up, but left me a note on my bedside table. *Take the day off.*

I read the note several times, lingering over each word in his sprawling handwriting. Then I crumbled it into a ball and threw it into my waste paper basket.

The past is easy to forget until it comes rearing its head again. And it did last night, right *in front* of him. Embarrassment still makes my head feel heavy.

I'm so stupid.

He knows now, and it doesn't seem like he's judging me... or he hides it very well. Maybe that's it. We only have two weeks left until the first draft is due. Two weeks until I have to send it to Aiden and get his thoughts on it. And then it's time for me to pack up my things and leave. Like with all of my ghostwriting gigs.

Maybe he's counting on that to be the natural end to things between us.

That's the nature of my job, after all. I stay for a few months, maybe half a year. Move on when the book is done. Add it to the others in my repertoire and then reinvent myself somewhere new.

Never stay long enough for people to figure out my past.

I failed this time.

I work outside again. I should be finishing his chapters, but instead, I'm writing the pitch I've been dabbling on for so long. Pages pour out of me. They're rough. I still need to do research and talk to experts, but the words suddenly flow for the first time.

It feels too personal, though. I sit back after lunch, looking over what I've written, and wonder if it's anything I could ever share with the world.

The city is bathed in bright, beckoning sunshine. I feel antsy. Like I can't sit still, can't stay here. I want to get into the car and drive into the hills. Maybe I should take a hike. Maybe I should go to the observatory again. Or that spot high up on Mulholland that Aiden loves.

He mentioned we could go to see his childhood home.

I call him.

He answers on the second ring. "Everything all right?"

"Yeah. I'm sorry to bother you."

"You're not."

I tuck my phone against my shoulder and pull up Aiden's schedule on my computer, the one Eric gave me access to all those weeks ago. "Are you free this afternoon? We could drive out to your family house. I feel like... I don't know. Going somewhere. Moving."

There's a brief pause, and then a muffled sound across the line. I hear his voice. Faint, but audible. *"I'll need to sit this one out. Continue without me."*

"Aiden?" I ask. "Are you in a meeting?"

"Not anymore," he says.

"You didn't just walk out of one."

"Okay. I won't tell you that I did." There's a smile in his voice. "I'll come pick you up. Half an hour okay?"

His calendar finally loads. There are meetings booked throughout the entire afternoon. "Yes, but... you're busy! I just saw your schedule."

"Nothing that can't be moved."

"Eric is going to kill you. Or me, actually," I say.

Aiden scoffs. "Nonsense. He loves you. We can stay overnight at the house, if you want. Watch the sunset."

"Okay. I'll pack a bag." I'm already closing my laptop. It'll be a short trip, but it means being on the road again. Seeing new things. For years, that's been the best way to soothe my anxiety.

Aiden picks me up right on time. His stubble is thicker today. Did he not shave this morning? Maybe he lingered in bed with me longer than he usually does. The thought makes my stomach flip over.

His hand slides up beneath my skirt, gripping my knee. "How are you?"

"Good. I've been working."

He hums. "No regrets after last night?"

I look out the window. "For telling you everything?"

"Yes."

"Maybe. I haven't really decided how I feel about it."

He chuckles, and it amazes me again, how easy everything is with him. "All right. Well, let me know when you do."

And that's that. Without saying a word, I somehow know we won't talk about it again until I'm ready.

"Tell me about the house."

"It's by the ocean in Malibu. Dad lost it in the divorce, and my mom doesn't want to stay there much. She mostly stays at her place up in Sonoma. She loves it there, and it gets her far away from the social circles down here."

We pass tall palm trees lining the residential streets and

the beautiful greenery flanking Canyon Road, and eventually, the ocean starts to peak on the horizon. Aiden has the radio on and his hand on my knee. I feel the sun and hum along to the notes of a song, leaving the receding city and all the obligations that come with it behind.

And the complications that exist between us.

They also fade away into the distance.

Aiden pulls up to a large wrought iron metal gate. It's anchored to a stone wall so high, I can't see what's behind it.

I peer out. "*This* is where you grew up?"

"Yes." There's a smile in his voice. He taps in a code, and the gate swings open for us, revealing a curved stone driveway. The large house is white with blue shutters on the windows. Beachy, huge, and nestled right by the beach.

He parks, and I exit the car just to marvel at the place.

"How," I breathe when he joins me, "could you ever leave this place? Your mom's house in Sonoma must be insane to beat this."

He wraps his arm around my waist and kisses my temple. "Come on. The back is the best part."

He's not lying. The porch opens up to a large deck, a terraced backyard, and then nothing but the beach and the deep blue ocean.

I set down my bag with a dull thump. "Oh my god."

Aiden changed his suit for a pair of navy slacks and a short-sleeved T-shirt, with a pair of square sunglasses on his face.

He looks painfully handsome. Athletic and like *himself*, the version he is when no none is looking. With the sun on his face and broad shoulders, he's ready to move.

"Chaos," he says and holds out a hand in my direction. "Let's get in the water."

"In the water?"

His smile widens. "Let me show you how to surf."

The air is warm, the water cold. It's a beautiful day on the waves, and I can't believe he has access to this. That he could do this every day if he wanted to.

Judging from the content look on his face, I bet he'd like to, as well.

I've surfed only once before and was terrible at it. I'm not great now either, but Aiden doesn't seem to mind. I borrow a spare wetsuit, and we stick closer to shore than the professional surfers riding the bigger waves further out.

"Why don't you do this every day?" I ask him.

A wave crashes over us. The water sparkles, and I taste salt on my tongue. I grin at him, and he grins back.

"What did you say?" he calls.

"Why don't you do this every day?!"

He laughs. "I honestly don't know, Chaos. I don't know."

I manage to get up on the board twice. He hollers at me both times, and I fall laughing into the surf at the end, adrenaline rushing through me.

"That was incredible!"

He grins at me. "You looked like a pro."

"Now you're lying."

He wraps his hands around my waist, under the water. "You looked *good*, Chaos. Happy. We should do more things like this. Fuck the office."

I kiss him. "Fuck the office."

He grins and turns his face up to the sky. "Fuck the world!"

Later, he wraps me in a towel and tucks me against his side on the wide Malibu porch, where I lean against his bare chest, with the sun bathing us in its warmth. I'm still in my bikini. It's dried by now, and my skin is salty.

He's humming with infectious energy—his touches are light and his lips are always against me. My hair, my temple, my cheek. I turn and wrap my arms around his waist. Press my lips to his still-unshaven jaw and whisper what I've felt since we left the hills of Bel Air.

"I don't want to go back to the city."

He presses me tighter against him, hip to hip, chest to chest. "Then we won't," he says simply.

I know it's not true, but I close my eyes and pretend it is.

Pretend that this can last forever.

"I have something to tell you," he says, and just like that, the moment is broken. "And something I need to apologize for."

CHAPTER 54

AIDEN

She stiffens in my arms.

In the distance, the sun has started to set, lighting up the sky in a glory of colors. I need to say this. Even if it breaks the bubble we're in. I need her to know.

"Aiden…"

"Jeff was fired. I told you that." I press a kiss to her temple. "I've spent a good deal of this morning in meetings. Blake won't work for us anymore."

She sits up straighter, her eyes flying to mine. "What?"

"He's fired, effective immediately. The season of *Expedition Island* he's on will still air. I can't get around that. But after that, he won't appear in another Titan Media production for as long as he lives."

She shakes her head slowly. "You're really doing that?"

"Yes. You don't mind?" I watch her face carefully. "You don't still… care?"

"Care about him? Of course not." She lets out a breath. "Wow. Thank you for doing that. It feels terrible, to thank you for making two people unemployed, but…"

"Don't feel bad," I say. "It was my decision. I'll take on that burden. It's not yours to carry, not after what they both did to you."

She exhales again and something softens between her eyebrows. "Okay. Thank you, Aiden."

"I also had a meeting with my financial advisers and accountants." I reach out and brush back some of her still-damp, salt-stiffened hair. "You didn't make enough money from *The Gamble*."

Her gaze turns cautious. "What do you mean?"

"The things you told me. The song? The T-shirts?" My voice rises, and I force it back under control. "You should have gotten paid for that."

"I don't want any money from that show."

"People exploited you and what happened to you, and you got nothing from it. The DJ, with the song?" I shake my head, anger making it hard to stay calm. "You're owed royalties. It was your voice they remixed into that music."

Pink highlights her cheeks. There are more freckles over the bridge of her nose, a testament to the sun we've been out in today. She's so beautiful like this. Bathed in the fading light, with her hair windblown and wild around her.

"It's been years," she whispers.

"Still, it wasn't right. Let me handle that part of it. Please, Charlotte. Let my lawyers look into it. You deserve more than what you got."

She's quiet for a long moment, and I see the rise and fall of her chest. But then she nods. "Okay. I... okay. Thank you. No one's ever thought about that. Except me, at the time. Now... Well, I believed it was a losing battle."

"It's not. I'll fight it for you, sweetheart." And I won't stop. I'm already in contact with a journalist, too, and I've fed her a story idea. To look into just how problematic some reality shows can be. I want to discredit Blake publicly.

I don't just want to fire him. I never want him to be hired by another TV network, either.

She blinks rapidly a few times, and then she falls onto my chest with a big sigh.

I wrap my arms around her. "Hey, what's the matter?"

"Why are you so nice to me," she mumbles against my neck.

I chuckle. "What do you mean?"

"You're making it very, very hard to stick to rule number one."

"Yeah. Won't apologize for that, Chaos."

She leans back and smiles at me. I smile at her in return.

"Is there a clear view of this patio from the beach?"

"Not if we move back a bit, no. Only the whales and the dolphins could possibly see us."

She brushes her lips over mine. "Good."

Charlotte kisses me, and I groan at the excitement of her touch. She's sweet. I won't use that word again, but there's no denying that she's sugar. Addictive and glorious. I grip her tightly and pull her onto my lap.

It's easy, so easy, to untie the strings at her neck. Her bikini cups fall down, and I run my thumb over the hard peak of her pink, pert nipple. We make out until she's boneless in my arms, her hands searching between our bodies to reach down to my hardness.

But maybe... it's time for me to make it up to her in a different way. To apologize properly.

I pull her up off the sun lounger and lead her toward the house. I turn us, and gently push her back so her back's to the wall.

She giggles, and fuck, I love that sound.

"What are you doing?"

"I want you to have a nice view." I start at her neck, kissing down to her tits. They're perfect.

I tell her that.

She shakes her head a little. "You don't have to say that. Now that you know..."

I take her hands and pin them over her head. "Chaos," I

tell her. "I was obsessed with your tits before I knew of the nickname. You know that."

Charlotte smiles a little. *Yeah. She knows.*

But I need her to believe it. "I've taken tequila shots off them, and it was because I wanted to. I'm *still* obsessed with them. Always will be. They're the perfect size for me to suck."

Her lips part. "Oh. Right."

I kiss across her jaw, neck, and down to find her nipples. They're perfectly pink, the crowning glory on top of her slight mounds. I slowly release her hands and let my own glide along her sides. Over her waist, her hips, as I continue to suck.

Her breathing speeds up. It catches when I bite down on a nipple, and I smile around the peak.

When her nipples are more ruby than pink from my touch, I drop to my knees in front of her. I kiss her stomach. She tastes like warm skin, and faintly of sea salt.

"I'm sorry, Charlotte." I slide my hands up her bare thighs, gripping her firmly. "I'm sorry about all of it."

"Aiden," she breathes. "What are you doing?"

I kiss her knee. The inside of her left thigh. "I'm so sorry. Let me show you just how sorry I am."

"You weren't responsible for the show." Her fingers tunnel into my hair, and I fucking love it when she grips me like that.

"I profited off your pain, and I'd gladly spend a lifetime trying to make that up to you." I kiss further up the sweet, soft skin of her thigh, moving my lips toward her bikini bottoms. "Starting with this, sweetheart. At your pace. Let me spend an hour on my knees and kiss you here. Let me convince you every fucking thing he said was wrong."

"Aiden," she whispers.

I use my left hand to stroke her softly through the fabric. My mouth is at her hip. "You can trust me. And you're in control."

Her other hand grips my shoulder, and I see her contemplating it, see the thirst for adventure and fear warring within her. "I might not enjoy it," she says. "Maybe there's just something—"

"There is nothing wrong with you. Say the word, and I'll stop. We don't have to do it if you don't want to try. But if it's because you're thinking about *him* and his stupid fucking words, I want to banish him."

Her breaths are coming fast. She wants this. I know she does, and I know it excites her, but scares her, too. And I want to help her overcome this anxiety. The idea that she doesn't taste good? That doing this to her won't be the best fucking experience of my life?

Outrageous.

"Okay," she says. Her eyes are alight. "I want to try it with you. But…"

"You say the word, and I'll stop," I repeat. "We can use your vibrator, too. Just let me convince you there is not a single thing wrong with you."

Her teeth dig into her lower lip. "I want to shower first."

"Sure. But you don't have to, not for my sake. And we were just in the ocean."

"I think I need it. For my own peace of mind."

"Anything you need, Chaos." I kiss her hip again and then rise to my full height. Charlotte walks ahead of me in nothing but her red bikini bottoms and that top that's tied only around her rib cage.

I follow her into the shower.

If she's surprised, it melts away as soon as I take her into my arms. "If you're clean, I'm clean," I tell her.

She's nervous.

But the nerves dissolve under the hot spray. I stroke her skin. Her arms, her lower back, shoulders, and legs. Let my fingers brush over her clit a few times. I kiss her beneath the cascading water until I'm so hard, it's inconvenient. My cock trapped between our naked bodies.

She giggles and gives my erection a tug. "Sure you want to go down on *me*?"

"Yes. I'm damn sure. This is an indication of *just* how much I want to."

Neither of us fully dries off. I throw on a pair of sweatpants, just to keep myself at bay.

She stands in front of me in a white towel, wrapped tightly around her frame. Her hair is wet, draped on her shoulders, and she smells faintly like soap.

I recognize her expression. It's one of determination, like I've seen on her so many times before.

"Come here," I say.

She takes a deep breath and steps forward, a flush cresting her cheeks. From the hot water or the kisses, I don't know.

"I'm turned on." She says it like it's a surprise.

I smile. "That's good, sweetheart. Wanna lie down? Wanna stand?"

She hesitates at the foot of the large bed, but finally sits on the edge and lies down on her back. The fluffy towel is still wrapped tightly around her.

"I think here." She spreads her arms out, touching the soft covers of the bed. "It's comfortable."

I look through the weekend bag I'd quickly packed. A few of the vibrators she has are in there. I grab two, a smaller one and its larger cousin, and put them in the pocket of my sweats.

I start at her thighs, slowly moving upward. Gradually, inch by inch, I fold the towel up. It spreads like the petals of a flower, revealing her stomach, her slender hips. The delicate pink folds between her legs.

I kiss her inner thighs, across her hip bones. Blow warm air across her pussy. The need to taste her is so overwhelming, it's making my cock ache again. But I don't rush this. I won't.

"Aiden," she whispers again. I could listen to her saying my name forever. It plays like a melody in my head.

I use my hands first. I brush the pads of my fingers up and down her seam, her legs still closed. I find her clit and circle it softly through the hood.

She watches me, her breathing quick. Seems like the anticipation is getting to her just as much as it is to me.

I part her thighs. "Bend them for me, sweetheart."

She spreads open easily, trustingly, before throwing an arm over her face. "I can't believe I'm doing this."

She's beautiful. All pink skin that glistens lightly in the overhead light.

She's wet.

I lean closer, kissing her inner thigh, pausing at the crease where her leg meets her pussy.

"Trust me," I tell her. "You smell so good, and you look perfect. Have I told you how pretty your pussy is?"

Her reply is muffled. "No."

I chuckle, my breath warming her already hot flesh. "Well, it is. You are. Prettiest fucking pussy I've ever seen. And I'm going to enjoy this." I bend and touch my lips to her. I kiss across her folds, the hood of her clit. The seam and just barely over her entrance. Soft, open-mouthed kisses. All the while, I stroke across her smooth skin. Her hips, her stomach, her thighs.

Her body slowly relaxes under my touch.

"Oh," she whispers. "That feels... okay."

I smile against her thigh. "Okay?"

"It feels better than I thought it would."

I grin. "A good start, but I can get that up a bit higher."

"You sure I taste all right?"

"You taste incredible. I could do this for hours."

I reach for the slim pocket vibrator. We've played around with it a lot, and I know she likes its vibrations. It won't hurt to keep things familiar for the first time she's let a man eat her out in ten years.

It's a fucking honor.

Charlotte's clit is swelling up. I let my tongue trace the outlines of it and hear her hitched breathing. "That was... better than okay."

I do it over and over again before brushing the head of the vibrator through her folds. Getting it wet before fitting it to her entrance.

"Aiden?" she asks.

"Trust me," I say.

CHAPTER 55

CHARLOTTE

The vibrations are low and pulsing, and he slowly pushes the slim vibrator inside me. I squirm beneath it, the pleasure increasing yet another notch.

"Oh."

"Feel good?"

"Yeah. Yeah… it does."

His damp hair tickles my inner thighs, and he dips to run a tongue along my folds. He does that several times, and I try to just relax, to feel nothing but pleasure. To focus only on being here.

With him.

It's like he can hear my inner thoughts. "You're perfect," he says against my clit. "There's not a single thing wrong with you."

My hand rakes his hair. "You can't know that."

He looks up, and there's pure confidence in those green eyes. The man I know well, one who gives orders, runs a company, and bought me a car. "I know."

This is Aiden. This is the man who has never given me any reason to distrust his desire for me. He wears it on his sleeve.

"Okay. I trust you."

"Relax," he whispers against my skin. His tongue does that thing again, skirting along my clit, and pleasure rushes through me. "Can you do that for me? Just focus on relaxing. I'm here with you, and I think you're so fucking pretty. Do you believe me?"

"Yes," I whisper.

"When I walked into that hotel room and saw you naked? It felt like a punch to the gut." He kisses my inner thigh again, giving me a break. "People say there's beauty in chaos, but sweetheart, those people have never seen you like you are right now. Spread out naked and wet in front of me. They're right, though." He kisses my clit. "Chaos is beauty."

This time, he leaves his mouth there. Kissing right over the sensitive nub.

It's *Aiden*. He's the one doing this, and the past is the past. I'm safe here, in this room. No cameras. No recorders. Just him.

I'm breathing too shallow and my head feels light.

He closes his mouth around my clit and strokes his tongue over it. Strong sweeps that feel good. Surprisingly good.

"That's it," he murmurs. "God, you're so sweet on my tongue."

But he continues, his hands sliding up my thighs to help spread me wider. It's so indecent it makes my heart clench. He kisses me there, too, lavishing his tongue and lips over my folds. I think he nudges the vibrator, and the stretch, the vibrations...

Pleasure pools like slow-dripping honey through my limbs.

Electricity sparks from his touches. The light, feathery touches, and then the firm press of his tongue against my clit.

I close my eyes. I can't handle seeing him there, between my spread thighs.

It feels scary. My toes are pointed, calves tense. But I also feel good. Better and better, like for every minute I relax, more desire sneaks into my veins.

"You're so pretty," Aiden murmurs. He kisses my inner thigh and looks up at me, giving me a break from the pressure. "Status?"

I smile faintly. "I'm enjoying myself. It feels good."

"What do you like the most?"

"When you sucked on… my clit."

A smile flashes across his face, and he nods. "Okay. Noted."

He bends his neck again and closes his lips fully around my clit. A jolt of energy surges through me, and I moan despite myself. He chuckles, and the reverberations make the same thing happen again.

Oh.

With my fingers tugging on his hair, I just surrender to the feeling of his lips on me. He's so good at using his tongue, the addition of his hands, the vibrator at the same time as he suckles on my clit…

And he's told me he enjoys this. He's licking so steadily between my legs that I know it's the truth, too. There's no obligation in the way Aiden touches me.

The sensations are deliciously nice for a long time, and then I'm suddenly on fire. I'm so close to coming that I even surprise myself.

"Aiden," I pant. My grip on his hair tightens. "I'm not sure, but I think—"

He flicks his tongue back and forth over my clit, and the orgasm consumes me. It forces me to arch off the bed, and I clamp my thighs hard on either side of his head.

Aiden doesn't stop touching me throughout the whole thing. His tongue softens, the press of his lips turns to kisses, but he doesn't stop.

I lie, wrung-out and limp, with Aiden Hartman feathering

lazy kisses between my legs. A shiver races through me when he touches a particularly sensitive spot.

"Perfection," he murmurs, kissing my folds again. "You're so good, Chaos... so sweet." He lifts himself onto his elbow. "And you thought there was something wrong with you."

I smile at him. "Let's never go back to the city."

"We can stay here for tonight." He kisses my thigh, his eyes still on mine. "And I can do this again."

————

Much later, I'm lying in his arms in the large guest bed. His hand strokes up and down my back, his touch slow and sweeping. I feel pleasure-drunk, tired, and happy.

"So, you weren't here that often?"

"After the age of seventeen, no." His left hand is on my thigh, moving up and down. Warm and big. "Summer vacations, sometimes. Winter breaks. Holidays."

"Did you miss coming here?"

"Sometimes." His voice is a bit raspy, his eyelids low. "But my parents fought a lot. They were really good at it. Either fighting or being so icy you couldn't be in the same room as them. This place wasn't always so fun."

"I'm sorry your parents weren't... better."

"Yeah. So am I. My mother isn't a bad person, she's just mindless sometimes. You know? Neglectful. She focused on other things than her kids."

"She moved away after the scandal."

"Sure did," he says. "Mandy and I are the only ones who've stayed in the city. Even Dad isn't in it anymore." Aiden chuckles, a dry sound. "He always used to talk shit about Fresno and now it's his home. There's some irony in that."

"I'm sorry."

"Don't be sorry for me, Chaos," Aiden says. He bends forward and catches my mouth with his. We've been trading so many kisses today that my lips feel swollen, and I'm in no way ready for it to stop. "I have everything I want right now."

I want to drown in him.

Snuggling closer to his chest, I close my eyes. "I have a non-sequitur."

"Shoot."

"Do you want kids?"

His hand resumes sweeping up and down my back. "That's right. We haven't spoken about that, yet. Important for the memoir."

"Absolutely crucial," I murmur.

"I think I want kids. Yes. But if I have them, I can't... I *won't* work as much as I do now. I want Titan to be better positioned by then. So I'm needed less."

"Uh-huh. That's smart."

"Do you want kids?"

I turn to look at his jawline. "I'm not sure. I used to really want them. But now, for the past decade... I haven't let myself think about that."

Kids would mean settling down somewhere. Staying in one place. The cat on the armchair and the annual gym membership. A stable group of friends. A house and a family car. Maybe a garage.

And a man to raise them with.

"You've got time to figure it out," he says.

"I'm almost thirty."

"You've got time," he repeats and presses his lips to my temple. "You're already figuring out loads of things."

"Oh. Am I?"

"Yes. Like there being not a single thing wrong with you, or your ability to enjoy things." He kisses me again. "You've told me before that you like to play roles."

"Roles? Yes."

"When you move from one ghostwriting gig to another. What role have you been playing here in LA? With me?"

I pause, my hand on his chest. The question catches me off guard. "I'm not sure," I finally say. "It's been one of the harder ones."

"Oh?"

"Yes. I've tried to play Charlotte of the Big City. Confident. Charismatic. Not taking any of your shit." I smile. "But, sometimes, I lose my focus, and I think I'm just... me."

Aiden's eyes grow soft. "I like that version best," he says. "The one that's just you."

"You know what? Maybe, I'm starting to, as well."

CHAPTER 56
CHARLOTTE

It's Thursday evening, two days after we got back from his Malibu house, and I'm sitting on the couch in his TV room.

It's 9 p.m. and we've just finished having takeout while watching another episode of *Friends*. Aiden is lounging beside me in a pair of gray sweats and a T-shirt, with my laptop open on his lap.

I play with the hem of the oversized blue T-shirt I'm wearing. It's his. I'd thrown it on along with a pair of pajama shorts after showering in his giant en suite bathroom. That was after he'd gotten home from work and we had fast, hot sex in his bed.

I'm getting very used to this intimacy. Every day, still, since we started having sex again.

"What do you think?" I ask.

Aiden smiles, eyes still on the screen. "I'm still on the first page."

"Your poker face is too good."

"It's interesting," he says. "It's very interesting."

I roll my eyes and fall back on the couch. "That's a *terrible* word. It could mean anything."

"Shhh," he says gently. "I'm reading."

I have bugs crawling under my skin. The pitch is something I've worked on for days, in between finalizing most of the chapters for Aiden's memoir. My plan is to get the pitch to Vera in a few weeks. If it's good enough.

If I think I can go through with actually writing it. Which is still a big *if*. Right now, I can't imagine putting it out into the world, but... maybe I can find the courage.

My phone rings. It jolts me off the couch and toward where it's lying on the end table. Next to empty boxes of Chinese.

"Shit."

"Who is it?" Aiden asks. He's still sprawled on the couch.

I rise and race down the hall to my bedroom. "My parents! I forgot we arranged to have a call tonight."

There's silence from the couch. I sit down on my bed and hit the answer button on my phone. And shit, I should have closed the door so Aiden won't be bothered.

My parents' faces fill the screen. They're a bit too close to the lens, Mom's reading glasses take up half the image. Dad's looking concerned. But then my camera must have finally connected, because they both smile.

"Honey!" Mom says.

"You're looking tan."

"You're not forgetting sunscreen, are you?"

"No, no, I'm wearing it every day." I smile at them. "How are you guys?"

They tell me about life in Elmhurst and fill me in on Dad's ongoing feud with their neighbor. This time, it's about the placement of a fence.

"Riveting," I say after a few minutes.

Mom laughs and nudges Dad. He rolls his eyes. "It's about common decency, which is in sharp decline these days."

"You sound like one of those *it was better in the good old days* geezers," I tell him with a smile. Every time we chat, I'm reminded of how much I miss them. They're closing in on retirement age, and I know they have plans to travel. I can't wait to see them flourish.

"No, I know that's factually incorrect," Dad says. "But it's true that fifteen years ago, Dave would never have pulled this fence stunt. He knew better—"

"John," my mom says with a laugh. "I love you, but I wanna hear what Charlie's been up to. How are you, sweetheart?" She leans closer to the screen. "You're somewhere else. Doesn't look like your apartment."

Panic races through me, and I remember that I'm wearing his shirt. Aiden's shirt.

"Yes, I'm not home," I say. My voice comes out perfectly calm and placid. I hope. It takes effort not to glance past my phone to the hallway. Is Aiden still on the couch, just steps away? He'd hear all of this if he is.

Mom wiggles her eyebrows. "Oh? Have you met someone nice in Los Angeles?"

The moment hangs in the air. I could go either way. Tell them I'm living in the house belonging to the memoir subject, or admit I'm staying over at a friends.

The first option dances on my tongue.

But it's only a matter of time before they'll learn just *who* I'm writing the memoir about. They're not going to like it. And even less when they realize I've stayed in his home.

For a split second, I want to hang up the phone.

"Yes," I say instead. "I have met someone. But it's still very new."

Mom beams a wide smile and leans in, nearly pushing Dad off the screen. "Really? Tell me more, honey."

"Is he a big, famous actor?" Dad asks out of view. "Is he in any of the movies I know?"

"No, but I did meet Logan Edwards the other day."

Mom draws in a breath. "You did?"

"Who's that?" Dad asks.

She nudges him. "The young boy who was so good in that space movie we saw after Christmas."

"Oh. Right." It's clear Dad has no clue who she's talking about.

"Anyway, honey. Who's the man?"

"He works here in Los Angeles," I say and pick at the hem of my T-shirt off-screen.

"In the entertainment industry?" Mom's face is equal part hopeful and equal part cautious.

I know what they want to hear.

"Not really. More on the corporate side of it." I shrug. "Anyway, it's still very, very new."

"LA is far, but it's not that bad," Dad says. "Have you asked your boyfriend if he'd be willing to move to Elmhurst?"

I laugh. "No, and I'm not planning to."

"Shoot."

We all know that I'm not comfortable in that town anymore. Not with everyone knowing what happened. The community is small, and my parents have been living with my shame there for nearly a decade.

But we like to pretend as if it never happened.

We've become good at it, the three of us. We had to.

"Do you think you'd want to come home? After your deadline?" Mom asks in a gentle voice. "It's Grandma's birthday, and we're inviting all your cousins, too."

"You don't have to answer now," Dad says. "Think about it."

"Maybe. Will you text me the date of the party?" I ask.

Mom smiles, but it doesn't quite reach her eyes. Like she already suspects I'm only asking to humor her, certain I won't come. It feels like a knife wound, that look. To know that I'm *still* disappointing them.

"Absolutely."

"Honey," Dad says. "We still don't know the name of the person you're writing the book about!"

"You know I've signed NDAs."

"Yes, but come on. We'll find out in a few months anyway, and we won't tell anyone," Dad says. "Is it someone I know?"

"Dad, you don't *know* anyone."

"That's not true. I know the guy who played Rocky. And the one who played Han Solo!"

"What are their names?"

He struggles for a few seconds, and Mom and I both laugh. "Okay, fine. Maybe I know their character names better," he admits.

"I'll tell you later," I say.

It's just a conversation I've been dreading for weeks.

"What about your boyfriend?" Mom asks. "How is he treating you? Is he nice?"

"Yes, tell us more about him," Dad says. "He hasn't asked you to sign an NDA, too, has he?"

I run a hand over the back of my neck. "No, not exactly."

The distance from my bedroom to the large couch in the TV room feels painfully small. There's no way Aiden isn't hearing this.

"So? What else?"

"He's a good guy," I say, my cheeks burning. "Funny. Has a good job. Works hard. I actually tried surfing thanks to him. But, like I said, it's still early. We're not really boyfriend-girlfriend."

"I see," Mom says with a knowing nod. "He sounds fantastic. And he's treating you well?"

"Yes, and you already asked that."

"It's worth double-checking," she says. "We care about you, honey."

I know they do.

And I know they don't entirely trust my judgment. *To this day.* Even though it's been years and years since *The Gamble*.

We chat for a few more minutes before I excuse myself and hang up. The silence in my room feels absolute, and I take a deep, calming breath before forcing myself off the bed.

Aiden is standing in the doorway. He's leaning against one of the jambs, hands in the pockets of his sweats. He takes up all the space in the threshold.

I grimace. "How much of that did you hear?"

His face is carefully neutral. "How much are you comfortable with me having heard?"

"I'm sorry about the boyfriend thing. I had to give them something, but I know we're not... that we're..."

He lifts an eyebrow. "That we're what?"

"You know," I say and wave between us. "That we're this."

"Right. And what do you think that *this* is, exactly?"

"Aiden," I say.

He takes a step into the room. "Your number one rule is for *this* not to be serious. That neither of us are allowed to want *this* to continue."

The blush had been there during my call with my parents, but now it singes my cheeks. "Yeah. I did say that."

"I won't hold you to it," he says. "You know that, right?"

I blink a few times. "You mean you... wouldn't mind? If I theoretically called you... that... again?"

"Your boyfriend?" A smile plays at the corner of his mouth. "I wouldn't, no. But we're not in a rush, either. I think you've felt that in the past. The rush. So we won't add any here."

"I have to hand in your memoir in a week."

"Yeah. But life will continue after that. You can stay here. Work on your book proposal, which is fucking fantastic."

"You think? Really?"

He nods. "It's spot-on for the time. You should use yourself, too, sweetheart. And your story."

I dig my teeth into my bottom lip, and then slowly shake my head. "I can't. I don't want to be back in the media, ever."

"Your story deserves to be told. Properly. The way you told it to me."

"Maybe. But I can't do it."

A furrow appears between his eyebrows. "Your parents don't know who you're writing a memoir about."

"No. I signed an NDA."

"Chaos, break it. Break it if you want to tell them." He sits down beside me on the bed. There's something measured about his movements. "Are you worried what they'll say when they realize *who* you're writing about?"

"They won't like it," I admit.

His frown deepens. "Fuck."

I shrug. "You weren't responsible for the show. I realize that now. And I think, in time, I can get them to see that, too. Maybe. But they hold a bigger grudge on my behalf than I do for myself. There will be… reactions."

"Do you want me there when you tell them?"

My gaze flies to his. "You'd do that? Why?"

"If I'm there, they can take their anger out on me," he says.

"I don't want you and my parents to get into a fight."

"I won't fight back." Lifting his head, he points his chin toward me. "I'll give your dad a free pass to clock me. Right here."

The stupidity of that makes me chuckle. "Thank you. But it's me they're going to… question. I should tell them, though. Better they hear it from me than when your book is released." I sigh. "I'll call them tomorrow and have the conversation with them."

"Okay," he says, his smile slowly fading. "But I don't like the idea of you getting any flack for something that you didn't even know about. You had no idea I was the subject when you signed the contract."

"If it'll make you feel better, I'll tell them about that."

"Please do." He pulls me to his chest, and the warmth is more calming than any words could be. "I do want to meet them, though," he says. "Someday."

My eyes widen. "You do?"

"Yes. They're important to you, so they're important to me. And I can be very charming, Chaos. I charmed you."

"Yes, but I feel like that's somehow in a *different* way than you want with my parents?"

He chuckles against my temple, just like I'd hoped. "Slightly, yes. But I want you to know, I'll be there if you need me, or if they want answers from me about the show. My face is available for punching."

A smile tugs on my lips. "I'll bear that in mind."

"Good. We can circle back to this next Tuesday."

My smile widens. "Add it to the agenda?"

"Yes." He leans down to press a kiss on my cheek. "It's a great initiative for Q3."

I kiss him back and surrender to the soft warmth of his lips. I love it when he kisses me like this. Slow and steady, like he could do it all night.

"I love it when you talk nonsensical business jargon to me," I say.

"Mm-hmm. What if I said..." He kisses my neck. "That I'm spearheading a new proposal... that has a hard stop."

It's hard to think with his lips right below my jaw. "I think we should workshop that. Invite some... other people... for maximum synergy."

He groans against my skin. "Invite other people?"

"Yes. Like five to ten useless employees who nod approvingly at your suggestions," I say, and he pulls back to level me with a look. I giggle. "What? That's exactly how your meetings look like."

"Are you saying what I think you are?"

"That you're surrounded by sycophants?" My eyes are wide, the picture of innocence. "Of course not."

"Okay, that's it." He grabs me and pulls me up to the center of the bed, into his arms.

I laugh again. "Oh no. Have I upset you?"

"I'm realizing," he says, settling against me, "that I've failed to make a sycophant out of you."

I wrap my arms around his neck and feel the worries of the last hour melt away. Even when they're related to him, he's so good at making them disappear. Shelving them for another conversation.

He's always been good at making me feel safe. Even when it would make no sense to anyone else, even when it made no sense to me.

"Are you going to convince me?" My fingers play along his cheekbone, up to his temple, into his hair.

He bends closer. "No. I like you disobedient."

"Disobedient, huh? That implies I'm yours."

He brushes his lips over mine. "And are you?"

I don't answer him. Instead, I kiss him, my fingers twining in his hair, and pull him closer. I wrap my legs around him, and it's not a verbal answer, but he groans low in his throat, like he's heard it regardless.

CHAPTER 57

CHARLOTTE

The city is alive around me, but I can't take it all in. It's like the noise is filtered through a shield. Can't reach me, can't touch me. I've been driving for the past hour. I took the Mulholland Drive that Aiden showed me and stopped at the scenic overlook.

But I couldn't handle staying still.

So I got back in the car and drove the roads around Beverly Hills. When that didn't work, I drove down Sunset Boulevard, all the way out toward the ocean, until it intersected with the Pacific Coast Highway.

The sun is setting outside my windshield. I can see it. Disappearing in the distance, dipping below the vast horizon. I could look at that view forever and never tire.

In my pocket, my phone rings. Once, then twice. I know who it is before I glance at it. Aiden. He's probably home from work now and is wondering where I am.

I stop at a red light and look back out at the ocean. It's so huge, it could swallow me whole. I could disappear out there and be no one at all. Not recognized, not seen. One wave among the masses.

My parents did not approve.

They asked if I knew what I was doing, writing this

memoir. Why I hadn't told them right away. Why I hadn't broken the NDA.

Honey, Mom glances at Dad with a worried look on her face, *you've been pushing yourself so hard for the past few years. Take a break.*

I don't need a break.

This doesn't sound good. I don't like the sound of it, not one bit. My dad, with his arms crossed over his chest and an angry concern in his eyes. The kind I'd seen so often in those first few months, years ago, when our lives turned upside down.

The media will get ahold of this when it's published.

I'd told my dad that I don't go by the same name. They *won't* put two and two together, when no one has in the past.

Mom's eyes flash. *The media always finds out. That company doesn't deserve an ounce of your time, and certainly not your writing! Honey, what are you doing?*

Nothing I said mattered. This was a dumb decision. *Again.* Mom used it as an excuse to pile on the guilt about wanting me to move back to Idaho. And Dad, he asked me to read the contract in case I missed something, some loophole in the fine print. They're both trying to get me out of Titan Media's clutches. Again.

Dumb little Charlotte, making another dumb mistake.

It's hard to imagine how much worse this could have gone if I'd also told them I was *living* with the CEO of Titan Media, not just writing a memoir in his favor.

Not to mention, *sleeping with him.* That the "boyfriend" they were so happy about just the day prior is the very same man. Now, they see him as someone who won't let me out of an NDA, the villain in the story.

Anger takes the place of numbness. It seeps in slowly, and I have no way to let it go. It builds and builds until it spreads through every limb. Until I grip the wheel so hard, it hurts.

Maybe I'm *not* making a dumb mistake.

Maybe I've grown.

Because I've realized Aiden isn't intimately involved with the shows the network produces. He handles big-picture things. He only became CEO *two* years ago, for Christ's sake, and before that, he worked in Titan's strategy department. He had absolutely nothing to do with my experience on *The Gamble.*

I drive until the anger slowly seeps out of me. I likely speed, too, a weak parallel to the jogs I like to take. Maybe that's what I should do instead. The LA air is much cooler at night.

I arrive back at Aiden's Bel Air home. It's late, almost midnight when I pull into the driveway. Maybe he's already gone to bed.

But when I open up the front door, the lights are still on. Footsteps sound across the hardwood floor.

"Charlotte." Aiden's hair is a mess, like he's repeatedly dragged his hands through it. His eyebrows are drawn low. "You've been out?"

"Went for a drive."

"A very long drive," he says. "Were you safe?"

"Yes. I'm always safe." I pass him and head into the massive kitchen to pour myself a glass of water.

"What's happened?" he asks. There's a cautious note to his tone, one that I've rarely heard before. Like he thinks I'm seconds from exploding.

That's just ridiculous.

I'm the picture of calm.

I set the now-empty glass down on his marble countertop a bit too hard. "I got a lecture today from my parents, after telling them about the memoir."

He grits his teeth. "They don't approve."

"Approve is a nice word. They're not the kind of people to express themselves that way. But yeah, they're questioning my sanity, which is worse." I close my eyes against a wave of guilt that punches through my frustration. "They're worried that I'm back to making stupid decisions."

"You're not," Aiden says.

That makes me smile. "You would say that, though. Wouldn't you?"

His eyes narrow. He's in a pair of dark slacks and a gray T-shirt that spans his broad shoulders, and I wonder if he's been worried. If he's been pacing the house waiting for my return. More guilt joins the already swirling whirlpool inside me.

"Maybe I should have been there," he says.

I throw up my hands. "Oh my god, Aiden. What would that have done?"

"They could have been mad at me, instead of you."

"They would have been mad at us both."

He braces his hands against the kitchen island. "Did you tell them about us?"

"God, no." I bury my head in my hands. "Can you imagine? I totally lied about living here, too."

There's complete silence across the space. Then he sighs. "They're not going to be my biggest fans, and I guess that's only natural."

"No." Numbness has seeped into me again. Chased out the strong emotions, leaving me with only hopelessness. "I've gotten more involved than I should've. I've *moved* in with you. And we only have about a week left until the memoir is due... and you don't do relationships. And I've *never* done a relationship."

Aiden pushes off the kitchen island. "Don't think too far ahead."

"Too far ahead? We're talking days!"

"Charlotte." He reaches for me and pulls me against him. I resist. Put my hands against his chest but I don't relax. I don't surrender.

Not at first.

But then his warmth envelopes me. His scent is uniquely his, like soap and cologne and man. His arms around me are familiar. I relax against him and bury my face against his shoulder.

"I've really fucked up this whole thing from the beginning," he mutters against my hair. "We hadn't even met yet when I messed up the first time."

"You didn't. You didn't work for Titan, then."

"No, but I was the heir to it. I was living off the money that came from it." His hands move down my arms, slowly up and down. "I'm trying to make amends, though. Whatever you want, sweetheart. Do you want me to cancel the show?"

I lean back and just stare at him. "What?"

"I'll happily do it, if you want."

"That's crazy, Aiden. That show employs hundreds of people." I push away from him and try to find my breath again. "It's not the show itself, it's... it's the way the shows are produced. It's so *exploitative.*

"I have the deepest respect for reality television, I really do. Especially for the people who share their real lives for entertainment. But it's never on equal footing. The producers will massage and twist a story during editing until 'you,' the actual real-life person starring on the show, no longer exists. And 'you' don't have a say in any of it."

"Charlotte," he says, his face drawn tight. "I'm sorry."

I wrap my arms around my chest. "I saw a few of the contestants in bad situations. Too drunk, hyperventilating, sleep-deprived. There were panic attacks, and no therapists around, or trained professionals to help with that sort of thing. Not to mention consent... That whole thing..."

He nods. "Changes need to be made to the production."

"Yes. They're young people, mined for content. If they're okay with that, great! They're adults. But just, you know... have some guardrails in place. Can you do that?" Hot wetness streaks down my cheeks, and I brush it away. "Damn it. I'm not sad. I'm just... feeling a lot right now."

Aiden takes another step closer. "Can I hold you again? I understand if you don't want me near you right now."

"It's not your fault." I shake my head slowly, and now, I'm crying harder. I didn't even know I was sad. But now that my tears have started, I can't seem to make them stop. "I tried and tried to hold on to my grudge against you because of the show, but I always knew you weren't the one directly responsible."

"It's okay," he says. "It's okay if you hate me forever."

"It's not. Because I don't, and never did. You aren't to blame for what happened back then." I take a deep breath and say the thing I've come to be most afraid of. "But it was safer to hold on to my bitterness than to face that I was falling for you."

CHAPTER 58
CHARLOTTE

"I don't want to make you cry. Ever." Those green eyes are liquid, and his mouth is tense.

"But you are," I murmur and smile a little. The numbness was safer than this, the bubbling of emotions inside of me. I wipe the tears off my cheek. "I haven't felt anything like this for someone since... him. I've been strict with myself. Only temporary arrangements, only men who don't... who aren't really interested in anything long-term with me."

"I know," he says. "Even if I find it hard to believe that men wouldn't be interested in you in that way."

I chuckle weakly. I'm standing at the edge of an abyss, unable to see the bottom. Not seeing a safe way across. "See? You say something like that, and I can tell that you actually mean it."

His long fingers wipe another tear away. "I do mean it."

"You don't do relationships, either," I whisper.

"No. I haven't had time." His lips curve. "But I'm willing to try, Chaos. Work isn't the only thing that's important to me. I want more days with you. I want to go surfing and hold you when you sleep. There is more to life than just work."

I look at the hollow at the base of his throat, where I see his throbbing pulse point. "It's all I know," I confess. For years, I've thrown myself into other people's stories to avoid dealing with my own.

Aiden's hand tips my face up, angling it toward his. "You know more than you think," he murmurs and kisses me. "You know what you mean to me."

My tears have slowed. Settled into a deeper emotion, flowing through me and into my grip on the fabric of his T-shirt. "I don't know what we're doing," I tell him, "but I know I don't want to stop."

"Sweetheart," he says, and his deep voice is achingly quiet. "Letting you go would kill me. You're mine now, for as long as you want to be."

I wrap my arms around his neck. The hollow inside me has transformed along with the sadness, and all I want is to fill it. And only he can do that. "Take me to bed," I murmur against his lips.

His arms slide down and circle my waist. "You're sure? You're sad."

"I'm emotional," I whisper. "Not the same thing."

He lingers for a moment, his touch warm against my skin, before he lifts me off the ground. I wrap my legs around his waist and grip him tight. Aiden walks up the stairs with me clinging to him like that, ignoring my whispered *I can walk*. He pushes open the door to his bedroom with his shoulder.

"Aiden," I say.

He lays me down on top of his duvet and climbs over my sprawling body, settling on top of me. Both of us are still fully clothed.

My heart is beating so fast that I can hear the thunder in my ears.

"Yes?"

I lock my knees around his hips and pull him close until most of his weight rests on me, deliciously crushing me into the mattress. I feel heavy and light at the same time.

Too many emotions are swirling inside me.

I need him. I need him so much that I think it might shatter me, the final blow in a fight I never knew I'd been waging. It cripples the control I've so carefully built.

"We've always used a condom."

His mouth hovers over my neck. "Yes. You prefer it, and it's safer."

"Yes. But I'm on birth control, and I'm clean. I took a test just a few months ago. And… I've never had sex without one."

Aiden is completely motionless for a good few moments, long enough for me to wonder if I've fucked up again.

"We could try it?" I ask. "If you want to?"

He buries his head in the crook of my neck with a groan. "God, Chaos. You're really trying to kill me. But I'll die happy."

I run my hands through his hair and use my nails the way I know he likes. He groans again. "I had a checkup a while back. Haven't been with anyone since. So yes," he says and lifts himself onto his elbow, "we can *try* fucking without a condom. Although I don't think there'll be much *trying* involved."

I love it when he looks like this, hair mussed, olive skin, those brilliant green eyes, and so big and warm above me. Like he belongs to only me. A version of reserved for my eyes only. Aiden, when he's no one but himself. Not the CEO, not the brother, not the figure in front of a crowd.

I reach for the hem of his T-shirt.

He lets me undress him and uses the moments in between to kiss me. To ease down the zipper of my jeans and to run his big hands over my body until the ache inside me spikes.

When I reach into his pants, he's already hard. I grip him tight and revel in the sound of his breath hitching.

"Charlotte," he mutters. "Say again what you told me earlier."

I arch into him, my nipples against his chest. "What part?"

"That you're… falling for me. That you don't want to stop what's happening between us."

I rest my forehead against his. "Okay," I whisper. I repeat the words and feel him twitch in my hand.

He groans again and then pulls away from me completely.

"I'm already too close," he mutters and reaches for my panties. He shimmies them down my legs and pushes my thighs apart. Any lingering self-consciousness in me is long since gone.

It's been replaced by the warm blanket of need he surrounds me with.

"So pretty," he murmurs and leans between my legs. This time, I surrender right away to the sensations his tongue produces. Let them sweep through me until tears well in my eyes for an entirely different reason. He curls his fingers inside me and sucks on my clit, and I break apart like he's taught me to do, effortlessly and without any shame. There's enough of it out in the real world.

It doesn't belong in bed with us, too.

I rake my hand through his hair. His dedication to my pleasure has been the most surprising thing in all of this. I had no idea sex could be like that.

"Come here," I murmur, pulling him between my legs. I want to see him. Feel his skin against mine.

Aiden braces himself on an elbow beside my face. His shoulders are broad, the hair on his head and chest the same brown color. In the dimmed spotlight, his green eyes are dark.

He reaches between us and grips himself. Notches against my entrance and then, slowly, with his eyes on mine, pushes inside me.

I love this part.

He groans when he's fully seated, his forehead resting on mine.

Both of us are breathing hard.

When he starts to move, it's with slow, rolling thrusts that

I feel deep within. I wrap my legs around him and lock my ankles behind his lower back. Run my nails all over his back.

Aiden reaches out to his bedside table and grabs my vibrator, the small one that has been my solo companion during all my trips.

He tucks it between our bodies, against my clit.

"Lowest setting," I tell him and stretch my arms out above my head. Luxuriating in him, in the heat, the feeling of being filled. "I want to come when you do."

Aiden groans. "It's like you were made for me."

The vibrations and his deep thrusts make my breath hitch. *Oh.* This won't take long at all.

He settles atop me, my nipples brush his chest. "Stay," he says in between thrusts.

"I'm here."

"After the memoir's done." He kisses my neck. "Stay in LA to write your own book. Live here. Figure it out."

A wave sweeps through me. It's desire, it's need, and it's something else I can't name. All I know is that it's big and terrifying and delicious.

The fire inside my chest is scorching, and I have to close my eyes against another sudden swell of tears.

"Stay here with me," he repeats. He's everywhere—deep inside me, above me, around me.

We have things to figure out. Things to talk about. But right now, all that feels trifling, and my brain can't hold on to a single thought.

I grip him tighter against me. Arms, legs. Flex my inner muscles around his cock, and he groans against my neck.

"I'll stay."

Aiden growls and his hips stutter. Once, twice, pushing the vibrator firmly against my clit. My climax takes me by surprise. My fingers turn into claws digging into Aiden's shoulder blades.

His body goes rigid, and then he groans against my flesh,

muttering my name in his hoarse voice. His hips stutter into me as he finds his release.

An eternity later, we lie sweaty and panting on his bed. He's still on top of me, inside me. Warm and handsome.

I run my hand over the muscles of his back. My eyelids feel heavy. "I didn't know you could feel it," I murmur. "When a man comes inside you? But I did, this time. Without the condom."

Aiden's still buried inside me, and I feel a faint twitch. He groans against my temple. "The death of me," he mutters again.

I nuzzle against him. "Are you gonna pull out?"

"No," he says and tugs me firmly against him. "We're gonna sleep just like this."

His mouth returns to my temple, and his hand sweeps in slow circles over my hip. Soothing and warm. I'm close to sleep when I hear him mumble in my ear.

"You said you were falling for me, Chaos?"

"Mm-hmm, yeah. I did."

"I've already fallen."

CHAPTER 59

CHARLOTTE

An unknown phone number is calling. I've gotten used to answering them. It could be someone on Aiden's team or from Polar Publishing. Might even be Aiden calling from a work phone I'm not familiar with.

"Hi, it's Charlotte," I say.

"Hi there! My name is Audrey Kingsley. I'm calling from the *New York Globe*. I hope I'm not bothering you."

I shake my head as if she can see me. "No, not at all." I rarely get calls from journalists about the books I've written. They'd usually rather talk directly with the subjects than me.

"That's fantastic. Thank you so much for taking my call," she says. "I would love to chat about a story I'm writing."

"Oh? What's it about?" I ask. The next memoir release isn't scheduled for months, yet. It's too early for the press, and besides, Polar handles all of that.

"It's a deep dive into the predatory practices of reality television," she says.

I pause, and my hand tightens around the phone. "I'm sorry?"

"It's an investigative journalism piece on the often exploitative nature of dating shows, especially what women go through on some of these programs," she continues. Her voice is professional, and I hear the flip of papers. "You were on *The Gamble* some years ago. I would love to hear your version of the story."

"My version… of the story."

"Yes. What really happened in terms of the relationship you were in," she says. "I've done some digging, and from what I've gathered, there were a lot of things that happened that season that were never aired."

I stare out the window, barely seeing the turquoise of Aiden's infinity pool. "And you want to… publish this?"

"Yes. You're the key piece in my analysis, actually." She gives a little laugh, almost like she's embarrassed. "All roads point back to that first season. Would you be willing to meet up? I'm happy to travel wherever you are."

She doesn't know where I am. She doesn't know I'm writing a memoir about Aiden. She's really not calling about my current job.

She's calling about the past.

I thought those calls were long over.

"Because you want to mention me in an article? I don't want to be included." My voice comes out harsh.

There's a brief pause on the other end. "I understand. I don't wish to cause any offense, but your name will be mentioned in passing, at the very least. The treatment of you on that show was a watershed moment in dating shows and reality television. Especially the media attention you received following your appearance."

My breath is coming fast. "What?"

"I want to hear your side," she says. "It's important—"

"Why are you investigating this? Why now? Why are you writing this article?" I demand. My voice sounds high-pitched, even to my own ears.

There's a helicopter flying out over the city. I watch it—a tiny, insignificant speck in the sky. But it doesn't deviate from its path. It's determined and persistent like a fly.

"Well," she says, and her voice has softened as if she's talking to a child. I can hear it and realize it's because of me, and my reaction. "This article is part of an independent investigation, here at the *Globe*, and it's integral in our initiative to tell more female-led stories."

I grip the back of the sofa. "You said you've done some digging. Who are your sources? Who have you spoken to?"

"I can't tell you that, I'm afraid. Not all of them. But I think it's worth noting, Charlotte, that I have been in direct contact with Titan Media."

I pause. "Sorry. You've *what*?"

"Titan Media is aware of our investigation," she says. "That is not something I wish for you to pass on, however. But I do want you to know that I'm confident you won't face any kind of legal backlash for speaking out. They're welcoming an independent investigation."

I scoff. "Really? When do corporations ever welcome scrutiny?"

"Normally I would agree with you," she replies, "but I've had personal reassurances. From the very top."

"From the very top," I repeat. The words come out slowly. "You're talking about the executive team."

"Yes, I am," she says. Her voice turns earnest. "I can assure you, you'll be protected through all of this. I would not ask you or any of the other contestants to tell their story if I wasn't confident about this."

My chest feels too tight. I take another breath, and then another, but the air doesn't seem to make it into my lungs.

"Charlotte?"

"Did you talk to the CEO?" I ask.

"I can't confirm that on the record," Audrey says carefully, "but I have spoken with an individual in the highest reaches of the company. You have nothing to—"

"I have to go." I hang up and throw the phone away, at Aiden's giant couch, like it's on fire.

He knows about this. Of course he does. But he must not have expected the journalist to reveal so much.

My skin crawls, bugs scurrying about beneath its surface. I'm already racing across his living room and up the stairs. I take them two at a time.

I spend the next hour googling. The newspaper in question, the journalist, finding her on social media, and the kind of stories she writes.

Everything checks out.

What the hell, Aiden?

I walk the length of the hallway between our two bedrooms. Back and forth. Back and forth. The itch is only getting stronger.

Why is he doing this? What game is he playing now?

My anonymity is *everything*. I thought we'd spoken about this. Why would he want a piece written that would expose his own production company's mistakes?

Whatever the reason, he's done it without asking me. Without telling me about it first.

I should sit down and write. Finish his memoir, yes, but also work on my book proposal. Which he's also been pushing me to write.

To tell my story.

Just like he's doing with this interview.

I put on my workout clothes.

There have been times when running is the only thing that got me through the day. Feeling my feet hit the ground and my lungs ache, like I could leave whatever was eating at me behind.

It's what got me out of my childhood bedroom, out of my parents' house, after *The Gamble* aired. I hid in bed for weeks. Barely venturing down for dinner, not talking to friends, hardly interacting with family. Until my best friend showed up outside my door in her workout clothes, insisting we go for a walk.

It turned into a run, and soon, I started going on my own. Listening to nothing but the pounding of my feet against the grounds.

The paved streets around Bel Air aren't as comforting as the dirt trails through the woods around Elmhurst. There are no sidewalks, only asphalt-covered surfaces made for speeding cars. I run to the trailhead I discovered earlier and hit the packed gravel ground. I jog up and up until I feel the high. Run until I have to slow to a walk, and walk until I can finally run again. I repeat the pattern until the buzzing in my mind dies down.

I don't have to be in the article.

I'll send Ms. Kingsley a text tomorrow or the day after, a kind but firm request that any mention of me be omitted. Of course, she warned me that might not be enough. It's open season for anyone to bring up my name. Lord knows I'm well aware of that.

But it's the only defense I've got.

I walk back to Aiden's house. My mind might have cleared from the low buzz of irritation, but my body has not.

Aiden must be home now. There's a massive bouquet of flowers on the kitchen island, with a small note attached. I glance at it.

To my favorite writer.

I let the card fall from my hands and set off in search of him.

CHAPTER 60

CHARLOTTE

I find him eventually, following the deep tones of his voice to the half-open door of his study. He's sitting at his desk, leaning back. His eyebrows are drawn low. "That's good," he mutters. "Nora Stone agreed just the other week. We have another meeting scheduled tomorrow."

I lean against the doorframe. He really is the king of his own world. Getting his way, giving his orders. Expecting everyone to fall in line.

He sees me and something softens in his eyes. "I'll have to call you back later," he says into the phone. "I'll think of a plan. We need to get the contract ready for signing later this week."

Then he puts the phone down and looks at me—skimming over my tank top and the leggings. There's appreciation in his gaze. "You've been working out?"

I ignore the question. "The Stones have agreed to sell?"

"Yes, but only verbally. We're nearly at the finish line."

"After I hand in the memoir, right? You need it for the Board to approve the purchase."

He takes a moment before nodding. "Yeah. That's right."

"And you'll likely cut some things out of the first draft before then," I say. "You don't want too many of your intimate secrets in there." My voice comes out too combative, and I don't know how to make it stop.

"Right." He gets up, a furrow between his brows. "But I can tell you anything you want to know, as long as it doesn't make it into the book."

"Right. Because you're protective of your personal life."

"I suppose, yes. And it involves more people than just me." He tilts his head slightly, like he's trying to figure me out. "Charlotte. What are you thinking?"

"I know that the deadline for the first draft is in a few days. I'm almost done. I'll just need tonight and tomorrow to finish it up," I say.

"Okay. There's no rush."

"We signed a contract. So there sort of is."

His lips turn down. "Not one I'll enforce."

"Mm-hmm." I dig my teeth into my bottom lip and look past him at the bookshelves lining the walls of his home office. Maybe my book will be on one of them in a few months. He still needs a picture for the cover. The photo shoot is next week, and Aiden asked me to go with him.

"I got an interesting call earlier." I look at a bookshelf instead of directly at him. It's easier to face.

"You did? Is everything okay?"

"It was from a journalist. Audrey Kingsley of the *New York Globe*." My gaze slides to his. "Do you know anything about the article she's writing?"

His face doesn't change. But there's a flicker of something in his eyes, there and gone again. "I know of her, yes."

My stomach sinks. I feel it drop, and disappointment tastes like ash in my mouth.

"How do you know her?" I ask.

"She's married to one of the owners of Acture Capital. Our paths cross from time to time," he says.

"Right. You're friends."

"I'm not sure I would go that far," he says.

"But you've never spoken to her about business things."

"What are you getting at, Charlotte?"

"She's writing an article. About exploitative situations in reality television." I cross my arms over my chest, and for a second, try to channel him. The commanding presence I've seen him put on like a cloak. "She thought of me, even though I've never spoken about my experience publicly."

"Did she?" He's standing very still. So am I. Like a sudden movement from either of us could break this stand-off.

"Yes. Even said that she would mention me regardless of whether I made a statement or not." I shrug and work hard to keep my voice under control. "Then, she assured me—and here's the weird part—that I wouldn't have to worry about Titan Media suing me for breaking the NDA I signed for doing the show. You know why?"

Aiden blows out a breath. "Chaos."

"Do you know *why*, Aiden?"

"I do. I made it clear to her that I won't stand in the way of an independent investigation."

"You made it clear to her. Or did you encourage this? You forget that I know you fairly well by now. Even if you've made it difficult to get close to you."

Aiden's jaw tenses. "You've gotten closer than I've allowed anyone else for as long as I can remember."

"Did you encourage her to write the article?"

There's a moment of pause. "I gave her the idea," he says.

The punch knocks the air out of me. I knew he was manipulative, in a way that most successful people are. He plans, he's strategic, his focus is always on winning.

But this?

"Why," I breathe.

He takes a step closer and reaches out. I react in kind, taking a step back until I'm in the hallway outside his office. "Charlotte, it was never meant to hurt you. Quite the opposite."

"Right. Because dragging up my past would help me *how*?"

"Because I want *him* discredited," Aiden says. His voice is tight with suppressed fury. "I can fire him from all our shows in a heartbeat. That decision has already been made. After this season airs, he will never be on Titan Media's payroll again. But it's not enough. I don't want him to work in this industry. Ever."

"Aiden," I say.

He shakes his head. "It's not fair, Charlotte. It's not fair that you had to suffer questions and embarrassment when you've done nothing to feel ashamed of. It's not fucking *right* that opportunists made money off *your* soundbite with a song, and you never got a dime. You should have had the choice."

"I've made my choice." My voice feels choked, and I force my feelings down. Bury them deep and lock them away. "I told you that I don't want this mentioned again. That I *hate* when people drag up the past. That I don't want my name to be associated with that time in my life ever again if I can help it. I changed my last name!"

His eyes are fierce. "I know that. And you shouldn't *have* to feel that way."

"But I do!"

"You did nothing wrong." His voice is hoarser than I've ever heard it, thick with conviction. He throws out his left hand. "*Nothing.* You were nineteen, and you were taken advantage of. I'm trying to make it right."

"Nothing will ever make it right," I say. "I've already come to terms with that."

"No, you haven't."

My breath catches, and he sees just how hard his words hit me. But he keeps going. "You haven't, Charlotte, not really. I've seen how you constantly look around wherever we're in a crowded room. How deeply those people who recognized you by the restaurant hurt you. You're still ruled by someone else's narrative. By Blake's narrative, and by Jeff's."

I take a step back, and then another. There's too little air in here. "You didn't just say that to me."

"Is it not the truth? You've told me over and over again to own my narrative, Charlotte. I've let you do it."

"Because you asked me to! Because I'm writing a *memoir*!"

"Yes, and I've learned just how powerful that can be, thanks to you. I've read all the preliminary chapters you've sent me, Charlotte."

The ones about him and his good qualities. His tenacity, his drive to overcome things. How broken he felt when the FBI charged his father. How he stepped up to clean up Alfred Hartman's mess when he didn't have to.

And how much the accusations and suspicions hurt.

That he was somehow involved. In the know. When he was, perhaps, the one person who had been deceived most of all.

"Don't believe your own puff piece," I tell him.

The words land. He pulls back, his eyebrows lowering. "Charlotte, the article is *for* you."

"I didn't ask for it."

"Maybe not, but you need it."

"That's for me to decide." I walk to my bedroom.

He follows. "Don't run from me."

"I don't want my name in the media. I don't *want* to dredge up the past. Isn't that my decision?"

"Yes. But if that's what you decided, you'll just keep burying it instead, Charlotte. And it will always catch up with you."

"It works for you," I call over my shoulder.

"It doesn't. It *hasn't*. That's what I'm learning." He blows out a breath, and I hear the frustration in it. "That's what *you've* been teaching me!"

His exasperation mirrors my own. "How could you not have asked me first?"

"I didn't know she was going to reach out to you directly."

I shake my head. "Not an excuse. How could you not have asked *me*, Aiden? If she hadn't called me, would you have admitted you were behind the idea?"

The answer is in his eyes. He knows I wouldn't have agreed if he'd asked. "I did it for you," he says.

I shake my head. "You should have spoken to me."

"I'm speaking to you now."

That makes me laugh. "Yeah, but it's a little too late, don't you think?" I move to shut the door, but he holds up his hand and catches it neatly.

"Charlotte," he says fiercely. "Don't run away from me."

"I need time alone," I say. "Can I have that in the guest room, or do I need to leave?"

He takes a step back. "It's not a guest room. It's *your* room."

"We'll talk tomorrow," I say and close the door. I lock it, too, knowing he can clearly hear the sound on the other side.

CHAPTER 61
CHARLOTTE

I don't leave my room until I know he's definitely left for work the next morning. It's well after eleven when I finally venture out and find the place deserted.

Walking down the elegantly decorated hallway, the decadently wide staircase, and into the spacious living room. His home has always felt too large for one person, too empty. It's beautiful but a bit soulless. Like he doesn't truly live here.

His family house in Malibu, the one he'd taken me to... that felt more like him.

Here, even with the mementos everywhere, ones that his sister must have left when she decorated, the space feels cold. I wrap my arms around myself and look at it all. The wine in his cellar. Years of vintage. The pictures on the giant bookcase by his living room couch.

Everything has changed. Everything *will* change.

Finally, when I can't delay it any longer, I sit down at my computer and click open the manuscript. The one that I've temporarily named *Titan, Rising*.

I've written the title in thick, bold font on the first page. Below, the outline of the various chapters.

Seventy-five thousand words.

It's as much about Titan Media as it is about Aiden. But

the chapters about him had been my favorite to write. I spent the past few days rereading some of the chapters and revising the weaker ones. The document needs to go to Aiden before it goes to the Board or my editor.

When I'm done, it's almost two. I send the entire manuscript to the closest printing house and let them know I'll pick it up within the hour.

My phone rings while I'm on my way back, and connects to my car speakers via Bluetooth. It's Eric.

"Hey. What's up?"

"Ms. Gray," he says. There's a long pause that's unlike him. "There's a picture of you and Mr. Hartman on the front page of *Star Buzz*."

"What?"

"A picture of the two of you. I'm not sure where or when it was taken, but it's unmistakably you. It has been connected to your… past."

The words land like a ton of bricks. Directly onto my chest, weighing me down.

"There's no mention of the memoir. Just that you two are now dating," he says.

"Does… Aiden know?"

"Yes. We're monitoring the situation. It was just published."

My hands tighten around the steering wheel. "Thanks for telling me." My voice sounds reedy and thin, and not like my own. I hang up and pull over into the first parking lot I spot in Westwood.

I type my name into the search bar of my phone with shaky hands. Charlotte Gray. The results are a few passing mentions of me as the ghostwriter of memoirs.

It was a pleasure to work with Charlotte…

All thanks to Charlotte…

I add Aiden's name, and then, after a second of hesitation, change the surname on my search.

Charlotte Richards.

And things start pouring in.

I click on the first video that comes up. It takes me to a social media app. One of the many I've been avoiding.

The world crashes around me as I listen.

A woman on the screen. Cheerful, in a bright-blue blouse. She talks over the rolling footage of blonde me at that Mexico resort.

And then, she cuts to an image of me with Aiden. We're walking out of the fancy restaurant. Our first date, where we later met a group of people who recognized me. The screen-me is looking up at Aiden.

It's clearly me. And obviously him. His arm is wrapped around my shoulders.

The headline is what makes my heart stutter.

The Gamble's Sugar Puff is now dating the billionaire owner of Titan Media, the production company responsible for the show.

The text below isn't much better.

Aiden Hartman, the billionaire son of the now criminally convicted Alfred Hartman (yes, that one), seems to have found a girlfriend. And it's not a supermodel or a European heiress.

Another picture. This time it's me—crying, hysterical, standing in front of Blake by a pool. My mascara is smudged and my mouth is open. I know what picture-me is about to scream.

But I'm your little Sugar Puff.

Charlotte Richards made The Gamble a worldwide sensation. Spoken about at water coolers across the globe, Sugar Puff is responsible for the series' unprecedented success. She's kept a low profile since her time on the show, but now it seems like she's not done with life in the spotlight.

My hands shake, holding the phone. *Spotlight.* I look around, but no one is paying me any attention. No one is staring or whispering to their friends.

Just in case, I pull my cap lower on my face.

The paranoia is the worst. It's something I've worked hard to overcome, to get rid of the feeling that there are always eyes on me, always murmurings, always attention.

It's lessened more and more with each passing year.

But this? Can I handle it starting again?

It won't take long before this makes its way to my family. These sorts of things grow, get big on social media. Someone sees it and sends the post to someone else.

Didn't you go to school with that girl?

In all of fifteen minutes, it could get forwarded to a family member or childhood friend back in Elmhurst.

Which means my parents will know everything in a few hours. Maybe in a day. But no longer than that.

Panic grips me with an icy hand. I pull out of the parking lot and start the drive up to Bel Air. But I go past Aiden's house and continue on.

Aimlessly taking curve after curve.

My phone rings. I hear it but ignore it.

The memoir is a thick bunch of papers, all stuck inside a manila envelope. Lying on the passenger seat beside me. I need to deliver it before I can... before I can do anything.

My phone rings for the fifth time, and I look at the console to see who it is.

Esmé. My best friend since childhood.

I answer. "Hey."

"I just saw it," she says. There's silence on the line, like there's nothing more to say. And is there, really?

Is there anything else that needs to be said?

"I don't know what you've gotten yourself into," she says in her calm, collected voice, "but I'm here if you need me."

The simple words make my throat squeeze shut. My eyes well up with tears, and I try my best to blink them away. But one escapes anyway, slides down my cheek.

"It's all such a mess," I whisper.

"Oh, Charlotte. I wish I could hug you," she says, and that

makes me cry harder. I don't stop the car, don't slow down. As I've done for years. *Just keep moving.*

"How did you find out?"

She hesitates for only a moment. "Tara saw it on social media and forwarded it to me. Some kind of video."

Tara is her sister-in-law. It's just like I expected. Friends sending links to friends—that invisible network that never fails to spread gossip around.

"I can't believe this is happening again," I say.

"Your parents," she says softly. "Do they know?"

"I'm sure some helpful soul will inform them. They know I'm... I'm writing his memoir. But not about..."

"Ah. I'm sorry, Charlotte."

There's a brief pause, and I use it to wipe my cheek. There are too many emotions running through me, and I can't parse them all out, can't handle the speed or intensity.

"Are you okay?" she asks. "I mean, why did this happen? He runs Titan Media, Charlotte."

And there it is. Even with the gentle tone in her voice, the judgment. *You should have known better.*

This is a dumb decision, Charlotte.

"I have to go," I say.

"Charlotte—"

"Thanks for calling. I'll talk to you later." I hang up and pull to a stop at a vacant cul-de-sac, fronted by high hedges. Hiding the million-dollar houses from view.

I open up the tabloid site again. The one that Eric had sent me. Ground zero.

It's been updated.

Star Buzz News reached out to Aiden Hartman's team for a comment. Mr. Harmann himself has told Star: "Ms. Charlotte Gray and I have no relationship beyond the professional. She is a fantastic writer, and I have every confidence in her skills for my memoir."

My eyes skip over the middle words. *No relationship beyond the professional.*

No relationship beyond the professional.

No relationship beyond.

None.

He's denying it.

The first punch is one of anger, and then my tears begin to flow. There's no controlling them this time. At least I'm not sobbing. It's a steady stream of emotions, leaking out of me. The way they always do when I can't restrain them.

The headline is an embarrassment for him.

He's made his opinion of reality stars loud and clear all too often. He doesn't particularly respect his company's production of dating shows, but he's tolerated it because it pays the bills. Keeps advertisers happy. Because his personal feelings don't matter—only the company does. Its survival. And his damn family name.

The one he so wanted to restore.

No relationship beyond the professional.

It didn't take him long to state that. What had it been, an hour? And he's already made his position crystal clear.

I glance at my watch. He'll still be at work, but judging by his repeated calls, he's trying to reach me. And soon, he'll be checking at his own home.

I press my foot on the gas.

SOCIAL MEDIA

@yogiyara: Remember Sugar Puff? She scored the man who OWNS The Gamble! Talk about playing the long game.

@digitaldaisy: Honestly, mad respect for this chick. Talk about upgrading and getting the last laugh!

@starbuzz: We can confirm that the billionaire Aiden Hartman (remember him sitting by his father's side during the infamous court case?) is now dating Sugar Puff girl from The Gamble's first season. Hard to know who got the short end of the stick there!

CHAPTER 62
AIDEN

The Board meeting is called on short notice.

It's the last fucking thing I want today. Charlotte isn't answering my calls or my texts. And she hasn't spoken to anyone on my team since Eric called to inform her of the current shitstorm.

He did admit that bit of information with a look of defiance on his face. Brave of him, considering how pissed I am. Why the hell did he not wait so I could break the news to her myself?

Give her time, he'd said, too, as if he knows her better than I do. Infuriating.

So now I'm sitting here, facing the Board. The people I dislike the most; the same ones who have consistently been interfering with my goals of returning Titan Media to its position of preeminence in the industry. Some members care more about their own reputation and status than the business.

"The point of this memoir," Richard Granthurst says across from me at the conference table, "was to show confidence in the company and in you as the CEO. This news directly undermines that."

"Romance the ghostwriter," Ingrid says with a wave of

her bejeweled hand. "But not publicly, and certainly not if she is a reality star."

"This whole thing was supposed to send a sign of maturity to the shareholders," Richard continues. "To show that the company has turned a leaf."

"That I am not my father. That's what you mean." My tone is scathing.

A few members shift uncomfortably in their chairs. But then, several of them nod. "Yes, to put it bluntly."

I brace my hands against the wooden tabletop. "Let me make a few points," I say. "First, you all vetted Ms. Gray and found her to be an excellent candidate to write this memoir based on her previous experience. Nothing about that has changed."

"We didn't know about her past as a reality star," Ingrid protests. "That could seriously damage the reputation of this memoir."

My tone is merciless. "Then you should have done better research. I don't need to remind you that this memoir was *your* idea, not mine."

Richard crosses his arms over his chest. He's one of two Board members who's been here since my dad's time. He's always been cautious, tentative, and obsessed with image.

"The idea was to project strength. Victory, if you will."

"I don't see how a tabloid headline would change that."

"It'll steer this book into things *other* than the story we want to tell," one of the board members says. Claire. Usually sharp, she's one of the few board members who's regularly had my back. Now her eyes are narrowed. "It's the wrong kind of publicity, and it will overshadow the memoir."

"I disagree." My hands fist as I lean forward. "If anything, it's an opportunity. Charlotte has her own story of overcoming adversity. Part of it is due to hardships at the hands of this very company. Despite that, she's an accomplished writer now."

"And your girlfriend?" Richard asks with raised eyebrows.

I meet his gaze. "Yes."

At least I still want her to be. But she might object to the title, especially after the last few days. It's looking less likely ever since the news broke and she stopped answering my calls. Frustration makes my jaw clench and my teeth grind together.

I force myself to project calm and competence instead. Set my shoulders straight as I look at every single Board member around the table.

"The memoir is almost complete. Don't forget the deal we have. Caleb and Nora Stone of BingeBox will be here for the final round of negotiations later this week."

"We need that memoir before we approve," one of the newest Board members says. She pulls up some papers and puts on her reading glasses. "And according to agreed timelines… it's due at the end of the week."

"The book will be finished," I say.

Richard steeples his hand on the table. "What we can all agree on, I hope," he says, and I hate the tone of his voice, "is that the overall focus has been slipping lately. The tax investigation is still ongoing. I know it's bogus—we all know it's bogus—but it received a lot of publicity."

"I denied it immediately," I say. "In the weeks since, I've also given several short interviews to continue refuting the claims. The rumors are dying down. The quarterly profit report will be released next week. That will change the direction of the conversation and help drive the stock price back up."

"The memoirist. Dating her…" Ingrid shakes her head. "It raises aspersions on whether you're taking your role seriously. Titan Media needs good publicity at this time. The stock price needs it. And it would certainly bolster the Board's general confidence in the CEO."

"In the CEO," I say. "You mean me."

She inclines her head, not looking away from me. Even as several of the people around her are quick to avert their eyes. "Yes."

I press my palm flat on the table. "I have been the CEO of Titan Media for two years. In that period, we have increased our profits. Balanced the books, and handled a significant investigation by the IRS into our tax filings. We've won back most of the advertisers that left us in the wake of my father's arrest. We're expanding the LA office, and yet our overhead has never been lower. I have made concession after concession to the Board for the sake of good publicity."

My voice turns sharper. "I have given interviews on our own talk show. I have made sure the Hartman name is associated as little with Alfred's reputation as possible. I have acquiesced to the Board's demands to be cautious with my expansion plans, even when I didn't agree. There is no reason for the Board to have anything but the utmost confidence in me.

"So I will make sure this purchase of BingeBox goes through. I will handle any bad publicity that comes my way in the same way I have dealt with this thus far. And I will date whoever I damn well please."

I rise from the executive chair and button my suit jacket. "The first draft of the memoir will be in your inboxes by the end of the week," I say. "Written by a fantastic author who has over-delivered on what you asked of her."

I walk out of the meeting.

I ask Eric to clear the rest of my afternoon. He doesn't hesitate before turning to his computer screen and letting his fingers fly across the keyboard.

Blowing off the Board is not something I've done before. Not so spectacularly. But right now, I want them and their focus on the stock price to go to hell.

"We got a few new requests for comments," Eric says.

"Continue to deny them." I look down at my phone. "Is the article done, the one Jeanette is working on?"

"I'll check in with her."

I'm already backing up toward the elevators. "Please do. And send me Vera Tran's contact number at Polar Publishing."

Eric's eyebrows rise. But he just nods. "Will do."

Possibilities spin through my head. I need to make this right. The one person who wasn't supposed to be hurt in all of this was Charlotte.

I speed on the drive back to the house. Her Audi is on the driveaway. Thank God.

But there's no sign of her on the first floor. I call her name, but there's no response. Taking the stairs two at a time, I race to the upper level.

"Charlotte!" She does not answer; my voice echoes through the empty rooms.

Her bedroom is neat.

The bed is made. Her two giant suitcases are gone. I stride to the closet and rip open the doors, but all that greets me are empty shelves and hangers.

There's a manila envelope resting on her desk.

I open it up. The title page has two words on top, typed in simple sans serif. *Titan, Rising.* Below, the subtitle reads: *A story of Aiden Hartman.* And at the very bottom, in a font size so small that it makes me grit my teeth, is her name. Charlotte Gray.

There's a Post-it slapped on top. It has her familiar handwriting, with only two words written on the note.

I'm sorry.

CHAPTER 63

AIDEN

She's not at her rental in Westwood. She never comes back to the house. And she refuses to answer her phone.

No calls, no texts.

She'd left behind her new car, and taken her old Honda.

Maybe she's at another resort, somewhere deep in one of the national parks

Sleep eludes me.

I sit all night on the couch by the giant living room windows, the shimmering view of Los Angeles as my only companion, and read page after page of Charlotte's manuscript. Halfway through the prologue, I had to get up to pour myself a glass of bourbon.

Fuck.

She opened with me walking into the courtroom for my father's trial. The eyes of the world, cameras, questions. Responsibility. She's captured all of it, but in her tone. The tone she's often used with me. No-nonsense, wry, sometimes funny, and at times ironic. Often sharp and exacting. Intelligent.

It might be my life she's written about, but I see her in every line, in every choice of word.

The next chapters were about the immediate aftermath.

Then, she started alternating structure, shifting between the past—mine and Titan's—back to the trial. What I had to do to satisfy the investigators and the Board. The people I had to let go and the new direction I'd taken the company.

She's included everything she's learned. Including the conversation with Mandy that I had no idea they had. My eyes pause on the passage, and I have to read it twice more. My sister said I've always taken it upon myself to protect her, protect our family, and that it's often come at a cost to myself.

Not that he listens when I try to tell him to do more for himself.

The man on the page is me.

It's a polished, slightly elevated version of me. The flaws mentioned are only those that make sense within the greater narrative. But it is me.

I'm nearing the end, and it's close to midnight when a knock sounds at my door.

In a few long strides, I'm at the front door and throwing it open.

It's not her.

Mandy stands on the other side. She's in a long silk trenchcoat, and she's frowning.

"You look terrible," she says.

"Fuck. We had dinner plans, didn't we?"

"Yes. With Mom no less, who is very peeved you haven't been answering your phone." She steps past me into the house. "What the hell happened here?"

I glance at my living room as if seeing it for the first time. Pages are spread everywhere. Half a bottle of bourbon on the edge of the coffee table.

"I'm reading the draft of the memoir."

"I can see that." She looks around. "Where's the author?"

My head pounds, and I know it's as much from the liquor as from the intense reading. I lean on the wall for a moment to steady myself. "She's not here."

"I saw the tabloids."

It's not surprising that she had. I look beyond the windows to the dark night sky. Mom must have seen the headlines, too. No doubt they'd spoken about it at dinner.

"Charlotte ran away," I admit.

Mandy crosses her arms over her chest. "Ah."

"You read the story, I'm assuming." My voice comes out bitter. "She was on *The Gamble*."

"I saw that. Funny, I didn't recognize her. But then, I never did enjoy *The Gamble*. I watch other series, like that show of yours on a deserted island? It's delicious." She shakes her head a little. "Did you know?"

"Yes."

Mandy's face drops. "Oh. You kept that close to your chest. Same as the fact that you're *dating* her. Thanks for letting your *sister* know."

"Charlotte didn't want it widely known. Either thing." I run a hand over my face. "She won't answer my calls. I've tried searching for her throughout the city with no luck. She fucking *hates* publicity, and right now, she's getting a ton of it."

Because of me.

The guilt had been gnawing at my bones since my PR team called me. I wanted to break the news to Charlotte myself but never got the chance. Eric beat me to it.

Mandy sits down on the opposite couch. "Okay. I think you need to tell me everything, starting with how this whole thing even *happened.* Because you being this distraught... Aiden, you care about her."

I sigh. "Yeah. I do."

So I tell my sister as much as I can, leaving out more than a few details she doesn't need to know. It doesn't take long. And in the end, I feel even worse.

"I knew from the start she was worried about publicity. I even tried doing something about it. Something that could help her in the long run, but..." I reach for my bourbon again.

It's been a long time since I've drunk this much. "I fucked up. I did something to set her on edge, and then the news hit."

Mandy carefully moves a few of the papers out of her way and curls up on the couch. "Right. Okay, let's hear it, then. What did you do?"

I tell her in short terms about the article. She listens, nodding every now and then, her eyes sharp.

"A hit piece," she says. "That's what you wanted the article to be, right? You wanted to expose Blake and his douchebaggery."

I sigh. "Yes. But I genuinely wanted her to tell her version of the story, too."

"I get it. You did what you've always done."

"And what's that?"

"Protect the people you love." She leans over the coffee table and waves her hand at the liquor bottle. "Hand me that, will ya."

Huh. I hesitate for a moment before handing her the bottle. "You can't drive if you drink that."

She hides it behind a cushion. "I won't. And neither will you. So. *Charlotte.* You wanted to protect her. Do you love her?"

I lean back against the couch and look at the image on the far wall. The one that Charlotte once commented on. The beach, the surfers. My happy place.

"Yes," I say.

Mandy swears softly.

"I know. I didn't expect it."

"No one does." She looks at the papers around us. "You're going to have to make it up to her, then."

"But being with me would mean being in the spotlight. Not always, but... from time to time. I can't see her ever agreeing to that." My hand fists at my side. "As much as I'd want to, I can't crush every single tabloid story."

"Have you told her you love her?"

I look at Mandy briefly before shifting my gaze to the backyard.

"That's a *no*," she says. "Look, I'm not an expert at relationships, you know that. My last one didn't work out, and the last few years have been… crazy. But in your place, I'd start with that. Say you're sorry and tell her that you love her. And, Aiden?"

"Yeah?"

"We didn't crush every news article about Dad." She smiles weakly. "And we survived. It's been tough, yeah. But we're tough people. Don't you think Charlotte is, too?"

"Yes. I do. But I'm not sure she believes she is." My fingers tap along the back of the couch in a hectic rhythm. "First I have to find her. There's one place she might have gone… but it's a bit of a stretch."

"Then what are you waiting for?" she asks. "Get in your car."

I start collecting the pages, stacking her memoir into a neat pile again. This draft is a culmination of months of Charlotte's hard work. Of turning the fractured mess of a person's life into something that can be sold as a compelling story. It's a book I needed, but it's one that she might regret ever agreeing to write.

"I have an idea," I say.

CHAPTER 64

CHARLOTTE

During the long drive from Los Angeles back to the small town I once called home, I think of all the things I've learned from the people written memoirs about. Whose lives I've seen up close and personal.

Odds don't lie. People do.

The cold only hurts if you let it.

People's opinions are like air.

I had to win. There was only victory or death.

Most people fear failure. I fear never having tried.

I usually listen to podcasts or audiobooks when I drive. But during the hours it takes me back to Idaho, I'm alone with my thoughts.

My parents know now. Their concerns had been palpable on the phone, especially when I confirmed that I had indeed been dating Aiden.

Their response hurt like a wound, a splinter I can't seem to get out. Knowing that, just as in the past, I once again made them targets of lunchroom speculations and embarrassment at work. That I've given them reasons to worry again.

My parents had had to endure televised scenes where Blake and I got intimate. Nothing explicit. Hints. Moving covers. Stupid smiles and winks.

I'd been so in love.

And then I'd been betrayed.

I'd been wrong to trust him. Wrong to trust my own emotions, to surrender to them so fully, and to let them lead me when I should have done more thinking instead.

I dodge more phone calls during the long drive. The latest is from the *New York Globe* journalist, Audrey. I saved her number the other day so I could easily screen it.

A little later, a text comes in. I read it when I stop to get gas, avoiding the other fifteen or so on my phone. Including more than a few from Aiden.

Audrey: I've seen the tabloid news today. I want you to know that it affects nothing, as far as I'm concerned. I still think you should tell your story. Or just have a chat with me, off the record. It's up to you.

The last few words are ironic. Nothing is "up to me" in all of this. I don't have any control, like so many times before. Just like all those years ago.

What emerged back then was a version of me I didn't recognize.

But many other people saw it as the real story.

Aiden calls again, just as I roll into Elmhurst. I ignore his call again. Let it ring and ring, each vibration in my cup holder echoing inside my little car. Each feeling like a tiny knife cut.

Elmhurst looks exactly the same. It always does, every time I get back. Nerves make my stomach tight.

My parents' house, the house I grew up in, is at the far curve of the cul-de-sac. Painted white wood, red brick, green lawn. Mom's planted daisies in the flower boxes outside the front door.

My tears well up at the sight. I have so many good memo-ries of this house. And then bad ones, too. From when I retreated inside its walls like an injured animal, hidden away to lick my wounds.

After that, I only returned between jobs. To go through the boxes of my things that Dad still keeps in his garage and to pack whatever I'd need ahead of my next adventure.

I've been without a home since I left this house.

Never stayed long enough to make a base, never bought my own furniture, never settled into routines. In some ways, I've been running from both my past *and* this place. From having to come face-to-face with people who know what happened.

I park my old Honda next to my parents' shining SUV. Mom rushes through the front door before I've even shut off the engine. She's got her reading glasses on, her hair in a giant claw clip, with a pair of rubber sandals on her feet.

I open the car door. "Hi."

"Sweetheart." She pulls me in for a hug, and she smells like the perfume she's used for over twenty years. I close my eyes and the tears spill down my cheeks.

"I don't know what I'm doing," I whisper.

"I know. I know," she says. "But it'll be all right. Come on in. There's food for you."

———

I meet up with Esmé the next day. We walk around Elmhurst. I was the one who suggested it, even if it chafes. I think better when I'm moving.

I ask her not to judge me.

"Charlotte," she says, her familiar smile wide. "I never judge you."

"I know. But... still. I needed to say it." Then I take a deep breath and tell her everything, from the very beginning. Every detail that's mine to share.

"I can't have it happen again," I pick at a fray on the hem of my jean jacket. "When I can, once he responds about the memoir and I get the green light to submit it to Vera, I think I'm going to ask her for another ghostwriting gig."

Esmé's eyebrows pull together. "But what about the pitch you told me about? For a non-fiction book of your own?"

I look past her to the green space at the center of Elmhurst. I've been to many Fourth of July celebrations there. School fairs, little league baseball games, and once when a circus came to town.

I haven't told Esmé I've already written the beginning of the book.

"I know, but I want to go somewhere. Be *sent* somewhere. Disappear for a while."

"Like you've done for years," she says softly.

I sigh. "Yes. I suppose."

"This guy… he wanted you to tell your story?"

"Yes. Forced my hand." I lean back on the bench and look up at the sky. Blue peeks out through the fluffy expanse of rapidly moving clouds. They never stay long in one place, either.

"He was wrong to do that," Esmé says. "No one should force you to give a tell-all interview or anything. Not even a guy you're dating. But I do think… And don't hate me for saying this, okay?"

"Okay," I say. "I won't."

"This guy could be bad news or the love of your life, I really don't know. But Charlotte, you've endured a lot without ever speaking up."

I look at her. "What do you mean?"

"You've never tried to change the narrative."

"Because I can't. I couldn't back then, and how could I now? People have already made up their minds."

"People can change them," she says. "Not that their opinions should matter. Not really. It's more that... people in production manipulated events so they could sell good TV. It wasn't the *truth*."

"I'm well aware of that." My voice comes out low. "It's just, how would it help if I tell my side of events? It would just attract even more attention."

"It would," she agrees. Logical, as always. "In the moment. But after, the hype will die down, and you'll be left with more peace." She nudges me with her elbow. "Maybe. Not that I know if that's true."

I shoot her a crooked grin. "Way to caveat your advice."

"I always do," she says. "Give someone very direct, potentially life-changing advice, and then bookend it with 'but what do I know?' so they can't hold it against me if it backfires."

"Clever."

"I know." She nudges me again. "This isn't like last time."

I raise my eyebrows. "Really? Because my parents have already gotten calls from two of my aunts and one uncle, wondering if I'm well. If I know what I'm doing. Why would I ever date the man who runs the production company for *The Gamble*."

"Right. And what happens later? They go on with their lives. And you'll have to go on with yours." Esmé wraps an arm around my shoulders.

I'm glad she's here.

She lives back in Elmhurst now, having returned just a few years ago. At the time I didn't understand the decision. Why would you give up Seattle for a small town?

But in the distance, birds sing high up in the trees. A couple of boys pass a soccer ball on the field.

"You can't make life decisions based on other people's fleeting thoughts," she tells me.

I'm quiet for a long moment. "You're right. It's just... it's scary to be vulnerable."

She chuckles faintly. "Of course it is. Do you think it's any different for the rest of us?"

"Why... do you all do it, then?"

"Because the cost of doing nothing is too high." She looks down at her hand, resting on her lap. Her wedding band glints in the sunlight. "It took me a very long time to open up to Tim. Somehow, he had the patience to let that be okay."

"I'm sorry I've been a shitty friend," I say.

She straightens. "What? Of course you haven't."

I nod at her. "I have. And probably a shitty daughter, too. And cousin, and granddaughter. I've spent so many years running and checking in only when it suited me. Not when the other people might have needed me."

"You're giving yourself too little credit," she tells me. My beautiful best friend, one who's helped me through so much of life's hardships.

A fierce desire to be there for her in return hits me. Her life is beautiful, happy, and safe—but I will be there regardless, should that ever change.

"I'm sorry." I grip her hand and take a deep breath. "I also think you may be right."

CHAPTER 65
CHARLOTTE

My parents and I are playing Uno in the living room. I haven't done this in years. But it used to be our thing during the summer and winter vacations at my grandparents' cabin.

The past few days have been…

I don't even know the right word. I'm drained. I feel it in the air, how weary my parents are, too. We've spoken about things all of us would rather have swept under the rug.

I told them about Aiden. About who he is as a person, and what he's come to mean to me.

And I apologized to them for what happened all those years ago. Again. I haven't been able to get away from the guilt, picturing Dad's students laughing behind his back about *me*, and Mom's colleagues peppering her with nonstop questions.

I cried. Mom turned into a statue, and Dad wiped his own tears with the back of his hand.

Now we're here, in a peaceful kind of truce, playing like I'm still fourteen and it's summer holidays.

"Good one," Dad says to Mom. His voice is begrudging as he reaches to pick up the cards she's dealt him. She chuckles a little and puts her cards down. "Does anyone want anything? I'm gonna get more tea."

"I'll take another cup," I say. "Thanks."

"I'm good," Dad grumbles.

She walks into the adjoining kitchen and I look through my hand of cards. Everything is so familiar, and yet so different, and it makes me feel heady with nostalgia. I could be twenty-eight or twelve. Eight or nineteen.

"A car is coming," Mom says. Living in a cul-de-sac, she and Dad have a habit of monitoring every car that comes by.

"Oh?" Dad asks.

It makes me smile. They do this several times a day.

"A huge one. It's really fancy, too. A Jeep of some kind." Then I hear her set a cup down. "It's stopping outside our house."

My cards fall to the table, the wrong side up. I'm showing everything. "Oh my god."

"Honey?" Dad asks.

"There's a man getting out of it," Mom continues. "I think—"

I'm already hurrying to the door. "Please stay inside. Okay?" I pull the door open and descend the steps in double time.

Aiden is standing by his massive Jeep, hands hanging loosely at his sides, eyes on mine. He's in that same leather jacket he wore in Utah. A pair of dark wash jeans, and not a suit in sight.

"What are you doing here?" I ask.

His eyes run over me. Like he's making sure I'm safe and sound. "I had to talk to you," he says. "I *want* to talk to you. There are things I didn't say the last time, things I need you to know."

I wrap my arms around my chest. "Aiden…"

He takes a step closer. "I know the last two days have been insane, ever since the tabloid published the story. I know that made you want to run. But Charlotte, you don't need to run from me."

The evening air is warm. The sun has started to set, but it hasn't fully dipped below the horizon. It's casting a soft light on the familiar street where I grew up. Tall trees play hosts to crickets that serenade around us.

There's no doubt in my mind that my parents are watching from the kitchen window.

"Come on," I tell him. "I know where we can go."

He follows me to the small path behind my house, down toward the creek. It's shaded and has a view of the meadow across the water.

Aiden's presence is heavy behind me. It's there in his steps, his barely audible breaths. I sit down on the bench that my father placed here when I was in kindergarten.

"How did you find me?" I ask.

He smiles crookedly. "You've told me about this place. Told me about the white house in a cul-de-sac, by a creek. There aren't too many cul-de-sacs in Elmhurst."

My mouth goes slack.

"What?" he asks.

"There are at least a dozen, I bet."

"I tried a few." He drapes his arm along the back of the bench. "Charlotte... I tried to get a hold of you when the tabloid news broke. I never wanted you to have to handle all of that alone. The calls, the questions."

I can't quite meet his eyes. It's far safer to watch the moving water instead. "You told *Star Buzz* we weren't a couple."

"Yeah, I figured the lie might help the speculations die down. You've mentioned being afraid that your family, your friends, your entire world would hate me. That it would make it harder for you." There's a note of bitterness in his voice, and he shakes his head, like he can shake off the ugly feelings. "I wanted to protect you. Again."

My breath whooshes out of me, escapes entirely. "Oh."

"I never meant it, though. Of course we're dating." He lifts his hand as if he wants to touch me, but pulls back only inches from my shoulder. "Fuck, I'm butchering this. Charlotte..." He takes a deep breath. "I'm sorry. I'm sorry that being with me has dragged you into the public eye again. I'm sorry that your family found out that way and not from us— together. That you had to face everyone alone." He shakes his head again, and his eyes narrow. "More than anything, I'm sorry I contacted Audrey about the article in the first place. I meant what I said. But I realize that I went about it completely the wrong way. It should be your choice entirely. At your pace."

"Yes," I say. Because that's the truth.

He nods, and his face is lined with tension. "I've called Audrey and asked her to put the article on pause."

That makes my breath catch. "You have?"

"Yes." His jaw clenches, and then he blows out a breath. "She wasn't happy about it, but she'll—"

"No. Don't," I tell him.

The words surprise us both.

"Charlotte?"

"Maybe... I don't know, yet. If I can talk to her. But I don't want her silenced. She seemed..." I shrug. "I don't know. Genuine? And she's not just reporting on my story. I've thought about it, and that's a good thing. Objectively. You were right about that."

His eyes are serious. "I still should have asked you beforehand."

"Yes. You should've," I agree. "Even though I get why you did what you did. But I don't want to be produced, Aiden. If I do this, either with Audrey or with someone else, *eventually*, I want it to be on my terms."

"I understand that now." He sighs. "Fuck, Charlotte... All I saw was how much it was hurting you, and I wanted to make it right. I've seen, week after week, how much what happened continues to affect you."

"Aiden." I shake my head. "You didn't do any of it."

"Maybe not personally, but I still feel responsible."

"You don't make show-level decisions."

He runs his hand through his hair. "Seeing how it's been eating at you... made me feel two inches tall, Chaos. All I've ever wanted, from the moment I first met you, is to give you everything. And here I am, starting at minus.

"I've spoken to my chief officer in charge of production. We'll make sure therapists are on set at each of our reality shows."

I shift on the bench. "You are? Really?"

"Yes. You've taught me a lot." His hand rubs a circle on my shoulder, and something shifts in his eyes. "I read the memoir."

"I added everything to the draft," I say quickly. "I understand if you want to cut out some things."

"Charlotte..." He shakes his head. "If you want, we can cancel the memoir entirely."

I pull back. "What?"

"If being associated with me hurts you, if it hurts your family, if you truly want the spotlight gone..." He swallows hard. "I can make the phone call. I'll make sure your editor at Polar knows it's my fault. Just another egomanicial CEO with whims, you know. You'll get out scot-free."

My breathing feels shallow. "But you'll lose your deal with the Board. You won't get approval for buying the streaming service."

He lifts a shoulder in a shrug. "Yeah. Not a big deal."

He's been working toward this for months. *Years.* The way he's described it, he believes it's the key to ensuring Titan Media stays relevant and competitive in the coming decades.

The cost is astronomical.

"You can't do that," I tell him. "That means too much to you."

His lips curve. "I found something that means far more."

"Oh."

"Anything you need from me is yours. Just say the words. If you want us to live in anonymity and obscurity, that's what we'll do. I can buy and kill news stories. I'll apologize to your parents. I'll do everything I can to convince them that you'll never suffer again because of me or Titan Media." His hand slides down my arm and finds my fingers. His entwine with mine. "Chaos, even if all you want is a 'no strings' kind of relationship that allows you the freedom to keep traveling and writing, moving from place to place, I'll be right there alongside you every step of the way."

"Your life is in Los Angeles," I whisper.

"Only because Titan's headquarters are there. There's no other draw for me, and I can work remotely." His voice turns fierce. "You're what matters. Ever since I walked into that hotel room, you've set my entire world ablaze. I've seen your bravery and your heart, and it's the most beautiful thing in the world. I want..." He shakes his head a little. "Fuck, I want everything where you're concerned. But I'll take whatever you're willing to give me."

"What do you want?" I tighten my grip on his hand. "Tell me."

"This is about you," he says.

I shake my head. "It's not. It's about *us*. And I want to hear what you want."

"I want you living with me," he says. "I want your laughs, your smiles. Your late nights and your early mornings. I want you by my side at events, and I want to get to know your world. I want you to show me around this town and meet your parents, and I want to kill anyone who's said a single bad thing about you throughout the years." His eyes burn, and I'm swallowed whole by his expression. "I want you to tell your story. I want everyone to know the truth about what happened on the reality show, even if it's my company that'll look bad. I want years with you. To walk beside you on whatever path your pen takes you. I want us to surf together, hike together. Hold you in my arms on the couch while you fall asleep to a movie. I want everyone to know you're mine, and I'm yours. I want to hold you at night, and I want your last name to change just one more time.

"That's selfish, all of that. But you asked me, so there it is, Charlotte. I am a selfish man. I've been given a lot in life, and here I am, asking for more. Asking for you. Because god help me, I'd give up everything else if it means you'll be mine." He brushes the back of his hand along my cheek. Finds a tendril of my hair and twists it gently around his finger. "You've been so unexpected from the start, Chaos. Turned me inside out at every turn until I couldn't think about anything but you. So here I am, so in love with you that it hurts. And while I know and *hate* the fact that I've caused you pain, I'm asking if you'll have me in return."

The moment feels like it lasts forever.

So much in love with you that it hurts.

I look at him and the strong planes of his face. He's always been handsome. Right now, he's so beautiful it breaks my heart. Cracks it wide open and his words pour in. They fill me up with warmth.

A tear runs down my cheek. Aiden's green eyes widen, and his hand slides down to cup my face. "Charlotte," he murmurs.

"You're in love with me?" I whisper.

He dips his head in a single nod. "You've ruined me entirely, Chaos. There's no one else for me."

I throw myself at him.

It surprises us both, I think. He catches me with a low grunt. His arms wrap around my waist, and he kisses me back. He tastes like mint.

His lips feel like coming home.

I lift my head, now halfway in his lap. "I love you, too."

Aiden goes very still. Every part of him, except for his hands on my waist. They tighten their grip.

"You do?"

"Yes. I've liked you since I first met you. Even when you were annoying, when you drove me mad, when you frustrated me... I always liked you. Somewhere over the weeks, it grew stronger than that. It felt like I was drowning and floating at the same time."

"I know what you mean."

"I tried to fight it for a long time. But it wasn't... it wasn't because of the show. It was because I was scared of getting hurt, I think." My forehead comes to rest against his, both of us breathing hard. "And I was scared of being found out. Of making a dumb mistake."

He strokes up my back in slow, reassuring sweeps. "You were hurt. And you were healing."

"I thought I was over it," I whisper. "But I didn't realize I'd just closed myself off entirely to the possibility of... *this*. It's scary."

Aiden chuckles a little. "It's fucking terrifying, Chaos. You could ruin me with a single sentence."

We breathe in silence for a few moments. Happiness is a slow syrup through my veins, heady and thick, until his words settle trigger a niggling thought in the back of my mind.

"Aiden," I blurt. "The thing I said, when we argued earlier in the week? About how you shouldn't believe your own... God, I can't even repeat it."

"My own puff piece?" His voice is easy, and his hands never stop stroking up my back.

I close my eyes in shame. "Yes. I'm so sorry, I was hurt, and I didn't mean it."

"I read the book," he says gently. "I know you didn't mean it."

I lean forward again, our foreheads touching. "What *did* you think about it?"

He smiles. I can almost feel the movement, we're so close. "I think," he says, "that you're the most talented writer I know. You made me sound infinitely better than I truly am. You also made observations that... I'm going to have to think about some more." He strokes his thumb along my cheek. "No one has ever known me quite like you, Chaos."

"I feel the same way," I whisper. "You figured me out so fast."

"I'd say that you read me like a book, if that wasn't terribly cheesy," he says. "And wrong. Because you've written the book."

"Mmm. I just had to learn to read between the lines."

He kisses my temple again, and I close my eyes, feeling his steady heartbeat against mine.

"Aiden," I say.

"Mmmhm?"

"I want to try living in Los Angeles for a bit."

He's quiet for a long beat. "Really?"

"Yeah. If that's okay."

"*Okay?* It's fucking perfect." His hands come to cup the sides of my face. "But are you sure? You're not going to give up anything because of me. I want to give you things. Not take things away."

That makes me laugh. "Aiden, in what world would me living with you be *taking things away?* I want to try staying in one city for a bit. I want to write my new book. And maybe... I want to try being a girlfriend."

A slow, wide smile spreads across his face. "My girlfriend."

"Yes. *Your* girlfriend."

He kisses me again, and then pulls me tight against him. I feel his heart beating. "I am very happy right now," he says.

I close my eyes against the welling of sudden tears. "So am I."

We sit like that for a long few minutes. There's only the sound of the creek behind us and birds in the distance, settling down for the night. Somewhere, a car engine starts.

"Do your parents like wine?" Aiden asks.

I laugh. "What?"

He leans back to meet my gaze. "I've brought a case of *Langley* wine for them. I know I'll have to fight an uphill battle to try to win them over."

I laugh again. It slips out of me, warming the little glade. He looks at me with a widening smile. "Wrong choice?"

"Wrong choice," I say and lock my hands behind my neck. "But I love you for trying. And so will they, once they get to know the real you. No wine, no fancy cars. Just you."

CHAPTER 66
CHARLOTTE

Two weeks later

"Aiden." My voice comes out hoarse.

His hair is dark between my thighs, his tongue moving over my clit. The toy inside me is pulsing with steady, tantalizing vibrations that have my nerves wired high.

He doesn't stop. I twist my hips and he follows, his lips suctioning around my clit.

My hands are tied to the bedframe using two of his ties.

It had been my idea, my old fantasy, one I'd confessed to him last night.

It didn't take him long to re-enact it.

"Please," I whisper. The pleasure is riding me hard and I don't know if I can come another time. I've come twice already and my nerves are shot.

He nudges the vibrator inside of me with his other hand, turning the angle so the sensations hit that spot inside of me.

Liquid heat flows through me and then rises so quickly, it robs me of breath. He flicks his tongue a few times over my clit and I break apart with a shout.

My orgasm is short and intense, spreading like a burst of

wildfire. It turns into pain at the end and I use my knees to try to force Aiden's head up.

He looks up at me, eyes ablaze and mouth smiling. "That was a good one, sweetheart."

I pant against the bed, my arms still locked above my head. "I can't do one more."

"Sure about that?" He blows down gently on my clit, and a shiver runs through me. Without looking, he lowers the vibrations on the toy still inside me.

"Yeah," I breathe. "I'm sure. If you make me come one more time, I think I'll start crying, and I'll be a mess for the rest of the day. And I have a meeting to get to."

Aiden kisses the inside of my thigh, up to the crook where my leg meets my pussy. He takes a deep breath before gently pressing a closed-mouth kiss to my clit.

A whimper escapes me.

"I'll let you go, sweetheart." He pulls the toy from me with a soft sound, and I feel abruptly empty. Unfulfilled. I might be done with my orgasms for the day, nerves too frazzled, but I haven't had him inside me.

He puts the toy aside and smooths his large hands over my thighs. He's in nothing but his boxer-briefs, his hair still a bit damp from his morning shower. It hangs over his forehead in a much messier hairstyle than his usual one.

He looks so good. Dark hair on his chest, a line disappearing down into his underwear.

He's hard. I can make out the shape of him, heavy against the fabric.

Aiden looks me over with those eyes that make me feel like the sexiest woman who's ever lived. I lift my back a little, tits up, and his eyes zero in on my nipples.

"I have a little more time," I say, "before I need to shower."

His hands come to rest at my knees. "Oh?"

"Yes."

His lips curve. "And what do you want, if it's not to come?"

"I want you to come," I say, and spread my knees wide in a clear invitation. "Inside me."

He pushes down his underwear, and I try to slide further down on the bed. My hands are still tied and they're loose, if I pulled I could get out of them, he had made sure of that. But the tug at my wrist still thrills.

"This was the final puzzle piece, right?" Aiden mutters. He sits on his knees between my legs, and pulls them up so the backs of my thighs are against his chest.

Tie me to the headboard, my legs on either side of your head... bend me double and go to town.

"Yes," I breathe.

Aiden's smile flashes, and he lines himself up. The first brush of his head makes me shudder.

"God, you're wet, sweetheart," he mutters. "I warmed you up real good."

I smile at him. "Hurry up, Hartman. I've got places to be."

"Brat," he says, and kisses the inside of my ankle.

Then he thrusts inside me with a strong push of his hips. I *am* really wet. He enters me easily, and we both breathe a sigh of relief at the feeling.

He doesn't let up. Using his weight to push down on my legs, folding me over, and driving into me. He growls while he does it, hoarse groans that shoot fire through me.

"God, I love fucking you," he mutters. "Best fucking part of my week."

I turn my hands around, so I can hold on to the head-board. I didn't think I'd be able to come again, but the way his pelvis is hitting me sends shivers of pleasure through my already too-swollen clit. It's like faint after-shocks of an orgasm. Delicious and just enough for my system to handle.

I love how much he swears during sex. Love it when he loses himself. As much as I've learned to relax during his focus on me, to crave his mouth between my legs, this part is my favorite.

Aiden, eyes near-black and body in a fury, seeking his own release.

"Come inside me," I tell him.

He groans and his hips stutter. "Fuck, Chaos. Say that again."

He thrusts deep, and another moan escapes me. "Come inside me. Please."

Aiden leans forward, and there's a stretch in my hamstrings when I'm folded double. His face tightens in pain as he thrusts hard. He gives a hoarse half-shout, and then he's spilling deep inside me.

"I love you," I tell him when it's over, when he's spent and still buried deep inside me. His hair is damp and soapy against my cheek.

He's let my legs down, and I've wrapped them around him.

Aiden chuckles weakly against my neck. "Fuck, I love you so much, Charlotte."

"I love you more," I say. "And I know how much you like it when I run my fingers through your hair after you come. I'd love to do that, but you're gonna have to help me."

"Shit." He pushes up on an elbow and easily undoes the ties with his free hand. "You okay, sweetheart?"

"I'm fantastic. Thanks for tying me up." I use my newfound freedom to rake my fingers over his upper back and through the thickness of his hair. I use my nails, too, and he groans.

Inside me, his cock twitches.

I love these moments. When he's spent on top of me, both of us are sensitive and slow, and nothing in the world exists outside of this bed.

"I don't want you to be late," he mutters between soft

kisses along my cheek, "but letting you get out from beneath me might kill me."

I hold him tighter. "I've got time."

"Mmhmm. I hope I distracted you well enough."

I kiss him. It's soft and messy and he's so warm. "Thank you," I whisper.

He sighs against my temple, and chest to chest, I feel the pounding of his heart. "It's going to be all right, sweetheart. You've got nothing to worry about."

———

Later that day, I meet Audrey Kingsley at a small café in Westwood. She's got auburn hair and a wide smile, and she asks if she can give me a hug. Usually, I'd find that sort of thing fake or an over-the-top attempt to win me over, but something about her genuine excitement rubs off on me.

It lessens the nerves roiling inside me like a winter storm.

She asks me what I want to drink and tells me it's on her. "No strings," she adds and laughs a little.

I order an iced coffee. "That sounds delicious," she says and orders the same, but asks for an extra shot of caffeine.

"I've got a toddler at home," she says with a small shrug. "I'm working part time now, trying to juggle both, and I'm *always* in need of caffeine"

"That sounds hard."

"It can be, so I'm really enjoying this trip to LA," she says. "But that also means I'm extra careful about the stories I choose to investigate. I want them to really mean something."

I look down at my hands, knotted together on the wooden table. "Right. What made you think of… well. Of this topic?"

The waiter arrives with our drinks, and I grab my coffee with grateful hands. Something to do, something to hold.

Audrey takes a sip of hers. "Good question. I mean, it landed on my desk as a tip from the beginning. But I'd been interested in the ethics of reality shows for a long time, especially dating shows. There are different kinds of them, right? *The Gamble* is definitely one of the…" She looks at me then gives an awkward little shrug. "Sorry."

"You can say it," I say dryly. "It's a trashy one. Alcohol, youngsters, hotness on the beach."

"Yes," she admits. "Exactly. With a focus on hookups for short-term gain rather than actually making meaningful connections."

I nod. It's easier than I expected, talking about it. To hear her mention *The Gamble* and know she must have watched my season in preparation for this.

"A lot of them are heavily produced. We're talking young people, often sensitive situations, unsupervised but constantly filmed—every drop of drama milked." She shrugs. "It feels like the industry hasn't been properly investigated. What are the safeguards in place? Especially for young women?"

"So you decided to take the job. When Aiden called you," I say.

A tiny frown appears on her lips. "He didn't offer me a job. He suggested I write a story and agreed to provide funding. I did the rest."

"Right. Of course."

"Unusual, to be sure. But it's not the first time a company's top executive has welcomed scrutiny of his firm. Some have done it to force the change they couldn't implement because of their Boards." She gives another shrug, and a smile replaces her slight frown. "I have a feeling, Charlotte, that so much of your story was left untold. It's there, though, if you look carefully between the frames of the neatly edited season you were on."

This is everything I never wanted to talk about.

All this time, to be naive felt almost worse than looking crazy. And to be so openly vulnerable, to share what happened and what it meant to me... To admit that I was told and believed that I was going to get vindicated once the show aired. And that while filming, I was egged on and encouraged by producers, and my wineglass always kept full.

But I find myself nodding to the woman across from me.

"There was a lot more that happened than was shown," I say. "But here's the thing... I've never told my story. And I'm a writer, too."

Audrey's eyes light up. "That's right. I did some searches on your name—you've written a lot."

"I'd like to tell my story," I say. "But I want to be a part of writing it, too."

She looks at me for a split second before she extends a hand. "Deal," she says.

I shake it, feeling better about myself than I have in a long while.

And then I tell her everything.

CHAPTER 67
AIDEN

Two months later

She's lying in my arms, on the large couch we've used so often in the past weeks. On the projector screen, the opening credits start to roll set to the notes of an upbeat pop song. There's aerial footage of a large villa, surrounded by towering palm trees. Then quick flashes between different faces—all of them tan and attractive. A group of young people. British, American, Canadian. There's an Aussie, too.

And then, the gold text. *The Gamble.*

Charlotte takes a deep breath.

"You okay?" I ask.

She's got a firm grip on the remote. "Yeah. I think. But I'm not sure how far in I'll make it."

"We can stop anytime," I say.

It had been her idea, a week ago. She'd said it so suddenly, over lunch at the Malibu house, on a beautifully sunny Saturday. *I think it's time I rewatch my season.*

It shocked me. But then, she'd explained why she thought it was necessary. Both for her book, but also to see... if it was as bad as she remembered. *It's grown in my head,* she told me. *I think it's a dragon I need to slay.*

So here we are. I know I'll get upset by what I'll see. I told her that, warned her about it. She said I didn't have to watch.

It'll be... Blake will be there. It will include—

I cut her off. I know very well what it'll include, and I don't feel jealousy when faced with that prick. It's a decade in the past.

What I do feel?

Pure and sheer anger.

But I'm not about to let her go through this on her own.

"There I am," she says softly.

On-screen, younger Charlotte stands at the edge of a pool. She's in a short blue sundress, showing off her tanned arms, and her hair is bleached to a wheat-blonde. It suits her, but nothing is as pretty as her natural color.

She's holding a colorful cocktail and watching a group of guys across the water. They're by some kind of shuffleboard, and the show is about to kick off with one of the inane challenges inherent to *The Gamble.*

"Oh. I'm kinda cute, actually," she says. There's true surprise in her voice.

I kiss her forehead. "Of course you are."

"I remember being so nervous about what to wear. My mom and I went to the mall before to get a ton of dresses." She digs her teeth into her lip, and we watch another few minutes in silence.

"Oh, wow," she says after a confession by a red-headed girl who said she really liked Charlotte. "I had forgotten about Emily. She was... out of all the girls, she was actually pretty nice."

"What happened to her after the show?"

"I don't know." Charlotte's voice is thoughtful. "I kinda lumped her together with the rest."

We watch several episodes in one evening.

Charlotte jumps ahead sometimes. Other times she pauses and sits up, as if to take a more thorough look at the scene. When Blake calls her Sugar Puff the first time, I want to bury my fist into a pillow.

But beside me, Charlotte laughs.

"What?" I ask.

She shakes her head, her eyes on the screen. "I don't feel anything."

"Nothing?"

"Well, a bit of secondhand embarrassment, I will admit. But it's because *he's* so cringeworthy. Entertaining, sure. But he's the cringey one. Not me."

"Of course he is, sweetheart. He's an asshole."

She laughs again, and it's a sound of such relief that it makes my fists relax against the cushion.

"I thought... I thought I wouldn't make it through five minutes. I thought I would be a sobbing mess on this couch. But I'm not. I'm not, Aiden."

"You're strong," I tell her. "And you've grown so much since you were that nineteen-year-old."

"I have." Her smile fades, and she tracks her younger self's movements on the screen. Looking tired and red from the sun, the Charlotte of a decade ago nervously looks around at the other, older contestants. "You know what? That girl? If she was anyone but me, I would feel for her." Her voice turns thoughtful. "Isn't that... I should feel for her, too. Past me. I was young and in way over my head, and I navigated it all as best I could."

"You definitely did."

She shakes her head slowly. "Compassion, maybe. Is that the answer? I didn't realize..."

"You've shown it to a ton of your memoir subjects," I tell her. "Curiosity to learn why they did what they did, and the empathy to understand them, even when you haven't necessarily agreed with their choices."

"Yeah. That's true." She leans back against me and looks at the younger version of herself on screen. The girl she once was is laughing at something the guys are doing. "Maybe it's time I do that for myself, too."

EPILOGUE

AIDEN

Eight months later

It's release weekend.

There's a large banner featuring the book cover. It's got a plain background and a black-and-white image of me. Embossed text below. *Titan, Rising*. The tagline is right beneath it. *A story of an American media empire, and the man behind its future.*

"This is torture," I say.

The woman beside me laughs. She's heard me complain for weeks in preparation for this day.

Her hand slides into mine. "One hour. Contractually, we have to be here for one hour."

"I'm going to throw all the attention on you."

Charlotte chuckles again. "No, you're not."

"For a release party, I think that's pretty expected," I say. I pull her in closer and press a kiss to her temple. "After all, this book wouldn't have been a success without you."

Vera Tran is standing by the drinks table, chatting with a few people. She sees us coming in and excuses herself.

I've heard a lot about Charlotte's editor at Polar Publishing. Especially in the last few weeks, ever since Charlotte submitted the outline for her non-fiction book. They've chatted weekly about what to keep, what to change.

Vera is slating it along next year's spring releases and wants to make Charlotte into one of their biggest debut authors.

"You both made it," Vera says. "Come in, come in. A few of your guests are already here."

I frown. "I didn't put anyone on the list."

But someone must have, because standing in the corner of the bookstore is my mother and Mandy. They're chatting with Charlotte's parents.

On the table between them is a stack of books. Of *my* memoir.

Charlotte chuckles as we walk up to our families.

I'm already groaning.

"My hero!" Mandy says and holds out the book to us. "Could you sign it for me, please, Aiden?"

"You're ridiculous."

She laughs and hands the book to Charlotte instead. "You're right, it's her autograph I want, anyway. The *actual* author."

Charlotte accepts the book from my sister. She turns the hardback over, studying the spine and the elegant cover. The design is nice, I'll admit that much.

And so is the content of the book. I've cut almost nothing of what Charlotte wrote. Even if the idea of people buying it and reading it, making the story their own, is terrifying.

Mom even likes it.

She was the hardest critic. The one I suspected would be most upset by some of the stuff in it. But she liked it. *You're getting your revenge*, she'd said.

Mandy and I have agreed not to chase any of the headlines that might come out after this book is released. She made me promise not to. That we won't continue trying to clean up the mess he made.

It's not our mess, she'd said. *It never was.*

We'd written him a letter together ahead of the book release. Each said our part, and it was a lot of anger. I'd made sure it was delivered there with utmost security—no chance of it getting leaked again.

I don't know what the future holds for him. Or for us, if there will ever be an us again, a relationship. But for the first time since he was arrested, I'm okay with not knowing.

And now, here we all are, at the release party. It once felt like we'd never reach this day.

"Hi," I tell Charlotte's parents and step past her to greet them properly. "Thank you both for coming. It means a lot to us."

Charlotte's mother hugs me. "We're glad to be here. Did you know, we've never been to a release party for one of her books before?"

"Really?"

"Never," she says again and motions for John. "Have we?"

"Nope." He extends his hand my way. "I read it. Charlie sent me an early copy."

"She did?"

"Sure did. I didn't realize... quite how much you've overcome." John shrugs his shoulders. I've gotten to know both him and Helen quite well over the past few months.

Charlotte and I have been back to Elmhurst several times.

And each time, I've had a few hard conversations with her parents.

I thought they'd be people I'd need to charm and impress. Instead... the relationship has developed into something far more genuine. They're like Charlotte. Honest, kind, and straight shooters.

They're people I respect.

"You've had some crazy years," he continues. "I'm sorry

about all of it. No child should be held accountable for the sins of their parents."

It takes me a moment to speak. "Right. Thanks, John. I appreciate that."

A lot.

He shakes my hand again and smiles at me. "Now let's get this party started. We're here to celebrate, after all. To celebrate you!"

"And Charlotte," I say. "You know this book wouldn't have happened without her."

He looks at his daughter. Laughing with Mandy and both of our mothers, with a copy of the book under her arm. She was nervous about her outfit for tonight, but she had nothing to worry about.

Charlotte is stunning. She always is.

"She has always surprised me," John says. "I'm not surprised that her choice of a man surprised me, too."

I chuckle. "I know. I'm sorry about that."

He claps me on the shoulder. "That's okay. I think we've all gotten over the initial shock by now, hmm?"

"We definitely have."

"And between you and me, I don't think Charlie could have chosen better. I was worried she wouldn't..." He clears his throat. "I've been worried about her. All part of being a parent, you know. Well, I suppose you don't."

"No. Not yet, at least."

His face softens with a smile. "Yeah. Not yet. But she's on such a fantastic path, and... I'm really excited about the book she's writing now."

"So am I," I say honestly. "I think we're only at the beginning of what she'll accomplish."

SOCIAL MEDIA

Two years later

@YvetteS: Just listened to the audiobook of Going Viral and now I'm feeling a little bit ashamed about buying a Sugar Puff t-shirt ten years ago as a joke gift for my sister.

@TwoGirlswhoReadPodcast: Hey everyone! We just started Charlotte Gray's book *Going Viral: What Happens After Fifteen Minutes of Fame,* and can we just say, wow! We were entirely wrong on what actually happened all those years ago to Sugar Puff! Plus, she talks to some of our favorites— remember the lady from the hurricane meme? Listen to our episode recapping the book. We're gonna try to get an interview with Charlotte, too!

@AuthorGraceEllington: It was my honor to write the foreword to Charlotte Gray's new book, *Going Viral.* She's a new and bright light in the investigative non-fiction space.

@GreeneyedGirl: Okay, so I've never seen this show, but watching the clips now? How did anyone think that was okay to air? Blake is CLEARLY the villain and somehow he managed to have a career afterwards? Do better!!

@NewYorkGlobe: Today's recommendation is the hot new non-fiction book: *Going Viral*. It's written by an investigative writer, Charlotte Gray, who went viral herself twelve years ago. It's a combination of excellent essays on the intersection of fame, media, and ordinary people who suddenly have everyone's eyes on them.

@TheRealFrankieSwan: I've known Charlotte for years. She's a beautiful woman, and I'm so proud she's finally telling her own story in *Going Viral*. If you remember, she helped me write my memoir a few years back. It's available in bookstores all across the country!

EPILOGUE II
CHARLOTTE

"Wait for me," I tell Aiden.

He leans out of the driver's side window. "I'll wait forever."

"Well, not that long. The hotel valets will get pissed."

He grins. "Then hurry up, Chaos."

"I'll be right back!" I hurry away from the Jeep we've rented and back up the steps of the resort. It's stunning here. The entire place is, nestled in a valley here on Kauai. There's greenery everywhere you look.

The reception is pretty busy. It's 10 a.m. and a lot of people are checking out. It's an adults-only five-star resort, and we have our own bungalow.

I could get used to going on a honeymoon to Hawaii every single month.

There's a small bowl of fruit in the middle of the lobby. It's free for guests to grab, and that's my goal. Aiden and I are hiking today. The four-wheel rental will take us to a trailhead over by the Kalalau Trail. We've got all the water loaded into the vehicle, but we've got no snacks.

I'm in a pair of workout shorts and hiking boots very at odds with the other people here in the lobby. They're in long summer dresses and linen shirts.

I grab two bananas and examine an apple when a woman comes up beside me.

She reaches for a pear. "Hey. I'm really sorry to bother you."

I look up at her with a smile. "That's okay."

"Are you Charlotte Gray?"

"I am, yes."

"Oh, that's so cool." She's wearing a purple dress and has tight, curly hair. She looks around my age.

"Let me guess?" I ask. "You're a fan of *The Gamble*."

She shakes her head. "No. Well, I have seen a few seasons, I'll admit. But actually, I'm..." She digs into the beach bag slung over her shoulder and pulls out a paperback.

It's a matte, white book cover with red letters. *Going Viral: What Happens after Fifteen Minutes of Fame.* Vera and I worked a long time with the graphics department to get the cover just right.

The shadow of the title is made up of tiny images, tiny faces. Each is a moment in time that has gone viral. Little moments—like a fly in amber—even though the person and society have moved on.

"I'm nearly done with this. My cousin recommended it to me, and it's been the perfect beach read. I keep bothering my brother with the anecdotes." She laughs a little. "You wouldn't... Do you mind signing it? I don't have a pen, actually."

"Oh, that's all right," I say. "Reception probably has one. That's so cool! Are you enjoying it?"

"Yes. I can't believe I'm seeing you here now, too." She shakes her head as we walk over to the reception. "You know, I... I did see the first season. I don't remember much of it, but I love that you included your own story in the book."

"Thanks. That means a lot to me." I mean every single word.

The receptionist hands me a pen, and I sign the first page of *Viral*.

It's not the first time I've done it. But it's definitely the first time it happened out in the wild like this, and I can't get the smile off my face.

The woman thanks me again when I hand the book back to her. "I'm going to have an even better anecdote to bother my brother with now," she says with a huge smile on her face.

For a brief second, I feel like hugging her. Or maybe crying. "I hope you enjoy your time here."

"You, too. Thank you again, truly."

We wave goodbye, and I almost forget the fruit I came in here for. By the time I make it out into the bright Hawaiian sunshine, Aiden has pulled the Jeep over to the side. I hurry to meet him. He probably *did* get told off by the valet.

"Hey," he says, his window still down. There's a wide smile on his face. "You're looking awfully happy."

"Can't a newly married woman be awfully happy?"

"I *hope* she is."

I open the passenger door of the badass Jeep and jump in beside him. "You will never guess what just happened."

"Tell me."

I explain the entire story to Aiden in excruciating detail as he starts the drive to the trail.

"She had the book in her bag?"

"In her bag!"

"That's fucking unreal." He laughs, and I look at him and his deep tan and messy hair and the smile that's wide across his face. God, I love him so much. "I can't believe that just happened. That's a sign, sweetheart."

"A sign of what?"

"Of you having a great day. A great month. A fantastic honeymoon, and, honestly, just proof of what a monumental success this book has been."

I chuckle. "Okay, it's been a very good, medium-sized success." I'm happy with how *Going Viral* is doing. Very happy, even, for my very first non-fiction book. The topic has garnered more interest than I thought it would.

Vera even booked me on talk shows.

Because I get to talk about *other* people's stories... I don't mind quite as much. I'm nervous, every single time. But it's also a new adventure.

And as Aiden likes to remind me, that's where I thrive. Every time I feel anxious to do another interview, he tells me: *You're in control. You got this. And you're going to love it when you're there.*

"It's a major success," he says and puts a hand on my bare knee. "My wife is a bestselling author. And, Chaos, just the fact that you were recognized? For your *book*?"

"I know. I didn't even feel scared when she approached me! Like, I wasn't nervous at all. I thought it would be about *The Gamble*, and I was just..." I shrug. The sun is shining, and I'm with my best friend in the world. Past Charlotte hasn't got a thing on Present Me. "Unbothered."

He laughs. "That's you. My unbothered queen."

"Wife, queen... you're full of compliments today." I look over at his hand on the steering wheel and the thick gold band on his ring finger. My husband.

Our wedding was a small, private affair. Only our closest family members and no press. The party after had been different. It was a much bigger affair, with all of our relatives and friends invited.

I've focused on making new ones in the last few years. After I decided to stay in LA, I've gained more than a few. It's been a rocky process. Building my own little tight-knit group, and settling into habits I used to scorn.

And I've loved every single day of it.

"Ever since we got rid of that 'no compliments' rule," Aiden says. "Do you remember that one?"

It takes me a moment. "Oh my god, yes. Early on in our relationship."

"Yes. You didn't want to develop feelings." He chuckles again. "It was a valiant effort, Chaos. But it failed."

"Badly. I liked you long before I admitted it to myself. Or to you."

He looks over at me. "You know, I suspected."

"You did?"

"Of course. You weren't terribly subtle."

"I can be, I think."

His smile widens, and he removes his hand to help steer around a sharp narrow curve, flanked by greenery. The island is stunning, and we've already decided this won't be our last time here. "Yes, with other people. But not with me."

I sigh. "No, you always saw right through me."

He puts his hand back on my knee. "Not through you. I just saw *you*. The real you."

I take his hand and weave our fingers together. My own ring is a slim gold band with a solitaire diamond. I didn't want anything big. Nothing giant, nothing fancy. I love the design he chose. Simple, elegant, everlasting.

"I like to think I saw you, too."

"You did," he says, and his fingers tighten around me. "At a time when I felt like no one else had in years. I didn't allow anyone in close enough to let them look. And there you were, with your notepad, asking questions and refusing to take *no comment* for an answer."

"You were tough to crack," I say with a chuckle.

His smile widens. "I think we were both tough to crack."

"Well, we're thoroughly cracked now and locked in for life." I turn toward him in the jeep and reach out to run a hand through his hair. "You're not scared?"

"Scared?" He's so handsome. Dark beard, sparkling green eyes, and that wide smile. I've looked and looked at him for over two years straight, and I don't think I'll ever get enough.

"Terrified, Chaos. As always. But we're going on this adventure together."

I tighten my hand around his. "And we love a good adventure."

ACKNOWLEDGEMENTS

Aiden and Charlotte's journey surprised me.

I had a different plan for this book, but it took on a life of its own. It didn't want to be part of a series. It didn't want to be set on the East Coast.

Aiden and Charlotte wanted to be in Los Angeles, and they wanted their own space and time for their story to be told properly.

I'm glad I listened.

My word for this year was chaos. It's been my guiding principle in making bolder plans, crazier decisions, trying new things. As someone who likes routines and organization...

Well. It's been hard to find the beauty in chaos, but I'm trying. So when Aiden called Charlotte Chaos for the first time, it just fit. Both for them and for me.

I hope you're finding some beauty in your own chaos.

Charlotte's story is one I've thought about for a long time. What happens when people get famous overnight in that viral, short-lived, often quite embarrassing way?

And how do we forgive ourselves for making mistakes? For being human? I have a lot more grace for others than I do for myself. Writing Charlotte's story, and how she learned to be kind to her former self, was a great exercise in self-reflection.

As a pretty new consumer of reality TV, it was fun to grapple with some of the aspects of the industry and how that might affect people. Of course, not all shows are like the fictional *Gamble*. I have a lot of respect for people who share their lives for entertainment.

And I really can't stop watching Below Deck.

As for Aiden, he walked on to the page with all of his troubles and concerns and deep, deep love for Charlotte.

He's one of the good ones and I loved getting to spend time with him chapter after chapter. I'll miss having him as my book boyfriend, taking shape every day on my screen.

Los Angeles is a city that's close to my heart. I once spent a year living in Westwood, and that inspired much of the story. Any mistakes relating to Los Angeles geography are mine and mine alone—I'm drawing from memory (and mine is often flawed!).

A huge thank you to my author friends who help make this lonely job so much more communal. You give advice, make me laugh, and definitely helped sort me out when this book challenged me. Grace, Kyra, Lily, Sophia and Stephanie. I don't know what I'd do without you all!

The fantastic beta readers; Alizé, Stefanie, Nikki, Conner, Anuska, Valentina, Sarah, Margaret, Laura, Jelena, Iqra and Emily. Thank you! I appreciate you reading this book early and giving your honest reactions as readers. It helped make it stronger.

Thank you to Andie, my editor, who polished and strengthened this story. Thank you Shannon, for your impeccable proofreading.

Bri, my assistant sent from above, thank you for helping me with all my crazy ideas and plans. Thanks for listening to my rambling voice notes on Slack. You're the best.

Yibi, you drew the perfect cover for this book. When you sent over the first sketches I literally squealed with glee and shared them with friends, who all wanted to know who you were. You're a gem of an illustrator and you captured Aiden, Charlotte and the background so perfectly.

But most of all, thank YOU for reading this book. Thank

you for picking it up, giving it a chance if you've never read me before, or coming back for more if you have.

I continue to be deeply honored to have this as a job, and it's all thanks to you reading.

Thank you.

BOOKS BY OLIVIA

The Connovan Chronicles

Best Enemies Forever
Gabriel and Connie

The Perfect Mistake
Alec and Isabel

One Wrong Move
Nate and Harper

The New York Billionaire Series

Think Outside the Boss
Tristan and Freddie

Saved by the Boss
Anthony and Summer

Say Yes to the Boss
Victor and Cecilia

A Ticking Time Boss
Carter and Audrey

Suite on the Boss
Isaac and Sophia

12 Days of Bossmas
Christmas anthology

The Seattle Billionaire Series

Billion Dollar Enemy
Cole and Skye

Billion Dollar Beast
Nick and Blair

Billion Dollar Catch
Ethan and Bella

Billion Dollar Fiancé
Liam and Maddie

Brothers of Paradise Series

Dark Eyed Devil
Lily and Hayden

Ice Cold Boss
Faye and Henry

Red Hot Rebel
Ivy and Rhys

Small Town Hero

Jamie and Parker

Standalones

Between the Lines
Aiden and Charlotte

How to Honeymoon Alone
Phillip and Eden

Arrogant Boss
Julian and Emily

Look But Don't Touch
Grant and Ada

The Billionaire Scrooge Next Door
Adam and Holly

ABOUT OLIVIA

Olivia is a hopeless romantic who loves billionaires heroes, despite never having met one. So she took matters into her own hands and creates them on the page instead. Stern, charming, cold or brooding, so far she's never met a (fictional) billionaire she didn't like.

She picked up the pen in 2019, and she hasn't put it down since. With over a million books sold, Olivia writes fast-paced, swoon-worthy stories filled with banter and spice. Join the heroes as they meet, clash with, or stumble into the ambitious heroines that make them fall, and fall hard.

Join her newsletter for updates and bonus content.
www.oliviahayle.com.
Connect with Olivia

f facebook.com/authoroliviahayle
o instagram.com/oliviahayle
g goodreads.com/oliviahayle
a amazon.com/author/oliviahayle
BB bookbub.com/profile/olivia-hayle